Du Rose Blaze

The Hana Du Rose Mysteries

K T BOWES

Dedication

For my mother,
and her friends in the belly dancing group.

Join Me

I have a reading group which you're very welcome to join.
You can do that by signing up on my website ktbowes.com
In return, you'll receive four free eBooks sent to your inbox and
an email from me once a month.
I'd love for you to join us.

Love from Kate x

1

Breastplate

"Oh, this is heaven." Hana Du Rose lay back in her deckchair and tugged her sunglasses over her eyes.

"Heaven." A little girl with bouncing dark curls skipped over the wooden deck with a knitted brown horse dangling from her right hand. "Heaven." She repeated the word on a loop, fondling the new sound with her lips and tongue and liking it.

"Clever girl, Edin," Hana murmured. She breathed out a heavy sigh and turned her face towards the sun's loving rays, soaking up the heat with satisfaction. "I needed this. Five minutes' peace."

Steel railings protected the child from the yawning precipice beyond the house, the distant shoreline of Port Waikato glinting like diamonds with its black, iron rich sand. Edin skipped up and down the steps to the deck, muttering to the toy horse in her arms.

Hana's mobile phone trilled from the pocket of her shorts and she grumbled as she tugged it free. "Yeah," she answered, recognising the caller's identity from their image on the screen. "What's up?"

"Nothing, my angel." Her mother-in-law's voice rang through the speaker, and Edin stopped. She tottered towards Hana and held out her hand.

"Nonie!" Her rosebud lips turned upwards into a beatific smile. "Talk a Nonie now."

Hana held up her index finger to ask her to wait, grunting as Edin clambered onto her knee. The wooden supports of the deckchair groaned beneath the extra weight. "Edin wants to speak to you, Leslie." She hissed as the child's elbow dug into her ribs as she wriggled into position.

"Edin peak a Nonie?" Her eyes widened, and she bounced her head up and down to indicate her refusal to take no for an answer.

"One minute." Hana wrapped her arm around the child and set the phone on the other knee. "No!" she warned as Edin lurched for it.

"Would you like me to fetch the others from school?" Leslie's cheerfulness crossed the distance between the hotel and the mountain with ease, her willingness to help easing a knot in Hana's shoulders.

"Oh, yes, please!" she gushed. "I just sat down about two minutes ago. Macky is finally asleep, so I'm trying to keep Edin outside to give him some recovery time."

"Ah, bless my wee mokopuna," Leslie cooed, using the Māori word for grandchild. They shared no DNA, but she'd adopted Hana's brood without question, anyway. "How is he today?"

"Tired." Hana dodged sideways as Edin stretched up a tentative hand and tried to snatch her sunglasses. "But his hearing is even better than last time. Phoenix dropped her cereal bowl on the kitchen floor this morning and he jumped into Logan's arms like he thought the world had ended."

"That's a grand sign." Leslie grunted in the background as she heaved her overweight body down the stairs from her apartment. Hana heard the muted strains of a vacuum cleaner as the hotel staff readied the rooms for the next wave of conference guests.

"It is a good sign," she admitted, "not that I enjoyed cleaning up all the smashed crockery, mulched cereal and tears."

"You're a good girl," Leslie soothed. "I don't know many other wāhine who'd take on other people's children like you do. Did Logan drive up to Auckland to attend her appeal?"

"No." Hana cringed and eyed the wriggling child in her arms. "Can we not speak about somebody's mother with them listening? She's already confused."

"Mama?" Edin pushed her forehead against Hana's lips. "Mama, tiss."

Hana kissed the faint line left over from her tumble the previous week. The child healed fast but enjoyed the attention, especially from Hana's older children. She sighed. Besides Mac, only one belonged to her. Leslie's comment about other people's children related to four of her eight offspring.

Thinking of grafted families reminded her of the two adult children from her first marriage. "I meant to call Izzie this afternoon." She peered at the phone screen and tutted. "She'll have started work by now."

"Did that wee one just call you Mama?" Leslie's voice rose on the last word.

Hana cringed. "I don't know how to stop her. She uses my name for a while and then, when she's around the other children, it just pops out."

"You're doing the best you can, kōtiro," Leslie affirmed. "Her real ma can't complain when you're feeding and clothing her tāmahine for free."

"She can and will," Hana sighed. "I hate visiting the prison, but Logan refuses."

Leslie's snort shook the phone with the explosive vibration, and Hana caught it as it slipped sideways off her knee. Not wanting Leslie's opinion on Edin's birth mother, she held the phone up to the child's mouth so she could regale the old woman with her burbled language.

Hana leaned back against the striped fabric of the deckchair and observed her latest family member. Edin chatted to Leslie with complete words interspersed in nonsensical sentences. With another prison visit looming on the horizon, Hana's chest tightened, and a chill rolled over her despite the bright sunshine. "Thanks for getting the children," she called during a momentary break in Edin's involved storytelling. "I'll see you in a couple of hours." She bounced her knees and the little girl released a high giggle. "We'll make dinner. You can stay if you'd like to?"

As Leslie killed the call, Edin bowed low over the phone screen and placed a dribbling kiss against the glass. Hana waited until she looked away to wipe it on her shorts. "What shall we make for dinner?" she asked and Edin squeezed one eye closed in concentration. She lifted the finger and thumb of her left hand and pressed them together as though making a beak. The knitted horse dangled from beneath her armpit, its ratty tail trailing flecks of cut grass and biscuit crumbs. Edin pursed her lips and jabbed at a point in mid-air. Hana frowned with concentration, trying to understand her words.

"Macaroni? Spaghetti bolognaise? Shepherd's pie?" She listed off the limited choices, not wanting the drama and mess of pizza or a stir fry.

"No, no." Edin closed her eyes, and her body convulsed as she tightened every muscle and gritted her teeth. She released her fists and breathed out in a whoosh as though the effort of searching for the word had exhausted her. "Heaven," she said, her eyes bright and her grey irises dancing. "Heaven. Nonie."

Hana wrinkled her nose and observed the child on her knee. "I'm not sure Uncle Logan would find those two concepts synonymous. How about I make macaroni cheese and we'll just call it Heaven?"

"Yep." Edin's huge nod almost rocked her off Hana's knee.

"Fantastic." She held out her arms, and the child snuggled against her chest. Her head rose and fell with the movement of Hana's breathing. The sun caressed their exposed skin, kissing Edin's and attacking Hana's porcelain tones.

"Nonie!" Edin sat up in a rush as Hana's phone rang.

Roused from a gentle snooze, Hana jerked awake and the device crashed onto the deck.

"Oh, no! Nonie!" Edin clambered from the chair and chased after the phone. Her bare toes caught the edge of the case as she bent and it skittered further across the deck. "Oh, no!" she cried, sounding like Phoenix through an uncanny twist of DNA. Her chubby fingers caught the device and clasped it against the flowery pattern of her frock. "Heaven!" she shouted at the ringing screen. "Heaven."

"Here, baby." Hana held out her hand and Edin thumped the phone into her outstretched palm and stepped back.

She stared at the unfamiliar number with a frown. Hana activated the call and pressed the device to her ear. Eden stood in front of her, observant and alert. "Yes, this is Hana Du Rose," she replied to the questioner. Her complexion paled, a waxen hue fading the blush of the sun on her cheeks. "What do you mean, he's missing?" Her tone sharpened, and she sat up straight, despite the sloping angle of the deckchair. Her peripheral vision blurred as she struggled to absorb the words spilling from the phone and into her ear. "He's missing." She dug the knuckles of her left fist into her eyes and clattered the sunglasses. They fell to the ground and Edin swooped to claim them. Hana's heart thudded in her chest and she gave a fleeting thought to the pace maker buried beneath her left collar bone.

"Look, Mama." Edin grinned from behind the sunglasses. She'd perched them on the end of her nose and given herself the appearance of a bug with enormous eyes.

The call ended and Hana dipped forward in the chair, shoving her head between her knees to discourage the pounding in her ear drums. "No," she hissed, her throat strangling the word. "Please, no."

2

Halter

Edin watched as Hana tried Logan's mobile number and then the land line for his office. When she received no response from either, she cast her net wider.

"Detective Inspector Johal." He picked up on the first ring, the cafe noises seeping around his greeting.

"Tama's missing!" Hana spread the fingers of her other hand across her eyes to negate the glare of the sun's rays. They heated her skin with merciless enjoyment, the gentle kisses changing to striped burns as she fidgeted in the deckchair.

"Right." Bodie's tone switched from pleasure at hearing his mother's voice to disappointment. "Thanks, Mum. I'm doing well at my job and my wife and kids are fine. Nice of you to phone."

Hana closed her eyes and forced herself to swallow. It prevented the stream of ready vitriol spilling from her lips. She'd called him at the weekend and enjoyed a long and lazy conversation about his life. It didn't matter how much effort she put into her relationship with her eldest son, it never seemed enough.

Her fingers balled into a fist as she shielded her head with her forearm. "Sorry," she breathed, the energy required to form another response failing her.

"Oopsie." Edin's exclamation followed a snap as the left arm of the sunglasses detached from the lenses. She raised the limp horse from beneath her armpit and glared at him. "Horsey done it."

Hana exhaled and ended the futile call with her son, not investing more into the conversation. "There's never a police officer when you need one," she remarked to the child, unable to keep the irony from her tone.

Edin's lips twisted and she shifted her lower jaw to the right, creating a guilty expression. "No smack horsey."

"No, baby." Hana held out her hand for the remains of her sunglasses. "We don't smack anyone. Even though we might want to cause certain people actual bodily harm sometimes." She blinked against the sun's glare and marveled at the speed with which her afternoon had slid downhill. "It would help if you didn't touch things that don't belong to you, though." She rose and turned her feet towards the house, holding her hand out for Edin to grip. Under her breath, she remarked, "But then, you wouldn't be a Du Rose, would you?"

It took a moment for her eyes to adjust after the glare of outside, and she closed the door behind her and walked Edin to the kitchen. The whirring of her brain belied her outer calm. When her phone trilled in her hand, she jumped and dropped the main body of her sunglasses, hearing a muted crack as Edin stepped on the lens.

"Ouch!" The child's elfin face crumpled, and she looked up at Hana with an expression of disbelief, as though asking how such a terrible thing could happen to her. Ignoring the ruins of her favourite sunglasses, Hana bent at the knees and scooped the child into her arms. Edin's wails deafened her as they settled at the kitchen table.

Hana laid her ringing phone on the table and accepted the call through the speaker. Logan's steady baritone vied with Edin's loud cries. "You after me?"

Hana imagined him jamming his index finger into his other ear and holding the phone away from him. "Sorry," she called over the din. "It's too hard to explain." She reached for Edin's bare foot and tilted the sole to inspect it. "It's a bruise, baby. Sit here and I'll get some ice."

"Ice cream!" Edin's face relaxed as though an artist had smudged out the original and redrawn it in situ. Tears glittered on her cheeks as she fixed her intense, grey-eyed gaze on the fridge.

"I'll call you back in about an hour." Tack clanked, and a horse blew out a long breath.

Her foot forgotten, Edin snatched up the phone and held it to her mouth.

"He missin' now!" she yelled. "He missin'. Heaven and ice cream. Now!"

Hana returned with an ice pack and liberated her phone. Spit and greasy finger marks dotted the screen. "Hold this on your foot," she instructed the child. "I need to speak to Uncle Logan."

"Ice cream," Edin complained. "Not ice cream." She winced as Hana pressed the pack against the sole of her tiny foot. A blue line spread out from a point in her arch. It looked painful.

Logan's continued silence exhibited his supernatural level of patience. He hadn't wanted to give Edin a home, making a valid case for the efficacy of social services. Why, he'd argued, would he want to house the offspring of two people he'd hated with just cause?

Hana took a deep breath and steeled herself. Her husband didn't respond well to hysteria. Mindful of that, she leveled her voice and delivered the news. "Tama didn't show up to work yesterday or the day before. Nobody knows where he's gone.

He didn't phone in sick and his station chief is worried about him. She got my mobile number from his personnel records."

Logan swore, the expected response still causing Hana to take a sharp intake of breath.

"Bugger!" Edin growled, mimicking his rumbling tone. She lifted the ice pack away from her foot and wiped it across the knitted horse's cream muzzle. "Bollocks!"

"Edin! No!" Hana exhaled in a rush and turned to face the window. The sea sparkled in the distance as though it contained a million tiny diamonds. Her craved five minutes of peace lost their lure against the backdrop of the phone call.

"Meet me at the office." Logan rapped out the command with his usual authority. In his capable hands, the terrible issue became something manageable. Solvable. The sense of disaster lifted enough for Hana to search the counter tops for her car and house keys.

"Okay," she agreed. "Give me fifteen minutes to round up Edin's gear and get down there. Where are you now?"

"Bollocks. Heaven." Edin dropped the ice pack onto the kitchen tiles and sat the horse on her head. Its legs dangled either side of her face, its tail giving her a ratty fringe. She blinked from beneath it and giggled up at Hana.

"I'm in the round pen trying out this new gelding." He sighed and Hana sensed his disappointment stretch across the distance between them. She missed Sacha too, the feisty white mare they'd turned loose to retire on the mountain with her sire. They'd found no sign of her last time they checked, just tail hair on the top of a fence post where she'd jumped it and seized her own destiny.

"Any good?" Hana forced her mind away from Tama. It welcomed the momentary relief from the loop of scenarios as she gathered up her keys and pushed her feet into her shoes. Not wanting to fight Edin into the truck parked under the porch, she snatched up a packet of mint chocolate biscuits and jerked her head towards the front door. "We'll take these for Nonie," she whispered, and Edin's eyes widened.

"And me?" Her brows knitted, and she lowered her head to observe Hana from beneath her eyelashes.

"Only for good girls," Hana replied. She added a nonchalant shrug to her statement, hating herself for bribing the child. "Not bribing, rewarding good behaviour," she muttered.

"What?" Metal clattered behind Logan's word, and Hana heard the gentle slap of a palm against a solid, furry neck. "He's okay, but he's not the one. I'm heading back to the office now."

"I'll see you soon." Worry and regret carved deep lines into Hana's delicate forehead as she killed the call. Her auburn hair swam around her face in a cloud of curls and frizz caused by the humidity. She persuaded Edin into the car seat behind her driver's chair and buckled her in, tying the knitted horse's legs through the straps to distract the child's busy fingers. Chucking the biscuits into the driver's seat out of sight, she closed the door.

Her hair resisted as she pulled it into a loose plait and jogged along the hallway to her son's bedroom, each step marking valuable seconds in time.

Mac snoozed over her shoulder as she slammed the front door behind her and yanked open the car. Edin grinned at her from her car seat, the red button still held fast and Horsey's leg's still knotted through the straps. "Got biccit." Edin waved the melting chocolate circle in the air and smiled around brown stained teeth.

"So you have," Hana breathed. Her shoulders slumped further beneath Mac's sleeping weight, intensified by the black cloud encircling her head.

3

Martingale

Hana parked the truck in her reserved spot in the staff car park. She reversed it to facilitate a fast getaway if required. A snap sounded from the back seat as Edin released herself from the safety straps.

"No!" Hana whirled around and pointed at her. "That's dangerous. The grown-up fastens you in and only the grown-up presses that button. Then, we know it's done right. Do you understand?" The ramifications unfurled before her like a rug, decorated with Bodie's distress as a road patrol officer when he arrived first on the scene of an accident. Unbelted child versus windscreen and road surface remained etched on dreams which even therapy couldn't eradicate.

Edin studied her with a furrowed brow, a fathomless depth in her coal black pupils. Dread snaked around Hana's heart as she found herself face to face with the essence of Caroline Marsh. She swallowed and strengthened her will. "I'm not losing this battle with you, Edin. You're beautiful and clever and I know there's a good girl in there." She pointed towards Edin's chest and sighed. "And I love that good girl very much." She just wished she saw more of her. The child required almost all her attention, her stunted speech development making a liar of the intelligence behind her eyes.

Mac's auburn head lolled against his seat, a line of dribble snaking from his lips to his shoulder. Complications from the first surgery for hearing in his left ear had demanded a second attempt to attach the implant to the bone. The coil and audio processor from his right ear peeked from beneath his auburn curls.

Edin gasped, and her eyes lit up like strobes. "Macky!" she hissed. She stretched out her left arm but couldn't quite reach him across the middle seat. "Macky!"

The boy inhaled, pink cheeked and fresh from slumber. He sat up straight and blinked, confused at his presence in the car when he'd gone to sleep in his bed. His green-eyed gaze settled on Hana, and he spread his hands in question. "I need to see Papa," Hana signed. She still used her fingers to speak to him, despite the right implant's lone ability to convey her voice.

He nodded in acknowledgment and lifted a delicate hand to touch the tender skin above his left ear. The shaved hair would grow to cover the scar as it had on the other side. Edin leaned sideways, grunting and stretching her body to reach him and only satisfied when he lifted his hand and tagged her fingers. She released a giant exhale. "All better now." Her head bobbed up and down to confirm her diagnosis.

Hana exhaled. "Right, this is what's happening." Both children watched her hands as she signed and spoke. "I'll walk you upstairs to see Nonie for a moment. We'll take what's left of the biscuits. Maybe Poppa Alfie would let you nap in his bed, Mac? I need to see Papa." She swallowed and turned to Edin. "Uncle Logan."

Mac nodded in understanding and Edin studied him before copying his movement. Hana stepped from the driver's seat and eyeballed Edin through the window. To her credit, the child remained in her seat as Hana pulled open the door. "Do it gain." Edin flapped her slender fingers at the button.

A glance at Mac for a translation showed him signing for her to fasten the button and then release it. An unexpected childishness rose in Hana, making her want to stamp her authority by ignoring the strange request. But as her fingers paused over the straps, Edin smiled up at her as though offering a compromise. "Good girl," Hana forced herself to say. "Nice waiting." She refastened the seatbelt button and then released it.

Realising she'd shot herself in the foot with her enforcement plan, Hana held Edin's hand as she walked around to Mac and released his seatbelt. She relied on the older children to unfasten themselves and had now caused confusion. He looked up at her and smiled, wisdom in his gentle emerald irises. Hana smiled back and kissed his warm forehead. "Thank you for waiting," she mouthed to him. He hadn't heard her rebuke Edin, but had employed his father's quick intelligence to read the situation with accuracy.

Hana held one of Edin's hands and Mac gripped the other as they crossed the hotel car park and entered the lobby. Gravel crunched beneath Hana's shoes and she glanced down at the children's bare toes. They showed no sign of discomfort, stepping across the rough surface like mountain goats.

The receptionist waved from behind his wide desk as they entered the lobby. Hana blinked against the dimness after the glare beyond the double doors. "Hi Mrs Du Rose," he called. "And hello little Du Roses." He never got their names right and had given up trying when Edin arrived.

Hana glanced down to see her jutting her tiny chin upwards and defiance flashing in her eyes. Her delicate fingers gripped Mac's until he released a hiss of pain. Somehow, throughout her short-lived journey of confusion, Edin had discovered a hidden security in her cousin. She clung to it and to him with everything she possessed. It formed another reason Hana couldn't send the girl to the distant relatives of Caroline, who had asked for her through a barbed lawyer's letter.

Hana released Edin's hand once they'd knocked on Alfred and Leslie's apartment door. Light flooded the attic room through skylights as they stepped over the threshold.

"Nonie!" Edin bolted for Leslie's legs and she tangled herself in the floral skirt, which hid them. She lifted her arms and the old lady laughed.

"I can't lift you, kōtiro," she snorted. "You're five. Much too heavy for an old whaea like me to carry." She took Edin's hand and walked to a sagging sofa, sinking into its folds and allowing the child to clamber onto her knee.

"Hana." Alfred Du Rose stepped from behind the partition to the kitchen. A drying towel hung over his left forearm as though she'd disturbed him in the process of tidying.

"Alfie." She kissed his cheek and accepted the embrace he administered despite his arthritic joints.

"Up! Up!" Edin sat bolt upright on Leslie's knee and stabbed her finger at the ceiling. She loved the excitement of accessing the roof garden through the narrow passageway, but she needed a more agile attendant to keep tabs on her than the two octogenarians.

"Not now, darling," Hana soothed. "I need to see Logan."

Alfred bent and pressed a soft kiss to Mac's downy hair. "How you doing, tane?" he demanded.

Mac smiled and lifted a thumbs up, standing on one leg and sticking close to Hana.

"He's good." She stopped herself from answering for him, biting down hard on her tongue. Mac's lips twisted and she sensed him resisting a grin. He didn't mind that she still forgot and acted as his unofficial mouthpiece. She forced brightness into her tone. "Please, can Mac stay with you for a little while? I woke him up to drive down here." Her gaze strayed to Edin, seeing the child's dark curls nestled against Leslie's copious bosom. "I'll take her with me."

"She can stay." Leslie issued the invitation with only a modicum of hesitation.

Hana winced and considered her answer. Alfred patted her shoulder. "She'll behave."

Mac tilted his head to observe her, his steady gaze containing no judgment.

"I'm not sure," Hana whispered. "She seems a little better, but what if she misbehaves and you can't cope?" She forced herself not to look at the French doors in her peripheral vision. The new veranda rail beyond them replaced the one Logan's brother took with him when he plunged to his death in the car park. Caroline had served six months on remand and six months of a thirteen-year sentence for pushing him. Manslaughter, not murder. Though no one in the family denied she'd intended to kill Neville Du Rose, the jury had failed to reach a guilty verdict beyond reasonable doubt. Edin's intense fascination with the veranda had traumatised them all.

"We're fine," Alfie assured her. "I hid the key. She can't get out there or on to the roof." He swallowed. "Not like last time."

"Okay," Hana breathed. She took a step towards Leslie and Edin, bumping Mac's shoulder with her hip by accident. He blinked up at her, his expression blank. "Edin?" Hana injected enthusiasm and seriousness into her tone in equal parts. "Nonie and Poppa Alfie said you can stay. If you're naughty, they'll phone and I'll take you away with me. But if you behave, we'll look at the horses from the roof garden when I get back. Okay?"

"Up?" Hope flickered in Edin's eyes. "Up."

"Yes." Hana stepped back and rested her palm on Mac's warm head. "If you behave."

Edin gripped the horse beneath her arm and considered Hana's bargain. She released a slow nod as Hana held her breath.

A countdown began in her head, moving backwards on an invisible stopwatch to the moment when all hell would break loose and Alfie would call, breathless and dismayed.

Hana kissed the top of her son's head and bolted, her feet drumming down the staircase before the door had clicked behind her. The sense of escape enveloped her, forcing her heart rate to hike and the pacemaker to stand guard over her life. She burst through Logan's office door on the ground floor of the enormous house, her breath coming in heaves and her legs trembling.

He started in surprise, dropping the fountain pen in his hand and rising to his feet. Grey speckled his hair like salt and pepper, making him even more striking and imposing than the glossy black locks of a decade ago.

Hana stopped at the sight of Lincoln standing next to him. "Where's the fire?" the stable manager asked with a smirk. Hana ignored him. She'd accepted his employment but hadn't changed her mind about him.

"I left Edin upstairs with Leslie and Alfie." She glanced down at her watch. "I have about five minutes before they call for help." The stopwatch ticked in her head.

"I'll leave you to it." Lincoln shifted the discarded fountain pen aside and pulled the sheaf of papers free. He gave an upward jerk of his chin to Hana as he passed her. Blond curls poked from beneath the cowboy hat he hadn't removed. The door closed behind him.

Logan met her halfway across the room, his boot soles half on the expensive Turkish rug, which buffered his steps against the wooden floor. Hana relaxed into his chest, the muscles hard against her cheek. She'd played her last hand with Edin, and they both knew it. She sensed him wanting to state the obvious.

"It's fine," she lied. "I'm coping. She's getting better." Hana pulled away from him and turned, knowing he could read her like an open book if she didn't hide her face. "Let's talk about Tama." Her gaze fell on an envelope lying on Logan's desk. The tattered corner showed he'd already opened it. The familiar stamp of the Auckland lawyer sent a dart of anxiety bubbling into her chest. It piled on top of her existing misery. They wanted to take Edin and they weren't giving up.

4
Surcingle

"Another letter?" Hana's finger trembled as she pointed to it. Logan brushed off her question with a jerky shrug of indifference. "Tell me exactly what the fire chief said?" He pulled up his visitor's chair and sat opposite her. She cringed beneath his scrutiny, knowing he expected an accurate account right down to the last full stop and comma. Horse hair clung to the hem of his jeans and she focused on the dark stain of worn saddle soap on the inside of his left calf.

"You need new chaps." She pointed to his leg, stalling as she recalled the conversation in her mind.

The crook of Logan's index finger warmed her chin as he lifted her face and forced her to look at him. "Start with the phone ringing," he commanded, his tone soft and cajoling but laced with authority.

Hana exhaled and her thoughts sorted themselves into order. "I didn't recognise the number. She asked for me and said Tama listed me as his next of kin." Her eyelashes fluttered as she peered at Logan from beneath them. "That's okay, isn't it? You're his uncle, so it should be you."

"It's fine." Logan dragged the chair nearer and stroked his fingers across her cheek and into her hair. His biceps bulged, and the veins rose from beneath his olive skin. The sight distracted her, and she lost her place for a second. "She said he didn't show up for his shift and they're concerned. A few guys visited his house but he isn't there." She swallowed. "What do you think has happened to him? Where do we start?"

Logan exhaled and sat back in the chair. He dropped his hand into his lap. "I don't know." His brow furrowed to a black line, merging with his fringe and casting his eyes into shadow. He tapped his right thigh with his fingers as he sifted through his thoughts. "He called me at the weekend." Logan tutted. "I couldn't hear everything he said because of the noise in the restaurant."

Hana's insides knotted into hard balls of pain. Her shoulders slumped. They'd taken the children to Auckland for the day to celebrate Edin's fifth birthday. She'd chosen to visit the aquarium in Mission Bay and then screamed all the way around it when Hana refused to buy her a second ice cream at the kiosk. Hana took her back to the car, and the others enjoyed her treat without her.

Tears pricked behind her eyelids and she covered her face with her hand. "So, he might have asked for help, and we missed it."

"I missed it." Logan frowned. "It's no one's fault."

Hana blew out a ragged breath. "It's mine. I agreed to keep Edin, and I'm not coping. She runs me in circles and the rest of the family is suffering. Just as I think I'm getting her on track, it's time for another visit to the prison and her mother lectures me on all the things I'm doing wrong. I feel backed into a corner and I can't find the exit."

Logan rose and slipped onto the sofa next to her. His arm wound around her shoulders and he kissed her temple. "Hallelujah!" he snuffed into her hair.

"What?" Hana swallowed and wiped her eyes with the back of her hand. Tension snaked around the crown of her head.

"You're happy now because you can wash your hands of her? I've failed and we can all go back to normal?"

Logan snorted, sounding like one of the stallions on the mountainside. "Really? I thought you knew me better than that."

"I don't know how to fix this," she breathed.

"Then, stop!" His grey irises twinkled with wisdom. "Let us help you, Hana. We're a team and we've spent the last eighteen months watching you ward off assistance like a lone ranger. You can't fix it, but we can."

"How?" Hana tipped her head back to stare at the ceiling. "I thought Bodie proved willful, but Edin makes him look like the model child.

Logan grunted to avoid commenting on Hana's eldest son. He twisted his lips to keep his opinion contained. "Right," he said, his tone definitive. "This is how it's going to go from today. You'll stop shielding Edin from anyone else's discipline and accept help. I'll make the next prison run and it will be the last for the foreseeable future. Caroline can't have it all ways."

Hana gasped and leaned back to gauge Logan's expression. "You can't keep a mother from her baby."

Logan shook his head, his neck stiff and the motion stilted. "Caroline should have thought about that before she shoved Nev off the balcony. She either accepts my terms or we hand the kid over to the family members who keep sending us nasty lawyer's letters. If they want Edin, they can have her. Caroline killed my brother, Hana. I owe her nothing. From now on, it's my way or the highway."

Hana exhaled. "Okay. If you're only bluffing. We keep Edin." Relief released a lightheaded sensation which caused her head to swim. "What about me?"

Logan rose and walked towards his desk. He gave a nonchalant shrug of his broad shoulders and a smirk slid across his lips. "You can behave too."

Hana tutted. "I mean, what about me and Edin? How can I change what's going wrong?"

"Easy." Logan tapped the keyboard on his desk and squinted at the computer screen. "Stop sheltering her like a delicate flower. Everyone else is scared to tell her off because you jump in and shield her. It takes a village to raise a kid, Hana. Stop mediating for her and making excuses."

Hana nodded. "I'm afraid she'll tell Caroline what a failure I am as a parent. She already criticises everything I do."

Logan snatched up a piece of paper and a pen and glanced up at Hana. "Which is why I'm taking the next visit. I'm sorry for the kid, I really am. But I won't continue jeopardising my family for her sake. It ends today."

Hana rubbed her stomach, sensing the knots constructed from each of Edin's tantrums disperse. Then she remembered Tama, and the tension flooded back into place like the return of the tide. "The fire chief is expecting me to call her back today." She sniffed. "What do I tell her?"

"That I'll find him." Logan stuffed the scrap of paper into his front pocket. "And I will." He tapped his pocket. "That's the address of the fire station. We'll drive up there tomorrow. Wait here a second. I'll run to reception and ask Raymond to cancel all my appointments and we'll leave as soon as we've dropped the kids at school."

Hana gulped. "We?" She edged forward on the sofa until her knees dipped towards her toes. "But what about Mac? He can't go back for a few days because of his stitches. And Edin? I'm sitting here waiting for Armageddon to start."

Logan strode across the room and paused with his hand on the door knob. "Mac can hang with Alfred tomorrow. He wants to drive up to check on Methuselah with Toby and asked if he could take him. I'll see if Leslie can fetch the others after school, in case we're late home." He turned his body to face Hana. "And Edin is going to have her first day in the reception class."

"No!" Hana rose. "Caroline doesn't want her at school yet. Edin can't string a sentence together. She already blames me for that, so she'll go nuts if I put her in school."

"Tough." Logan shrugged. "Caroline is in prison with no power, yet you give her total autonomy over my family. The school said she can start, so she's going. It's time for her to sink or swim."

"But that's cruel!" Hana closed her eyes and imagined Edin's blonde mother glowering at her across the table in the visiting hall. She flipped the scene and put Logan in the hot seat, hating that scenario even more. "You can't go to the prison, Logan! She still loves you."

"You mean, you don't want me to go in case I see her in her prison sweatshirt and decide I'm in love with her. At least tell the truth, wāhine."

"It sounds ridiculous when you say it like that." Hana sighed and clasped her knees. "But I've seen how manipulative she is."

"Yep, first hand, it seems." Logan closed the door behind him and Hana see-sawed between relief and terror. She didn't doubt that Caroline would relish seeing Logan again and cringed at the thought of the other woman's delight. But the weight of the prison visits and the endless stream of criticism she endured while there seemed to lose their heaviness.

Hana turned her palms downwards and opened her fingers, allowing the emotional load to cascade to the ground and dribble through the cracks of the floorboards. "We're a team," she murmured. "Start being one."

Logan returned within minutes, having instructed Raymond to empty his calendar. "I'll call the school," he said, reaching for his desk phone. "She can wear one of Phoenix's old uniforms. They can stop writing to us now." He searched for the number online and dialed.

Hana held her breath as he dealt with the unfortunate school receptionist, whose squeaked protest issued through the gap between the handset and Logan's ear. When his mobile rang in his pocket, he hauled it free and frowned at the number.

"She's just gone to fetch someone," he remarked to Hana, smirking as he jerked his head towards the land line. He answered the mobile in his other hand. "Hi, Pete. Hana's here. She'd love to talk to you." He lobbed his phone through the air, giving her no other choice but to catch it.

"Pete who?" she demanded. At the grin on Logan's face, she shook her head and held the device away from her body. "Logan, no!" she hissed. She lifted it in her fingers, ready to throw it back to him, but she'd faltered too long and lost the bluff. Temper burgeoned in her chest as her husband laughed and turned away to answer a question on the other phone. He'd let the mobile smash on the floorboards if she threw it, knowing someone else would order him a new one and spend the time making it fit for his use. Material items held none of his affection beyond their usefulness in the scheme of his day. At that moment, Hana hated him for it.

"Hi, Pete. Can I call you another time? We've got stuff going on here."

Mouth noises issued from the device as Hana activated the speaker. She'd force Logan to listen one way or another. "No." He huffed and puffed, the offense obvious. "I want to talk to you about our wedding. Henrietta's very upset. Logan said we could hold it at your hotel, but the receptionist told her there isn't a single weekend free between now and December."

"We shut in December." Hana stated the obvious and then groaned. Logan turned towards her, one eyebrow raised and a smirk spreading across his lips.

"Logan said we could hold it at your hotel. He offered us a discount."

"Phoenix is seven!" The sentence blasted free without consideration, causing Pete to pause in his complaint.

"Happy birthday to Phoenix?" He didn't sound sure. "Many happy returns?"

Hana rose and shook her head at her husband. "Logan made that offer eight years ago. You can't turn up now and demand he fulfill an obligation which you didn't value at the time. We don't do weddings anymore, Pete. This is a hotel and conference centre. You need to find another venue."

Her fingers shook as she stabbed the flashing icon on the screen. Pete's indignation ended with an abrupt silence. Hana hung her head and closed her eyes. Her heartbeat thrummed in her ear drums, rhythmic and steady. Healthy. For now.

Logan's slow clap forced her to open one eye. He hung the handset back in the cradle. "Mrs Du Rose, you are the new taniwha." His lips quirked upwards on one side and admiration sparkled in his grey irises. "You're scary when you get going. Anyone ever told you that?" He exhaled and rubbed his eye sockets with his knuckles. "Welcome back, I've missed you."

5

Hackamore

Edin clutched Hana's hand as they walked across the playground. An old skirt of Phoenix's bumped the back of the child's skinny calves as she pressed against Hana's legs.

"School now?" Edin's voice held an uncharacteristic waver as Hana bent to kiss both Phoenix and Wiri's foreheads. The older boy pinked with embarrassment at the routine and brushed a hand across his skin as though wiping away the kiss.

"Yes, darling." Hana forced a beam of enthusiasm onto her lips, making her eyes wide to hide her misgivings. "You're five, aren't you? They sent you an invitation to register through the post, remember?"

Three invitations, to be exact, each a month apart. Caroline had insisted Hana reject them all, citing Edin's poor speech as a factor to keep her at home. Hana pursed her lips together as she waved to another mother. She'd confessed to Logan the previous afternoon how Caroline had demanded she home-school her daughter. Pity for Edin had fanned the flames with which Caroline had surrounded her. Logan's intervention laid waste to the scheme. He'd obtained a visiting order for the prison and would break the news to Edin's mother. He'd also phoned Tama's station chief.

Hana held Edin's hand as they stepped onto the porch of her new classroom. Children milled around outside, hanging lunch boxes and cardigans from named pegs. She searched for Edin's name and sighed at the spelling. "This is yours," she said, keeping her tone bright. "Let's hang your lunch on here and find your teacher." Edin cast a knowing gaze at her name and frowned. Doubt clouded her grey irises, and she blinked up at Hana.

"Isn't."

"We'll get it changed," Hana promised. "It's warm today. You might not need to wear your cardigan."

"Mrs Du Rose." A tall woman with gentle blue eyes emerged from the classroom. She held out her hand to Hana. "I'll introduce Edin to the class and then we'll have a quick chat?" She framed the statement as a question and Hana winced, wishing she'd press ganged Logan into doing this part. The woman squatted down in front of Edin and addressed her at eye level. "It's nice to meet you. We were very excited to learn you could join us. I'm Mrs Tomlin. Mac is usually in our class, and I'm sure he'll look after you once he comes back next week." She glanced up at Hana. "How is he?"

"Good," Hana whispered. Guilt ravaged her heart as Edin's fingers shook in hers. An inexplicable urge to cry pushed tears onto her lower eyelids and she turned aside and blew out a shallow breath to hide her emotion. She'd thrown the child to the wolves to save herself from insanity.

A frown lined Mrs Tomlin's forehead, and she rose and offered her hand to Edin. "Angela is excited to meet you," she whispered. "You can sit with her and Mrs Forrester, if you like?"

A low keening noise began in Edin's chest, revving like a motor as she sensed her world tilting out of control. Hana saw the scenario unfold like it had many times in the last months.

"Could you draw me a horse?" Hana bent down to whisper in her ear. "I bet they have better art materials here. Draw the perfect horse for Uncle Logan to ride. He's desperate for one of his own."

"Horsey." Edin bumped the knitted toy against her stomach, and his legs danced as though electrified. "Paint." She gritted her teeth as she issued the command about the type of art she might consider.

"How did you know we were painting today?" Mrs Tomlin clapped her hands together and Edin studied her enthusiasm with interest. She called through the classroom door to her teaching assistant. "Mrs Forrester, we have another artist joining us."

"Fantastic." A round woman looked up from a child's tiny chair. Her thighs spilled over its edges like muffins. Her expression didn't match the word.

Anxiety set Hana's tongue flapping and she couldn't contain the burble of excuses which broke free. "I know we missed all the tester days last term, but somebody's mother didn't want her to come. I can't manage her at home full time and my husband put his foot down yesterday."

She clapped a hand over her mouth as Mrs Tomlin's eyes widened and she raised a finger in warning. "Let's get Edin fixed up with a painting overall, and Mrs Forrester can take the register while we chat."

Hana swallowed as the teacher offered Edin her hand. The child stared at it and then into her face. Her irises glittered with a raft of emotions Hana couldn't read. She held her breath and waited for the expected tantrum.

Edin's head bobbed once, and she allowed Mrs Tomlin to take her hand. Horsey's legs dangled almost to her knees as he bumped her thighs with his knitted hooves. They moved off and Hana stopped breathing, blood thudding through her eardrums as she froze in position.

It seemed a relief when Edin's sandals ground to a halt on the floorboards of the classroom. Like a suicide bomber grateful for the finality of the dreaded moment of explosion, Hana watched as Mrs Tomlin jerked in surprise. The child whirled around and sped back to the porch.

"Tiss it." She jabbed a slender finger at her forehead. "Tiss it now!"

The other children turned to watch as Edin rose on tiptoes and batted Hana's thigh.

"Here you go." Her voice wavered and her knees knocked together as she bent at the waist and pressed a kiss to Edin's head. The girl's eyelashes fluttered, and then she raised Horsey and swiped him over the spot. She smiled at Hana and jabbered something nonsensical.

Hana blew out a slow breath and forced her lips to curve upwards in response. Her hand lifted in a shaking, feckless wave. Edin had spent eighteen months observing Wiremu dodging Hana's kisses and produced a version of her own. Mrs Tomlin retrieved her and put her under the care of the capable Mrs Forrester.

"Let's stand away from the windows," she advised, as she returned to Hana. She steered her off the porch and around the corner after closing the door behind her.

Hana floundered, not sure where to begin. "I'll fill in the paperwork now," she promised. "We have a copy of her birth certificate and the guardianship papers." Her fingers fumbled with the zipper of her handbag as she tried to extract them.

Mrs Tomlin rested her hand over Hana's and halted her action. "You can do that at the office. Someone from your family put her on the school's waiting list last year, so you just need to complete the process." She glanced over her shoulder as a reedy voice piped a reply to Mrs Forrester calling out their name. "Tell me whatever you can to help me today."

Hana swallowed. "She doesn't speak well. I took her to the doctor, but she wouldn't allow her to examine her ears. She didn't think the problem was auditory."

Mrs Tomlin cocked her head. The toe of her practical right shoe scraped a pattern in the grit and she stared at it for a moment. "You mentioned her mother. Is this the woman in prison?" She raised a hand at Hana's blink of surprise. "It's a small town, Mrs Du Rose. I taught the Year 6 class last year, but the case hit the news media."

"Yes." Hana nodded. "Well, Caroline doesn't think she's ready for school. I drive Edin to the prison once a month to visit her. She loves seeing her mother but hates the environment, and her behaviour deteriorates for around ten days after each trip."

"Thank you." Mrs Tomlin turned to leave but glanced back at Hana. "Anything else?"

"Her lunch is on her peg. Logan primed Wiri and Phoenix to help if she gets distressed or can't make herself understood." Her lips moved and her chin wobbled of its own accord. "Obviously, if she gets hysterical, you can call me. We have an appointment at the prison, but we're an hour away at most." The verbal diarrhoea threatened again, and she bit her lip. The prison wasn't the main reason for their trip. Her mind performed somersaults as it drifted to Tama.

Mrs Tomlin's soles tapped against the porch steps and Hana tutted as she remembered another important fact. "Edin! She spells it with an 'i', not an 'e', as in Dunedin. It's where she was born."

"Not a problem." Mrs Tomlin gave a wave and continued through the door to the classroom. Hana imagined her instructing a grumpy Mrs Forrester to assemble a bevy of new labels.

The school fell silent but for the gentle hum of low voices as the children settled into their rhythm. Hana imagined herself as a helium balloon released into the sky by careless fingers. Then guilt crashed into the vacant space, berating her for abandoning the defenseless child against her mother's wishes. Concrete weights dragged at her feet as she turned towards the school office, her ears listening for the shrill tones of Edin's condemning screams.

6

Longeing

“I forgot to tell her Edin can read.” Hana tapped a nervous beat on her right thigh as Logan turned his truck onto the motorway. “She asked me to give her the most important information, and I burbled on like an idiot about Caroline. I should have told Mrs Tomlin she’s been reading for over a year.” Trees and bushes blurred in her peripheral vision as they sped towards Auckland Region Women’s Corrections Facility and certain doom. “I don’t think she’s deaf. Do you think she’s deaf?”

Logan’s palm settled over her writhing fingers and though he said nothing, it calmed Hana enough to draw breath. “Sorry,” she whispered. “I’m sorry.”

“They’ll find out she can read pretty fast,” he mused. “And there’s nothing she can throw at them they haven’t seen before today.”

Hana exhaled and leaned her head against the seat. “Am I the problem, Logan? If it’s nothing physical, is it something I’ve caused?”

Logan's face clouded, and he stared at her as though replaying her question. "No!" He sounded appalled. "It's one thing to accept other people's children, Hana, and another to take the blame for their baggage. Phoenix and Mac are fine. Don't accept guilt for factors outside your control." He withdrew his hand, and a chill moved through Hana as he cut himself off from her downward spiral of recriminations. He'd accepted Wiri, pushing aside his misgivings about the boy's parentage. But Edin proved a step too far. She and Wiri shared a father but having Logan's ex fiancée as her mother acted like a knife through his chest. Yet Hana had taken her anyway, giving her a home when Alfred and Leslie couldn't cope.

"What a mess," she breathed. "I'm sorry for not listening to you at the start."

Logan released a sigh but didn't respond, watching the traffic as he pulled into the outside lane. The diesel engine rumbled beneath them, steady and reliable.

"What will you say to her?" Hana pushed herself upright and turned in her seat. "What will you say to Caroline?"

Logan shrugged, the motion nonchalant. It jarred with the nervous jitters Hana experienced for days before each trip to the prison. "I don't know yet." His reply caused her eyelids to give a series of rapid blinks. It amazed her he could remain so calm, relying on his wit and intelligence to furnish him with immediate responses to Caroline's demands. She leaned against the hard edge of the door handle and sifted through her memory of previous visits. She'd rehearsed every possible conversation before she even stepped through the door of the prison.

Her gaze dropped to her ring finger, and she spun the gold band hanging loose below her knuckle. Stress had caused weight loss. Her engagement and eternity rings kept slipping off when she washed her hands. Hana sighed and pressed her palms together, sliding them between her thighs to stop them trembling. "There's a dog," she said, her voice a whisper. "He has to sniff the car and everyone entering the prison. They're looking for drugs and weapons."

Logan gave her a nod and a smile, which didn't reach his eyes. "Good job I took them all out then, isn't it?" he assured her.

But as they drove the rest of the way in silence, she rebuked her selfishness. They didn't need to take Edin. That was on her. She'd insisted. "I'm sorry," she said again. "You shouldn't have to do this."

They queued to enter the prison car park, subjected to the customary searches of vehicles and persons. Hana recognised the corrections staff from her other visits. Eighteen other visits, to be exact. They nodded to her and moved on, the tan dog with the floppy ears showing no interest in them or their truck.

Logan parked where the officer directed. Hana pulled out her phone, preparing to answer some emails while she waited. But the officer approached the truck and knocked on the window. "You can't wait here, miss," he advised.

"But I'm not going in today." Hana pushed the door ajar and stared up at him.

"Wait over there." He pointed to a metal shelter where a group of women gathered. They smoked and bickered in low voices, occupying the bench which ran the width of the space. They stared at Hana as she walked towards them, assessing and judging her based on her appearance.

"What are you looking at?" a slender woman snapped. Bleached hair hung in dead tresses from grey roots. She glared at Hana, challenging her to enter their space.

"Leave her alone!" An olive skinned grandma perched at the very end of the bench, her clacking knitting needles incongruous against the surroundings. Soft pink wool passed through her fingers, jarring with the razor wire and aluminum backdrop. Hana followed the twin lines of her thread into a copious bag nestled between her feet. "Sit by me," she demanded, patting the metal. Her rings created an eerie click against the bench.

"Thank you." Grateful, Hana settled next to her with a sigh. The phone in her jacket pocket caused the garment to list to one side on her shoulder, but she didn't dare get it out in front of the women. The blonde one chain-smoked and flicked ash without consideration, the fumes drifting into Hana's nostrils and irritating her lungs. A tightness built in her chest and she imagined the hostility a coughing fit would cause.

"What's yours in for?" The kuia looked up from beneath bushy grey brows.

"Sorry?" Hana leaned closer to listen.

"What's your prisoner in there for?" She jerked her head towards the queue snaking from the front doors.

"Oh. Assault with a deadly weapon. Murder. Well, manslaughter."

"There's a difference, you stupid bitch!" The blonde woman shook her cigarette at Hana. "One's accidental and the other isn't." She pointed at Logan as he stood head and shoulders above the other visitors. "Is he with you? He's fit."

Hana nodded, her insides quailing. The women jeered and made coarse remarks about conjugal visits, remarking on the unfairness of New Zealand prisons not allowing them.

Hana ground her teeth. She'd had courage once, nursing it like a tiny flame and finding it when she needed its assistance. It seemed so long ago when she'd galloped around the property on her white mare. Sacha had given her confidence. A sharp pain snaked through Hana's chest. She missed her with a physical ache. The last year and a half had sapped her courage until even the spark had flickered to nothing. Her fear of the women caused a flush of embarrassment to stain her cheeks.

"Ignore them." The kuia reached the end of her row and turned her knitting over to begin again on the other side. A baby's pink sleeve flopped against her thigh. "My mokopuna is on remand," she said with a sigh, referring to a grandchild. "She's pregnant." She lifted the needles and two sleeves bounced, a delicate cable pattern snaking through the middle of each. "I can't go in today. They waited until I got here to tell me she got put in solitary for fighting."

"Pregnant? A baby girl?" Hana kept the other women in her peripheral vision as she spoke to the kuia. Despite the cameras mounted on metal struts, they oozed a restless trouble.

"Yeah. She can keep the baby here until she's two." She nodded and smiled, tugging on her woollen threads to loosen the tension and then resuming her gentle clacking.

"I don't think anyone offered Caroline the choice," Hana mused. "Her husband died of cancer, so I took her daughter."

The blonde woman stubbed out her cigarette, crushing it into oblivion with the rubber sole of her trainer. "I've seen you here," she remarked, raising an invisible eyebrow. Black pencil formed a thick line in the general area, missing the mark and giving her a startled expression. "With a kid." She jerked her head towards the queue as Logan disappeared through the door into the bowels of the prison. He'd left his phone and wallet in the truck and she had the keys. The driver's license in the front pocket of his trousers identified him to the guard at the entrance. "Is she his kid?"

"No." Hana watched the queue shrink as the waiting visitors snaked into the prison. "Niece."

The woman snorted and jeered at Hana. "Na. She's his kid. He did you dirty, babe. Now he's going in for a bit of conjugal bliss." She laughed at her own joke and the others with her tittered.

Hana turned her face aside and kept her expression impassive. A latent fury fired up in her gut, stoking itself into a slow burn, which she struggled to contain. Her fists balled by her thighs on the metal bench until the kuia elbowed her in the ribs. "Don't bite, honey," she murmured. She darted her gaze at the group within kicking distance. "Seen their like before, a million times over."

The blonde's eyes flared, but she didn't challenge the elderly woman. The matriarch's quiet authority suggested she returned home to a whānau. Du Roses bickered and fought among themselves, but they stood as one against outsiders. Hana imagined the kuia surrounded by strapping sons and grandsons ready to take up her cause. Her mind flicked to memories of Tama's laughter, his dancing grey eyes and the mischievous tilt of his chin.

The blonde lit another cigarette, arguing with an officer who asked her to extinguish it. "No smoking." He pointed to a sign inside the shelter and stood his ground. "Why are you here?" he demanded as she continue to hold the lighted cigarette out of his reach. Smoke funneled into the atmosphere in wispy lines.

"I'm seeing my partner," she snarled. "But that dude won't let me inside today. So, I'm waiting with my mates."

The officer beckoned to the colleague she'd pointed to, and the women became engrossed in an ensuing discussion. The officers led the group back to their vehicle and saw them off the premises. Hana breathed a sigh of relief as they took their latent sense of threat with them. "I hate this," she admitted in a rush.

"Me too." The kuia sighed. "It's not how I ever imagined I'd spend my weekdays." Her needles paused as she inspected the hands of an analogue watch face. "My husband will come for me soon."

"Where do you live?" Hana concentrated on her heartbeat, regulating her breaths and forcing herself into a calmer state. "We're going as far as Parnell if you'd like a ride?"

The old lady waved her needle, keeping hold of her knitting with the yarn tucked beneath bent fingers. "I'm good, honey. My tāne dropped me outside the gate and he's coming back for me." She smiled without looking at Hana, finishing her row and ramming her knitting to one end of the needle. Dipping forward, she shoved her creation into the bag at her feet with a grunt. "Good luck, honey," she wheezed as she rose. "You do right to pick your battles." She hefted her bag and weaved through the parked vehicles towards the exit.

Hana gnawed on her lower lip and considered the kuia's words. She'd provided encouragement instead of dwelling on her obvious lack of courage. A memory surfaced of her at school and wearing hockey pads. She'd frozen in place as an unforgiving match ball soared through the air towards her face. She hadn't moved a muscle, rooted to the spot as the ball clanged against the metal post of the goal and ricocheted into the field. It dropped at the feet of a defender who bore it away, out of danger.

"Well left, Hana!" the coach had called from the sideline. "Great judgment."

She always wondered if he'd seen her fear and converted it into feigned wisdom, allowing her to receive the praise and save face. She experienced a moment of delayed gratitude for his kindness. Time allowed her to pay it forward and heap her appreciation onto the shoulders of the woman lumbering across the car park. Her grand-baby's knitted jacket peeked from the top of her bag.

Hana's phone vibrated in her pocket and she pulled it free and peered at the screen.

7

Rein

"Hey, don't hang up on me, Mum." Her eldest son's tone held a faint plea. "Amy gave me a serve when I got home."

Hana's eyelids fluttered as she battled with the rebuke on the end of her tongue. He saw no error in his behaviour but phoned because his wife pointed it out to him. She half-wished the blonde woman would return and pick another fight so she could redeem herself. Venting her disappointment on Bodie always proved futile, but it burned in her stomach like a knot of flaming rope. "Right," she replied, the word stiff and jerky as she released it into the atmosphere. "I can't talk to you now. We're at the prison."

"He got himself locked up. Wow!"

"I should go. Bye." Hana killed the call and stuffed the device back into her pocket. She drummed the toes of her boots on the concrete to funnel the pent-up aggression. Her nature demanded that she forge comfort and safety amid adversity, and she'd done that. Edin had turned their family life inside out, and

Hana placed herself in the firing line, holding back the tide with her slender fingers. To no avail.

Doom washed over her. She'd missed something important with Tama, blindsided by the demands of the mini tornado occupying her home. Worries about Edin dominated every waking moment until the facade slipped and Logan noticed. She couldn't cope.

Hana rose and paced the shelter, digging her hands in her pockets to stop them from shaking. The need to be in two places at once picked at her loyalties.

Tama needed her.

Edin needed her.

They were other people's children, while her own tiny son needed her most but wouldn't ask.

"Are you all right, miss?" The female voice startled her to a halt. She wore a guard's uniform and a German Shepherd waited by her left leg, its tongue lolling from one side. Ears pricked, it stared at her with gimlet eyes.

"I'm waiting for my husband." Hana freed her hands, and they wrung at her chest.

"Are you strung out, miss?" The officer cocked her head, and Hana waited for her to finish her sentence. She didn't, and it occurred to her that perhaps there wasn't more to the question.

She swallowed and faced the officer, her eyes wide and unblinking. "What do you mean? Strung out. What is that?" She took a step forward, and the woman raised her hand.

"Just stay there, miss. I'm asking if you're coming down off a high. Drugs. Do you need a paramedic?"

Hana's lips moved, and no sound emerged. Her mind went blank behind her staring eyes. She gaped at the officer and then at the dog as though looking for help from the animal's inquisitive face.

"You ready?" Logan appeared behind the officer, staying out of range of the dog.

"Is this lady with you?" The woman eyed Hana through narrowed eyes, placing her body at an angle to form a corner between them.

"Yep." He beckoned to Hana with a jerk of his head and waited for her to slip past the dog. The officer didn't move her body, but her head swivelled on her neck and the dog mirrored the action like a furry twin.

Logan caught up Hana's hand and led her across the car park, starting as her boot soles ground to a halt on the asphalt. "What's wrong?" His brows met over the bridge of his nose as she released his fingers.

"I'm a door mat," she announced. "I'm everybody's bloody door mat!" She spun on her heel and stamped across the car park, weaving around the vehicles until she reached the shelter. The officer had moved on, walking the dog towards the front door of the prison.

"Hey!" Hana called.

The officer spun, her stance stiff and on instant alert. "Just stay there," the woman said, her tone even. "You don't need to run at me." Her left hand strayed to the radio at her chest.

"I just wanted you to know that I'm not on drugs." Hana ground out the words as though spitting glass. "I'm frightened and sad and guilty. My little boy just had surgery and my big boy is missing." She lifted her left hand to squeeze the bridge of her nose, sensing no sympathy in the officer's stance.

"You're wasting your time." Logan's steady voice rumbled through her confusion and his strong fingers gripped her elbow. "She doesn't care, Hana. We're leaving."

"But she thinks I'm on drugs. She wanted to string me up a minute ago."

"No, that's not right, miss." The woman's words remained respectful, but she exchanged the detachment for concern. "I did not threaten to hang this lady." A glance to her right showed her a colleague coming to her assistance. "I asked if you were strung out, is all, miss?"

Logan released a groan alongside a vile expletive. "She's not on drugs, lady." His grip intensified around Hana's elbow and he tugged her against his side. "She wouldn't know where to start." He bent his head to whisper into his wife's ear. "We're leaving. Now."

"Why wouldn't I know where to start?" Hana protested in a loud voice. Logan steered her between two parked cars and directed her steps towards their truck. "Asprin, paracetamol, ibuprofen. I could overdose on all of those if I wanted." Logan blinked at the seriousness in her expression. He shoved her into the passenger seat and slammed the door. Long strides took him around the vehicle, and he started the engine with a side glance at Hana. She lifted her left hand and counted off her fingers, beginning with the index. "White stuff," she listed. Her brow furrowed, and she raised her middle finger. "Other white stuff."

"Hana, shut up." He shook his head and laughed as he steered the truck through the gates. "Did you want to get yourself banned?"

"What?" She sat up straight in her seat and turned to him, her lips pouting in dismay. "I could get banned? Why did no one tell me that's all it would take?"

She slammed her spine against the seat and descended into a sulk which lasted as far as the next service station.

8

Roller

"I need coffee." Logan stepped from the truck and stretched, pointing his fingers towards the matte azure sky.

Hana pouted and jumped from the runner board, not waiting for him to open her door. "I need the bathroom," she announced, seizing her chance to dash across the busy car park. She lurched into the nearest stall, hissing in annoyance as her sleeve became entangled with the latch. Then she crouched without touching the walls and buried her face in her forearms like a child. The pose lasted thirty seconds before her thigh muscles atrophied and she rose with an equal measure of difficulty and disappointment. "You never could pull off a spectacular sulk," she rebuked herself with a sigh.

Hana used the toilet and washed her hands at the sink, primping her hair and dragging her feet to avoid Logan's scrutiny. As the hands of her watch stole away the minutes, she felt the vibration of her phone in her jacket pocket. Other travellers milled around her, coupled with the jarring clang of the toilet doors as women moved through their ablutions like automatons. Hana lurked by the hand dryers and tugged her phone free.

'Got you a coffee to go. Waiting in the truck.'

Logan's thoughtfulness stung her. She sensed the familiar dance begin, the unconstrained notes already chiming in her mind. He'd recognised the storm brewing in her heart and chosen to bide his time until the complaints spilled from her lips like a burst dam. Then he'd deal with the fallout in his gentle, authoritative way.

Hana washed her hands again and exited the bathroom, knowing he observed her crestfallen trudge from the service station to the truck. She slammed the door behind her and sank into her seat, reaching for the cardboard cup in the holder.

As her hand curled around the warm surface, Logan's fingers arrested the movement. The sun's rays refracted through the windscreen and bleached the colour from his skin, revealing the myriad fine scars. Hana's chest tightened and the list of petty grievances pushed from behind her lips.

"It's still hot." Logan released his grip and lifted a napkin from the dashboard. "Use this."

Tears prickled the backs of Hana's eyelids and the damn burst as she accepted his offering. It wasn't just a scrap of flimsy tissue in that moment, but a truce flag. "I didn't want you to see Caroline. Ever again." Her lungs shuddered and her breath hitched, as her misery lowered a blade onto the last strings of her composure. "She'll never give up on you. She told me that every time I took Edin to the prison."

Logan said nothing, but his grey irises absorbed Hana's tumult. They morphed from a stormy sea to a gunmetal hue. "I know." His admission stripped away the remains of her weak resolve and she dropped her hand into her lap. "She phoned me after her appeal failed yesterday. I sent her call to voicemail."

"You knew how she felt and yet you let me keep driving up here for her abuse?" Hana shuddered, the motion starting at her shoulders and ricocheting through her torso to end in the depths of her roiling stomach. Pique entered her tone.

Logan threw back his head and laughed. "I don't stop you doing anything, Hana. It's best to oversee your madness and wait until you run aground." He sighed and his dark fringe bounced with the movement of his lashes. "You're just like Sacha; all misguided loyalty and grand plans. She'd gallop anywhere without thought about how she'd stop when she got there."

"Thanks." Hana wiped her nose with the edge of her sleeve and grimaced. "You loved Sacha," she murmured, reaching for the hidden compliment instead of the rebuke.

"I also despaired of her." Hana experienced the force of his perceptive gaze as he turned to face her. He raised an eyebrow and dipped his head. "How many times over the years have different people wanted to put a bolt through her brain?"

Hana gasped, and a flush crawled up her neck. "That's just rude!"

"Drink your coffee." Logan jerked his head towards her cup. "Do you think we should drive to Tama's house first, or to the fire station?"

Hana reached for her cup and pursed her lips. "I don't know." She sipped and her eyes glazed as she turned her thoughts to Logan's wayward nephew. "We might find him hiding out at home, but we don't have a key. The fire chief didn't seem to know much, only that he hadn't fronted for work and didn't answer either his phone or his front door."

Logan slugged the last of his coffee and held onto the cup, tapping the fingers of his other hand on the steering wheel. "Yeah, she said the same to me. Know any cops?" He narrowed his eyes to slits and squinted sideways at her.

Hana avoided his gaze and busied herself with her drink. When she didn't respond, Logan dipped forward to study her expression of guilt.

"Right." He exhaled. "I guess we're on our own, then."

Hana nodded. "I tried to speak to him, but he assumed the worst as soon as I mentioned Tama. Maybe you could try?" She issued the question without enthusiasm. Logan had long since abandoned any hope of establishing an amiable relationship with Bodie. They avoided each other, circling Hana like moons, sharing the same orbit but destined never to engage.

Logan dumped his cup in a nearby dustbin, stretched again, and then started the diesel engine. As Hana mirrored him in fastening her seatbelt, she imagined them as paragliders leaping in tandem from a high ridge and diving into the thermals. "Where are you, Tama?" she whispered beneath the rumble of the engine. "Did you leave us any clue?"

9

Harness

"What did Caroline say?" Curiosity forced Hana to engage with her husband as he navigated the streets of Parnell.

"Will it help you to know?" He leaned forward to judge the gap between two cars before easing into it.

Hana exhaled. She lifted her voice into an irritating whine meant to mimic Caroline, though it sounded nothing like her. "You can't keep my child away from me. How dare you send her to school. I'm phoning her tonight and I expect you to let her talk to me. Why did you marry that stupid woman, Logan, when you could have had me?" She wobbled her head on her neck and turned her lips down before acknowledging her runaway imagination. "Is that what she said?" She flapped her hand, a feckless movement drained of energy.

Logan squinted sideways at her through one eye. "She got mad about Edin going to school. Even madder about you not driving her to the prison for a while. She didn't compare herself to you though, possibly because she's wearing prison sweats and you're not. But perhaps also because she's learned she can't come between us."

Hana rolled her eyes, not believing a word of it. "Whatever," she sighed.

"Is it possible that you've tied yourself in knots by taking on her daughter and then mitigating the inevitable damage?"

Hana gaped but couldn't think of a suitable response. Caroline's spiteful influence clouded her days and filled her nightmares. Until she looked at Edin, and then she saw only hurt and a latent, indecipherable terror. "Maybe," she whispered.

"Look," Logan said, his tone carrying a note of appeal. "These relatives are asking for access to the kid. Why don't we let them take her?"

"Did Caroline say it was okay?" Hana narrowed her eyes at him.

"No." He shook his head and tapped the steering wheel. The car in front stalled at the traffic lights, a learner driver at the helm. "I've checked my grandmother's diaries and she says Antoinette left Caroline with family from Kerikeri after she gave birth to her. Somehow, Reuben ended up with her back at our place after Antoinette died, even though he wasn't her father. He raised her, anyway. Why would a man take care of his wife's illegitimate kid unless the family she left her with turned out to be a worse bet?"

"You read the diaries?" Hana's body stiffened and she turned in her seat. "Can I have them back again? I didn't finish."

Logan narrowed his eyes and pursed his lips. "Let me think about it," he said with resignation. "I've read them all now and Will's catalogued them. I don't suppose there's much harm you can do."

Hana wrapped her arms around her chest, hugging herself and wishing she felt more delight in Logan's concession. But Edin's issues and Tama's disappearance cast a pall over her victory.

Tama's double storey townhouse nestled in a quiet suburban street. Logan parked the truck on the road and they sat and observed for a moment.

"His car is on the driveway." Hana pointed to the smart, secondhand Toyota Rav4 with its nose parked a metre shy of the garage door. "Who do you think owns that other vehicle?"

"Dunno." Logan activated his phone camera and pointed it at the scruffy saloon parked next to Tama's truck. He snapped a photo of the registration plate, frowning as he texted the image to a number Hana didn't recognise. She glanced sideways at her husband.

"We could just knock on the door." She left her sentence hanging as Logan pushed his phone back into the pocket of his jeans.

"We could." Logan settled with his hands in his lap. "But we won't."

Hana exhaled, leaning her head back against the seat and closing her eyes. She fought the desire to rush in where angels feared to tread, meeting the situation head-on and damn the consequences. "So, why are we here?" Petulance laced her tone and her lips tightened into a sullen bow. When she squinted at Logan through one eye, she found him shaking his head. "What?" she demanded. "It's a legitimate question." Her fingers smoothed the leather seat beneath her. "I could ask Bodie to check who owns that other car."

"You could." Logan's smile didn't reach his eyes. "But he'd get fired for misconduct unless he had a good reason for doing a personal search. My way is better and no one loses their job."

"A hacker?" Hana raised an eyebrow and sat up straighter. "Do I know them?"

Logan curved his knee and turned sideways in his seat. He licked his lips and stared at the ceiling of the truck before answering. "Would it help you to know their identity, or would it concern you? Would you find yourself less hospitable to someone who provided information if you knew they had a financial relationship with me?"

Hana folded her arms and stared at Tama's front door. "That's a good question," she admitted. "Are they male or female?" She glanced sideways at Logan. "It makes a difference."

He nodded. "Male and he's on Liza's payroll. We became friends at school and I introduced them."

"Okay." Hana nodded, the action drawn out as though in slow motion. Her mind ran wild, adding names to faces and trying to remember the crowd which arrived with the judge last time she used the hotel for a meeting. Their features blurred. Liza surrounded herself with men willing to serve her. She disliked Hana and they avoided each other. "Fine," she conceded. "As long as it doesn't come back to bite you. Or Bodie." She added the last with a wince, recognising that any delving into police databases would automatically put him under suspicion.

"It won't." Logan moved aside an auburn curl which snaked across her neck. He laid it behind her shoulder with care and let his fingers coast over her cheek. "Are we good?" he asked.

Hana nodded. For the first time in months, she felt their familiar connection. It pulsed through her veins like an electrical current. She lifted her hand and clasped his, pushing his fingers against her cheek and closing her eyes. Relishing the moment gave her energy coupled with a sense of inexplicable hope. "I've missed you," she whispered. "I've let everything slide. This black cloud sits above my head just waiting to descend and cover my eyes. It's impossible to see through it to the other side. I'm holding it back with my hands and it's so heavy."

Logan pulled her shoulder against his chest and kissed her temple. The seatbelt dug into her collarbone as it tried to keep them apart. The phone in his pocket vibrated, sending a low rumble through his body. Hana tensed, expecting him to drop his hand and answer the call but he didn't. His thumb stroked the crest of her lips and he gave a sigh which held regret. The leather seat crunched like footsteps in the snow as he kissed her, soft and slow to savor every second. His phone vibrated again and he tutted and dug in his pocket. "Sorry," he whispered.

"Du Rose." He answered without preamble. As though to acknowledge Hana's faith in him, he activated the speaker button after listening to the caller for a second. "Go ahead. I'm looking at the vehicle now."

"That plate is registered to an address in Ponsonby. Jordan Rafferty owns the vehicle." Tapping sounded in the background. "Ah, the owner changed the address of their driving licence to 153 Dominion Road, Parnell last week. It looks as though they're on the move."

"That's where I am now." Logan frowned. "I'm looking at the vehicle parked on the driveway of that Parnell address."

"Well, the car is registered to the previous address but the licence has updated to the Parnell property. People don't always remember to change both, so it could be an oversight."

Logan's fingers twitched as he thought. "Does Jordan Rafferty have any outstanding warrants or convictions I should know about before knocking on the door?" He dipped his body to peer at the house.

The male voice issued from the phone on Logan's thigh and echoed around the truck's interior. "Two parking infringements for downtown Auckland. Both settled in full. A speeding fine later attributed to a Danielle Rafferty. Also paid on time. There's nothing else in the system."

"Thanks."

"All good, mate. See ya around." The call ended to leave silence.

Hana studied her husband as he sat next to her. His eyes glazed while he sifted scenarios and probabilities. "I didn't recognise his voice," she said. "I guess I don't know him."

Logan smiled but didn't answer. If he sensed her fishing for information despite what she'd agreed, he didn't take the bait. "I think Jordan Rafferty is Tama's flat mate."

Hana nodded. "He rented two of the bedrooms to help pay the loan. Last time I visited with the children, he shared with two firemen. I don't remember him calling either of them Jordan." She closed her eyes and pictured the inside of Tama's kitchen. His excitement at entertaining them in his first home clouded as angst sullied it. Hana sighed. "I drove up with Wiri and Phoe. Leslie and Alfie kept Edin and you took Mac to the sale yards. Edin got upset and threw a tray of seedlings off the roof and Leslie called me back early. I remember meeting Stephen and Joe, but not Jordan. Perhaps he referred to Jordan as Joe."

Logan nodded and his fringe bounced with the movement of his eyelashes. "You know this can't go on, don't you?" His voice held authority and kindness.

Hana nodded and tears rose, turning her irises to glittering emeralds and sending a flush into her neck. "But I can't just throw her away because she's too hard. Not if that's what happened to her mother."

"I hear ya," Logan conceded. "But we need to do something. She's terrorising our family, Hana. At some point, you need to put them first." His words tore at the fabric of her reason, severing her already divided loyalties and blackening her vision. Then, he reached his hand across to still her writhing fingers. "We'll sort it out, babe," he promised, sharing responsibility for the first time since Edin's arrival in their home. "We'll find a solution."

Hana nodded, unable to choke out her gratitude. Fear lurked at the fringes of her relief, bearing the knowledge that Logan's solution might not prove acceptable to her. She fixed her gaze on Tama's house across the street, watching the sunlight speckle against the wooden siding and blossom the gentle cream into vibrant hues. "What shall we do now?" she asked. Pinpricks of anxiety roused her heart on his behalf.

Tama's name meant 'son' and Tama the boy had dragged himself to adulthood with Reuben's assistance. He'd been as much of a cuckoo in Reuben Du Rose's nest as Caroline, of no direct relationship to the man who fed and clothed them. Tama. No one's son.

But Hana's mothering had nurtured a gentler soul than the one who'd burst into her life. And he needed her. She released her seatbelt and stared at Logan with expectation.

"Okay," he said. "Plan A. Knock on the door."

10

Snaffle

Hana stood to the right of the front door as Logan depressed the button for the bell. When nothing happened, he knocked hard enough to wake the dead.

Hana sensed movement within the house, although she heard nothing. Then, heavy footsteps thudded downstairs and the front door whipped back with a curse.

"What?" The owner of the voice stood almost as tall as Logan, her muddy brown hair hauled into a loose ponytail. Frizz rose around her face and one pink cheek didn't match the other. Sleep creases splayed to create a fan across the reddened skin, and Hana winced.

"Sorry. We didn't mean to wake you." She kept her gaze on the woman's face and avoided looking at the rumpled pyjama shirt and the shorts hanging askew from her hips. "We're looking for Tama. This is his house."

The woman blinked into the sunlight and released a sigh. "I'll tell you what I told the last lot. I don't know where he is. Go away!" She stepped back and seized hold of the door, her sole focus on returning to her bed.

Logan lifted his foot and jammed his cowboy boot against the frame, catching the door as she pushed it and causing it to rebound. The woman's eyes widened in shock and her mouth dropped open as words failed her for the millisecond it took Logan to act. His index finger raised, and he jabbed it at her. "My tāma owns this house, lady!" He edged forward until he'd stepped across the threshold. He'd claimed Tama with the Māori word for son, and Hana's chest tightened with a surge of pride. She followed him over the step and into the hallway, closing the door behind her and leaning against it.

Terrified, the woman backed towards the stairs, looking from one to the other and shaking her head. "I'm calling the cops." She dug in the sagging pockets of her shorts and glanced towards the stairs when her fingers emerged empty.

"No need." Hana fixed a warm smile on her face. "We're Tama's whānau. His fire chief phoned me when he disappeared. We're worried about him." Hana lifted her hand and held it towards the woman. "I'm Hana Du Rose. We haven't met."

"Oh." The woman's shoulders sagged. She stepped forward, skirting Logan as she reached for the handshake. "I'm Jordan. Tama's flat mate. I've just finished a week of nights and am trying to catch up on my sleep."

"Tama says the transition from nights to days isn't much fun." Hana leaned against the door and relaxed her stance. Her phone vibrated in her pocket and she ignored its buzzing urgency. Logan shot her a frown, and she gave him a nonchalant shrug.

Jordan covered a yawn with the back of her left hand. "I don't know what to tell you," she said with a sigh. "We work opposite shifts most of the time. He let me move in when Joe went back to his wife. Stephen transferred to the south island last month."

"Right." Hana nodded and pushed herself upright. Her gaze tracked up the stairs to the hallway she could see just beyond them. "Please, may we look in his room? I need to work out if he took clothing or his passport. It might be a planned visit he hadn't mentioned."

"He doesn't have a passport." Logan's growled statement resulted in a nod from Jordan.

She exhaled. "You stopped me asking for proof of your identity. But no, he doesn't own a passport. It came up in a random conversation a few weeks ago. I guess only his family would know that."

Hana reached into her pocket for her phone. The screen showed a missed call from Bodie. She dug into the hidden flap behind the cover and pulled out her driving licence. Her bank card came with it, tumbling to the parquet floor with a gentle slap. She retrieved it and stuffed it back inside the flap before offering Jordan her licence. "You should ask for proof of identity," she stressed. "Especially at the moment." She waited as Jordan studied her photo and handed back the card. "Tell us about the other people who came looking for Tama."

Jordan checked a digital watch on her wrist and released a sigh. Hana imagined her calculating the hours left for sleeping and pitting the result against the number required for her to function as a fire officer. Edin's nightmares had stolen the last eighteen months of sleep for her and robbed her of joy. Hana forced her thoughts away from wondering if the child needed her. Did she hate her for putting her with strangers in a school environment? Was she coping?

"Tell us what we need to know, and we'll leave you in peace." Logan's command broke the deadlock. He jammed his hands into his pockets to create a less combative air, although the tension in his shoulders told Hana he wanted to rush upstairs and take Tama's room apart until he found answers. Jordan winced and still appeared unsure.

"My husband owns this house." Hana kept her tone soft. "Tama didn't borrow from the bank, but from us." Her lips flattened into a line as she softened the edges of the threat in her mind. "I don't want to break Tama's confidence, but I have a bad instinct about this." She pressed a hand over her heart. "You can let us search with you here or we can give you an eviction notice. I don't want to play that card, Jordan, but we're searching his room even without your permission."

Jordan's shoulders sagged and her body lost its stiffness. "He said you gave him the loan." She raised her hand, the palm facing outward in placation. "It's not common knowledge. We've sort of been seeing each other."

Logan raised an eyebrow at Hana, not needing to speak his thoughts out loud for her to know them.

"Sort of seeing each other?" she repeated, knowing what that meant for Tama.

"Yeah." Jordan nodded and swallowed. She didn't look at Logan, perhaps sensing his vibes of disapproval stretching across the narrow hallway. Instead, she appealed to Hana's solidarity as a woman. "It's nothing serious." She faltered, seeing the error of her words. "I'm going back to bed." She flapped a hand in dismissal. "Try not to make too much noise and close the front door on your way out." Her gaze flicked to the heavy lock attached to the frame and her features relaxed. "Leave the latch down and it'll lock behind you."

Hana glanced at Logan's impassive expression. He knew how the mechanism worked because he'd helped Tama to fit it. He bypassed sarcasm in favour of information. "Before you go, tell us about the others who came looking for Tama. Please," he added, cocking his head.

Jordan walked towards the stairs and paused at the bottom, her hand on the banister. "Woman and a man." She turned her body enough to address Logan, but raised her left foot to the first step. "Well dressed. She was, anyway. Looked familiar, though I'm not sure where I've seen her. Dark hair pulled back in a bun, tall and thin. She had an odd manner. Quite rude. The guy held a briefcase and seemed scared of her."

"What exactly did they say?" Hana demanded. She stepped in front of Logan and followed her up the stairs to the upper level.

With a sigh of exasperation, Jordan drifted along the corridor to an open door before turning. "She said, 'Tama Du Rose lives here. I know he does. Where is he?' I told her I didn't know, she called me a skanky little tart, and I slammed the door in her face."

"Right, thanks." Hana exhaled and turned away from the sound of Jordan's bedroom door clicking shut.

11

Stable

Logan met her in the master bedroom. He stood with his back to the window and surveyed the rumpled double bed. Hana wandered around, reluctant to touch anything and yet desperate to manufacture some vicarious contact with Tama through his possessions.

"Who do you think matches that girl's description? Could she be Tama's latest mistake?" Logan folded his arms and his gaze roved from the bed to the closed wardrobe door. "Stop moving around, Hana. I'm looking for anything out of place."

"Sorry." She stood next to him, her wrist bumping against his hip as she sought comfort. She sighed. "Tall, thin, dark, and rude. That's not his girlfriend."

"She sounds scary." Logan winced, and his lips flattened into a line. "Although he's always been a strange boy."

"She is scary." Hana stared at the floor rug she helped Tama choose. She closed her eyes and became silent.

Logan turned his body to face her. She sensed his gaze burning her cheeks. "And?" His rough tone commanded her to purge her thoughts. She shivered.

"It's like an accurate description of Liza."

"Our Eliza?" Logan's lip curled and his grey irises flickered. "My sister."

"Yep." Hana turned in a full circle and rested her palms on the windowsill. "It must be bad if the judge is looking for him with one of her legal lackeys. You should call her." She gave Logan's arm a gentle push. "Do it downstairs. I already have a headache."

He flinched and his lips parted for a moment before his fingers dug into his pocket for his phone. "Okay." He pressed a kiss to her temple and light footsteps carried him down the stairs to the ground level.

Hana released the sigh building in her chest and sank onto Tama's mattress. The room contained his essence, even without him. She dipped forward and retrieved an offending sock from beneath the bed, lifting it in finger and thumb. She didn't need to sniff it to know sweat stained its black folds, overlaid with male fragrance from one of Tama's famed deodorant showers.

Rising, she located the laundry hamper in the tiny bathroom attached to the master bedroom. She lifted the wicker lid and dropped the sock onto a creased shirt. It lay there like a swish of black paint on a whitewashed wall. Hana paused, the lid still held up by her left hand. With a frown, she leaned down and snagged the shirt. The sock tumbled into the bottom of the hamper.

"Where are you, Tama?" Hana whispered. She lifted the shirt to her nose and breathed in the faded scent of the boy she'd grown to love. But he'd taken his looks, his dry wit and his issues into manhood. The maternal parts of her nature spoke into her subconscious, urging her to take care of the little within her reach. She dropped the shirt onto the lid of the hamper and searched around for a bag with which to carry away his dirty washing.

"What are you doing?" Jordan's voice startled her as Hana pulled the bottom sheet off the bed.

"Sorry." She stuffed it into the bag with the pillowcases and a quilt cover. "I'm taking his washing. It's smelling in here." Wrinkling her nose, Hana darted into the bathroom and collected the shirt and the lone sock. She dug into the bottom of the hamper and pulled out smart trousers and a fire service tee shirt. "Jordan?" Jerky movements took her back into the bedroom and she lifted the items in her hands. "Do you keep your uniform at work or here?"

Jordan yawned and leaned against the door frame. "We show up ready to work, so I keep mine at home. I have two of everything, but I have a spare in my locker. Just in case."

Hana dropped the smart white shirt onto the rug while she pushed the other items into the plastic bag. When she retrieved it, the white fabric hung limp from her fingers. "This isn't an everyday work shirt, is it?" She pointed to the brand stamped on the label inside the crisp neck. "This is his best uniform."

"Yeah." Jordan stepped into the room. "Blue Watch attended a community event on Monday night and had to wear their best. A guy from another station won an award, so they all showed up to support him. Tama wanted the free food." She grinned before her lips straightened into a line. "Sorry," she conceded. "This is serious, isn't it?"

Hana exhaled. "I don't know. It feels like it." She pressed the shirt to her chest and stared at the ceiling as though searching for inspiration on the white surface. "He wore this on Monday night, took it off and put it in the wash. Then, he missed two shifts, one on Wednesday and one yesterday. His chief called me in the afternoon."

Jordan twisted her lips and gave a shallow nod. "His watch didn't work last weekend. They were rostered to start back on Wednesday for a twelve-hour shift. Four days on and four off. He should have worked Wednesday to Saturday this week. He's the opposite rotation to me. I got home on Tuesday morning and found the house empty. I assumed he'd come home later as usual, but he didn't."

Hana turned on the spot, the shirt still clutched to her chest. She imagined Tama moving around the room and tried to follow his pattern. "He disappeared between late on Monday night and seven o'clock on Wednesday morning." She unfolded the shirt and ran a finger across the collar. Her brow furrowed. "There's a pink lipstick stain on here."

"Oh." Jordan exhaled and long strides took her to Hana's side. She lifted the fabric and inspected the collar. "Great." Her shoulders slumped. "I worked a night shift. Guess he got busy in my absence." She dropped the shirt as though it held a contamination she didn't want on her fingers.

Guilt budded in Hana's chest. Loving Tama had cursed her with a parent's vicarious responsibility for his actions. "I'm sorry," she breathed. "If you like him, tell him. He won't treat it as a serious relationship if you pretend it isn't."

Jordan nodded and turned away, hiding her misery by leaving the room without speaking.

Hana balled the shirt into the bag, stopping as her fingers registered something hard within its folds. Logan's footsteps moved up the stairs, and he released a sigh as he made the turn at the top. He walked into the room and stopped at the sight of the stripped bed and the pillows set neatly in front of the headboard. His gaze fell on the plastic bag.

"I found this." Hana extracted the business card from the top pocket of the shirt and she peered at the tiny font.

"Let me see." Logan crossed the room and took the card from her palm. His brows furrowed into a line of salt and pepper grey. "It's just a name, number and the logo of an insurance company." He turned the card over and squinted at the writing on the back. "And a handwritten first name and mobile phone number."

"Male or female?" Hana quirked an eyebrow and pointed to the faint pink mark on the shirt's collar peeking from the bag.

Logan wrinkled his nose. "Female. What a surprise. The kid's a rabbit."

"I think it's significant." Hana replaced the shirt in the bag and tied the top. "I'm taking his bedding and dirty laundry, so it's all clean for when he comes home." She pursed her lips and surveyed the room. "I'll need a key to replace it all."

Logan shrugged. "That girl is downstairs in the kitchen. We should leave. She's slamming things around."

"Yeah." Hana raised her eyebrows. "What did Liza say?"

Logan leaned against the wardrobe door and dug his hands into his jeans pockets. "Not much. He phoned her for legal advice last week, but she had a court case running. Her clerk arranged a dinner meeting last night, and he didn't show up, so Liza drove around here this morning. She moved some other engagements to see him and assumed he blew her out for that girl."

"Ah." Hana sank onto the mattress and smoothed her fingers over the ornate wooden acorn set into the post of the foot board. "Hence the skanky tart comment to Jordan. She opened the door in her pyjamas and Liza didn't realise she lived here."

"Yeah." Logan turned his wrist to look at his watch. "Let's get some lunch and head home. If Edin kicks off, it'll be over food."

Hana rose and collected the bag. Logan took it from her in the doorway. "Try the bedside cabinet," he advised. "You might find a spare key."

Hana's fingers sifted through socks and boxer shorts, wincing as she moved aside unopened packets of condoms. She found a set of keys in the middle drawer and lifted the bunch up to Logan. "One of these?"

Logan squinted at them and pointed to one near her thumb. "That one. It's the original from the lock we fitted. I told him to keep that and get others cut from it. He obviously listened to me for once."

Hana closed the drawer and looked around the room. "Do you think we're overstepping by raiding his home and taking his stuff?"

Logan snuffed out a laugh. "We're not burglars, Hana. You're doing his laundry and we're trying to find him. I don't care if he's grateful or mad because if he's either, it means he's okay."

12

Pelham Bit

Logan saw no point in driving to the fire station. He took Hana to lunch at a cafe in Parnell and they discussed reporting Tama missing.

"That's one of the things I wanted to ask Bodie." She pushed away the remains of her cheese sandwich and picked up her coffee. "He assumed the worst as soon as I mentioned Tama's name."

Logan shrugged and set his cutlery on his empty plate. He shifted the fork with his index finger to make it parallel to the knife. "He's formed an opinion of us and we have one of him." His sigh held more sadness than disgust. "It's ironic that he borrowed money he never paid back, but my whānau wouldn't dream of behaving in the same way. If your word counts for nothing, then what's left?"

"I know. I'm sorry." Hana ran her hand over her eyes. "He never used to be so money grabbing. He paid for the gate installation at Culver's Cottage when I felt so unsafe. I'm not sure where it all went wrong."

Logan raised one eyebrow, and Hana sensed his boredom with the familiar conversation. Loyalty to her son made her continue, long after she should have quit. "I think his mindset changed when he invested the trust fund from Vic in that terrible deal. He struggled with the shame of it when he'd already promised Amy a big wedding and a new house."

Logan's jaw tightened, and Hana's voice faded. Her son borrowed a thousand dollars from Logan to auction his wife's house and buy Culver's Cottage. He'd never paid him back, and the amount hung between the two halves of her family like a swinging axe. Nothing she said would stop Bodie from seeing Logan as an interloper in Hana's life. He weighed every interaction on loaded scales. Despite numerous promises, he wouldn't pay him back the money because he didn't believe Logan needed it. Or that he should have to.

Logan groaned as his phone vibrated. He hauled it from his jacket pocket and peered at the screen. "Pete again!" he spat. "Far out! I don't hear from him for years and then I'm the devil because I won't give him a free wedding at the hotel."

"Give it here." Hana rose and held out her hand. "I'll speak to him." She flattened her lips. "Outside."

Logan paid the bill while she retreated into the sunshine to deal with Pete's over-inflated sense of entitlement. His attitude resonated with Bodie's and while her proximity to one situation hamstrung her, distance from Pete meant he got both barrels. "We owe you nothing!" she snarled. A couple walking along the street blinked in surprise and the woman edged sideways until her companion stepped into the road. A car honked him and they skirted Hana with care. She turned sideways to avoid their non-verbal recriminations. "Logan made that offer years ago. We don't host weddings at the hotel anymore and haven't for over eighteen months. You've missed your window of opportunity and don't even think about asking for the equivalent in cash. I swear I'll drive down there and punch you on the nose myself!"

Shame flushed her cheeks and neck as she heard herself, as though through the view of an astral projection. She saw her rigid stance and screwed up features, anger leaking from every pore. "Go away, Pete, please." Killing the call didn't remove the sense of dirtiness and she wondered what would. She never vented on others, preferring to see their good points shining through the silt. Pete had a good heart, and there would be a reason for his request.

Tears stung behind her eyelids and she closed her eyes to keep them contained. The weight of her cares bore down on her shoulders, causing a bone-deep ache to blossom as far as her heels.

Mac.

Edin.

Tama.

And now Pete. They piled on the pressure, demanding the nectar of unicorn blood and some other magical solution she couldn't provide.

"I feel useless." The admission burst free as soon as Logan exited the cafe. She handed back his phone. "It's all spiralling out of control. I don't know what to do."

"It isn't. I promise." His muscular arms enfolded her, his body cutting off her view of the street and dulling the hum of the traffic. He encased her in love and certainty and that other thing she couldn't name. His kisses patted the top of her head. "Trust me." Those words again, the same ones which forged a marriage, carried her back from hell and defended her when no one else could.

"Okay." Her shoulders relaxed as she relented. She tapped her phone in her pocket. "At least the school didn't call, so Edin hasn't burned it down or run away. Yet." She looked for positives amid the circling cloud of doom.

"You'll find life is easier now you're no longer dancing to someone else's tune." Logan kept an arm around her shoulder as he turned her towards the truck.

"What exactly is the deal with that?" Hana winced at the thought of Caroline. She allowed Logan to pull open the passenger door and offer his hand to steady her as she climbed up to her seat. She kept hold of his fingers as she waited for his reply.

"She can speak to Edin on the phone for ten minutes every week. I'm supervising the call. I said we'd discuss a suitable time, and she's phoning tonight to see what we've decided. No more prison visits for six months until Edin settles. Then we'll revise the situation. She has another thirteen years to serve before parole, so she plays it our way or not at all."

Hana nodded. Logan walked around the truck and settled into the driver's seat with a sigh. "You must have threatened her with something," she concluded. Her lips pinched into a thin line as she observed her husband's rugged profile. "Why did she agree?"

He started the engine, not looking at her as he delivered the cruel salvo. "I told her I'd hand Edin over to the Alderbank family's lawyer. I'm only doing this if she stops making it impossible. The bitch tried to shoot me. She needs to remember that fact."

Hana nodded, and a blanket of relief rode over her legs. It started at her toes and warmed her thighs before nestling against her chest. Logan had this. She swallowed. "I should have asked for help sooner. I'm sorry."

He snuffed out a laugh. "Yeah. But it's always the same story, isn't it? You're too ready to believe I'll trade you in for a different model. I can't criticise you for it because I once foolishly gave you reason for that belief, but it's faulty, Hana. I've never cheated on you and never will." The engine roared as Logan pulled away from the curb and slotted the heavy truck into the traffic. His phone trilled again, picked up by the car speaker, and Pete's number flashed across the screen.

Hana leaned forward and depressed the call button, watching as the strobing red receiver switched to green. "Right," she said, her tone determined. "Drop the guilt tripping and the hard-done-by attitude and start at the beginning. Why are you ringing us now and what is really the problem?"

13

Stable Rubber

Pete cleared his throat, his reedy voice piping through the speakers. Familiar enough to conjure an image of the sports teacher, it presented a skinny, unappealing man with wispy hair, dandruff and a skin complaint he'd never explored other than with his fingernails. Hana forced her muscles to unclench one at a time, leaving the ones around her knees until last.

"Henrietta had breast cancer." He coughed into the phone at his end, not bothering to spare them the wet hawking. "We delayed getting married while she went through surgery and chemo."

Hana ground her teeth and leaned into the surge of guilt which doused her like a storm shower. She cut her gaze towards a warmth on her right thigh and found Logan's hand resting there. "Stop," he mouthed to her. "Not everything is your fault."

Pete continued his tale of woe, accounting for the past year but not the five which preceded them. He detailed his partner's health, treatment and desire to get married sooner rather than later.

Logan's brows drew into a frown as he slid the truck onto the expressway, heading south towards Rangiriri. "But you got married Pete. Years ago."

Hana sat up straighter as she remembered the happy Facebook photographs from a honeymoon in Rarotonga. She stared at Logan, her emphatic nodding backing up his assumption.

"Yeah, about that." Pete sighed. "I forgot to post the paperwork to the court. It didn't get filed and we aren't legally married."

Logan wrinkled his nose and bit his lower lip. He shrugged and winked at Hana. "That's unfortunate, Pete. When did you realise?"

"It sorta wasn't me who realised." A fortifying breath rushed through the speaker, and Hana imagined biscuit crumbs dotting Pete's chin and lips. Unless he'd changed. She bore little resemblance to the woman who'd shared an office with him years earlier. It seemed possible he might finally have reached adulthood at the age of fifty.

"Right." Logan drew out the word. "Henrietta discovered your error."

"Yeah." Pete swallowed. "So now she wants another wedding with all the bells and whistles. Big. Like I promised her the first time."

"And that's where I come in, is it?" Logan craned his neck to check the outside lane as he pushed the truck around a heavy goods vehicle.

"Kinda. I need to dig myself out of this hole somehow, mate."

"Mate?" Logan snorted. His eyes narrowed. "Is this the same one you never want to catch up with when he's in town? The one who stopped calling you after you didn't show up to your last pre-arranged meeting?"

Hana turned her head in surprise. She recalled wondering when Peter North dropped off Logan's narrow friendship map, not realising he'd tried to hunt him down or resurrect the relationship. He'd released the jibe as a half joke, but she sensed the vat of pain beneath his litany of criticisms. It seemed an age since he'd mentioned Pete, his name drifting out of their lives like a fine mist.

Until now. When it suited Pete to phone and demand something of him, tugging on the fragile remnants of a lifelong friendship as though entitled to do it. Hana bridled as she watched her husband's impassive profile. His warm fingers twitched on her thigh and she pressed both her hands over his. Covering. Consoling. Offering her solidarity. He didn't reply, and Pete cleared his throat again as an awkward silence gnawed at the sketchy signal over the Bombay hills. "Are you there, Logan?" he asked.

"We're here." Hana inserted herself into the conversation. A latent fury beat in time with her heart. Her voice wavered as she battled the urge to call him out as yet another parasite in their narrowing circle of relationships. "I'm sorry Henri's been unwell. Please give her my best wishes."

"She's fine now. But how about the wedding at your place? Henrietta's keen to send the invitations soon. We thought about two hundred guests. She's got a menu she'd like and a date in April."

"April!" Hana exhaled the word. "Next month? Of this year? Dream on, Pete. Seriously!"

"The date is negotiable." She heard the familiar whine enter his voice as he scrabbled to regain his perceived upper hand. "Maybe June, but early, so it's not too cold."

Hana looked at her husband, but he kept his gaze on the road and didn't respond. She wanted him to explode, to tell Pete where to stick his expectations and his two hundred strong wedding. But he just kept looking forward, as though the conversation didn't involve him.

"We can't do it, Pete. Logan leased the hotel facility to a company who uses it for conferences. We're responsible for the maintenance under the terms of the lease. That's all. They book the rooms, employ the staff and run the venue."

"What?" Pete's spluttering induced memories of his fits of indignation when he sat behind Hana in the tiny office at the school in Hamilton. "Logan loved that hotel. Why would he give it to someone else?"

Hana closed her eyes against the wave of misgiving which had ingrained itself on her heart as a stain. Months of soul searching had preceded the signing of the lease. They'd retained ownership of the entire property and sole control of one guest room, two staff motel rooms, and Alfie's apartment. Logan kept his office in a wing of the main building. The events company ran the hotel and campground on a five year agreement which had three and a half years left on the clock. They'd wanted twenty. They got five.

"Because it works for my family." Logan's voice contained no emotion. "And I didn't give it to someone else. I leased it."

"But why?" Pete protested. "That hotel meant everything to you."

A sad smile curved Logan's lips. He'd thought so too. Releasing the running of the vast building had proved difficult at first, until the weight of responsibility slipped from his shoulders like the shucking of a heavy coat. He loved the farm, the horses, and the money.

Letting go of the hotel had changed his life in ways Hana hadn't foreseen. She'd made her decision from beneath a cloud of exhaustion, bowed down by Edin's tantrums and worried about Mac. Logan made a spreadsheet of reasons for and against, adding data and weighing them against mathematical algorithms which promised certainty. The lease uncoupled him from a shackle imposed on him by his parents. It set him free.

"We love the mountain." Hana corrected Pete's wrong assumption. "We now love having the time to enjoy it."

"So, what do you both do for work, then?" Envy filtered through the speaker, green and sticky like leaf sap. "That seems unfair to the rest of us if you're enjoying a permanent holiday."

Hana snorted. "I work in the family museum besides raising four children. Logan runs the Charolais business and breeds stock horses. He also teaches two days a week at a high school. It's hardly a holiday."

"Four children!" That's all Pete took from Hana's list of activities.

She leaned her head back and stared at a blade of hay stuck to the fabric ceiling of the truck. Her tongue lacked the energy to catalogue and verify her rag taggle band of infants for Pete's benefit. She squeezed Logan's fingers where they lay on her thigh, imploring him to come to her aid.

"Gotta go, Pete," Logan said. His tone held an airy quality as though he'd shaken off the disappointment of a one sided friendship dripping in serial abuse. "Nice to catch up with your news. All the best to Henrietta and good luck with the wedding. We probably won't make it, but give us the details. I'd like to send a gift." His thumb depressed a button on the steering wheel, and Hana heaved a sigh of relief.

"Thanks. I was drowning."

Logan gnawed at his lower lip. "Who gets married and forgets to post the paperwork?"

Hana gave a slow nod. She turned her emerald gaze on his handsome profile, and he shot her a look of incredulity. His lips stretched into a grin. "Yes, Hana. I filed our marriage certificate." He laughed. "Don't think you can get away from me that easily."

14

"Up, up!" Edin pointed at the ceiling, and her body tensed. Her gaze tracked towards the door which led from the attic to the apartment.

"I'll take you." Hana held out her hand and conceded defeat. "You went to school like a big girl and drew amazing pictures with your teacher, didn't you?"

Edin nodded and pointed again at the door. "Up. Up." Her bare feet pattered across the rug to Hana's side and she slipped her fingers into her palm. Her liquid grey eyes sparkled like mercury as she stared up at Hana with that frustrating, unreadable expression which betrayed nothing of her thoughts.

"Anyone else coming?" Hana searched the room, her gaze settling on each of the adults and children.

"Too tired," Alfie sighed. His gnarled fingers rubbed at the arthritic knee, which pained him.

Mac didn't answer, his concentration fixed on the electronic device in his fingers. He frowned as he swung his legs and twitched his fingers, feeding the hungry puppy on the screen.

Phoenix shook her head, but Wiri rose to his feet. Edin pointed at him, and her expression clouded. "No, no!" she protested.

Hana tensed. "It's not your garden, Edin. He can come if he likes. Poppa Alfie doesn't mind." She lifted the latch on the door and it opened to reveal a narrow passage leading upwards via wooden stairs.

"Remember when we had to crawl, Ma?" Wiri held the door as they passed through the gap and then closed it behind him. He flicked the new switch on the wall and the space flooded with light. "It was a secret garden where Poppa grew weed in the greenhouse without Uncle Logan knowing."

Hana's eyes widened, and she gave a slow shake of her head. She raised a finger to her lips. Logan had employed a builder to increase the height of the doorway and make the space more accommodating for two geriatrics to navigate. He'd done it without the local council's knowledge of the alteration to the heritage building. A frieze of a bush scene covered the wall of the apartment and masked the existence of the doorway. It remained invisible as it always had, only more accessible.

Edin insisted on going first, glancing behind her at those following and pushing her feet up too fast. She gave a cry as she stumbled, and Hana caught her around the waist. Producing a warning sound like a low growl, Edin thrust away her helping hands.

"Steady!" Hana cautioned. "We'll go back down unless you hold my hand and behave."

Edin stared at the bolt holding the door closed, knowing she couldn't reach it and resentful of the lack of control it condemned her to suffer. Hana read the stiffness of the child's body and, for the millionth time, wondered why she insisted on venturing up to the roof when she so obviously hated the experience.

"Want me to hold Horsey?" Wiri offered.

Edin met his suggestion with widening eyes and reached out to shove him away from her. She turned her body aside and tucked her toy under the other armpit. "Push." She shook her head and frowned with such vehemence that her eyebrows occluded her eyes. Shadows hid in her down-turned face, giving her a ghoulish appearance.

"What do you mean?" Offended on Wiri's behalf, Hana pressed the point home. "You think Wiri would push Horsey off the roof? Why would he do something so horrible?"

"I wouldn't!" Resenting the accusation, Wiri turned and clumped back down the steps to the apartment. His heavy footed descent accentuated Hana's foolishness at allowing Caroline's devil-child to invade her family.

She squatted on the tiny landing and faced Edin. "He wanted to help you. What's going on in that head of yours?" When Edin continued to stare at her without answering, Hana pushed against the heavy weight which settled on her shoulders and tried to stand. Needing something stable to pull herself up with, she reached for a protruding nail. Specks of rust coated her fingers as she flexed her thighs and hauled.

The pop came first as the nail wiggled free of the beam and surprise caused Hana to overbalance. She teetered on the narrow landing, imagining for a split second her body bumping down the twelve wooden steps to the bottom and exploding through the bush scene next to the sofa.

Her arms flew wide, the nail still clutched in her right hand, and the rough surface of exposed beams grazing the heels of her hands. A small cry escaped her lips as she braced herself, logic telling her not to panic.

Time seemed to halt as she relaxed her fingers and flattened her palms against the beams, pausing a moment before stabilising herself enough to stand. The nail fell from her grasp and bounced down the steps with a thin clatter. Then she noticed the pressure against her chest and, for a horrible moment, imagined the tiny hand pushing against her and willing her to fall. But a look into Edin's face painted a different picture.

Hana righted herself, but the child's grip on the front of her shirt prevented her from rising. She used the moment to catch her breath, noticing the knitted horse lying discarded on the top step. She clasped her fingers over Edin's and forced a smile onto her lips. "Thank you," she managed. "You saved me."

Edin nodded, and her eyes filled with tears. The saline danced and swam on the precipice of her lower lids before plunging down her cheeks. "No push," she whispered.

Realisation doused Hana with an icy chill which locked her joints and caused her tongue to fill her mouth. She collapsed onto the top step and pulled the girl into her lap, silent tears soaking into Edin's hair as she held her tight and tried and failed to breathe life into the little girl's soul.

Later, Hana held Edin's hand as they walked around the roof garden in silence, comprehension painting each of the child's actions in a different light. She lifted her countless times, waiting as she pushed her face between the iron railings to stare at the ground from every angle.

"We should go downstairs to see Nonie and Poppa now," she suggested, her tone gentle. "See if they've left us any biscuits."

Edin blinked up at Hana and gave a nod of acceptance. Horsey's dangling legs dragged against the paving slabs as they circled the greenhouse, which once contained Alfred's stash of contraband. Instead, potatoes and lettuces occupied the raised beds. She frowned to herself as they headed towards the door to the stairs, but for once, Edin made no fuss. Hana opened the door and Edin turned to her with a ferocious glare, jabbing an index finger into her stomach before stepping onto the landing. "Careful!" she snapped, her tone severe and her movements jerky.

"Okay," Hana replied, injecting brightness into her tone. She shot the bolt and followed the child down the steps, picking her way with more care than she had on the upward journey.

Edin stopped and turned towards her after each step as though assuming the role of parent and monitoring her progress. Something had shifted between them and Hana half wished it hadn't. Ignorance had offered her a welcome shelter without her realising, and now she had no place to hide.

Edin ran towards the French doors to the balcony, arriving there even before Hana had closed the secret door.

"Why'd you wanna go out there?" Alfred demanded. "You've just seen everything there is to see from the roof."

"Just let her," Hana soothed. Her tone carried a sadness which replaced the earlier frustration. She unlocked the doors and pushed open the left one, offering her hand as Edin teetered on the threshold. The child clasped her fingers, Horsey buried beneath her other arm, and they stepped onto the small veranda together. Edin edged towards the railing and touched it with a delicate index finger. She exercised more caution than on the roof, squatting down to peer through the slats. Wrought iron filigree snaked around her head as though sealing her in a frame as she raked the gravel car park with her gaze.

A voice carried from indoors, and Hana addressed Edin. "Nonie asked if you'd like to stay for dinner," she said. "Would you like pumpkin soup?"

Edin rose without touching the railing and bent her head towards Horsey's muzzle. Bobbles of worn wool between the white lips and brown body gave him a quizzical expression. She whispered something, her lips touching his plastic black eye, and then she nodded. Hana smiled and offered her hand, leading the child back inside and locking the doors. "Pumpkin soup sounds wonderful, please, Nonie," she announced.

"I've made some fresh bread." Leslie bustled around the kitchen with a serrated knife, spreading crusty crumbs across the counter with a flourish. "It's still warm. Get the butter from the pantry, please tāne." She jabbed the knife at Wiri and he obeyed, slouching to the cupboard in the corner and retrieving the dish and a knife.

Hana seated Edin at the table, easing Horsey from the girl's lap and winding his legs around her chair. She sensed Wiri studying her movements and met his perceptive gaze with a fake smile. Mac gaped at her as she confiscated his digital pet from the top of the table and she placed it beneath his chair with a wink.

"I just need to speak to Logan," she said, forcing calm into her voice despite the shaking of her hands. "Please, may you excuse me for a moment?"

"Ooh, shall we?" Alfie sought a consensus, his tone light as he hefted his old bones onto the seat next to Mac. Hana feigned ignorance and escaped from the apartment before the debate got started, plunging down the stairs to the third storey and navigating her way to the spiral staircase and privacy.

Uncertain of Logan's whereabouts, she dialled the number for his mobile phone and waited, relief flooding through her at the click as he answered. He'd gone to his office after their return from Auckland and the familiar woody echo betrayed he'd stayed there. Her words gushed free like flood water, staining everything they touched. "She's a bloody liar!" she shouted. "She's a rotten, bloody liar!"

15

The Hunt

Hana slouched on the sofa in Logan's office, the aged leather creaking like dry bones beneath her. She dipped forward and rested her forearms on her thighs to suppress the nausea rising into her throat. Logan nudged the dustbin aside with his foot, rubbing her spine with gentle, fortifying fingers.

"I can't believe it." Her chest hitched and acid burned her throat. She rubbed the back of her hand across her dripping nose.

Logan swore. His hand moved to her shoulder, and he pulled her close. His lips pressed through her hair to kiss her head, not fazed by the dampness of her scalp. "You okay now?" His voice rumbled through his chest and along his arm, infusing Hana with vicarious courage.

She nodded. "Yeah. Sorry." Her gaze tracked to the dustbin she'd only just made it to after running headlong through the hotel corridors. She hadn't realised she needed to vomit until it happened, rising like a tide in her stomach and consuming her.

Logan brushed her fringe back from her forehead. "Good job I love ya," he said, his tone even.

"Good job you had a bag in it." Hana pushed herself upright. "Please, may I have a drink of water?"

Logan rose, and his long stride took him to a bathroom hidden behind a panelled wall. He rinsed a glass under the tap, the gushing water waking the pipes to resume their air locked hammering. Another panel revealed a kitchenette, and he pulled a jug of cold water from the bowels of a fridge. Beer bottles tinkled as he slammed the door, their song dulling as the seal locked them inside.

"Here." He dipped in front of Hana, holding out the glass like an offering of some rare gift. With one knee on the rug, he remained there as she gulped the water. His hands cupped hers and he confiscated the glass when she took too much. Rivulets spilled on either side of her lips. "Steady," he commanded. He set the glass on the rug at her feet, where it dribbled condensation to form a dark ring. Then he slid into the seat next to her. "Start at the beginning."

Hana faltered through the incident on the stairs and her realisation. Guilt filtered through her words at having missed something so obvious, so significant. She wanted to beat her own head against a wall. "Edin saw him fall from the balcony." Her chest hitched, and the nausea threatened. She gripped her upper arms and squeezed her torso as though crushing herself might provide redemption for her gross negligence. "That's what the fascination with the roof and the balcony is all about. She's looking over it to see if he's still laying there mangled on the ground. It's an impulse to check and recheck because it's playing over in her mind like a film reel. She's traumatised, and I missed it."

Hana bent double and moaned in agony. Her forehead touched her knees.

"Stop!" Logan raised his voice, and the last threads of her sanity and logic sought the surety of his command. She sat up too fast and her vision blurred. Logan's fingers twitched as he reached for the dustbin again. Hana shook her head and dashed away the tears from her cheeks with a shaking, careless hand. The dustbin listed at an angle, constructed from flax harvested from the garden. Logan hadn't cared about its wonky base or leaning structure. She'd made it for him using traditional raranga methods, and he'd displayed it in his office with pride. Now she'd puked in it.

"What a mess." Hana pressed her fingers into her eyes, meaning the dustbin, the child, and her life in general.

"The opposite, in fact." Logan gripped her wrists and pulled her hands away from her face. The edge of his leather cowboy boot touched her bare toe as he moved to face her and their knees bumped. "We know where to start now. Edin needs a psychologist."

"We tried that." Hana shook her head. "She wouldn't speak to her."

"Then we try others until she finds one she likes." Logan caressed her cheek with his thumb. "This is salvageable, Hana. You've found the key to unlocking this whole sorry mess."

Hana closed her eyes and leaned her cheek against his touch. "Maybe. All the pieces are slotting into place. The prison is filled with metal doors, grates, and keys. The whole place clanks. Maybe it reminded her of the sound of the balcony giving way. What do you think?"

Logan pressed his lips against her forehead. "I think someone qualified needs to unpack it with her. But at least they're starting from a better position this time. There's more information."

"Okay." Hana closed her eyes and allowed the peace of the office to wash over her. "Do you think we were too hard on Pete?"

"Dunno." Logan's voice drifted up with a lazy lilt. "Perhaps." He sighed. "He's the least of our problems."

"Leslie said Mac had a good day." Hana rubbed her cheek against his fingers. "We understand Edin a little more. If we can find Tama, things might work out for us after all."

Logan pressed a kiss to her forehead and smiled. "We're Du Roses," he whispered. "They'll always work out for us."

Hana sat up straighter, drawing on his unlimited optimism to carry her forward in the moment. "Do you want dinner upstairs with us? Leslie cooked."

"Na." His eyes narrowed and Hana sensed his mind drifting away on a thread she couldn't follow. She faltered, expecting him to shroud his plans in secrecy and lock her out of the loop. He surprised her. "I'll call that number on the business card we found in Tama's gear. What do you think?"

Hana nodded, mute but grateful for his inclusion. Logan nodded and rose. He fastened the ties of the bag nestled inside the flax basket and gave her a lopsided smile. "I'll get rid of this but I'll make the call from home later. It's more private there." He winked at her. "Just sit there and recover for a while."

The door closed behind him with a click, and Hana sighed. She used the tiny bathroom sink to wash her face and located some toothpaste. The tang of the mint made her cringe as she used her finger to clean her teeth. She wished Logan would let her listen while he phoned the number, but knew he wouldn't. His cajoling might veer into threatening and he wouldn't want her to hear and become complicit.

Not yet ready to return to the attic apartment and face its occupants, she wandered around the familiar office. Logan's fastidious neatness extended to his work space, and she ran a finger over the spines lining a wall of bookshelves. Keats, Austen and Dickens nestled against other faded greats, reclaimed from what had once been the original library. The event company had turned it into a lounge, embellishing the stacks with artfully placed ornaments.

Flecks of degraded colour dotted Hana's fingers as she caressed the authors' historical view of the world through their embossed titles. She frowned, wondering if Will would consider them old enough to offer them sanctuary in the museum. He'd respected Logan's ultimate decision about the house's fate, but wheeled through the corridors and halls in search of artifacts worthy of rescuing as the interior designers ripped through the rooms. She retrieved her phone from her pocket and snapped a photograph of the spines, knowing without asking that Logan would resist the curator's rampage through his office.

Arranged in height order, the spines rose in thickness to occupy more of the depth and loft of the shelf. Hana moved along it with unseeing eyes, her mind in Tama's bedroom still looking for answers. Her index finger stroked each stationary soldier, coasting over the arch of the spine and crossing the divide to the next. The spines grew shinier, newer and gaudy. *An Accountant's Guide to Capital Gain's Taxation* leaned against *Teaching English in a World Without Conscience.*

A battered cash box acted as a bookend, and Hana wrinkled her nose as she tapped its metal lid. Pocks and craters covered its surface, the colour of its original paint indeterminate. Hard, bubbled plastic and glue covered a space where a label once sat. Two rusty plates of its lid mourned the absence of a handle long gone. Its roughness repelled her fingers, and she understood the box's purpose as a heavy bookend. A line of jagged grooves around its lip revealed a futile attempt to open it. She pried at the lid and it resisted.

Hana paused and smoothed her hand over her thigh, depositing the specks of brown rust onto her jeans. When she glanced up, the spiral binding of a notepad called to her, its flimsy, temporariness incongruous against the published books. Trapped between two copies of the same novel which Logan taught his Year 13s in the last term, the notebook cried out to her as though imprisoned between them.

With a glance back at the closed office door, Hana lifted her finger and thumb, fitting them around the metal arcs and pulling.

16

Summer Sheet

Hana jumped as the door clicked. Logan strode across the rug towards her. "Puke crisis averted," he said with a smile. He stopped and cocked his head. "Why do you have a guilty look on your face?"

Hana pushed the notebook between the waistband of her jeans and her underwear. She feigned an expression of offence. "Charming." She pointed to the metal box. "What's that?"

Logan shrugged. "An old cash box. It's been knocking around for years. You look better now. Aren't you hungry?"

Hana nodded. "I'll take the truck keys and then I can load the children before texting you." She offered her husband a winning smile. The keys jangled against her palm as she hefted the bunch from the desk.

"Okay." Logan paused before her and cocked his head. "Could you lock the office door from the outside and I'll just slam it when I leave?" His hands reached for her and a lascivious twinkle sparkled in his irises. "Unless you can think of another idea? We could leave together."

Hana thought of plenty of exciting ideas, reaching for them with eagerness. She released a laugh infused with giddiness, quickly followed by regret. She dodged sideways, conflict blinding her to her objective. Time alone and undisturbed with Logan had become a craving, and the offer sent a dart of pain shooting through her chest. She wanted it more than he would ever know.

The metal coils of the notebook dug into her right buttock as though to remind her of the subterfuge. Hana winced and hefted the keys, resenting their innocent, lighthearted jangling. "Hold that thought, cowboy," she said, keeping her tone upbeat. "I want wine and candles. A quickie over the boss's desk isn't very romantic." She wrinkled her nose and backed away from him. The cardboard edge of the cover rubbed against her ribs.

"You want romantic?" He raised an eyebrow and pushed his tongue behind his top row of perfect teeth as he thought through scenarios. "So, do we drug the kids first or hit them over the head?"

Hana snorted and made it as far as the door. Her right hand closed around the brass knob. "I have an idea," she said. "Just leave it with me."

Logan turned and shoved at a pile of documents held down with a jade paperweight. Hana didn't hear whatever he muttered, but winced at the disappointed list of his left shoulder. She clattered from the room and retrieved the notebook from underneath her shirt. It amazed her how he hadn't noticed the sharp corners protruding through the fabric, but lust and longing had clouded his vision in time for her escape. She used Logan's keys to lock his door against unwanted disturbances.

The taste of toothpaste infused a chill into Hana's mouth as she breathed in the warm air in the corridor. She pattered past the industrial kitchen, her steps punctuated by the dull clunk of a huge saucepan against the Belfast sink beneath the window. The event company had retained the hotel's staff, redrawing their contracts under Logan's watchful eye. They hadn't wanted the young man who washed dishes part time, arguing for an appliance which cost half the price. Logan resisted, knowing the man's history and disabilities. It had become a deal breaker.

Hana slipped through the reception and down the front steps, jogging to the truck. She leaned in and pushed the notebook into the pocket behind the passenger seat for retrieval later. A satisfied smile crossed her lips as she locked up the truck behind her.

Running across the car park in the heat brought sweat budding across her forehead and her stomach roiled. She waved to the face, which peered at her through the kitchen window. The man lifted a hand covered in a yellow rubber glove and returned her greeting. His long tongue touched his chin and his slanted eyes narrowed in a wide grin.

17

Discarded Stirrups

Edin dozed on her booster seat between Mac and Phoenix. Her head sagged sideways until it touched Mac's wiry shoulder. Wiri took refuge on the spare pull-down seat in the truck's boot, his profile thoughtful as he gazed through a side window. Logan drove and Hana planned her evening in her mind, running through scenarios which might lend her time with her husband.

It was all academic in the end.

School had wiped Edin out, sapping all her effusive energy and leaving her an empty husk of limbs and tired eyes. She sank into her bed without fuss, her eyes closed before the story finished. Hana dropped her arms and stopped acting out the Bear Who Didn't Care tale for her benefit.

"You okay?" she whispered to Phoenix, rising and crossing the room to her daughter.

"Yep." Phoenix nodded, her hair shuffling against the pillow.

Hana squatted next to her and leaned close to whisper. "Did you see Edin today?"

Phoenix wrinkled her nose as though about to sneeze. Her eyes grew round. "She's not the same at school, Mama." Her cool, toothpaste laced breath warmed Hana's cheeks.

"What do you mean?"

Phoenix turned on her side and lowered her voice. "I saw her at interval and lunch. She held the teacher's hand and cuddled Horsey. Some girls let her play their game for a while and she seemed calm, not like herself at all."

Hana exhaled and nodded. "You think she'll like school?"

"Maybe." Phoenix's gaze strayed across the room towards the gentle snores issuing from Edin's bed. "I liked her better today."

"Good." Hana pressed her lips against her daughter's warm cheek and closed her eyes. Floral hair conditioner and little-girl sweetness filled her nostrils. "I'm glad," she whispered.

"She upset Wiri." Phoenix's parting salvo destroyed Hana's illusion of rightness with her world, and she frowned. A glow bloomed from beneath the bedsheets and she stiffened.

"It's late. You're not reading tonight." Hana dug beneath the sheets and retrieved the eReader, closing the flap on Phoenix's addiction for books. She sighed. "I know what happened with Wiri. I'll speak to him."

Phoenix's lips twisted into a pout. With her bargaining chip confiscated, she no longer wished to play the role of Hana's informant. She turned on her side and released a dramatic sigh which could have won her an Oscar in its delivery. Hana stroked her shoulder and left the room, closing the door behind her.

Logan met her in the wide hallway. "Mac's snoring and Wiri's reading."

Hana tutted and glanced towards the girls' door. She waved Phoenix's device in her hand. "I just said no to Phoe."

"Sorry." Logan gathered her into his arms and his chest moved beneath her cheek. She closed her eyes and sensed her muscles relax.

"I should speak to Wiri about what happened on the steps to the roof garden. Phoe said he's brooding."

"Already done." Logan's arms tightened around her back. "I told him the truth. He's a realist, and it helped him to understand her better. She's his half-sister. We forget that sometimes when we're trying to fit a square peg into a round hole."

"Wow." Hana gulped, stamping on the ready litany of reasons for disagreeing with her husband's methods. He'd taken the initiative and shouldered the emotional load. It seemed churlish to criticise the outcome. "Is that how you feel? Like Edin's the square peg?"

"No." He exhaled and leaned his chin on the top of her head. "Her mother makes her that way. Without Caroline's influence, we'll see a vast difference in her ability to settle."

Hana groaned at the mention of Caroline. "Isn't she phoning soon to iron out the details for speaking to Edin each weekend? I'm not looking forward to that conversation." She tilted the hand still holding Phoenix's eReader and glanced at the time. "When will she call?"

"Already done and dealt with." Logan dropped his hands and wrestled the device from her fingers. He placed it on the long wooden sideboard which dominated the hall. He viewed her confusion with a benevolent smile, the glitter of the crystal light fitting overhead throwing sparkles across his face. "She phoned while you were sorting out clean pyjamas for the girls. She's agreed to play things my way. Edin can write to her and send drawings when she feels like it. I haven't committed to anything regular. She'll call your mobile every Saturday evening, and Edin can speak to her if she wants to."

"Did you tell her we know Edin was in the apartment when she killed your brother?"

"Yeah." His voice hardened. "I think that's the reason she's tried to micromanage our parenting of Edin. In her own way, she thought she could make it better. She feared being judged for something else."

Hana nodded. "It's hard not to condemn her for that. We knew Edin suffered trauma, but assumed it stemmed from separation anxiety. That's why I continued with the visits to the prison and bowed to Caroline's constant demands. She could have told the truth at any time, but didn't." A bite entered Hana's tone, and she baulked at hearing her own criticism of another woman. She sighed. "Let's not talk about her anymore."

"I'm happy with that." Logan stilled, and he stared up at the ceiling. His black eyelashes fluttered as he cocked his head. "Can you hear that?" he whispered.

"What?" Hana concentrated, following his gaze to a spot above her head. She stared and saw nothing unusual in the soft cream paint. "No. I can't hear anything."

His eyes crinkled at the corners as a smile freed itself from his soul and covered her in its glow. Bowing his head and leaning closer, he whispered in her ear. "Exactly." The rumble of his baritone stampeded through her body, producing an effect like successive dominoes falling in a predetermined line from her brain to her stomach. She gave a sharp inhale as Logan dipped his knees and caught her up into his arms. A girlish giggle bubbled up from her chest and she clapped her hand over it to halt its escape. Her husband's scent enveloped her; meadow grass, sunshine, and masculine deodorant.

Hana let her cares fall to the tiled floor like a discarded cloak as Logan bore her away to their bedroom. They'd still be there waiting when she emerged later with her forehead damp and her legs trembling like jelly. She'd pick them up again then and restart her continuous cycle of worry. Going nowhere fast.

18

Swingletree

Hana disentangled her legs from Logan's and he gave a contented sigh from his sleep. The candles he'd lit while she shed her clothes spluttered and spat on the dressing table. She slipped his discarded shirt over her naked arms, fitting her head through the gap and shivering as it slithered over her breasts and stomach. Then she looked back at her husband with a smile of satisfaction.

The thin sheet covered his midsection, unable to mask the defined muscles of his stomach and the knotty hip bone which protruded through the fabric. His salt and pepper fringe covered his eyes, and he slept with one arm flung above his head as though making a statement of careless abandon. The fingers of his other hand twitched against the pillow where Hana's head rested until minutes earlier. She waited a moment to see if he'd wake and sit up, searching for her through bleary eyes still filled with lust and longing.

He sighed and settled again, and she dipped her head to blow out the spitting candles. The tiny flames gave minimal resistance as they clung to life on their drowning wicks.

Darkness shrouded the silent house as Hana slipped into the hall and closed the bedroom door behind her.

Leaving the house presented a significant challenge. Although sleeping, Logan would sense the opening of the front door and rouse, alert and ready to face any potential intruder. This particular skill caused Hana stress, as she paused before the nearest exit point to the truck. She tapped her fingers against her lip and pondered the dilemma. The car keys tinkled in her other hand. Her mind ran a mental check of all feasible routes to the outside. The front door needed slamming since the hinges dropped, and the ranch slider onto the deck made a hissing sound which would carry across the back of the house to their open bedroom window. Hana wagged her index finger in the air and grinned into the dark hallway. "The laundry door," she mouthed without sound.

Her bare feet padded through the house to the garage and she skirted the ride-on lawnmower and an open toolbox. She stepped on Wiri's abandoned trainers, which hadn't made it as far as the shoe rack, hopping on one foot and cursing in her head. Moonlight created a puddle of light through the glass in the door, and Hana used it to hobble the rest of the distance in safety. She retrieved the key from on top of the freezer and winced as it ground in the lock. The house remained silent, and she eased the door open and slid her left foot over the threshold. The still warm concrete slabs formed a path around the house and Hana eased the door closed behind her.

A possum growled from the bushes nearby and her tiptoeing became a strange pecking jog. She cleared the side of the house and emerged next to the kitchen window. A wandering pūkeko screeched in alarm, stalking away from her before rising into the air on black wings streaked with sapphire highlights. Its white bottom bounced with the motion of its hasty flight, legs dangling like empty wire coat hangers beneath it. Hana clutched her chest and blew out a ragged breath.

The gravel driveway posed a problem, the crunchy stones cutting into the soles of her feet. Hana hissed and complained under her breath as far as the truck, walking on the sides of her feet and still suffering from the relentless bite of the grit.

The subtle click of the central locking allowed her to open the door and retrieve the notebook from beneath the seat. The lemon grass air freshener shrouded her in its intense tang, warmed by the sun and then sealed into the truck's interior. It clashed with the mustiness of the bush scents, fern and damp undergrowth, which always smelled to Hana like a wet dog.

The spiral binding dug into her palm as she climbed from the truck and closed the door. The interior light flickered as the catch caught, but not enough to seal the door. Hana groaned and stamped her foot, regretting it as another shard of grit dug into her big toe. She stood on one leg and tried to close the door again, concerned by the clunk which echoed off the side of the house. But the light faded to nothing, and she used the fob to activate the central locking again.

A warm breeze circled her calves as she turned towards the house. It shifted the loose shirt, stirring it around her thighs and bare stomach. Hana clutched the notebook and held down the hem with the other hand, setting off back towards the covered porch and the safety of the paving slabs.

She relaxed as her sore feet trod the warm concrete and her shoulders lost their rigidity. Until a voice disturbed the quiet of the garden.

"So, here we are again."

Logan stood in the gap where the front door had been only moments earlier. He leaned against the frame, arms folded across his muscular chest. A St Christopher nestled in the valley between his pectorals, moonlight creating glitter through the downy hair which kissed his skin. Hana froze, unable to read his expression beneath the shadows which hid his features. She twisted her lips and pushed her knees together, gripping the car key in one hand while pushing the notebook behind her back with the other.

"I forgot something." She stuck her chin higher in defiance and contemplated stuffing the notebook under the back of her shirt. Without underwear, she didn't have many places to shove it to stop it from falling back out and betraying her.

"Oh yeah?" Logan stepped forward to reveal bare legs and a midriff clothed in boxer shorts. He splayed his legs and kept his arms folded to issue a silent challenge.

"Yep. And I heard a noise." Hana turned her torso to search for the pūkeko, grimacing at the empty garden. She swallowed. "There's a possum in the bushes over there." She jabbed the key in the general direction and fixed a smile on her lips. "I thought you'd like to know. You don't want them to get out of hand again." Hana dropped her gaze to her feet and waited. When Logan still said nothing, she stepped sideways and sidled past him, keeping the notebook behind her back and her body facing him. "I'll go back in the side door," she said, her tone light.

She almost made it.

"I know you took the diary." He turned to follow her progress, his grey irises glittering beneath the caress of the half moon. "Why do you always believe you can outwit me?"

Hana's shoulders slumped, but she kept hold of the notebook hard enough for the metal spirals to dig into her palm. "I want it." She heard a catch in her voice. "You took the other diaries away from me. I didn't get to finish reading them."

Logan sighed. He dropped his hands to his hips and shook his head at her. "It's one thing to learn stuff, Hana. But it's a whole other thing deciding what to reveal and what should stay hidden. Your conscience threatened our family. Will and I stopped you reading Kuia's diaries until we'd vetted them first."

"I'm not a child." A prickle began in her chest as she sensed herself hitting a brick wall.

"No, you're not." She looked up at Logan to find him smiling at her. "But you're a decent person, Hana. You love the truth, but not all truths are good for all people. There's a reason Kuia kept secrets. Look at what's already happened."

She nodded and avoided his perceptive gaze, hating the rightness she heard in his words. She couldn't be trusted not to blurt damaging facts, and they weren't just damaging. Some of them were cataclysmic. To others who were blissfully innocent. Like Edin.

The prickle in her chest intensified as she brought the notebook forward and held it out to him. The woodenness of her movements demonstrated her reluctance to release it back into his possession. She hadn't known it existed, but now that she did, it rankled at the back of her mind as an obsession. Just like the others. "It's your mother's," she said, her voice little more than a whisper. "It's Miriam's."

"I know." Logan sighed. "And if you'd asked me, I would have let you have it."

"You would?" Hope and dread mingled in Hana's chest, adding tears to the prickling sensation. They rose into the back of her nose and her eyes glittered with the threat of expelling them.

"Yeah." Logan shrugged. "I trusted you."

Hana's eyelashes fluttered closed, sealing her soul against his perceptive gaze. "Past tense," she said. Bitterness laced her tone. "And now I've blown it."

Logan cocked his head. "What are you doing, Hana?"

She swallowed, choking back regret at having lost something precious in her continual crusade to know everything. The urge to bring the truth into the light plagued her, like a cleaner who ransacked cupboards in pursuit of a mysterious smell. "I'm sorry," she conceded. "I loved reading Kuia's diaries. It connected me to your family and to this country's lost history. It helped me to understand why things happened and how we got to this." She spread her left hand and the truck key tinkled against the gravel. Hana bent to retrieve it and the loose shirt fluttered around her buttocks.

Logan nodded. "I understand, babe. Believe me, I do." He blew out a breath which contained irritation and sadness. "But your quest for truth comes with a massive responsibility and that's when I find I can't rely on you."

Hana exhaled and tipped her head back. A smattering of stars twinkled above her in lieu of the Milky Way, which would be directly overhead in a few months. "I understand," she conceded. "I haven't yet decided whether discovering the truth about Caroline has helped or hindered my relationship with her daughter. Sometimes, I wish I didn't know and other times, I wonder if it's a vital clue to her behaviour."

"It isn't." Logan's teeth ground in his jaw. "I don't want to believe that it has any influence at all. Because if it does, then I'm condemning myself. Hemophilia is enough of a curse without wishing anything else on myself. Can you imagine what it's like growing up to keep a secret of that magnitude? Jack told me he was my grandfather. He didn't tell me the identity of his son and let me believe it was Alfred. I built my life on a lie."

"Do you wish you had known none of it?" Hana asked. She studied her husband's face as he considered her question, realising that much of their disagreement hinged on the next thing to emerge from his full lips.

"Yeah." He nodded and dropped his fists to his side, taking a combative stance as though about to perform his family's haka. "All or nothing, Hana. Not half truths and confusion. It creates only strife."

She held out the notebook, understanding sending a muted electrical current surging through her muscles and sinews. The back cover sagged, and the pages rustled in the breeze. "Okay," she said. "I get it." She shook her head. "Are you disappointed in me?"

Logan's eyes narrowed and his lips quirked upward on one side. "A bit," he admitted. He held out his hand to her, and she winced as she took a step forward, a piece of gravel still digging into her left sole.

"I'm sorry," she said, lifting her foot and brushing off the loose grit. "I shouldn't have sneaked around. It's not the stuff of solid marriages."

Logan snorted and his fingers closed around her wrist, steadying her as she brushed off the other foot. "That's not why I'm disappointed." Humour rippled through his voice. "We thought you'd find it sooner. Will bet me fifty bucks you'd find that one first, but I banked on you finding the other three." He shrugged as she stared up at him. Her lips parted and her eyes widened. "I even put them at eye level," he said. "Trust you to go for the least obvious find. He'll never let me live it down now, will he?"

19

Hacking

Logan let Hana keep the diary, and that fact alone caused her disappointment. It meant it contained nothing of interest or potential devastation. It pained Hana to realise that his assertions proved accurate. She hunted the truth with the sole purpose of revealing it. And he couldn't trust her.

Saturday morning slid by amid the chaos of breakfast for three amiable children and one picky marauder. Edin sat next to Mac, her spoon poised as she watched him make patterns in his rice bubbles. Wheat flakes disintegrated in her milk and turned to mush as she ignored them. Phoenix shoveled porridge into her mouth in slow motion, her attention absorbed by her eReader.

"Why can't I have bacon and eggs?" Wiri rested his hands on his hips and pouted. His dark fringe bounced against the movement of his eyelashes. Hana exhaled, noticing how his jeans rode up over his ankle bones.

"I can't keep up with clothing you," she joked, forcing a lightness she didn't feel in her tone. "You might end up taller than Logan."

Wiri peered down at his bare feet and frowned. "That's why I need bacon and eggs for breakfast. It makes me big and strong."

"And it makes me late," Hana bit. "I don't have time to degrease the kitchen after a cooked breakfast. If I make it for you, I need to do it for all the others and I don't have time today. I'm sorry, Wiri. It's cereal or microwaved porridge."

"Or nothing." Logan ran his hands through his hair as he entered the kitchen. He kissed Phoenix on the top of her head and closed the cover of her device, at the same time miming to the other two to eat. His solidity and capable authority flooded the room, chasing away the tension with his presence. He pulled out the toaster and dumped two rounds of bread into the slots.

"Toast?" Wiri stood in the centre of the room, his brow furrowed as he pushed the negotiations. "Toast and peanut butter."

Hana navigated around him, carrying drinks for the children at the table.

"Sit." Logan pointed towards an empty seat and Wiri slouched across the tiles, dragging his feet in a silent protest.

"What's the rush?" he demanded. "Why did I have to get up so early? Why did you make me get dressed? It's not even seven o'clock yet. Why can't I have bacon and eggs?"

A switch flicked within the consciousness of the other children and they turned their attention to him. Mac studied Wiri's body language with the intensity of a psychologist and Edin took his cue, picking out wheat flakes with her fingers. Milk dribbled along the handle of her waving spoon and her grey irises sparkled. Sensing trouble, they shot covert glances at one another.

"Why is the sky blue? Why is the grass green?" Logan retrieved the browned bread as it popped free of the toaster. As Hana emptied the dishwasher of the previous night's crockery, he snagged a knife and spread peanut butter over the slices. He winked at her as she dug in the bottom rack to retrieve an escaping teaspoon, and she pursed her lips and blushed. They'd lingered in bed too long, taking advantage of the children sleeping late for a change.

Wiri huffed out an exaggerated breath. His body crumpled in the chair, and Mac and Edin giggled in unison. "Why are you asking dumb questions?" he grumbled. His eyes widened as Logan's large hand rested on the top of his head, keeping him from knocking the plate out of his hand as he laid it before him.

"My thoughts exactly," Logan replied. "We're mustering the middle slopes today and I thought you wanted to come."

"I'm going," Phoenix asserted. "Excuse me." She pushed her chair back and left the table, taking her bowl over to the sink. "Do we need sandwiches, Mama?"

"Already by the front door." Hana smiled at her daughter and dumped knives into the cutlery drawer. "Two lots of sandwiches each, fruit and snacks. Wear your body protector and a proper riding hat today, please. It'll be chaos out there. Make sure you drink lots of water."

"Okay, Mama." Phoenix stood on tiptoes to kiss Hana's cheek. She screwed up her eyes and her body jerked with involuntary excitement. "I can't wait. Papa taught me to cut and block on Dotty. She's quite fast."

"She's also a long way off the ground for a little girl. Take care."

"She will." Logan shot her a sideways glance, warning exuding from the storm water grey of his irises. He lowered his voice beneath the chatter which erupted between Phoenix and Wiri. "David Allen will keep her back with the other green ringers. He'll tail the mob and supervise the mothering up when we get to lower ground."

"What about him?" Hana jerked her head towards Wiri, frowning as he folded a whole slice of toast in half and shoved it into his mouth.

"He's rounding up the Micky bulls with Toby. He came out with us last season. Cocky little sh-"

"Logan!" Hana jabbed her elbow into his ribs. She pursed her lips at his ready smirk. "Knock it off."

He stepped over the lowered dishwasher door and wrapped his arms around her. "You spoil all my fun, Ms McIntyre."

She replied into the folds of his denim shirt. "It's not fun when he's suspended from school for copying you."

"This is true." He lowered his head and pressed his lips over hers. The toaster clicked behind him, disgorging his second attempt at breakfast.

"Tust!" Edin shouted. "Edie's tust."

Logan groaned. "Sometimes I miss the old days, babe. Nipping into the hotel chiller and grabbing breakfast on my way to the stables. Ma and Leslie feeding the stockmen through the kitchen window and everyone sitting in their own muck and eating on the front steps."

"Careful what you wish for," Hana whispered. "I'll tell Leslie how much you miss her."

"Don't!" Logan's eyes flashed with amusement, and his lips curved upward into a smile. His teeth clamped over his lower lip. "Don't encourage her."

Wiri rose, shoving another hunk of toast into his mouth and high fiving Mac. His unintelligible sentence became lost beneath swallowing and choking as he clattered out of the kitchen.

"At least he won't puke bacon and eggs through his nose this time." Logan grinned and stared after him. "That was entertaining."

Hana shuddered and drew her lips back in disgust. She changed the subject. "Leslie wants to forage for kawakawa leaves this morning for her balm. The little ones can come with us. I'll carry the radio, so flick me occasional updates?"

"Okay." Logan pressed a last kiss over her open mouth. "We're aiming to get back around seven tonight. Two quad bikes are following with spare gear and water. I'll radio you when we're getting near the yard."

"And to tell me how Phoe and Wiri are doing?"

Logan's eyes narrowed. "No, Hana. Not unless you want life to be even harder for them than it already is. They need to learn their trade and earn respect. No one else's helicopter mummy gets radio updates."

"Did you really just call me a helicopter mother?" Hana's jaw dropped open.

Logan laughed and spun towards the table. He dropped a kiss on the top of Mac's head, and she watched the conflict in his eyes as he forced himself to mirror the gesture for Edin. The child's head bobbed beneath the pressure and she glanced up only in time to see the closing kitchen door. "Papa." She puffed out the sound and smiled at the popping of her lips. Patting Mac's thigh with her milky hand, she leaned forward until he looked at her. "Papa," she repeated. Her greasy index finger pointed towards the door in a jabbing motion. "Papa."

Hana's phone trilled on the counter, the vibration carrying it far enough to pull its charger cord tight. She set a stack of dinner plates next to it and examined the screen, seeing Bodie's number flash beside the ringing green icon of a receiver. She blew out a breath and connected the call, lifting the phone to her ear.

Edin's gaze tracked to Logan's abandoned breakfast, and she pointed at the toaster with the tantalising brown crusts poking over the slot. "Edie's tust!" she yelled. "Tust!"

20

Weymouth Bit

"Hey Bo." Hana yanked the bread from the toaster and dumped it onto a plate. Edin's racket stalled as she studied the movement. She ditched the spoon and hauled Horsey from her lap, positioning his muzzle so he could view Hana over the tabletop with his mismatched button eyes.

"Mum?" Bodie paused, as though waiting for something. "How are you?"

"Yeah, good. We're going into the bush with Leslie this morning to collect leaves for her balm. Did it work on Hope's eczema?"

"Yes, thanks. We're keen for some more once it's brewed or cooked, or whatever she does with it."

"She boils it in a rice cooker." Hana put the phone on speaker and the sound altered, gaining a tinny, disjointedness. She spread butter onto the toast and frowned across at Edin. "Jam? Peanut butter?"

"What?"

"Sorry, I'm giving the little ones their breakfast. Logan took the others mustering. Which do you want, Edin?"

"Cheese." She conferred with Horsey, who gave a waggling nod in response.

"No." Hana dashed their dreams. "Jam or peanut."

Edin closed her eyes and refused to engage in negotiations. Her eyes snapped open with indignation as Hana dumped the plate in front of her. "No!"

"That or nothing!" Hana turned her back on her and returned to the phone. Edin complained about the poor parenting to Horsey, but the index finger and thumb of her left hand clamped around a toasted corner and lifted it to her mouth. Mac had produced his device from under his chair and stared at the screen, his eyelashes flickering as he studied a fascinating insect in his game. He caught Hana's eye as she turned and pursed her lips. "One hour a day," she reminded him, the phone almost flying from the counter as she signed her warning. "Thirty minutes left."

"You sound busy." Bodie blew out a sigh and Hana held her breath, expecting him to drop into the usual pattern of self-pitying.

"I'm fine," she lied. She forced herself to still, watching the children with her back to the counter and lifting the phone.

"Are you on speaker?"

"Yeah, why?" Hana frowned at the screen. "Want me to switch?"

"Yes, please."

She complied, fiddling with the buttons and returning the phone to her ear. If Edin threw the toast, there was nothing she could do to stop it. The child's gaze slid towards her as though reading her mind. She pushed a crust at Horsey's lips, butter running up her wrist. "What's wrong?"

"I wanted to apologise for the other day." Bodie heaved out a breath. "Have you reported Tama as officially missing?"

"Not yet. Logan nipped to the local watch house while I picked the children up from school yesterday. The officer on duty said Tama's an adult. He can take himself off on a tiki tour whenever he likes. They won't worry about him for a few weeks unless there's a particular reason. He's not suicidal, so they don't care."

"It's not that we don't care, Mum." His tone held tiredness at reciting a familiar mantra. He added his solidarity to his colleague. "We need some unusual circumstances, or something to indicate foul play."

"He didn't take his car. It's still outside his house. He didn't tell his flat mate, and he's missing his shifts at work. The fire chief phoned me on Thursday, which is what sent us up to Auckland. He isn't answering his phone."

"You checked his place?" An intensity entered Bodie's tone as though some magic sentence had sparked his interest.

"Yes. He went home after a community event on Monday night but wasn't there when his flat mate returned home on Tuesday morning. He started missing work on Wednesday."

"Did you find his phone or wallet when you checked his house?"

"No." Hana frowned. "We checked his bedroom, but not the rest of the house. His flat mate was sleeping off a night shift and wasn't happy about us being there."

A tapping sound issued through the phone as Bodie remained silent. Hana sensed the cogs turning in his brain as he considered the information. He shared similar tendencies to Logan, and it pained her they'd never reached a consensus, which lasted more than a few tense exchanges. "If I had flat mates, I wouldn't leave my personal stuff lying around in the common areas. I'd keep it in my private space. Did you see a phone charger anywhere?"

Hana closed her eyes and pictured Tama's room. She tutted, remembering the black bag still leaning against the washing machine. "Yes. I remember seeing the cord lying across his night stand. The plug socket must be behind it."

"So, he possibly slept in his own bed on Monday night and then left the house sometime on Tuesday. I don't suppose you'd know if he'd taken clothes with him or what he might have worn when he left."

"No." Hana sighed. "Sorry. I haven't done his washing for years. I brought his laundry home with me, but I saw nothing unusual about it." She lifted her index finger and wagged it at Edin. "Eat it yourself, or I'll take it away. Horsey isn't hungry." Edin made a pincer movement with her finger and thumb and prepared to flick the toast across the table.

Hana inhaled and readied herself for battle, but Mac saved the day. He turned his screen towards her and pointed at something moving through his battle scene. "Bug," he said, the word distorted by his residual deafness. "Lay-bug."

Edin forgot the toast and knelt on her chair, pressing her temple against his to share the experience.

"Sorry." Hana listened to herself speak and realised how many times a day she issued the apology. She'd grown tired of hearing it. "There is one thing. I found a business card in the pocket of the shirt he wore on Monday night. It had a woman's name and an insurance company logo on it."

"Can you remember the details?"

"No. Why?"

"I'm not sure. She might be the last person to see Tama. Text me her details when you have them. But just prepare yourself."

"What for?" Hana gulped and her fingers fluttered over the pacemaker embedded beneath her left collarbone. "In case something terrible has happened?" she whispered.

"No, in case he met some new love interest and went off on a bender with her."

Relief left the flood of adrenaline with nowhere to go, and it surged through Hana's bloodstream. "He wouldn't do that." Her voice wobbled. "He hasn't missed work without a reason since he started. That's why his chief phoned me."

"Fair enough," Bodie relented. His voice softened. "Go back to the watch house in Rangiriri and file a missing person's report. I can't do any personal checks on him until you do; it's a disciplinary offense. Once you've filed the report, I can liaise with whoever gets assigned to it. I'll do what I can from this end."

"Thank you." A flush of gratitude started at Hana's toes and worked its way through her body. "I'll do it today."

"The satellite watch houses aren't open at the weekend. Do it on Monday and text me. I won't tell you not to worry because I know you will. Make the report in person and take a photo of him with you. Let's hope it's nothing."

"I appreciate it." Somehow, Bodie's interest made Tama's disappearance seem more serious. She wondered if she preferred it when he dismissed her concerns as trivial. "I'll do that and let you know what happens."

"Okay." He exhaled. "I love you, Mum. Send me a photo of the business card when you get it. Let's not panic until we know something concrete."

"I'll try," Hana promised. She pressed the edge of her phone against her lip and bounced it twice after her son disconnected. Bodie's final sentence sent an alert to some latent early warning system in her subconscious. It was the kind of thing someone said when they had only partial information about a looming disaster. They knew it was bad, but not yet how bad. "Oh, God," Hana breathed, issuing her silent prayer for a favorable outcome. "Please, let me be angry at him tomorrow when he surfaces from some random girl's bed with a hangover."

21

Blinkers and Blinders

Hana answered her phone without checking the identity of the caller. Voices sounded in the background of the call and a door banged. A gasp sounded as a woman's voice rose through clenched teeth. She swore and issued a threat to someone Hana couldn't see.

"Hello? Are you there?" She sounded breathless. "I don't have long. This bitch behind me won't stay down for more than a few seconds."

"Caroline." Hana's fingers froze, Tama's shirt clasped tight enough to release a haze of his aftershave. "You're not meant to call me. Logan promised."

Caroline snorted. "Yeah, thanks for sending him to see me instead of your insipid face. I enjoyed it."

Hana swallowed and pulled the phone away from her ear. Her fingers shook, the tremor taken up by the rest of her muscles. She considered ending the call and blocking the prison number. Only her recent progress with Edin stopped her following through and doing it. "You lied about Nev's death." She lifted the phone to her ear and choked on the words. "Edin saw you push him."

"Shut up!" Caroline growled. "Shut up and listen."

"I don't have to!" Hana's voice rose. "You're dealing with Logan now."

Edin played on the laundry floor with Mac. They crouched together to watch a lone ant stride across the tiles. "Mama! Look!" she insisted, her breath blowing the ant a few centimetres further than he'd intended. The children giggled.

Caroline swallowed loud enough for Hana to hear the gulp. "She calls you Mama," she snarled. "You promised you wouldn't let her do that, and I heard it with my own ears."

"I'm sorry," Hana breathed. "I've tried to stop her. We all correct her, but she hears the other children." Her voice trailed off as she found herself on the back foot against Caroline's inimitable force. Guilt sent a dart of pain into her heart.

"You need to do something for me," Caroline urged. Her voice grew muffled as she swore again. Another female tone rose alongside one with more authority. "I have to go." She exhaled.

"You've had your time," the authoritative voice stated. "Say your goodbyes." Keys jangled in the background. Caroline hadn't spoken to her for five minutes and Hana's mind distracted her with thoughts of who she'd called before her. Logan, perhaps. Jealousy rose in response to her fears that letting him take over had forced him to establish contact with Caroline. Her weakness had caused the very last thing she wanted.

"Don't let the other family have Edin," Caroline snarled. Her tone rose at the end of the sentence. "They're coming for her. Don't let her go."

"Why?" Hana dropped the shirt into the washing machine and fought the urge to drag it back out and lift it to her nose. "Who are they?"

"Just don't!" Caroline rose through gritted teeth. "I swear, if you let them take my daughter, I'll ruin your relationship with yours." She snorted. "I might do it anyway, just for the hell of it."

"Phoenix?" Hana lifted a hand to her sternum and pressed. "Don't you dare threaten my children!"

"Not that one," Caroline scoffed. "The other daughter. I have friends in Invercargill. How would she like to know her daddy cheated on her perfect mother? He planned to leave you the day he died. Pity Logan hasn't wised up and taken the easy way out yet."

"How do you know about Vic?" Hana whispered. Her gaze darted towards the door as Edin and Mac ran through it. She heard the front door slam and Leslie's voice in the hallway. Giving in to her need for comfort, she hauled Tama's shirt from the washing machine and pressed it against her cheek.

Caroline swore again, and the call ended. She lost her fight for domination of the communal telephone at the prison. Hana imagined a line of women snaking behind her as they waited their turn. Caroline's narcissism would persuade her she had the right to talk for as long as she wanted.

Silence surrounded Hana as she sank onto the lone camping chair abandoned after their last beach visit. A streak of dirt stained the fabric, the reason for its separation from the other three as it awaited cleaning. Tama's shirt brushed the edge and orange clay transferred to his sleeve. Hana blew out a ragged breath and hugged it against her stomach. "How does she know about Vic?" she whispered into the empty house. "How does she know?"

Giggling drifted to her from outside as Leslie readied the children for their foraging. Her voice rose as she instructed them in the karakia they needed to say to appease the ancestors before they began their task.

Grief mingled with fury to bend Hana double. She lifted the shirt to her nose and inhaled Tama's masculine scent. Caroline's threat swirled around her brain and her fingers gripped her phone. She considered telling Isobel the truth for the millionth time since Vik's death, but the words stuck in her throat. She'd left it too long to destroy her daughter's respect for a father she idolised. Years too long. A lifetime, in fact.

22

Tail Guard

The children enjoyed the bush foraging. Leslie took time to point out the many plants available for rongoā medicine. Edin proved a fast study, peering at the heart-shaped kawakawa leaves and pointing out many more bushes for picking. She absorbed the rules for harvesting with respect, her delicate fingers pinching off grandparent leaves and sparing the mamas and babies for the next season. Mac carried the basket, his angelic gaze flicking from Leslie to Edin and back again. A floppy hat covered his red curls and protected his fair skin from the ruthless sun, which sparked shafts of yellow through the canopy. He epitomised peace and contentment within his elfin frame, and Hana yearned for even just a taste of his relaxed state.

"I need some manuka," Leslie said. Hana jumped as she touched her arm with a cool hand. "You have the snips."

"Sorry." Hana delved into the cloth bag and retrieved a set of dangerous looking secateurs. Her nose wrinkled at the thought of the harsh, phlegm busting tea created from the twigs and leaves.

Leslie smiled. "I know you don't like it. I'll make kanuka too, just for you."

"Kanuka for kind, manuka for mean." The sentence spilled from Edin's lips without fault, and Hana blinked. Mac giggled at his cousin.

Leslie waggled her eyebrows. "School is excellent for te tāmahine. She's flowering like a wee bud."

Hana swallowed and gave a jerky nod. "It's complicated."

Leslie snorted. "It always is with her mother involved. That wahine doesn't have a good bone in her body. Always trouble, right from the minute her mother bore her, God rest her soul whoever the poor tūpuna wahine was."

Logan's wisdom returned to haunt Hana. Knowing the identity of Caroline's parentage burned in her chest. It fought to sear through her porcelain skin and expose itself like a maggot eating its host. Caroline deserved it for threatening her when she'd taken her child without protest. She imagined what the revelation might do to her and savoured the momentary flush of victory.

Instead, she choked on her fumbled reply and Leslie rubbed her smooth hand over the knotted ridges of Hana's spine. "Sounds like you need some kanuka tea," she diagnosed.

Hana nodded and fixed a meek smile on her lips. The children remained close to the track as they foraged, already familiar with the dangers the native bush presented. They kept the gable end of Hana's house in sight and the boundary fence within easy reach. Though the mountain bore much useful flora and fauna across its craggy ranges, it pleased the women by presenting it to them on their doorstep.

"Enough now," Leslie called as Edin's fingers reached up towards a low-hanging branch. The child stopped and turned towards Mac, pushing her face near enough to kiss him.

"Nuff now," she repeated with authority. She wagged her finger at him. "No more!"

Mac shrugged and turned, the basket bumping against his knees.

"It's too hot." Leslie wiped her forehead with the back of her hand. "I wanted bush lawyer for Alfie's tonic, but I don't have the energy to get scratched up today."

Hana contemplated the hooky leaved shrub with its savage spikes and nodded in agreement. "We can grab some weeds from the lawn on the way to the house."

"Yes," Leslie agreed. "I need plantain and comfrey for a muscle rub."

Hana turned and moved off the narrow track, allowing Leslie to shuffle past her while she waited for the children. She held out her hand to take the basket from Mac, but he frowned and shook his head. Edin stared up at Hana and pursed her lips before running after Leslie.

Mac's steps laboured beneath the weight of the basket, though he refused twice more to relinquish it. Hana followed him along the winding track, inhaling the familiar bush odours of silver fern and damp undergrowth. Her mind grounded her in thoughts of her powerful husband, reminding her of how intoxicating she found his meadow and sunshine scent in those first heady months. He'd used the muscle rub his whole life without question to soothe the bruises caused by hemophilia. "Garden weeds and lemongrass," Hana whispered. "I fell in love with a man who smelled of garden weeds and lemongrass." She sighed to herself, raising her eyebrows at Mac as he turned to observe her. He blinked at her, his glittering emerald irises dancing in a shaft of light. They shared their silent conspiracy with a smile and continued their journey.

Hana winced as she closed the wide driveway gate and noticed Edin digging on the lawn with a trowel. She'd given up on creating the fine lawn of gardening catalogues. "What's another hole among friends?" she breathed. Deep hoof prints betrayed a recent visitor who showed up just to raid Hana's ailing herb garden. Sacha's addiction to parsley worried Logan, indicating some form of internal gut inflammation. But the vet refused to go near her dinner plate hooves and so, she trekked up the long driveway and jumped the fence to self-medicate. Logan tried adding it to her feed, but she didn't enjoy it quite as much as when Hana caught her trampling the lettuces. Apparently, there were different kinds of therapy involved in Sacha's penchant for parsley.

"Sorry." Leslie shrugged as Hana walked towards her. "This wee girl is so sharp. I showed her plantain last time, and she remembered." Her irises misted in thought. "Do you think it's too early to train her in rōngoa? She could take over from me one day."

Hana gave a noncommittal wave of her hand. If she took after Caroline, such knowledge would give her a leg up as a serial killer. Hana ground her teeth together and dismissed the notion with another wave of her hand. Caroline had killed one person, not a multitude. "Let it go, Hana," she berated herself as she unlocked the front door.

"Let it go." The little voice piped the words, and Hana jumped. The keys tumbled onto the mat as the door swung open. Mac stared up at her through eyes acting as windows to a soul far wiser than his years. He'd struggled across the lawn with the basket and still held it, his fingers white from gripping the handle.

"Thanks, baby." Hana took it from him and jerked her head towards Leslie. "I think Edin's digging her way through to England."

"Hole." Mac followed her gaze and his eyes widened. He sidled closer to her leg and slid his arm around her thigh, seeking shelter from the scorching sun. Looking down at the basket, he flicked a kawakawa leaf onto its back with a nonchalant finger.

"Yep. Big hole." Hana pursed her lips and shuffled over the threshold with the child still hugging her leg. She set the basket on the hall floor and tapped Mac's shoulder. "Wash your hands." She signed the action for him, even though the flicker of his eyelashes showed he'd heard her the first time. Lifting the sun hat from his head, she frowned at the scar from his implant surgery. "We'll put some more of Nonie's medicine on that," she said, forcing a smile onto her lips. "Then we can plug in your other magic ear."

He kissed the front of her leg at the same time as kicking off his boots. His feet padded along the hallway and light bloomed as he opened the bathroom door. Hana listened for the tap to spit running water, also hearing the plop of the soap falling into the sink.

"Who wants cake?" She leaned through the front door to call to Leslie, stifling a snort at the speed of the old lady's movements. "Don't leave the trowel in the middle of the lawn," she shouted, pointing as Edin abandoned her tools and followed Leslie's ungainly run. "I ran over the last one and Logan had to take the mower for repair."

Leslie backtracked to scoop up the fallen trowel and hefted it along with the dangling green leaves of an uprooted plantain sprout. Edin's slender legs carried her to the front door, where she protested against removing her rubber boots. "Cake," she grizzled, the merry girl of earlier gone in the face of food. "Edie wants cake."

"And you'll get cake," Hana promised. "Take off your wellies and wash your hands first and I'll get it for you."

Mac appeared from the bathroom, darker patches showing on his tee shirt. Water ran down the sides of his face and parts of his auburn hair flattened itself around his scalp. Hana exhaled as Leslie reached the door. "I hope he didn't dunk his entire head. He can't put his scar under water until the doctor says it's okay." She groaned. "And the other processor isn't waterproof."

"Na." Leslie wiped her feet on the mat and flicked off her boots. She grunted as she bent to set them upright side by side. "He's had a bushman's wash. He's been watching Alfie at the sink."

Hana's jaw hung slack. She very much hoped he hadn't. Another cursory glance revealed the evidence. "A bushman's wash," she repeated with a sigh. "Great."

Edin seemed unable to contain herself as she set her wellies next to Leslie's. Every part of her shivered and shook at the anticipation of cake. She sped to the bathroom and Hana doubted the efficacy of her hand washing. "Can you make sure she does a good job, please?" she asked. "I don't want her to have diarrhoea for a week."

"Ha!" Leslie snorted. She set off towards the splashing noises on bare feet and solid legs. "The kids have the sense to know what happens. It's just Englishwomen who weave flax and forget to wash their hands. They're the ones who get stuck on the toilet for days."

Hana closed her eyes and breathed out a steadying breath. "I'm not English!" she snarled. "I'm half Scots and half Irish."

"You still got the shits," Leslie replied with a birdlike cackle.

The pantry door squeaked from the kitchen and Hana groaned as her son hurried along the proceedings. The cake tin clattered against a cupboard as he wrestled with the lid, releasing the chocolate sponge she'd promised.

Hana stilled at the sensation of vibrations running through her soles. She glanced towards the gate as a vehicle laboured up the last of the steep rise, its engine straining. Her breath caught in her lungs as the police car stopped outside the gate and her adult son emerged from the passenger door. He closed it with a click and nodded to the driver. His fingers plucked at the cap in his fingers, turning it in a nervous, circular motion. The faint rustle of the evidence bag drifted across the lawn.

She knew what he'd come to tell her, what he'd driven all the way from Auckland to say. And she didn't want to hear it. Not even from him.

23

Crop

The chatter of Leslie and the children faded to background noise as Hana waited for her son. He approached the gate with exaggerated care, fumbling with the catch beneath the spotlight of her gaze. The driver remained in the vehicle, his head down as he studied something out of view. As Bodie closed the gate behind him, the noisy diesel engine ceased its rumbling.

Bodie offered a feckless wave as he navigated the gravel drive. No longer in uniform, he dressed in the awkwardness of someone unfamiliar with smart-casual. The hems of black jeans kissed the tops of shiny insteps, and his tee shirt showed the creases from an iron on the sleeves. As he scrunched across the gravel towards her, Hana realised the hat gripped in his left hand wasn't police issue.

She spent every second of Bodie's careful journey praying. Māori and English prayers melded together in a seamless plea for mercy. But the set of his shoulders in a slump of defeat dashed her false hopes as he stepped over the threshold and gathered her into his arms.

"I'm sorry, Mum," he said. "We found a body. I think it's him."

White noise erupted into Hana's brain, obscuring the sentences which followed in Bodie's gentle tones. Her mind snapped her back to the sobbing police officer, forced to give her the bad news about her first husband. She heard her words as an echo of Bodie's.

Hana blinked, finding her cheek pressed against her son's shoulder. A soapy scent shrouded him, as far removed from the bush and the ocean as the city which claimed him. Her right hand lifted and her fingers smoothed the outline of the pacemaker beneath her skin. A sheer act of will kept her standing upright while her stomach threatened nausea and her head thudded enough to drive her to the tiled floor, face first.

She took a step back and forced a smile onto her lips. "It's not him," she asserted, shaking her head. "It's not him. I'd know." She avoided looking at the cap still clutched in his left hand, the peak dented and bent and the fabric lacklustre and limp. An evidence bag surrounded it, condensation misting the inner surface.

Bodie's irises flickered with an eerie fire, which consumed the sympathy radiating from their maternal link. "Right," he said. "Well, there's a process. I need to speak to Logan. He needs to identify the body."

Hana shook her head, backing away from her son. "He's mustering with Phoenix and Wiri. He can't leave them." She blew out a ragged breath. "Leslie's here. I'll ask her to mind the little ones while I come with you." Her ponytail slapped her shoulder as she turned her head, staring back along the hallway as her feet refused to budge.

Bodie took her arm and steered her towards the kitchen, the warm breeze from the open front door licking Hana's fingers as they fidgeted in perpetual motion.

Mac released an exaggerated inhale and clapped both hands over his mouth as he spied Bodie, his green irises glittering with delight. "Bobo! Bobo!" he squeaked. He slithered from his dining chair, cake crumbs speckling his lips. Wrapping his arms around Bodie's thigh, he cocked his head to show his half-brother the wound from his surgery.

"Awesome, mate!" Bodie released Hana's arm and dipped to pick up the slender boy. He sat him on his hip and leaned back to study Mac's face. "I heard you were really brave. You take after me, don't you?" His smile widened as Mac gave a single nod.

"Love Bobo." Mac clasped Bodie's face in his delicate fingers and planted a wet kiss on his cheek. Crumbs dotted the space where his lips touched the olive skin. "Miss you." Mac released Bodie's face to sign his sentiment with fast moving fingers, and Hana watched the scene with a rigid spine.

"Kōtiro?" Leslie touched her elbow and she jumped. "You look sick. What's happened?" Her gaze slid to Bodie. "Did he bring trouble?"

Hana nodded, and the words stuck in her throat. "The police found a body. They think it's Tama."

Leslie's brown eyes grew enormous in her face. Her lower lip flapped like a stranded fish. "Our Tama?" she hissed. Her flax earrings bounced as she waggled her head. "No, that can't be right. He spoke to Alfie on Sunday. Asked him how the appointment went for his hip replacement surgery." The dangling strands shunted the beads against her neck as she continued her denial. "No, not our boy." A strangled sound entered her voice, and Hana shot a glance at Edin. She'd licked the crumbs from her plate and her fingers strayed across to Mac's abandoned cake.

"Shut up!" Hana hissed. She leaned closer to Leslie. "Say nothing! I'll go with Bodie and sort out this mess. I need you to keep this to yourself."

She dug her phone from her jeans pocket and unhooked the radio from her belt. Leslie's hand trembled as she accepted it. "What should I do?" she whispered.

"Please, look after Mac and Edin for me? Don't tell Logan or the others anything yet." Hana touched her pacemaker and exhaled. "We'll carry this burden alone for now, okay? We're strong wahine, yes?" The fire in her eyes forced a nod from Leslie. Hana gripped the old woman's shoulders in her hands and gave her a shake. "Make some balm with Edin. She'll love it."

Leslie's head began to shake even before Hana finished her sentence. "No, not today. I can't touch the rākau now. I'll taint it with sadness." She blew out a breath and frowned at Edin. "Do you think something is wrong with that moko? Worms maybe. She's eaten Mac's cake."

Hana exhaled and extracted herself from the problem. "Please, just give them both another slice. Try to avoid drama with her, but I know it's difficult. I'll deal with everything when I get back here. Listen to the radio but keep the sound low. Logan said he won't report on the children but he might relent." Her breath caught in her chest, but she planted a kiss on Mac's cheek and faked a bright smile. "Nonie will look after you for a few hours," she said, her hands trembling as she signed the instruction. "Behave for her, please." She tapped a kiss on the top of Edin's head as the child flattened her tongue across Mac's empty plate. "Be a good girl for me? I'm coming back soon."

"School. Cake." Edin frowned up at her, black brows drawn into a straight line. "Edie cake!"

Hana shot an agonised glance at Leslie and backed away from the child, trying not to anticipate the mess she'd return to. "Be good for Nonie," she reiterated and left before either child could complain. She winced against the wail of anger which issued from between Edin's lips.

"Wow!" Bodie hissed. He caught her up near the gate. "She's a banshee, isn't she? Do you think the old lady can cope?"

"Leslie." Hana stressed her name in rejection of her son's description. "I hope so."

"Logan should do this." Bodie's tone softened as he latched the gate behind them. The metal jangled with a jarring clang. "Can't you call him or something?"

"No." Hana tugged on the handle for the rear door. "Where are we going?"

Bodie exhaled and climbed into the passenger seat in front of her. He spoke in hushed tones to the driver before turning to face her. "The mortuary at the Waikato hospital. I'll stay with you while you see him."

Hana closed her eyes as an involuntary shiver seized her muscles and shook her slender frame. She reached a shaking hand forward. "Can I have it?" she asked. "The cap. Please, can I have it?"

Bodie winced. "It's linked to the crime scene, so no. Sorry. It's bagged as evidence. I wanted you to see it, but it didn't seem right in front of the kids." He handed it through the gap between the front seats. "I need it back, Mum."

The engine revved as the driver executed an unimpressive turn at the top of the hill. Hana glanced up at the kauri tree lofting overhead as a brown leaf fluttered down onto the bonnet. The car backed towards a clump of kawakawa bushes and she sighed. The driver spun the wheel and ended up back at the bottom of the kauri. "Why don't I just open the gate and let you turn around on the lawn?" she said.

"All good, miss," the man replied and faced the car downhill. "Fasten your seatbelt and we'll get going."

Hana's fingers trembled as she clicked the belt into its anchor. She imagined her husband's fury when he saw the tyre tracks rolling across the tapu site of his ancestors. "It's sacred," she said out loud over the rumble of the diesel motor.

"What is?" Bodie frowned and glanced at the cap balanced on her thighs.

"The tree and its roots. Didn't you see the rāhui pole next to it?"

The driver shook his head and released a hiss. "Sorry, miss."

"It can't be helped." Bodie dismissed the cultural offense with a wave of his hand. "Do you recognise the hat?"

Hana nodded. The plastic moved on her thighs, but her hands seemed reluctant to catch it up and stop it sliding into the foot well. If she touched it, she might somehow make it true. The vehicle lurched and instinct made her clamp her right palm over the bag. It shifted beneath her fingers as though alive, the smooth surface cool despite the day's heat. The brim of the cap bent beneath her grip, the substance inside it wilted and without strength. "It's a fire service cap," she said, her voice wavering. "Tama has heaps of them." She refused to speak in the past tense, denying the possibility that his disappearance held more sinister depths.

Bodie took it back and Hana leaned against the leather seat, registering nothing of the passing countryside.

24

Horseshoe

"**W**here did you find him?" Hana leaned against the corridor wall, her knees knocking inside her jeans. The bloated face swam before her vision and she sensed she'd remember it until her dying day.

"Sorry you had to go through that." Bodie wrinkled his nose and released a sigh. "The paperwork described a tattoo, but you needed to see it, to be sure."

Hana nodded and nausea threatened in her gut. "Same place on his ribs." Her faint snuff of laughter morphed into a sob. "Tama's is spelled wrong." She swallowed. "It's a whakataukī, a proverb. Tama sneaked off without asking Logan's advice and the artist made a mistake." She ran a shaking hand over her mouth and tasted acid. "Thank goodness!"

"Let's go for a coffee and something sugary." Bodie cupped his hand beneath her elbow and led her along the clinical corridor towards an exit. Hana dragged feet encased in concrete as she concentrated on each step. She lost all sense of direction as Bodie walked her through the hospital and into a bustling restaurant. Men and women wearing white coats occupied every seat, their noisy conversation rising to a point in the vaulted ceiling. "Are you okay to sit outside?" Bodie jerked his head towards a vacant table on the balcony. A waving umbrella cast a narrow shadow across one of the seats, offering the reason everyone else had avoided sitting there.

Hana nodded and accepted Bodie's direction as she wove her way through medics sitting, standing and walking. The sun baked the veranda with relentless heat, driving sensible diners inside the tinted windows and artificial ventilation. Hana concentrated on navigating to the double doors, pushing away the memory of another woman's son lying on a mortuary slab. Her chest tightened, and she fumbled for the door handle, finding empty air as someone else yanked it ahead of her. "Sorry," she murmured, though the fault wasn't hers. She stumbled onto the veranda and lurched into the nearest empty seat.

Her phone rumbled in her pocket and she tugged it free and inspected the screen. Leslie's name strobed and Hana answered her call, lifting the device to her ear. "It isn't Tama," she said, not waiting for Leslie to speak. "It's somebody else."

Leslie's audible gulp crossed the distance between them and obscured the busy chatter around Hana. "How was it?" Leslie's concern stroked Hana's forehead as though she sat next to her and wrapped her in maternal love.

"Horrid," she admitted. "I'm trying to forget."

"Aue," Leslie conceded. "Yes. I'm sure. Thank the Good Lord it wasn't him."

Hana nodded and squeezed her eyes closed. "He's someone's son."

"But not ours."

"No. Not ours." She glanced up as a shadow darkened the screen. Bodie dumped a numbered metal spindle on the table and the surface wobbled. He winced and looked around for something to stabilise it, folding a wad of napkins and wedging them beneath the offending leg. His bowed head and insatiable need to fix everything reminded her of Vik. A wave of regret tore through her chest and left her breathless. "I need to go now," she told Leslie. "Is everything okay?"

"I'm surprised to admit that yes, we're all behaving. Did you realise you had Ake ake on your property?"

"No." Hana exhaled as Bodie stood next to her. He nudged her arm and indicated that she move out of the sun. She levered herself upright and listened to Leslie detail the amazing tea she could make from the purple leaved variety. "The littlest moko is a natural," she concluded with pride. "She has the gift of rongoā."

Hana ended the call and took the seat beneath the umbrella.

"I ordered coffee and muffins." Bodie lifted sunglasses from the top of his head and sat them on his nose. "They do nice scones here, but they ran out."

Hana nodded and doubted she could eat anything. The poor man's bloated face drifted past her inner vision and she winced and squeezed the bridge of her nose. "I don't understand how you dived for so long," she admitted. "Day after day of pulling bodies out of lakes and rivers. How did you not go crazy?"

"Who says I didn't?" His glasses hid the wink he gave her, but she read the movement in the lift of one side of his lip and the crease in his cheek. She stretched her hand across the table and clamped her fingers over his wrist.

"I need to apologise," she said, her tone sad.

"What for?" Bodie leaned forward, but didn't wriggle free of her grip.

"I married Logan despite your warnings. You tried to help, and I ignored you and disrespected your wish to keep me safe. It's the root of whatever is wrong between us. I started it and I'm sorry."

Bodie stiffened part way through her confession and his jaw hardened. "What did he do?"

"Nothing." Hana exhaled. "I'm not sorry for marrying Logan. It's one of the best decisions I have ever made. He loves me with every fibre of his being and I'm grateful he never let me push him away. But I'm sorry for how I behaved towards you. I hate how crunchy our relationship is. I take responsibility for it."

Bodie swallowed and his lips parted before clamping shut. His chiseled jaw worked against his brown complexion as he weighed an internal battle. "Thank you," he managed. "I see how much he loves you, and I think I understand. It felt as though we lost you to his family. They swallowed you whole and left nothing for me and Izzie."

Hana frowned, bristling at how he dragged his sister into the pit of rejection with him. The Du Roses had embraced Izzie and Marcus and their brood with ease. But she reminded herself that she'd begun a path of healing after viewing that other poor woman's son. She refused to relinquish it at the first hurdle. She squeezed Bodie's wrist and left her hand there, her porcelain skin blushing beneath the sun's rough kiss. "What happens now?" she asked, her tone infused with softness.

Bodie shrugged. "I'll pay Logan back the money I borrowed, I guess. Call a truce."

"Oh." Hana blinked. "I meant about the poor boy in the morgue."

A man wearing a crisp apron interrupted the confusion with a tray containing two mugs of coffee and a plate of wilting muffins. The blue icing slid sideways the second the plate clattered to the table. Hana reached for the coffee, but the shade of the icing reminded her stomach of its trauma.

"Eyes bigger than belly." Bodie wrinkled his nose. "I'm glad they look horrible because I shouldn't eat that much sugar, anyway."

Hana smiled and nodded. She sipped her coffee, licking her lips when the white fluff left a trace. She imagined Logan speeding across country on a borrowed gelding, his hat clamped to his head and his expression serious. Her soul ached for his touch, for him to just know she was in difficulty and call her.

The phone sat on the table next to the tray, the screen dark. Hana swallowed her drink and told herself she'd rather he concentrated on Phoenix and Wiri's safety during the muster. She longed to see them clatter through the front door, filthy, exhausted and full of tall tales of their bravery and usefulness. Full of stories and alive. Breathing, pulses beating, unlike the poor boy on the slab with the sheet draped across his collarbone.

She connected back with reality and realised she'd missed Bodie's explanation of a process. "Dental records," he said. "DNA, medical records. We'll look for a next of kin and break the news."

"He's a fireman." Hana cleared her throat of the cloying frothed milk and set her mug on the table. "Those hats are issued. Either he's in the service, or he's related to a person who is. I'd start there."

Bodie leaned back in his seat and grinned. "Go, Miss Marple," he said. Hana smiled at his gentle mocking and shrugged.

"Logan is the most analytical person I know. I guess something good rubbed off along the way."

Bodie wagged his finger at her. "It's a great thought. I'll get the guys onto it." He lifted his mobile phone from his back pocket, leaning forward as he tugged it free. His fingers coasted across the keyboard with the ease of a teenager. He finished the text and set his device next to Hana's.

The surrounding conversation backfilled the awkward silence as Bodie nudged the sagging muffin with his index finger. "Mum, I need to tell you something."

Hana's ribs tightened in response to the breath she held onto. "Okay," she said.

Bodie licked his lips and paused before dropping his bombshell. "I've converted to Sikhism."

It wasn't what Hana expected, and she found herself without a response. She gaped at him and gave a jerky nod. Bodie frowned. He lifted his sunglasses onto his head and squinted at her as though needing to abandon the filter between them. "Say something."

Hana blew out the breath. "I don't know what to say. Has it made you happy?"

Bodie nodded and leaned forward. The table lurched beneath his elbows. "Yeah. It's connected me with my father's heritage somehow. I've spoken to Dādā lots since Bibi ji died. I thought you'd be upset." His black eyelashes fluttered as he studied Hana's expression.

Hana watched a magpie's lazy trajectory as it flew across the city. A sparrow streaked behind it, screeching a warning into the azure sky. She shook her head. "It's not my job to make you holy, Bo." Her eyes narrowed as compassion leaked through her wavering smile. "You must find your own way, sweetheart. Do I wish you'd found a great church and worked in a soup kitchen every weekend?" She shrugged. "I don't know, baby. I've sat at the back of a lot of churches and felt like the loneliest woman on the planet. Love and rejection can come from the same place sometimes. I won't complain about you seeking a relationship with God. If he doesn't like the vehicle, he's quite capable of telling you so. You'll always be welcome in my life and my home. It changes nothing."

Bodie sat back against his chair with a bump. The hand he swiped across his mouth shook. "That's not what Izzie said," he breathed. "She thought you'd go mental."

Hana exhaled and smiled at her son. "Well, I don't get out much." She shielded her eyes from the sun as it peeked around the umbrella to scorch her left arm and the side of her neck. "You'll accept anything when you get to my age." Thoughts of Caroline's threat against Izzie made her hand shake, and she dropped it onto her knee and out of sight beneath the table.

Bodie's bark of laughter drew the attention of a nearby group of white-coated men. They glanced at him before returning to their heated ethics discussion. He shook his head and his glossy black fringe fell into his eyes. "You always do the last thing I expect."

"Like marrying Logan?" Hana lifted her left eyebrow and dropped her chin.

Bodie shrugged. "Touché."

Hana wiped sweat from her brow with the back of her forearm. "I should get back to Leslie before Edin eats her way through the pantry." She drained the last of her coffee and rose.

"Mum?" Bodie snatched her wrist. "About that. There's something wrong with that little girl." He released her and nudged a sugar sachet with his fingernail, studying Hana's pained reaction.

Her tight smile walled off a growing pile of failures. "I know."

Bodie cocked his head and frowned. "Before I got diagnosed last year, I ate like her. If Amy didn't get to her food fast enough, I'd grab it off her plate. The hunger was insatiable. I understand now that I wasn't converting the glucose into energy and so my body demanded more and more. Has anyone checked her for diabetes?"

Hana floundered, and she shook her head. Another shock jolted her, adding itself to the hefty list she'd accepted when she took Edin into her home. She swallowed and her voice wobbled. "I'll take her to the doctors as soon as I get back. Thank you."

"I've got my gear in the car if you think she'd pee on a stick?" Bodie rose and snagged the tray. Deft movements piled the empty mugs next to the uneaten muffins.

"Who knows what she'll do, Bo?" Hana sighed. "I don't know from one moment to the next."

25

Horse Whispering

Edin didn't pee on the stick.

But Hana made a phone call to her brother's partner as Bodie pushed the police car around the hazardous bends leading to the hotel. The paediatrician provided her with a raft of great ideas and she arrived at the house with a tentative sense of hope.

"Oh, dear!" she announced as she stepped into the kitchen. Edin turned to her from her precarious position balanced on a dining chair. She snipped up kawakawa leaves with a pair of round bladed scissors and dumped them into a rice cooker. Leslie had obviously decided to continue with her rongoā in view of the joyous news that Tama wasn't at the morgue. Hana ignored the fact Edin stood on one leg and forced her eyes to widen in alarm. "All the toilets are broken," she announced. "But the good news is that Bodie's an expert, and he can fix them for us."

"What?" Leslie turned towards her from the sink, a fistful of dripping leaves in her brown fingers.

"Yes!" Hana emphasised, nodding her head like a maniac. "We all need to use the potty for a little while."

Leslie's mouth opened and closed, but fortunately, no words emerged. Her eyes glazed as she perhaps imagined herself lowering her sizeable rump onto a floor level plastic bowl adorned with Donald Duck's head.

"Bobo!" Mac crawled from beneath the table, his device clutched in his fist. He righted himself and rushed for Bodie's legs, clamping his arms around the left one. Bodie lifted him onto his hip and kissed his flushed cheek.

"Hey again, little bro. What are we playing?"

Hana tightened her lips into a grimace. Crumbs beneath the table showed where Mac had spent his day, but she couldn't complain. Edin appeared relaxed and busy, exuding a regal calm. She held her head at an angle as she snipped, and her tongue poked from between her lips. For every two pieces of kawakawa she dropped into the pot, three went into her mouth. Hana winced. Their designation as medicine made the leaves sacred and tapu, whereas Edin scoffing them at the same time made them noa, or ordinary. It broke every tikanga rule in Māori lore. She glanced at Leslie, wondering if the elderly woman hadn't noticed, or if she planned to dump the afternoon's creation.

"Poo," Mac announced and slithered from Bodie's arms. Hana's eldest son released a snort, which exploded from both his nose and mouth. His eyes watered as he stared at his mother.

"I'll see if I can fix these toilets," he said, his words barely audible. "I'll check all four." He snorted again and dived into the hallway. His laughter rang out, echoing against the high ceilings.

"Fantastic." Hana exhaled and tried not to roll her eyes. She held out her hand for her son and stopped him from bolting to the nearest bathroom. "Let's find Donald," she said, mouthing the words with emphasis.

"No." A crease formed between Mac's fair eyebrows. He shook his head from side to side and his lower lip turned down to form a ledge. "Not him." He lifted his right hand and pointed his middle finger towards his chest. He waggled his wrist up and down as the sign for the toilet.

"Broken," Hana mouthed. She hated lying to him, but her concern for Edin's welfare needed to take precedence. Again. "Bodie's fixing it."

She dredged poor Donald Duck from the back of a cupboard in the garage and Mac hopped around in discomfort while she wiped dust off the plastic bowl. Reluctant to concede defeat, she left her son sitting on the potty between the ride-on lawnmower and the shoe cupboard. He glared at her and folded his arms, his tufty orange curls sticking up like flames. "Okay!" she agreed. "I'll fetch your game. It might take your mind off it."

Bodie called her from the family bathroom as she dashed past the open doorway. He sat on the side of the bath with a bored expression on his face. "What am I meant to do?"

"I don't know." She rubbed her eyes with the back of her hand. "I've left my son in the garage egg-bound because he doesn't want to use the potty. Meanwhile, the child who should sit on it isn't. She's happily self-medicating behind Leslie's back."

Bodie clapped both hands over his mouth to stifle his laughter. Hana closed the door on him in disgust as he bent double and his shoulders heaved.

"Hana?" Leslie winced as Hana retrieved Mac's device from the kitchen table. She bobbed her knees and frowned with obvious discomfort. "I don't think I can get down as far as the potty. But I really need to go, kōtiro. I'd have been okay if you hadn't mentioned it, but now it's reminded me." She flicked water off her wet hands and avoided watching Edin pushing a whole leaf into her mouth. "What's the story with the bathrooms?"

Hana gritted her teeth and used her husband's familiar adage. "Trust me, please. It's important. I'll explain as soon as I can, but not with little ears listening."

"Okay." Leslie turned back to the sink but stuck her rounded bottom out and pushed one knee in front of the other.

Hana returned to the garage with Mac's game and discovered an empty potty and a missing child. She backtracked and found him seated on the ensuite toilet. He grinned and waved at her from the doorway. "Not broke," he cackled, raising his shoulders and lifting his hands.

Hana released a groan and shut the door. "This will never work," she said with a sigh.

Her luxurious ensuite bathroom became a hive of activity as Leslie followed Mac in and Bodie brought up the rear. She swore them all to secrecy and tried to wait out Edin's need to use the potty.

"I should leave soon." Bodie sat at the kitchen table two hours later, with a mug of coffee in front of him. "And I should do my bloods."

"This kid has a cast iron bladder," Hana sighed, resignation in her tone. She appeared to deflate on the chair. "Do you feel unwell? Sorry, I didn't ask."

"I'm fine." Bodie shook his head. "In view of the circumstances, do you think I should test my bloods here? We can either make it a normal feature of life or I can go to the car. What do you think?"

Hana squeezed the heels of her hands against her temples. "What do I know? My husband is about to arrive home and demand to know why our ensuite is locked from the inside, and I sealed the other toilets with duct tape. What a day!" She turned towards the child, still engrossed in snipping medicinal leaves into tiny specs. "Edin, would you like to sit on Donald?"

Bodie whimpered. "Please, Mum. Can you stop saying that? I'm a police officer."

"Oh, stop it!" Hana hissed. "Right, I'm about to break all the rules. If any of you repeat this to Logan, you'll wear Donald as a hat, and I won't clean him first."

"Stop personifying the potty. It's weird."

"Would Edin like a chocolate bar?" Hana rose and lifted the coveted tin from the top shelf of the pantry. She turned to discover Mac watching her with avid concentration. His fingers stilled over his screen. He sat on Bodie's knee, showing his older brother how to race his virtual go kart around a cartoon track.

"Oops, you crashed." Bodie tapped the screen, but Mac's gaze remained glued to the tin of chocolate bars.

Edin dropped a leaf into the rice cooker, and the scissors plunged in after it. She turned on the chair and her eyes widened like saucers.

"This is awkward." Hana halted. "I haven't thought this through, have I?"

"Then do it fast," Leslie whispered. "I need to go again."

"Right." Hana made her decision. "Bo, I'm leaving one for Mac up here." She laid a caramel bar on the counter. "Keep hold of him until we leave the room. I've got Donald set up in the family bathroom, so I'll lead her there and try to persuade her to sit on him." She bounced her legs a few times before striding across the kitchen, still carrying the tin. "Come on, Edin," she said, filling her voice with feigned brightness and frenzied enthusiasm. "Let's take a chocolate bar to Donald."

"Yuk." Bodie shuddered. "That's wrong on so many levels."

The little girl clambered from the dining chair and followed Hana into the hallway. Her feet pattered as she ran to catch up to her disappearing treat.

A groan followed Hana's whoop of victory five minutes later.

"Poo!" shouted Edin.

26

Bitless

Before Bodie left, Hana broached the subject of telling Izzie about Vik's infidelity. She lowered her voice in the echoing hallway as he laced up his shoes. Joyful sounds issued from behind the closed kitchen door as the children helped Leslie wash the rongoā equipment.

Bodie's negative reaction dispelled any notion of easing her daughter's pain and extracting herself from beneath Caroline's blackmail. "Hell no, Mum!" His brown eyes widened in horror and he seized her shoulders and administered a gentle shake. "Why would you do that after all this time? Please, don't! She doesn't need to know what he did. Promise me you'll never tell her. It messed me up, but it would destroy her. She adored Dad."

Hana nodded, pushing away her motivation and hoping Caroline wouldn't do it just because she could.

Leslie appeared, bearing a batch of cookies as an acknowledgement of the gentle truce which had occurred within the family unit. She enfolded him in one of her bear hugs, which made his eyes water, and not in a good way. Bodie left with a warning nod in Hana's direction.

"So, she's not diabetic?" Leslie slumped at the kitchen table and eyed Edin's activity. She leaned across and tapped the table. "Stop eating them, honey. We don't mix the rongoā with the kai. It's against the rules." Edin frowned and dropped the snipped leaf into the rice cooker. Her lips twisted in conflict.

"Will you actually use any of that?" Hana asked, lowering her voice.

"Not sure yet." Leslie rubbed her chin in thought. "There's nothing so pure as a child's desire to heal their world. I'll have to weigh it all up, won't I?"

Hana nodded and sank into the chair next to her. "Might be your best batch yet, mightn't it?"

"Āe," Leslie agreed. "That's true." She rested her elbows on the table. "Tell me about today."

Hana shuddered. "Please, don't make me. I'm trying not to think about it. It wasn't Tama, and that's all that matters."

"I've tried calling him, but an automated voice says his phone is not in service." Leslie's velvety nose wrinkled at the bridge. "Do you think he's messed up in something bad?"

Hana shrugged and spread her hands. She'd reasoned herself in circles and had nothing further to offer. She tipped her wrist to examine her watch. "Have you heard from the others yet? What time are they due home?"

"Wiri fell off." Leslie's eyebrows waggled. "He's fine, but his pride is dented." Her cackle betrayed her lack of concern, and Hana relaxed.

"Just a bump then?"

"Yeah."

Hana turned her attention to Edin's activity, gratified to see that she continued to snip the leaves but had stopped eating them. "What do you think is wrong with her?" she whispered. "She gorges until she's almost sick and yet she's as skinny as a broom handle." She sighed. "At least we know we can do urine samples if we need to. She kicked the doctor last time she tried to take blood, and it didn't happen."

"Let me know before you take her to the surgery next time." Leslie gave an exaggerated wink. "The bush grows some effective sedatives. No side effects."

"Right. I'm not sure that's ethical."

Leslie shrugged. "Sometimes, the end justifies the means."

"Thank you, Mrs Machiavelli." Hana smiled at Edin, gratified by the twitch of her lips in return.

Peering beneath the table revealed her son, still sliding his fingers over the tiny screen of his device. She heaved out a sigh, lacking the energy to confiscate it despite his exceeding his weekly allowance of screen time. Her eyelashes fluttered closed as she savoured a moment of peace.

Her phone chirruped from her pocket and she started, knocking the table as she lifted her hand.

"Ouchie!" Edin bugged her eyes and cocked her head, holding the scissors aloft.

"All good," Hana said with a sigh. She fished out her phone, peering at the screen and hoping to see her husband's name flashing across it. "Oh." She sat up straighter, her lips flattening into a line. "I don't know the number."

She connected the call and frowned as she lifted the device to her ear. "Hello?"

"Helloooo!" Edin parroted. "Helloooowwww!"

"Ma!" The voice rasped as though the speaker battled with a throat injury. "Ma, it's me."

"Tama!" Hana shot to her feet fast enough to send her chair skittering across the tiles. Leslie rose in a mirror of her shock. "Thank goodness!" Hana gushed. "We thought you drowned."

"Listen." Urgency filled his voice. "Stop looking for me."

Hana silenced and her cheeks paled as the colour drained from her porcelain complexion. "What?" she whispered. "We were worried. Your fire chief called me."

"Say nothing." The rasping quality increased. "You can't help me. This is a burner phone, so don't call it. Ask Logan to deal with my house and the tenant, please. Just for now."

"Bodie's lodging a missing person's report for you."

Tama swore and Hana dodged Leslie's outstretched hand. "Stop him!" he ordered. "Leave it alone."

Hana's heart hammered in her chest and sweat beaded on her forehead, though her fingers ached as though frozen. "Tell me what's happened!"

"I need to go." Tama exhaled. "It's about the fire, Ma. That's all I can tell you. It's about the fire."

"What fire?" Hana's voice hitched. "What fire?"

"Reuben's fire." The call ended, leaving Hana drowning in confusion.

27

Trace

Hana's fingers jerked and shook as they stumbled across her screen. "He said I mustn't call him," she whispered, though her hands disobeyed him.

"Then don't!" Leslie snatched the device before the call could connect, pushing it behind her rump. She held her other arm outstretched to ward off Hana's attempts to retrieve it.

"No fightin'!" Edin screeched, jabbing her index finger towards the women. She parodied Hana's frequent rebuke to her and Wiri, complete with the forward dip of her torso. The chair rocked beneath her, distracting Hana as she lurched to right it with a trembling hand.

"But he's in trouble!" she hissed at Leslie. "Give me back my phone!"

"No." Leslie dropped the device between her shuddering breasts and it disappeared into her cleavage.

Edin cackled like a magpie. "Boobies!"

"Nothing's changed." Leslie squared her shoulders. "He's in no more trouble than five minutes ago. The difference is that we know he's alive and not hāmate." Her chunky fingers formed the sign of the cross in a rapid, jerky movement.

Hana nodded and accepted Leslie's reason. She pushed her fingers behind her, seeking the chair without turning around and surprised at how far it had travelled with the force of her rising. "You're right. He's not dead. It's fantastic news." She sank onto the seat and her right hand fluttered over her pacemaker. "But I don't know how to help him."

Sensing her distress, Mac crawled from beneath the table and slithered into Hana's lap. He used her legs as a climbing frame, reluctant to release his device. His eyebrow raised in question as her gaze coasted over the scrambling cartoon figures on the screen, expressing the risk he took in comforting her. "You can keep it for now," she said with a nod. Her arms wrapped around his warm body, drawing him against her stomach and using his peace to ground herself.

"What did he say?" The shivering fabric of Leslie's skirt obscured Hana's view of Edin as the last of the leaves fluttered into the rice cooker. She pushed a metal skewer between the child's finger and thumb. "This is gonna get hot!" she warned, leaning close. "If this is your rongoā, you need to do it properly. No more eating it and no messing with it. Gentle stirring. Like this." She flicked the switch for the rice cooker to heat, and Edin's eyes widened. Her irises switched from slate grey to the hue of a stormy sea. She accepted the metal skewer with intense care and dabbed it into the water.

Hana groaned. "I'm not sure that's a good idea," she whispered to Leslie. "I don't think adding scalding water to the mix with a five-year-old and a metal spike is sensible." She tightened her grip around her son. He sighed and let the weight of his damp head lean against her breastbone.

"Give the girlie a chance," Leslie rebuked. She tapped Edin's shoulder. "Nonie will stand right here. Prove to us you can behave."

"Beehive." Edin nodded, and her legs rigidified as she clenched every muscle in her body. A tremor of excitement ran through her.

"Gentle," Leslie urged. "Gentle with the leaves. Be kind with them and they'll give their healing to you. Close your eyes for a moment and we'll give thanks for them."

Hana watched as Edin bowed her head. Her dark eyelashes flickered and her lips pursed as Leslie whispered through the karakia. A tiny smile slipped onto her face and altered her appearance. She looked like her father and the thought laid like a lead weight in Hana's chest. Edin had worn the rough edges off Kane Du Rose in the short time she'd had to affect him. Hana imagined Logan robbed of the ability to grow through his children and her mind flicked back to worrying about the muster.

"They're fine." Leslie growled a warning as she read Hana's mind. "Last radio call said they were tired and filthy, but all well. Tell me what the tāne said on the phone."

"He said I wasn't to call him on that number." She frowned and pictured her phone sliding lower between Leslie's sweating breasts. "He said it was about Reuben's fire."

Leslie's expression clouded and her brows joined in the centre of her forehead. "That was years ago! Dodgy Christmas tree lights set the curtains ablaze and the pine tree fuelled the fire."

"And the cedar wood exterior." Hana watched her son's deft fingers smooth across the screen. His go kart crashed, and he gave an audible groan.

"No, not cedar. Reuben hewed that house himself out of rimu from the mountain. He never got building permission from the council back in those days. Flung it up himself with his boys. That's why he never bothered insuring it. He always said he'd just build it again."

Hana sat straighter and Mac tipped in her lap. "So, what's the connection? Tama met some kind of insurance agent because he had her card in his shirt pocket. But if the house wasn't insured, nobody committed any kind of fraud. I don't understand why he's gone into hiding."

Leslie screwed her neck around, facing Hana while keeping vigil over Edin and the boiling water. "If someone's killing firemen who look just like him, that would be a good reason to disappear."

Hana nodded. Her mind drifted back to the bloated grey face in the mortuary and the contrast between the filmy white sheet and the chiselled brown chin. "Tama blamed himself for the fire. He put the Christmas lights up and it's the reason he joined the fire service. Could something have triggered his guilt?"

"Do you know the name of this woman he's meant to have met?" Leslie's shoulders waggled and Hana sensed her mind straying along the same thought patterns as Logan and Bodie. Tama's reputation as a gigolo negated the seriousness of any female connection before it began.

"Logan kept the business card," Hana replied. She closed her eyes and remembered seeing it lying on his nightstand when Mac waved to her from the toilet. She winced and her lower lip slipped into a pout. "He said he'd deal with it."

She lifted her gaze to Leslie's wicked grin. The old woman's eyebrows waggled in a salt and pepper dance. "Yeah, but he ain't here, is he?"

28

Mouthpiece

Time seemed to stop while the call rang out through the speaker. Hana's fingers shook as she held the device between Leslie's round face and her own. Edin murmured as she stirred the kawakawa leaves, unaware that Leslie had turned off the heat.

Ring, ring.

Ring, ring.

Hana inhaled as a bubbly female tone filled the air. She tried to cut across the airy greeting before realising she'd fallen foul of the woman's answering service. She winced at Leslie before ending the call and dropping the phone to her side. "I couldn't think what to say," she gushed. "And what if she phones back when Logan's here? He might be cross that I interfered."

"Then why did you?" Leslie shrugged and turned away, leaving Hana speechless.

She blustered a strained reply. "Because you told me to."

Leslie snorted. "If I told you to stick your head in the gas oven, would you do it?" The childish rebuke touched a spark in

Hana's breast and her fingers balled the business card into her fist.

Hana swallowed the various rude replies running around her brain and selected the only polite one available. "We don't have gas up here." She slumped into a dining chair and hissed at the folds she'd added to the card. She smoothed it flat by pressing it against her thigh. Then her phone trilled in her hand and she dropped it.

Mac caught the device as it skittered beneath the table. He connected the call and held it to his working ear, nodding as though engaged in a scintillating conversation. Lifting an auburn eyebrow, he smiled to reveal all his teeth in a display of pure joy. "It's Papa." He dipped his head and held the phone out to Hana.

"Thanks," she whispered, taking it and forcing brightness into her tone. "Hey, babe. How's your day gone?"

Silence greeted her in reply. An unfamiliar throat cleared and Hana tensed. "Erm, you just called my number," the voice said. "Did you mean to call someone else?"

Hana floundered, shooting glances of dismay at Leslie's turned back. "I'm not sure. I wanted Melissa Stratton."

"This is her number."

Hana gulped. "My son had her business card and, well, it's complicated." She exhaled and slumped into a kitchen chair. The voice had Logan's resonance and similar traces of the commanding mana which ran through his genes. Even Mac had misinterpreted the vibrations. She sighed. "I'm sorry. It's Saturday and I realise I should have waited until Monday, but it seemed like the right thing to do at the time. Please, give Melissa my apologies and tell her I'll call back during working hours." Hana lifted the phone away from her ear and prepared to kill the call. Guilt rampaged through her chest at having upset Melissa's significant other. Her finger hovered over the screen to end the conversation when she realised the man had continued speaking.

"Sorry?" Imagining she'd heard wrong, she squinted through one eye as though that might help her to understand. She pressed the phone against her ear. "Can you say that again?"

"I'm Melissa Stratton." Hana squeezed her eyes closed and then opened them again. She'd heard correctly. The him was a her. But the voice sounded very different to the one on the voicemail message.

"Right." She exhaled. "Then, I'm very sorry to have disturbed you at the weekend."

"It's fine." A sigh. "Tell me who your son is and then I might understand why you're calling."

Hana pursed her lips and filtered the information in her mind. Tama's phone call had alerted her to the stupidity of revealing too much. "He's a fireman," she began. "And he's missing. I found your business card in the last shirt we think he wore before he disappeared."

"Oh." Melissa's clipped answer held a sudden wariness. "Tama Du Rose?" She hissed through her teeth. "Damn. I asked him to leave things alone."

Hana's spine straightened, and she sat up fast enough that Leslie turned to face her with a frown. "Leave what alone? Do you know where Tama is?"

Melissa cleared her throat again, a strangely male sound against Hana's attempts to redraw the voice as a female in her mind. "We should meet. Am I speaking to Mrs Du Rose?"

"Yes." Hana swallowed. "Yes, that's me."

"We've met." A thread of apology worked its way through Melissa's tone. "You won't remember. Seven years ago last Christmas."

Hana's brain whirred. Last Christmas marked the seventh anniversary of Phoenix's birth, tainted by the memory of Miriam and Reuben's death. Hana worked hard for her daughter's sake to keep the two events separate. They'd gone to the urupā the day before Phoenix's party, laying flowers on the shared grave where Logan's parents spent eternity together. They'd hidden their relationship while alive, but their headstone told their secret. Logan. "I don't understand," she stammered. "I'm sure we haven't met." Amid all the chaos and the smoke which drifted over the mountain as a reminder, she would have recalled a woman with such a male voice.

"You were pregnant," Melissa continued. "I investigated the fire on the other side of the mountain."

Hana cast through the disjointed scrapbook of faces which gathered on the periphery of the waves of grief associated with the tragedy. She exhaled. "I'm sorry. I really don't remember too many people from that time. The stress of the fire sent me into labour early and the rest is a blur."

"Well, I remember you," Melissa said, her tone sombre. "You made tea and fed biscuits to everyone who showed up at the hotel." She sighed. "I think we should meet and I'll explain what I know."

"Okay." Hana stared around the kitchen, registering Leslie helping Edin to stir her rongoā with endless patience, and her son still hiding beneath the table with his device. "Where and when?"

"Are you still in the same place? The hotel outside Rangiriri?"

Hana blew out a ragged breath. "Yes. We built a house on one of the higher slopes. Would you like me to meet you somewhere half way between us? Are you in Auckland? I could drive to the motorway cafe at the Bombay Hills."

"No." Melissa's emphatic reply filled Hana with an eerie sense of foreboding. "That's not a good idea. I need to speak to you off the record and out of public view. We'll meet tomorrow morning at ten o'clock in the car park at your hotel. I drive a green Landrover Discovery." She paused and considered her next words with care. "I'm glad you called, Mrs Du Rose. I look forward to meeting you again. Alone."

The call ended, and Hana stared at Leslie's bowed head. She whispered words of encouragement to Edin. The child noticed Hana's interest and grinned. She dangled a knot of blackened leaves on the end of her spindle. "Look, Mama," she said. "Medicine. For you."

Hana forced a smile onto her lips. "Clever girl, Edin. You're good at rongoā." Her fingers shook as she forced the business card into the slender pocket built into her phone case. She watched as Leslie helped the child ladle warm kawakawa tea into a mug and deliver it to Hana. Despite filtering it through a sieve and a cloth, specks of green and black leaf floated around on the surface.

Edin pursed her lips as Hana tasted her work, her heart-shaped face tilted upwards in eager search of approval.

"Delicious," Hana concluded after the first sip. She spoke the truth, holding on to the sensation of the gentle healing the leaves brought to her throat and stomach on their journey through her system. "This always calms me," she remarked with gratitude, taking another slurp.

Leslie winked at her and nodded. "You looked like you needed it." She jerked her head towards Hana's phone and waggled her eyebrows. "I heard some of that conversation, but there are gaps."

The next sip seemed to slide down Hana's throat too fast for her to control, and she coughed. Repeating the conversation to Leslie would be easy.

Logan?

Not so much.

29

Barefoot

The riders returned home after dark. Successive showers and the whir of the washing machine tripled the family's daily water consumption in the space of an hour. As Logan came in the front door, Leslie slipped through the back.

"Wiri fell off." Phoenix rested her chin against Hana's arm and whispered the words. She glanced at the kitchen door, careful to prevent him from overhearing.

"Leslie said." Hana stirred spaghetti and leaned sideways to kiss her daughter's temple. "What happened?"

"A steer cut sideways and he couldn't stay in the saddle. He landed hard and his horse bolted." Her brows creased into a frown and tears sparkled in the corners of her grey eyes. "Papa snatched him from the ground just as the herd reached him. They would have trampled him."

Hana ceased her activity and wrapped her arms around her daughter. Wiri's defeat had dampened the buzz of Phoenix's sense of fulfillment. Her empathetic nature had absorbed his pain and embarrassment at needing rescue. He'd sloped into the house and taken the first shower, examining his bruised body and ego in private. "Poor Wiri," Hana mused. She leaned her chin on the top of Phoenix's head and breathed in the scent of clean hair and floral conditioner. "At least he broke nothing."

Phoenix tutted. "No. But Papa grabbed him by the back of his shirt and dumped him over his horse's neck. All the men laughed. I saw him trying not to cry."

Hana closed her eyes and screwed up her face. The mountain spared no mercy for hurt feelings, least of all those shrouded in humiliation. Logan's male dominated workforce ran on bravado and laughter intermingled with hard physical work and pain. The boy's misfortune would have entertained them all day.

"I don't know how to make that better," she admitted with a sigh. "Did Papa not tell them to stop?"

Phoenix twisted her lips into a grimace. "He tried very hard to protect him. At lunchtime, he sat with us and I saw him move around to block their view of Wiri. He was kind and gave him time to recover while he told us a story about Poppa Alfie falling off Methuselah and landing face first in a cow poop." She tittered. "I'm gonna ask Poppa about it."

"The men will forget by next time," Hana assured her. "I'm sure bigger things will crop up between now and then."

Phoenix nodded and stood on tiptoes to peer at the spaghetti. "Is it ready yet? I'm starving."

"Almost." Hana gave her a final squeeze before releasing her. "Wash your hands and call the others."

Dinner proved a silent affair. The children ate without fuss or conversation, and Logan appeared distracted. A small spat occurred over the loading of the dishwasher as Wiri denied it was his turn. "I did it all last week!" he protested, throwing out his chest as Phoenix disputed his selective memory.

"Easily sorted," Hana declared. She hauled open the pantry door and ran her finger over the typed list of jobs. Logan switched the tiny, laminated names each Sunday night and her eyes narrowed at Wiri's name hanging at an angle over the tab entitled 'Drying.' She sighed and switched it back into its allotted position. "Nice try, Wiri. Stop moving the names around, please."

His eyes widened to create a mask of pure innocence. His torso bristled with indignation. Logan's voice cut across his squeak of protest. "Do as you're told. Edin and Mac did the dishwasher together last week and you know it." Hana knew it, too. She'd supervised the haphazard operation, which involved a broken plate and a near miss with a steak knife. But Logan maintained they all needed to learn life skills to equip them for whatever the future dealt them. Hana tapped her index finger over the list and winced at the sight of Edin on 'Washing up' and Mac on 'Drying.'

Wiri's teeth ground in his jaw, but he remained silent. Phoenix collected the dirty crockery from the table, scraped off the remnants, and piled it all onto the draining board for Wiri to perform his task. He did so, having adopted the path of least resistance while still displaying his general protest. Operating at a snail's pace, his inching movements made Hana want to scream. She fought the urge to tell them all just to leave it so she could clean the kitchen in the ten minutes she knew it should take.

Mac scraped a dining chair across the floor so that Edin could reach the washing up water. Hana edged nearer to her husband as Wiri and Phoenix sloped from the kitchen. "I need to talk to you," she said, lowering her voice. "About Tama."

Logan nodded and leaned back in his chair. He ran his hands through his damp hair and, as his tee shirt rode above the waistband of his jeans, it exposed a line of bruising beneath his ribs. "Okay," he said. He frowned and dropped his arms, the faint flicker of his irises registering Hana's dismay. Dark circles shadowed the olive skin beneath his lower lids. His left arm snaked around her waist and he pulled her against his side. "I'm fine," he soothed. "The kid fell during the muster and I could see him getting trampled. I grabbed him by his waistband and threw him over the saddle, but his shoulder caught me in the ribs."

"Did you take arnica?" The line across Hana's brow deepened. Her fear of the hemophilia hadn't lessened, even after years of watching him suffer and then recover.

"Yep." He gave her a sultry smile. "And I used the balm you got from Leslie." His irises twinkled like diamonds. "Yey, for garden weeds and coconut oil."

A peal of giggles followed a loud splash from the sink. Edin turned on the chair and faced Hana, her gaze tracking to Logan in a sliding motion. She kept her hands in the sudsy water, but her lower jaw protruded as she worried at her bottom lip. "Oops," she whispered.

Mac huffed and dried his wet hair with the dish towel. Hana winced and shrugged free of Logan's arm. "No," she said with a sigh. "It's not play time, not when we're standing on chairs and handling crockery."

"She wet me." Mac dabbed at the processor behind his ear and frowned up at Hana. Edin's eyes narrowed until she noticed Logan appear in her peripheral vision. His likeness to the father she remembered caused her constant confusion. He treated her the same as the other children, but Hana wondered if she sensed his intense dislike for her parentage beneath the facade. Edin's eyes widened, and she apologised without prompting.

"Sorry Mac."

"Sokay." He appeared from beneath the dish towel. "Don't do it again."

Edin's dark eyelashes fluttered, and she turned back to her task. Her lips twisted into a mischievous smile, which told Hana she wasn't sorry at all. She sighed and resigned herself to policing the washing and drying effort.

Logan's proximity ensured no more silliness as the children finished their task. They scurried to get ready for bed as darkness obscured the panoramic view of the ocean. Hana leaned against the counter and stretched, hearing the small bones crack in her shoulders and spine. "Do you think we can trust them not to flood the bathroom?" she asked, her tone tinged with doubt.

"Him, yes. Edin, maybe not." Logan exhaled and stood next to her. His hip bumped her waist as he wrapped his arm around her shoulders. "Tell me about Tama. And maybe explain why the toilet seats were duct taped closed."

"Okay, but can you do the story tonight?" Hana yawned into her cupped hand. "It's Hairy Maclary again and they prefer your funny voices." She tilted her head and stared at the ceiling while she studied an imaginary calendar. "It's in the girls' room tonight." She ran a gentle hand over his chest. "Sorry, not if you're sore. I can do it."

He pressed strong fingers over hers to hold them in place. "Tell me about Tama first," he demanded.

Hana winced and swallowed. "Yeah, about that," she began, "I'm meeting someone about him tomorrow. And before you say anything, you're not invited."

30

Concho

"Not happening. No how, no way." Logan's jaw set into a firm line, and he folded his arms. His head began shaking before Hana finished recounting the horror of her day. "I can't believe you went to the morgue without me." He spun away from her and clasped his hands behind his neck. His long arms formed muscular triangles on either side of his head.

Hana's voice rose with indignation. "You make it sound like I went somewhere nice. I can assure you, it wasn't!"

"You could have called me!" Logan's angry brows formed a single black line.

Hana let her hands fall to her sides and they slapped against her thighs. "Yeah, because it would be so easy for you to just walk away from a muster, wouldn't it? It's not like you had two novices with you or anything."

"Fine! Sorry! Geez!" Logan sank into a dining chair. "But you're not meeting this person alone tomorrow. You don't even know them."

Hana folded her arms, warding off Logan's common sense from a distance. She squared her shoulders and braced her slender frame against the anticipated verbal onslaught. "She knows me. We met after Reuben's house burned. She insisted I come alone and if we want to know what happened to Tama, we don't have a choice."

"But Tama called you." Logan spread his hands and released a tired sigh. "We could just trust him to sort things out and resurface when it's safe."

Hana screwed up her delicate features into a grimace. Her shoulders rose to brush her earrings. "Can you hear yourself? If this was Mac who'd gotten himself into trouble, you'd feel happy just leaving him to his own devices?"

Logan snorted and his head shook from side to side. "Mac wouldn't get himself into stupid scrapes like Tama. My boy will think with his head instead of his dick."

The kitchen door squeaked on its hinges as it opened by slow degrees. Wiri's face poked through the gap. "Edin's saying rude words which end with poo." He glanced from Hana to Logan and back to her, his brows furrowing as he assessed her combative stance. "Why are you arguing? Is it about Edin again?"

Hana exhaled. "No. It's not about Edin."

"We could get rid of her." He stepped across the threshold, his pyjama bottoms hanging low enough to expose his stomach. "We could send her to live somewhere else with other people who don't mind naughty children."

Hana pursed her lips and closed her eyes. His solution stunned her and she daren't look at her husband. It seemed she'd done a good enough job at grafting the boy into their family that he'd forgotten the obvious fact that he didn't belong there, either.

Logan's chair scraped across the tiles as he rose. Hana heard him give a faint grunt of pain. "Come on," he said with a sigh. "Find the book for me. I think we're having story time in the girls' room tonight." Hana opened her eyes in time to catch her husband's glance as he left the room. He lifted one quizzical eyebrow and shrugged in a communication of disbelief.

"Yeah, great job there, Hana," she whispered to herself as she set the dishwasher on a cycle that would clean the dishes without draining the water tank.

31

Twitch

She hadn't expected Logan to back down from his protective stance and so wasn't disappointed when he continued the dispute in bed. "Why don't I remember her?" he demanded. He leaned up on one elbow and surveyed Hana's face against the pillow. She fought tiredness and irritation.

"Can we not talk about this now, please? I need to picture happy thoughts if I'm to get any sleep tonight." Her mind wandered unbidden through the corridors of the hospital until she faced the heavy fire doors to the mortuary. She groaned as they opened to reveal the sheet covered corpse of the poor dead man. "Too late." She pushed herself upright and rubbed her fists across her eyes. Her palms slapped against the light sheet. "Thanks for that, Logan! Now all I can see is that poor man they thought might be Tama." Her voice wavered.

"Sorry." Contrition furrowed Logan's brow, and he reached for her, tugging her against his chest. His fingers smoothed her hair away from her cheek. "Relax." He gave her a gentle shake to counteract the rigidity of her shoulders. "We can talk tomorrow before you go to church."

Hana winced and sat up again. "I can't go. Melissa is meeting me in the hotel car park at ten. You'll need to take the children to Sunday School. Phoenix is reading something in the service."

"Oh, no!" Logan shot upright in the bed, his head already shaking from side to side. His shoulder bumped hers. A sardonic smile lifted the corners of his lips. "Nice try, Mrs Du Rose. Not happening." He lifted the fingers of his left hand and counted off his reasons. "One, I'll get struck by lightning if I go to church. Two, your weekly tales of Edin's behaviour in public have put me right off ever seeing that for myself. And three, you're not meeting a strange woman in a car park by yourself. End of story." He hurled himself back against his pillows with a dull thud.

Hana opened her mouth to protest, but he snagged her around the waist and dragged her down to meet him. "We'll sort it out in the morning," he promised. His lips were hard against hers, but as she wriggled, they softened and he released her.

"I need to sort it out now," she whispered.

Logan's hair swished against the pillow as he shook his head. "Let me sleep on it and I'll find a solution," he promised.

Hana yawned and gave a reluctant nod. She doubted she'd like whatever solution he provided, but it bought her time to sift through a few of her own which might prove possible. With a little delicate subterfuge.

"I've missed you today." Logan hauled her onto his stomach and tucked her head against his neck. "I want you and Mac on the next muster."

Hana's muscles tightened, and she winced. She pursed her lips to stop the ready comment from exiting her brain. Edin showed no interest in horses and couldn't be left for an entire day with anyone else. She shelved the objection and prayed the next quarter might bring an answer which wouldn't see her caught between a proverbial rock and a hard place.

Running her lips along the jutting tendon beneath Logan's jaw caused enough of a distraction for him to drop the subject.

She giggled as he flipped her onto her back and attacked the buttons of her nightshirt. "I thought you hurt your ribs," she protested in a hushed whisper.

"Mmn hmn," he replied, but he wasn't listening. He reached between the folds of the shirt and teased his fingers beneath the elastic of her underwear. And tugged. A flush of heat surged through Hana's stomach, beating a path to his expert fingers.

"Logan," she whispered. But his lips covered hers, making it clear he wasn't in the mood for chatting. She hoped it no longer mattered that she'd forgotten to take her contraceptive pill that morning. Especially as Logan disappeared beneath the sheet and demonstrated his lack of interest in anything quick. Hana pressed her fingers over her lips to stop herself making any sound as her husband banished all thoughts of mortuaries, missing sons and wayward, disobedient children.

32

Double Bridle

"Oh, hi." Hana frowned as she pulled the front door open. Her visitor stepped over the threshold and kicked off his shiny shoes.

"Pastor Sam!" Phoenix stood in the hallway, still undressed. She paused in horror, tugging her vest low enough to cover her knickers, but exposing her neckline beyond decency.

Hana turned and blocked Sam's view as he bent to straighten his shoes on the mat. She raised her eyebrows at her daughter. "Just wear a dress, Phoe," she instructed. "Any dress. I don't think God has any particular preference today." She added urgency with a jab of her finger towards the bedroom end of the house. The debate, which had begun before breakfast, ended without the same fanfare. Phoenix fled, no longer caring about her favourite blue dress still crumpled in the bottom of her wardrobe where she left it.

Hana turned back to Sam with a smile plastered over her face, hoping to banish the air of awkwardness which shrouded his unexpected arrival. She cocked her head in question. "Have

I forgotten something?" she asked. Her right hand patted her chest. "I'm sorry if I have, but I can't come to church today."

Sam shrugged and sniffed the air. "Is that bacon I can smell?"

Hana nodded. "Yeah, Logan's doing a bit of a cook up for the children."

"Awesome! That's what I hoped." He rubbed his stomach and set off towards the kitchen in his socks. He collided with Phoenix as she scuttled around the corner. Her fingers scrabbled behind her, holding up the dress which cascaded over her bony shoulders. Colour flared into her cheeks, her earlier mortification not quite banished. She shimmied towards Hana, turning her body and walking backwards. Sam spared her dignity by pretending not to see her. He let himself into the kitchen, and Hana heard him demanding breakfast in a jovial voice as the door closed behind him.

"Why is Pastor Sam here?" Phoenix whined. She stuck out her bottom in an unspoken request for help to zip up her dress. "He saw me in my undies!"

Hana straightened the two halves of the garment and lined up the zip before tugging it to the rounded neck. She leaned down to fasten the flouncy bow around Phoenix's waist. "I told you four times to hurry and get ready. Maybe try putting your dirty dresses into the laundry hamper instead of stockpiling them in the bottom of your wardrobe." A smirk stretched her lips behind Phoenix's back.

The child turned and her grey eyes glittered with tears. "I can't go to church ever again." Her lower lip wobbled. "I wish I was dead."

"No, you don't." Hana exhaled and folded her daughter into her arms. "You have battles to fight and things to do, Miss Du Rose. Don't wish yourself gone before your time. Sam goes to summer camp every year. I'm sure he's seen far worse."

The kitchen door opened and Mac pushed his way through the gap. Bacon grease covered his mouth and chin. He waved to

Hana without embarrassment, despite being buck naked. She laughed.

"What?" Phoenix followed her gaze and tittered. "Oh."

Hana waggled her eyebrows. "I worry about that child," she mused.

"Boys don't care, do they?" Phoenix wiped her nose on the back of her hand. She gave a disgusting sniff and blinked up at Hana. "Do you think Pastor Sam has forgotten seeing me in my undies now he's seen Mac rudey dudey?"

She offered her daughter a reassuring smile. "I think everything else paled into insignificance the second he spotted your nudist brother eating bacon at the kitchen table."

Phoenix performed a perfect eye roll. "I hope so." She set off towards the laughter echoing from the kitchen, leaving Hana shaking her head at her husband's deviousness.

Determined not to assist in Logan's abuse of clerical good nature, Hana busied herself getting ready for her meeting with Melissa. Realising he'd press ganged Sam into shipping their children to church alone, she didn't wish to see the resulting drama when Edin dug her heels in and refused to go. "Have it your way, hot shot," she said with a smile, shoving her lipstick into her bag and closing the front door behind her. She left her truck keys on the hall cupboard and snatched up Logan's bunch. Sam's saloon sat in front of the garage, not equipped to carry four children with varying booster and car seat requirements.

She'd managed to open the gate and close it behind her before the front door whipped open. Logan covered the lawn on his long legs, and a jolt of fear caused Hana to send up a shower of gravel in her haste to stop him thwarting her escape. He halted to avoid the grit peppering the ground in front of him. His black brows formed a line of annoyance across his forehead, and the sun cast his eyes into shadow. Hana shot a hasty glance in her rear-view mirror and saw his lips rise in a smile. He jabbed a finger towards his left eye and then at the truck. Hana gave a nervous laugh at his warning. "You're watching me, are you, Du Rose?" she hissed. "Yeah, watching me leave without you."

She took the first bend too fast, and the truck jerked as she hauled the wheel to right herself. The heady sense of danger sobered her victory, and she took more care reaching the hotel. Her early arrival presented a different issue, giving Logan time to dispatch Sam with the children and still catch her. She parked in her reserved spot and tapped the steering wheel with her index finger.

A knock on her driver's window made her start. "What are you up to?" Toby ran his fingers through his hair and leaned his backside against the wheel arch. He folded his arms and Hana's insides clenched.

She clambered out onto the gravel. "Why are you asking?" She pursed her lips and blinked against the bright sunlight. "Did Logan send you?"

Toby smirked and a fresh cut above his top lip glinted in the glare. "Maybe," he replied. "I can neither confirm nor deny your suspicion."

Hana stamped her foot in temper. She always underestimated her husband's lengthy reach when engaging in battles she couldn't win. She exhaled and released a growl of exasperation. "What did he say?"

Toby's grin widened, and the cut opened, appearing painful. He pursed his lips and refused to answer. A low chuckle rumbled in his chest, making his loyalty clear. Hana cast her gaze around the car park. Melissa wouldn't arrive for another hour, by which time Logan would have regained control. Not that he hadn't already.

Toby's truck sat opposite Hana's, the driver's door not quite closed. He'd waited for her, able to see her emerge from the lane leading to the house. If she hadn't turned into the car park, he would have followed her to her destination, anyway. His cocky stance oozed victory.

Hana turned away from him and the indicator lights flashed as she locked Logan's truck. Without speaking, she set off in the direction of the hotel's main steps, passing close to Toby's vehicle. Her sandals scrunched against the gravel and the folds of her light dress swished around the backs of her knees.

Toby realised he'd underestimated her when she hauled open his driver's door and bounced into the seat of his truck. She slammed her hand over the button for the central locking before the smile slid from his face. He reached her too late, and she used the controls to adjust his seat for her shorter frame.

"Open the door, Hana!" he demanded. His palm thudded against the window.

She fastened the seatbelt around her and clipped it into its anchor. "This car is disgusting!" she shouted through the glass. A waft of her left hand indicated the discarded fast food wrappers littering the dirty floor mat on the passenger side. "Must I remind you this is a company vehicle?" She dropped Logan's keys next to Toby's in the cup holder.

"Just open the door!" Rapid blinking betrayed his anxiety as his mind ran through scenarios involving her furious husband. He couldn't follow her without transport. "Please, Hana!"

She lifted the bunch of keys he'd abandoned in the cup holder. She dangled them in front of his face and twisted her lips into a pout. "You should be more careful," she called. "Anyone could nick your car."

The diesel engine fired as Hana pressed the ignition button to the left of the steering wheel. Toby drove a newer version of Logan's truck and she cast her eye over the controls. He stepped back as she released the brake and rolled it forward. A sassy wave of her hand completed his devastation.

At the end of the long driveway and with no idea of where she was going, Hana realised the massive keyring contained Toby's house and office keys. Guilt prickled the back of her neck. She wondered where he'd go to avoid Logan's wrath. "I hear church is open," she said, wincing at her feigned lack of sympathy. She turned left and headed away from the hotel and Logan's ire.

33

Harness

The needle on the gas tank showed almost empty as Hana drove through the township. She groaned and pulled into the petrol station to remedy it. "Bloody Toby!" she spat as she spilled diesel onto the ground from the dripping nozzle.

"I'll do that, Mrs Du Rose." The garage owner's retired father stepped across the forecourt to relieve her. Diesel snaked up her wrist in an icy, methylated line, drying instantly. "Off to church, are we?" He smiled and glanced into the back of the truck, expecting four faces to peer from the rear seats. "Going alone today?" A drip plunged from the end of his nose onto the concrete unnoticed.

Hana shook her head. "I have an appointment." Her lips flattened into a line. "Logan's taking them.

The old man barked out a laugh. "Oh, he is, is he?" He chuckled to himself as the pump whirred and gas spewed from the hose into the car. "Will I fill her up?"

Hana mopped at her arm with a tissue and grimaced. Though her purse contained a business fuel card, she fought the urge to put in ten dollars and force Toby to fill his own damn vehicle.

But she sighed and nodded. "Yes, please. I'll wash my hands and pay."

She returned smelling of cheap, strangely chemical hand soap and jangling the key fob over her fingers. Her bag swung from her shoulder. "Thanks, Reggie," she said with a smile. The old man winked at her and continued cleaning soapy water from her windscreen with slow, even scrapes of the wiper. Hana settled herself in the driver's seat and waited for him to finish.

Agitation set in as the dashboard clock ticked through the minutes. It might take Logan a quarter of an hour to round up the children and get them into the truck for Sam. She'd taken his vehicle, but he could hitch a ride down the mountain with them and then grab one of the other farm trucks. She tapped a nervous beat on the steering wheel and waited for Reggie to step out of danger. His eyes widened at the sudden roar of the engine as she fired it up and floored the truck out of the bay. "Thanks!" she shouted through her open window, her tyres screeching as she shot onto the main road.

Her phone trilled in her bag. She'd never driven Toby's truck and so it couldn't connect with his hands-free system. Leaning sideways, Hana upended her handbag onto the seat and lifted her phone. Logan's number flashed on the screen, the icon displaying his unsmiling face and intensifying her guilt. "He never smiles for photos," she reassured herself, tucking the phone back into the bag. Hand sanitiser and a lipstick rolled around as she took the tight bends away from the township.

Almost at Rangiriri, she pulled into a lay-by and covered her eyes with her hands. "What are you doing, you crazy woman?" she murmured. A glance at her watch showed she'd wasted twenty minutes. Melissa would arrive at the hotel in another forty.

Hana retrieved her phone and dialled the same number as the previous day. Melissa answered, her baritone voice echoing against the rumble of asphalt beneath tyres. "I hope you're not calling to cancel," she said, no humour in her tone. "I'm almost at the turn off towards Matakitaki."

"Oh, thank goodness!" Hana breathed. "No, but I've had to leave the hotel. I'm in a lay-by just before Rangiriri. You're about ten minutes away from me. There's a golf course up ahead on your left as you get off the expressway. Why don't we meet in the cafe there? If it's not open, we can sit on the deck outside."

"Okay. I'll see you soon." Melissa killed the call and Hana worried in the resulting silence.

Spinning the truck around in a messy three-point-turn, she backtracked before swinging left into the golf course. Sunshine stroked the short grass on the fairways and turned the greens into a healthy lime. Hana navigated the long driveway with care, cautious of stray golf balls. "I'm glad I didn't bring my own truck," she mused as a ball bounced off the roof with a loud bang and slid down a bank to her right. A tall man in a knitted Fair Isle vest abandoned his bag and trolley to set off after it, crossing the driveway behind her. Hana glanced in her rear-view mirror and noticed the green Landrover make the turn off the main road and edge in her direction.

Hana exhibited some good sense by parking in front of the club room. The two storey building housed an exclusive restaurant and hotel rooms. Logan took her there for their honeymoon night, and her heart softened at the memory of those first tentative explorations. She turned off the engine and her fingers coasted across her phone screen, wondering if she should text him and let him know she was okay. It bounced from her fingers as his number and icon flashed again on the screen. The photo hadn't changed, but it somehow managed to look angrier. "Sorry," she whispered to his furrowed brow as she sent his call to voicemail and stuffed the phone back into her handbag. She collected up her lipstick, hand sanitiser and other paraphernalia and wedged it into an inside pocket.

Hana emerged from the truck at the same moment the Landrover crunched into the space beside her. She pretended to fiddle with Toby's bunch of keys to give the driver time to gather herself and step from the vehicle.

"Hana Du Rose?" A flash of bright blue shifted in Hana's peripheral vision as a tall woman rounded the back of the Landrover. She held out a slender hand with long fingers and protruding knuckles.

"Yes." Hana accepted the hand, hers disappearing inside it. She looked up into the face of a middle aged man and forced herself not to react. Dangling earrings tapped the collar of a vintage 1950s dress and she'd scraped mousey coloured hair back from an angular forehead. As Melissa turned her head, an azure blue clip glinted at the back of her ponytail.

Hana glanced down at male shins which ended in wedged blue sandals. Bright pink nail polish covered the toes which protruded from beneath the straps. She swallowed and schooled a smile onto her lips, desperate not to cause offence through her reaction. She sensed the woman studying her expression for traces of judgement or animosity. "Hi, Melissa," she said. "I'm pleased to meet you."

34

Wisp

They walked up the steps and onto the deck together. A waitress appeared from an open door, carrying plastic chairs under both arms. She smiled at Hana, but frowned at Melissa. Hana sensed her stop and turn to watch them as they went inside the building and out of the glaring sun.

"Tea, coffee, or something stronger?" Melissa clapped her hands together and smiled down at Hana. She'd made up her face with enough enthusiasm to suggest she wished to bury herself beneath a solid layer. A livid scarlet lipstick added the finishing touch to the flawless effect. Hana imagined the difficulties Melissa faced each day and determined not to do anything to make it worse for her. She chose coffee, paid the bill, and selected a corner table away from the primary thoroughfare.

She waited for Melissa to settle opposite before submerging herself back into Tama's plight. "When did you see my son?" she demanded. "And what do you know?" She tucked a strand of hair behind her ear and pursed her lips. Lipstick transferred itself from the top to the bottom, overlapping onto the pale skin beneath her lower lip. It created the effect of a bow, and Hana sensed the wetness even before Melissa stared at her mouth. She lifted a hand to her face, using her forefinger to smudge it away.

Melissa frowned as Hana continued her dabbing action, smearing a line across her chin. She checked her fingers and groaned. Hana's fumbled clean up operation spread the lipstick onto her cheek and she grew more embarrassed by the second.

Melissa tried not to stare and began her story. "Tama tracked me down through an old fire service contact," she said. She glanced behind her at the sound of the barista firing up the coffee machine. "Would you rather go outside?" she asked, her tone kind.

Hana altered their order at the counter and collected the two cardboard cups. Then she followed Melissa onto the deck. Digging in her handbag, she found a packet of baby wipes and a tiny mirror. They sat on a bench facing the first tee while she used the mirror and wipes to banish the lipstick. "It's a new brand." She sighed. "This rarely happens, but I left in something of a hurry." She squeezed her eyes closed and pinched the bridge of her nose between finger and thumb. "Please tell me about Tama."

Melissa leaned back against the bench with a sigh. "Okay. I'll trade you the information."

"For what?" Hana sat up as indignation puckered her features. "I have nothing to offer. If you knew the lengths I'd gone to just to meet you today, you'd tell me what you know and let me go home to face the music."

"I'm sorry." Melissa gave her a sideways smile. Her fingers moved to the clip securing her ponytail.

Hana groaned. She dipped forward and covered her face with her palms. "You don't really know anything about Tama's disappearance, do you?"

Melissa exhaled. "I do actually. Tama phoned me a few weeks ago. He wanted information about the fire which killed his grandparents."

Hana stared at the moss which grew in the cracks between the paving slabs and watched a cricket lope onto the grass. She lacked the energy to explain the family's confusing genetics. She allowed Miriam and Reuben to keep the title, though only one of them deserved it. "What information did he ask for?" she demanded. "A faulty connection in a set of old Christmas lights started the fire. Reuben built the house himself in the 1970s. He didn't get planning permission and none of it would have passed the council's regulations."

Melissa tutted. "That's the thing. Tama said he'd requested the official paperwork and nobody could find it. In recent years, New Zealand introduced an incident reporting system. Anyone can look online and see which fires required attendance in the last week. It didn't exist seven years ago, but we can now obtain full incident reports under the Official Information Act. He'd done all that and found no record of the fire."

"Right." Hana ran her forearm over her sweating brow. "I remember someone telling me the fire truck couldn't get up the driveway. Reuben hadn't kept it maintained. Alfred and I walked back down the mountain when the water tanks ran dry. We didn't want to see it razed to the ground, not after watching Miriam run into the inferno."

Melissa nodded. "I'm sorry. This must be very difficult for you."

"I gave birth the following night. The stress made Phoenix come early. Much of that period is a blur in my memory." Hana blinked. She shook off the shiver which ran along her spine as though a ghost had tickled the nape of her neck. Her fingers trembled as she reached for the cardboard coffee cup balanced on the arm of the bench. The hot liquid burned her lips. "Reuben owned the land but never insured the house. His sons couldn't afford to rebuild. They didn't realise how much debt he'd left hanging over them. My husband bought the land and paid off the creditors. He built a new house at the bottom of the mountain." She avoided Melissa's gaze. "No one gained anything from that fire. But everyone lost something." Her voice trailed off as she contemplated the black grief which had consumed Logan. He'd lost more than most.

"But the fire department attended." Melissa leaned forward and balanced her forearms across her thighs. Her gaze traversed a group of octogenarians sizing up the first tee from their carts. "Because the fire department attended, even though they couldn't assist, it generated a report on the old system. The police came because the fire caused a loss of life. There should be a coroner's report and the results of the inquest. I've double checked and your son is correct. The information is missing."

Hana tilted her head back and exhaled. She closed her eyes against the fury of the sun, still feeling its burn on her eyelids. "Tama always blamed himself for the blaze. He put the lights on the Christmas tree for Reuben. It's why he joined the fire service, to stop anyone else going through the same agony." She turned her head and squinted at Melissa. "Why would he start digging into it now?"

Melissa shrugged. "He didn't say. We met at a cafe in Parnell to talk about it. I work for an insurance company nowadays, which is where he contacted me. Tama asked what I remembered about our investigation. We drank coffee and parted company. Then the trouble started."

"What trouble?" Hana sat up straighter.

"Someone broke into my apartment. I heard from my ex-wife a few days later that someone had also burgled her. I lost nothing, but she missed some minor items as though the burglar meant to distract us from their real motive."

"Which was?" Hana leaned closer, desperate not to miss something important.

"I believe it related to my meeting with Tama. The police dismissed my theory that someone searched the apartment for records. The burglar emptied a filing cabinet from my spare bedroom. It's taken weeks to put everything back in place. I've heard nothing more from the police since their standard letter claiming there wasn't enough evidence to pursue their enquiries. They've closed the incident number."

"Can we walk for a little while?" Unable to control her fidgeting, Hana shot to her feet. She glanced at Melissa's unsuitable sandals and winced. "I couldn't walk in those. Do you have something else in your truck?"

"I do," she admitted, parting her knees and peering at her vibrant feet.

Hana smiled and nodded. "I love vintage styles and colours." She fingered the fabric of her own dress. "I have to stick to washable and practical nowadays." A scuff on the side of her sandal revealed Phoenix's habit of clumping around in Hana's nicer shoes.

She maintained a slower pace to allow Melissa to totter next to her. "Will you help me?" The sadness in the other woman's voice tugged at the empathy tucked beneath the surface of Hana's frustration. She held out her arm to offer assistance, and Melissa frowned. "No, not now. I want to know the number for your hairdresser."

Hana stopped beside Melissa's Landrover and waited for her to unlock the rear door. "I cut it myself," she admitted, mindful of the earlier allusion to an information trade. "I shove it into a ponytail high on my head and then snip. The layers just sort of happen." Her fingers made cutting movements. "I'm not sure I'm brave enough to do someone else's."

Melissa grunted as she lifted a pair of white plimsolls from the back of her truck. She bent to release the buckles on her sandals. "Damn. I need a hairdresser I can trust. Sometimes I wear a wig, but it's unbearable in this heat."

Hana fought the panic rising in her chest. She felt under qualified to offer any help to someone in Melissa's situation. She decided the truth would serve her best. "I've met no one going through what you are," she said, worrying about every syllable as it emerged. "I'm afraid to recommend someone in case it sets you up for a horrible experience."

Sweat beaded Melissa's forehead as she rose. Her blue irises glinted as though lit from within by an unseen fire. "Thank you," she said. "I appreciate your honesty."

Hana exhaled and rested her hands over her hips. The relentless sunshine dampened her armpits and made her wish for another shower. She hesitated before speaking. "I know one hairdresser who might help you, but she lives in Hamilton. Let me call her later and come back to you." She touched her collarbone with her fingers. "I promise I will. If she says no, it's because she's busy and not because she's prejudiced. She manages two children around a demanding job." Hana exhaled. Pride entered her tone, and she rose onto her tip toes for a second. "She's my daughter-in-law."

"Lucky." Melissa finished fastening her laces and stood up straight. She pulled a tissue from a patched pocket and dabbed at her forehead. "Where's her salon? I know Hamilton a little."

Hana's smile slipped from her lips. "She qualified as a hairdresser after leaving school. But she's a police officer now."

35

Crop

Melissa's easy snort of laughter lightened the mood and Hana smiled. "Sorry," Melissa acknowledged. "There's nothing funny about a hairdresser becoming a police officer. I just didn't expect the punchline."

"Amy is lovely," Hana affirmed. "My daughter won't let me cut her hair anymore, not after an accident with her fringe. Either I drive to Hamilton every couple of months or Amy visits us. Logan takes the boys to the local barber." She watched as Melissa fitted a floppy, wide-brimmed sun hat over her crown and wished she'd also planned ahead and brought a hat.

"I'm in a support group," Melissa said. She slammed the rear door of her Landrover and pushed the keys into the patterned pocket in the front of her dress. "As you perceived, visits to hairdressing salons can be fraught with conflict. We share recommendations of safe places to buy make-up or get haircuts. I can get most things online, but hairdressing isn't one of them."

Hana raised an eyebrow as they wandered along the path winding around the clubhouse. "If Amy agrees to cut yours, she might not want you to share the fact." She raised her hand as

Melissa frowned. "She cuts our hair as a favour. That would be the basis she operated on for you."

"I understand." Melissa dipped her head, and the brim cast her eyes into shadow. The plimsolls and longer legs allowed her to glide along the rough path, forcing Hana to hurry to stay level with her.

They followed the path past the first tee and meandered through the wooded area alongside the ninth. When a ball thudded against the bark of a nearby tree, Hana ducked.

"We should go back," Melissa suggested, her face creasing into a smile. "We shouldn't really walk here. It's dangerous." Another ball landed nearby, and Hana covered her head with her arms.

"Okay." She agreed with ease. Despite the prettiness of the course, it wasn't for ambling along and chatting about vintage dress shops. "I thought we'd find it safe in the trees. Aren't they supposed to bat the ball thingy onto the green parts?"

Melissa chuckled, a gentle, lyrical sound dampened by the trees. A golfer shot past on a cart, his eyes wide as he careened down a hill and almost into a waiting bunker. "I take it you're not married to a golfer?" she remarked.

"No." Hana wrinkled her nose and loitered in the shade created by a pine tree. "He thinks all open spaces are for galloping across, although he might still have shares in this place. I'm not sure anymore."

They turned back towards the car park, waiting for two more carts to make a less chaotic journey down the slope. The female occupants waved to them, and Hana smiled. "Tama disappeared sometime between last Monday and Wednesday. When did you meet him?"

Melissa raised a manicured fingernail and pulled her phone from her pocket. She scrolled through a digital calendar and read out the dates. "We met twice, once at the start of this month." Elegant movements made the words blur on her screen to dizzying degrees. She gave a nod of satisfaction as she found what she wanted. "Tama phoned after his house suffered a burglary. We met again last Monday." She frowned and two vertical lines appeared on her forehead. She caught Hana's eye and tilted her head in sympathy. "We met after he attended an awards ceremony at the Civic Centre. After a quick drink at a nearby bar, we parted."

"Can you remember what he wore?" Hana asked.

Melissa closed her eyes and tilted her head. She paused on the gravel path as she recalled an image of Tama. "A white shirt with a logo on the pocket." She tapped her front left breast. "Uniform shirt. Dark blue slacks." She shrugged. "He looked smart, but he did last time, too. We talked about the burglaries. He asked me if I'd kept any of the paperwork from my fire investigation days and I told him I hadn't. I had no reason to do that." She tutted and glanced around her at the bright green grass and the idyllic setting. "He promised to call me if he found more information, but didn't."

Hana's chest deflated. "We suspect he disappeared after speaking to you. I've heard from him and I know he's alive and hiding out somewhere, but he never stays in communication long enough for me to glean more details." Her green irises glittered with fear, and she gnawed on her lower lip. The remnants of her lipstick felt greasy on her teeth. "You're sure the Christmas lights caused the fire?"

"Certain." Melissa bobbed her head in a movement which indicated confidence in her reply. "They were old and someone left them on too long. We found traces of rubber around the wiring which shows their age. It's a common cause of house fires around Christmas time, although importers are sharper about electrical regulations nowadays." Melissa set off walking and Hana followed, dragging her feet.

Back in the car park, Melissa prepared to leave. She swapped her plimsolls for the sandals and rose with a smile. "When will I hear from you about the hairdresser?" she asked, blinking up from beneath her hat brim.

"I'll call her today," Hana promised. "I might need to leave a message if she's on shift. What do you suggest I do about Tama?"

Melissa shrugged. She slammed the rear door of her truck. "You know he's okay, because he called you." She leaned her hip against the bumper before frowning at the resulting line of mud which attached itself to her dress. "He's definitely onto something, though. It's a pity the police won't link all the break-ins, but we can't change that. Could you speak to your daughter-in-law and see if she can help?" She snapped her fingers. "Sorry, you already said your other son drove you to see the poor man in the morgue." She exhaled. "It sounds as though he might go digging, too. He needs to be careful. I didn't want to risk meeting you anywhere we might be overheard. Tama seemed scared when we met last Monday. He asked me not to speak to anyone about the missing paperwork. Now, someone else is dead." She shook her head and her hair tapped her shoulder. "Let's stay in touch over this. If I think of anything else, I'll text you. But you'll need to read between the lines. I can't risk having any more attention pulled my way."

"I understand." Hana took a step back as Melissa rounded her truck and pulled open the driver's door. She paused with half of her bottom on the seat. "Are you heading off now? Do you need me to wait for you?"

Hana's shoulders rounded and she gave a slow shake of her head. "No thanks. I'm okay. I'm putting off the moment of leaving because I know I'll get home to an argument." She dug in her handbag and saw another three missed calls from Logan, flashing red telephone icons at the top of her screen. She groaned. "Do I call him back and let him yell now, or put it off until I get home?" Lifting her hand, she shielded her eyes from the sun. "I could stand in the middle of the course and let someone hit me with a golf ball. It might induce sympathy before he scolds me."

"Not a good idea." Melissa's lips turned down in sympathy before a line furrowed her brow. She stared at a point behind Hana, and her expression darkened.

"No. It's a dumb idea."

Hana's eyes widened at the sound of the familiar, gravelly voice. She froze and stared at Melissa in the faint hope of assistance, but received none. A slow turn on the spot took her to within centimetres of her husband's broad chest. His white tee shirt stretched across his pectorals like a second skin. "Oops," she whispered.

Melissa's question sounded from behind her. "Would you like me to wait with you, Hana?" she said, an edge to her tone.

Hana turned back and offered her a watery smile. "I'm good, thanks." She gave a feckless wave which dislodged her handbag from her arm. "I'll call or text you with Amy's answer."

Then she turned back to Logan and stiffened her spine, preparing to face his wrath.

36

Horseshoe

Logan gave an upward tilt of his chin in acknowledgement of Melissa. She offered Hana an awkward wave before slamming her door and firing up the heavy engine. Logan's hands clamped around Hana's shoulders and he edged her sideways, out of the path of Melissa's wheels. The Landrover rumbled as it reversed from the parking space and ambled back along the driveway to the road.

Logan exhaled and left his hands on Hana's shoulders. "At least she offered to stay with you," he said. "That's something. Did she think I might get physical?"

Hana shrugged and kept her gaze on his cowboy boots. She studied the intricate threads which criss-crossed the instep and disappeared beneath the hem of his jeans. Logan moved next to her and slipped his arm around her shoulders. "We have time for a coffee if you're interested?" The sentence sounded casual, but his arm tightened to betray his hidden anxiety.

Hana glanced at her watch and sighed. "It'll take me half an hour to drive back to the township. Church finishes at twelve o'clock. That gives us another half an hour's grace." She nodded and her sandals scrunched against the loose grit as she allowed Logan to lead her back to the clubhouse and the smell of roasted coffee beans.

It took a moment for her eyes to adjust to the dimness after the glare of the golf course. She noticed Logan's leather jacket hugging a chair, his motorbike helmet resting on the floor next to it. Guilt prickled in her chest at the realisation he'd left without his protective trousers or boots. His jeans and regular cowboy boots seemed to condemn her as he left her by the table and walked towards the counter. Hana slumped into the empty seat and pushed away a stained coffee cup and saucer. Logan returned to retrieve it, the crockery rattling as he placed it on the counter without comment.

Hana leaned back and released a tut of exasperation. "You've been here long enough to have a drink?"

He nodded and his customary smirk lifted the left corner of his lip. "Two coffees and a muffin."

"Right." Hana wrinkled her nose. Her frenzied escape from the house and subsequent nervousness about meeting Melissa meant she'd missed breakfast. Her stomach rumbled as though in disgust. "Why didn't you join us if you've been here half the morning?" It sounded harsher than she intended.

Logan dipped forward and rested his forearms on the table. His bulk blocked her view of the counter and reduced Hana somehow to the size of a child. "I haven't been here that long. Only an hour. I followed Sam down the mountain after Toby called. Sam then met Leslie at church and she agreed to bring the children home in your truck. He'll fetch his own car later."

"How did you find me?" Hana frowned and cocked her head. "I'd arranged to meet Melissa at the hotel car park."

Logan grinned. "But then you ran into Toby, didn't you? And things changed."

Hana pinched her lower lip between her teeth. "Is he angry at me?"

"Just embarrassed." Logan released a rumbling laugh. "Didn't you realise all the fleet vehicles had GPS tracking installed?"

"No." Hana's shoulders slumped as her bravado deflated. "So, you followed me straight here?"

"Yep." Logan nodded to the barista as he delivered two coffees and another muffin. He waited until the man moved back behind his counter before continuing. "You can eat that if you want it. But tell me what this Melissa knows about where Tama's gone."

Hana exhaled and shook her head. She reached for the muffin and broke it apart, staring at the exposed walnuts and flecks of chopped date. "Tama tracked her down through a colleague at her old workplace. She attended the fire at Reuben's when she was still a man. It's why I don't remember her, although I can't recall much about that time. She looks different, obviously."

Logan's expression clouded. It had taken him a long while to recover from the overwhelming sense of loss which the fire caused. The ripple effects of that night had continued in diminishing degrees, but all disasters seemed to lead back to it and begin the grief process anew. "I don't remember any of the officials from that time," he admitted. "Unless, like the volunteer fire fighters, I'd known them before that night." He paused to sip his coffee and to consider his next question. "Did you ask her why Tama picked now to dig around in something that happened over seven years ago?"

Hana nodded. "Yes. Melissa said there should be documentation on file relating to the incident. Police and fire service personnel attended, which generates a report. Tama told her he'd applied for the information under some piece of public legislation, but the reports didn't exist. He didn't say what precipitated his search, but it's as though Reuben's fire didn't happen."

Logan frowned and leaned back in his seat. He ran a scarred right hand through his fringe. "That's not possible."

Hana cringed at the darkness which seemed to consume his irises and turn them to a smoky grey. "I'm sorry, Logan," she breathed. "The last thing I wanted was to drag all this up again. I don't know why Tama started looking into it, but something set him on this trail. He seems to have abandoned everything in favour of it, which means it's important."

"Yeah. I'm starting to understand that." Logan's boot heels scuffed the tiled floor, and he pursed his lips into a troubled line. "What should we do?" he asked, spreading his hands. "Wait for him to appear again, having solved the mystery, or investigate it ourselves?"

"We might get in his way," Hana conceded. "But what if he needs our help?"

Logan tilted his head to one side and his fringe covered his left eye. "What if we lead someone else right to him, when he's asked us to leave him to figure it out himself?"

They sat in silence and finished their coffees. Hana's appetite faded, and she ignored the rest of the muffin. Her instincts demanded that she rush in and rescue Tama before obliterating the unnamed threat. But Logan's caution stunted her mental search for a plan. "I don't know what to do," she admitted. The thought of driving home to the expected chaos without a resolution churned her stomach.

Logan lifted an eyebrow and dipped his head to look at her through his lashes. He reached forward and his hand covered her writhing fingers as she caressed the handle of her cup. "I think this is where we trust our kids to make good decisions," he said with a sigh. "We've put the right stuff into them, so surely it should eventually rise to the surface."

Hana's wistful smile accompanied a reluctant nod. Her mind performed an involuntary head count of the small people in her care. She realised she trusted Phoenix, mostly Wiri and sometimes Mac. Edin, never.

But Tama? Trust Tama Du Rose?

Hana groaned and Logan smiled as though reading her thoughts. "Let's go pick up our little darlings," he said.

37

Spurs

"Edie wanna stay. Eat. Edie eat!" The plaintive voice echoed from the speaker and ricocheted around the truck.

Hana jerked the steering wheel in fright and then glanced in her rear-view mirror at Logan following behind. She knew he'd seen when he edged the motorbike closer to her bumper, as though in concern. "Pardon?" She reduced the volume after searching for it on the screen. She wished she hadn't paused to connect her phone to Toby's truck as Edin's voice rose to a deafening volume. "Please put Nonie on?" Hana demanded. She'd answered the call expecting Leslie to bemoan a list of complaints, not put the child in charge of relaying them.

Clattering and a minor dispute occurred before Leslie gave a gusty greeting. "Kia ora, Hana. What did you find out about Tama?"

"Not much," Hana conceded. She looked in her mirror again and gave Logan a reverse wave of her hand. His black helmet bobbed once, and he dropped the bike back to a safer distance. "We can talk about it when you get home. We're about twenty minutes from the turn now. Are you okay to drive the children to the hotel and I'll wait for you in the car park?" She glanced around at the unfamiliar interior and winced. She'd need to return Toby's truck first, anyway.

"The church is having a potluck lunch," Leslie replied. She huffed out an irritated breath. "Did you forget?"

Hana groaned. "Yes. Sorry. Are the children ravaging the table?"

"Not yet." Leslie harrumphed. "Pastor Sam let the adults go first. But they want to know if they can stay for a while? The Sunday School teachers are taking them outside for games after they've eaten."

"Oh. Yes, that's fine." Shock nipped at the fringes of Hana's reply. "What about Edin? Did she behave?"

"Mac brought her out of Sunday School grizzling about half way through. She sat on my knee in the service and fell asleep. Now, she's complaining she's starving."

"Yeah. Right. Stay then," Hana said. She'd expected chaos and complaints and didn't know how to respond to peace and harmony. "Text me before you set off and I'll meet you. It saves getting them all out of the truck and back in again."

"All righty then." Leslie killed the call before Hana could say anything else. The prospect of an extra hour free filled Hana with an unusual giddiness. A moment of lost-ness clouded her brain. She'd won Lotto and didn't know how to use her winnings.

Glancing in her rear-view mirror, she saw her husband gliding his sleek bike around a tight bend, his chest tucked close to the arch of the gas tank. She gasped as she crossed the centre line and yanked the vehicle back to her side of the road. Logan's helmet lifted higher as he studied the evidence of her distraction.

Hana cleared her throat and dismissed her lascivious train of thought. She lowered her speed and drove with care, making the turn onto the hotel's winding lane without incident. With no sign of Toby, she parked his truck in the space she stole it from and retrieved her handbag from the front seat. Logan dismounted from his bike and stood it up next to her. The glare from the sun had super-heated his black helmet and his hair stuck up on end as he removed it. He shook himself free of the heavy jacket as soon as he could and laid it across the seat.

"You look so hot," Hana commented. She slammed the driver's door and slipped the strap of her bag over her shoulder.

"It's the humidity." Logan tugged his tee shirt away from his neck and flapped it to encourage a through draught. "I'm boiling."

"Not that kind of hot." Hana pursed her lips. She wafted her hand between them. "I meant the other kind. Like, gorgeous, good looking, sexy. That kind of hot."

"Oh." Logan let the fabric fall from his fingers. It popped back against his chest muscles and stuck there. "Ohhhh." His lips lifted on one side. Glancing up at the first-floor balcony, which used to be his bedroom, he wrinkled his nose. "I think they let my room this weekend. The manager texted me on Friday. The housekeeping staff might not have changed the sheets yet. Damn." He exhaled and his shoulders sagged. "Sorry."

Hana smiled. "You've become a lightweight, Mr Du Rose." She jerked her head towards the main steps. "You have an office, don't you?"

Logan raced her up the steps, carrying his helmet and jacket. They dodged right and followed the long corridor past the kitchen. Hana giggled and pushed him from behind as he fumbled his key into the mechanism. His office door swung open, and he slammed it behind them.

"Lock it!" Hana insisted, twisting her wrist as though performing the action herself.

Logan turned the key and dropped his gear onto the floor boards. His helmet rolled to one side, the visor turned towards Hana like unseeing eyes. A grin split Logan's face, and he took two strides across the room before a sharp rap shook the door.

He froze and irritation darkened his irises to the depths of a stormy sea. Then he shook his head and ignored the three knocks which followed the first.

"Logan, are you in there?" Toby's plaintive tone made Hana wince. "I need my truck. Rawiri said he saw you arrive back. Do you have my keys?"

Logan crossed the rug and met Hana in front of the desk. He placed a hand over her mouth and lifted his other to press his index fingers over his lips. She nodded, and he removed his hand. His fingers dropped to her thigh, finding the hem of her dress and travelling up to her underwear. His eager kisses brought the sensation of waves hitting the shore, determined, relentless, and insatiable.

38

Twisted Snaffle

"So, why Reuben's fire?" Leslie sat next to Hana on the bench in Miriam's rose garden. Will's son hadn't yet pruned the bushes back ready for autumn, but he would over the next few weeks. Wilted petals covered the mulch beneath their knotty trunks, spreading onto the lawn like a carpet of pink and white.

Mac squealed as he clung to Logan's head, covering his father's eyes as they spun in ever decreasing circles. He'd eaten at church and then again in the hotel restaurant, and his eyes bulged as he laughed. Hana bit back the suggestion that Logan stop twirling him before disaster struck. She'd learned not to be the voice of doom in their relationship. Anyway, he'd find out soon enough when the child puked on his head.

Wiri and Phoenix sat on the grass and licked ice lollies from the hotel restaurant while Edin chatted with Horsey in the shade. She muttered something in lowered tones and dripped sticky lolly onto his embroidered lips.

"We're not sure what set him off investigating." Hana lowered her voice and smiled at Wiri as he glanced in her direction. His eyes narrowed, and she sensed he'd guessed all wasn't well in the adults' world. "Melissa didn't know what made him look for the information in the first place, but once he realised the records didn't exist, he contacted her."

Leslie frowned. She leaned back and crossed her legs. "I don't remember a woman coming up here after the fire. Not one with such a deep voice."

"No." Hana licked her lips and chose to keep Melissa's trans journey to herself. "Perhaps you missed her. She investigated the fire with a colleague. She submitted the report as usual and it should have been treated like every other incident which caused a loss of life. For some reason, it wasn't."

"And someone broke into Tama's place and then hers?"

"Yeah, and her ex partner's house." Hana tapped her bottom lip with her index finger. "But we know that Tama's okay and just in hiding. Logan thinks we should trust him to know what he's doing."

"But what about his job?" Leslie's voice rose as she demanded answers. "They'll fire him and then replace him. He loves his job."

Hana jumped as Wiri spoke from beside her. "What's happened to Tama?" He lowered his chin and dared her to lie to him.

"What's going on?" Phoenix appeared next to him, her shoulder brushing his upper arm as she offered him solidarity.

"Edie wants more." Edin arrived, draping Horsey over Leslie's knees and directing her question towards the weakest link. She jabbed a finger towards her open mouth just in case Leslie hadn't understood the demand.

"No." Hana answered for her. "One each is enough. Have some water." She lifted the child's drink bottle from the bench next to her and offered it.

Edin shook her head and backed away on leaden steps. "Want juice." Her body deflated as though stripped of bone and muscle. Horsey slithered off Leslie's knees, pulled by fragile fingers around a black knitted hoof.

Hana cocked her head and frowned. "No more sugar for today. Have nice water." She lifted the bottle again and Mac rushed forward and grabbed it from Hana's hand. Edin let out a scream of protest and tussled it free. She glared at him and lifted the lid to suck at the nozzle.

Mac turned and grinned at Hana. He'd resolved the situation in seconds. Sweat beaded his forehead from his frantic game with Logan, and he appeared unsteady on his feet. Logan lay on the lawn, groaning from the circling, and Phoenix beamed. "Let's all pile onto Papa!" she shouted.

"Let's not!" Logan protested too late as she flew through the air and landed across his stomach. His grunt of pain appeared genuine. Edin held back, sucking at her water bottle and frowning. She never felt confident enough to join in the rough housing, though it clearly fascinated her. Mac clambered onto Phoenix's back as though she were a pony. His giggles mingled with hers as they double bombed their father.

"Just tell me." Wiri's demand forced Hana to deal with him.

"Mac's gonna puke," she announced to no one in particular. Wiri let out a humph of irritation and Hana folded. "We don't know enough to worry you," she admitted. She glanced sideways at Leslie, and the old woman shrugged and rolled her eyes.

"So much for keeping it quiet," she murmured.

"I won't tell anyone!" Wiri planted his hands on his hips and faced her. "Don't treat me like a baby."

Hana peered at him from beneath furrowed eyebrows. "Don't speak to Nonie in that tone." She waited while he muttered an apology. "Tama didn't show up to work last week. Logan and I drove up to his house, and he wasn't there either. But he's okay, because he called me and said he was taking some time out."

"Whatever, Ma." He pressed the finger and thumb of his right hand together and zig-zagged them in front of Hana's face. "Your lips are saying one thing, but your whole body is saying the opposite. If he's fine, then why are you worried about him?"

Hana exhaled. "I worry about all of you." She cocked her head. "Have you heard from him?"

Wiri's cockiness faded as though an artist had redrawn it in seconds with a daub of well-placed paint. His body vibrated with an instant shiftiness and he turned his feet away from Hana as though preparing to bolt.

"Wiremu Du Rose!" Hana hissed. She lowered her voice and glanced at her husband's head peeking from beneath the pile of wriggling bodies. "Tell me what you're hiding right this minute!"

Wiri bent his knees in acute discomfort. "I don't want you to take it away."

Hana glanced at Leslie and then back at the boy. "Take what away?"

"My email address." Wiri turned his body to locate Logan and, seeing him indisposed, relaxed a little. "We did a computer class at school last year and set up email addresses as a practice. We wrote to each other, and it was fun. Some of the girls sent me love letters, and it seemed funny at first. Then they got stupid and wanted to follow me around at break time and stop me playing soccer." He paused, and his irises flared at a raucous giggle from Phoenix. She'd somehow ended up on the bottom of the pile, battling with Mac's bare foot in her face. Hana imagined her daughter's reaction to other girls fluttering their eyelashes at Wiri. Their unspoken alliance showed no sign of wilting as life encroached on their friendship.

Hana shook her head. "Those are internal email addresses. It's on the school Intranet." She tried and failed to recall the exact wording of the standard letter she'd signed the year before, dredging up a sentence about not tolerating bullying or hate speech. "You can't email anyone outside that system."

Wiri twisted his lips until the top one disappeared completely, sucked into the vortex of his guilt. "I made a Gmail address." The words exhaled in a rush and collided with Hana's groan.

Her shoulders slumped. "We explained why you don't have mobile phones and external contacts outside of the family. We supervise your interactions with other people because you're not mature enough yet. It won't always be like this, but those are the rules for now." She clambered onto her high horse, and only Leslie's sharp nudge in her thigh silenced her tirade.

"What do you know, tāne?" Leslie demanded. "Have you been talking to Tama?"

39

Whip

"Yes." The single word hit Hana in the face like a whip. Her sharp inhale sent guilt stampeding across Wiri's expression and he caught his lower lip in his teeth. "Sorry, Ma." His fingertips brushed her shoulder as he sought solidarity again. "I just wanted to see if I could do it. I tried to set up a Facebook account, but the school blocked it." His nose wrinkled in disgust until he realised he'd compounded his error by admitting the latter crime.

Hana shook her head. "You're not old enough for social media," she grumbled. At Leslie's warning tut, she moderated her tone. "I suppose we never named Gmail addresses as forbidden, but you understood the spirit of the rule."

Wiri pursed his lips and nodded. His grey irises flashed, and he seized his advantage. "I'll delete it at school on Monday."

A prickle moved along Hana's spine as she sensed herself snookered. Leslie took the bait before she'd formulated a way of extracting herself from the corner she'd let herself get backed into. The old lady grunted as she leaned forward and snagged Wiri's spindly wrist. "What did Tama say?" she demanded.

"You're having no more of my special blackberry and apple crumble with custard until you tell us."

Wiri snorted, but didn't attempt to free his wrist. "Is that the best you can do, Nonie?" he whispered. "Ma makes it just as nice."

Leslie's eyes bugged, and she dropped his wrist. She wiped her palm on her skirt and drew her lips back in a snarl. "Well," she gasped. "Well!"

Her loud remonstrations caused Phoenix to glance at her from beneath Mac's armpit. "Papa!" she shouted. "Nonie's having a heart attack!"

The bodies disbanded into separate parts, Mac's leg tangled through Logan's arm and his lips grinning with maniacal enjoyment. Hana winced at the prospect of his cochlear implant dislodging and gave a feckless swipe at Leslie's rounded thigh. "Well done!" she hissed.

"I'm fine!" Leslie croaked, though she narrowed her eyes at Wiri. "Just learning how my baking is rubbish."

"He didn't say that!" Hana protested. Leslie had demoted the inquisition to a complaint session. She snatched at the woman's skirt as Leslie hauled herself upright.

"You're raising a deviant!" she snapped, jerking her head in Wiri's direction. Her chins wobbled as she stamped across the rose garden and squeezed herself through the narrow gap in the hedge.

Phoenix extracted herself from the twisted limbs and tried to run after her. Mac clung to her wrist and pulled her back into the mass.

Logan groaned and rolled onto all fours. "Just leave her, Phoe. She looks fine to me."

Phoenix's gaze turned towards Hana in mute appeal, her lips parting wide in a squeal as Mac attacked the ticklish spot beneath her armpits. Hana gave her a wave and a smile, reinforcing Logan's diagnosis. But her left hand shot forward and grabbed the hem of Wiri's tee shirt as he turned away from her. "Oh, no you don't, buster!" she snarled. Her knees creaked as she rose from the bench. Wiri's fingers closed into a fist as she curled his hand into hers. "We're going for a walk."

Hana directed him towards the gap in the hedge, tapping Edin's shoulder as she passed her. "Wanna see the horses?" she asked in a gentle voice.

Edin frowned. "Cows. Want cows."

"Okay," Hana conceded. "Horses, then cows." She glared at Wiri and didn't release his hand as Edin joined their expedition.

The little girl skipped ahead as they walked across the car park. She chose a circuitous route which made no sense to an onlooker, backtracking and turning without taking a straight course. Hana knew she sought the glittering red stones hidden in the gravel, and which she picked up and collected in her pockets. Dents in the washing machine drum bore testament to the latest obsession.

Hana released Wiri's hand, not wishing to humiliate him in public. "Right," she began, "is my blackberry crumble really as nice as Nonie's?"

"Better," he admitted. "She uses too much fruit and not enough crumble."

"Thanks." Hana shot him a smile of appreciation. "Now, tell me what Tama said to you."

Wiri sighed and dug his hands in his pockets. His shoulders rounded into identical slopes along his collar bone. "We just chatted at first, everyday stuff. I told him about the girls acting all dumb and he enjoyed it. He sent smiley faces and told me to make the most of it. Then, a couple of weeks ago, he started asking me about Poppa Reuben and if I remembered the fire at his house." Wiri shrugged. "I was a little kid. I remember standing on the lawn and watching the house burn. A lady screamed and screamed." His brow furrowed, and he stopped walking. He turned to face Hana. "You were there, weren't you?"

Hana swallowed before nodding. "Yes." Miriam's animal wails returned to her mind as an echo and she shuddered beneath the caress of the sun's rays.

Wiri drew closer, his shoulder bumping Hana's upper arm. Her fingers itched to fold him into a fortifying embrace, but she stopped herself, knowing he'd hate it. She took a deep breath of the clean air surrounding the hotel. Kōwhai and kawakawa scents laced it, turning it into a healing inhalation. "What else did he ask?" Her voice trembled as she sought to push past the ghosts, despite their presence remaining at the centre of this new mystery.

Wiri shrugged. "I remember moving into the motel unit with my parents." His jaw clenched. "My other parents, the ones I started with." A lazy smile slid onto his lips as he glossed over his mother's incarceration in a mental facility and his father's demotion to uncle. "You smacked Kane in the face to stop him fighting with Logan." A chuckle followed. "You made his eyebrow bleed."

"I'm not proud of that." Hana winced. "Not my finest moment, for sure."

Wiri shrugged. "I know he was my dad, but I didn't like him. He didn't care about me, not like you and Logan do." He exhaled. "And Tama." In a rare moment of affection, he reached for Hana's forearm and linked his fingers through the crook of her elbow. "Will Tama be okay?"

She offered him a reassuring smile. "Yes, he's resilient and agile, and Logan believes he knows what he's doing."

Wiri frowned. "I don't know what half those words mean. But if Logan believes in him, then we should, too, shouldn't we?"

"Absolutely," Hana agreed. "But I'd feel better if you log on to your email account when we get home and check to see if he's contacted you again."

"Okay." Wiri disengaged his hand from her arm, leaving a warm space where his fingers had rested. "Maybe he's written me a secret message and we can rescue him."

40

Trappings

Edin napped on the lounge sofa, a blanket pulled over her head. Hana tried everything to postpone the impromptu snooze without effect. "She won't sleep tonight," she complained to Logan. "She'll be wide awake at midnight."

"I'll deal with her," he promised. Phoenix lay on her stomach on the rug and read a storybook, while Mac snuggled on Logan's knee, using up his half an hour of tech time. "You do what we talked about." Logan raised an eyebrow, and Hana nodded.

"Okay."

She found Wiri on the deck wielding a pair of binoculars. He turned to greet her with a wide grin. "I just saw a falcon," he announced. "I thought it hunted alone, but when I raised the glasses, I saw her mate flying high in the sky. It's like they each have different views of the same thing and one helps the other find the food."

Hana stroked his damp hair back from his fringe and nodded. He'd described her relationship with Logan. Her husband favoured the big picture while she scrambled around in the weeds. Somehow they made it through each situation, although she doubted the degree with which she helped, or rather hindered. "I'd like to look at the emails now," she said, lowering her voice. "Please, will you show me?"

Wiri nodded and clutched the binoculars to his chest. "But what about the others?"

"They're busy. Let's find Logan's laptop and you can log in there. We have about ten minutes before Mac comes looking for me."

"Why ten minutes?" Wiri stepped away from the railing and moved across the deck.

"Because his tech time will run out, and he'll want me to entertain him."

It took seconds to locate Logan's laptop, but only because he'd left it on their double bed. Hana sat on the mattress and used his password to unlock the screen. She called up a Google search and then passed the device to Wiri. It tipped on his slender knees. His fingers moved with a pecking action as he put in his email address and used his password to log onto the Gmail site. Hana watched the keys as Logan instructed, committing Wiri's sacred details to memory and hoping they remained there until she could relay them to her husband.

"Nothing." Wiri's exhale contained relief. He clasped the screen and made to fold it closed before Hana intervened.

"Show me his last email," she demanded.

With slow reluctance, Wiri clicked on an address half way down. Grey instead of black, it showed he'd read it another time. A brief communication from Tama leapt from the white space, his language simple and unfettered by propriety. Hana swallowed back her disappointment at realising her relationship with him of late contained far less honesty.

'Hey bro,' it began. *'Hope those girls are leaving you alone. They act dumb when they like you. It's annoying, but us handsome Du Roses can't help it. We're just too fine.'*

Hana blinked at his lack of embarrassment and wondered if the sentence summed up his existence. He never sought female companionship. They fell at his feet like blown leaves. She sighed and skim read the inappropriate details of his rental agreement with Jordan. "He shouldn't tell you this stuff," she hissed. "You're too young and he should know better."

Wiri shrugged and his chin bumped her shoulder as he leaned sideways to look at the screen. "I know it all, anyway," he replied.

"That doesn't reassure me. Wait, what's this?" Hana used the mouse pad to drag the cursor lower on the email. '*Sorry if I upset you with the questions about the fire. It's worried me all these years that I caused it with the dodgy Christmas lights, when that's not true.*' She stopped herself from reading the words aloud, not wanting to voice Tama's concerns when Wiri had already borne them himself in silence. She looked at the date at the top of the message. Tama sent it a week before he stopped showing up to work.

"Can we log out now?" Wiri frowned towards the bedroom door. Mac's voice drifted along the corridor, raised in complaint. His tech time had ended and his disciplined father hadn't fallen for the same gags as she usually did.

"Okay." Hana gave him a reassuring smile and watched as his deft fingers logged out of his account and closed the browser. He slipped the laptop from his knee with care and left it on the bed. "Thanks," Hana said with a sigh. "You understand we need to talk about this, though, don't you? We have good reasons for keeping you away from social media and private email accounts. There are things happening out there in the world which are hard for me to understand sometimes, and I've had half a century to process things. You're nine, Wiri. You've already seen too much for your age." She jerked her head towards the laptop. "Having too much information can be a burden."

He nodded, and his irises shone from behind his dark eyelashes. "It feels better that you know," he admitted. "All the sneaking made my heart hurt, but I wanted to talk to Tama."

"I understand." Hana ran a hand across his shoulder, forcing herself not to linger. He seemed so small and frail, ill-equipped to face a humanity determined to extinguish itself.

Wiri remained sitting on the bed next to her, his complexion pale as he picked at a thread in the bedspread. "Will you tell my teacher?" His voice shook and his eyes widened. "Please, don't tell Uncle Logan."

Hana tutted. "You've sneaked around at school using the computers in ways that are against their policy. Remember the paper you had to sign with me? That was a contract, and you understood that. When did you check the email account?" She clenched her teeth and prayed he hadn't been hacking into the teacher's computer.

"We have technology class on a Monday morning." He flicked at the thread. "I already learned how to do the stuff he's teaching us. It's boring."

Hana exhaled, part relief and part self-doubt. She'd made a mess of raising her eldest son, desperation evolving into permissive parenting and making excuses for his behaviour. Gritting her teeth, she prepared to do better second time around and reached for the truth. "There will be a consequence," she said, her tone soft. "But I need time to think about it. I'm willing to make it less of a punishment because you owned up, and because you put Tama's interests before your own. We'll talk again later today and I'll tell you what I've decided. But I need assurances you won't just make another Gmail address or a social media account as soon as you get the chance."

"I promise. And I'll delete this one now." Wiri reached for the laptop and Hana froze.

"Don't. Let's leave it for the moment." She smoothed his fringe from his eyes as Mac stampeded through the doorway. "Please, can you check if the dishwasher has finished its cycle?"

Wiri jumped to his feet, eager to escape. "Okay. I'll put everything away in the cupboards if it's dry."

"Good boy." Hana couldn't resist placing a kiss on his smooth forehead. His palpable relief created crow's feet at the corners of his eyes as he smiled. He didn't wipe it off or complain about her show of affection.

"Mama!" Mac rubbed his eyes and pouted, pushing his way onto Hana's knee. He wrapped his arm around her neck and raised his head to meet her lips. "Kiss me," he demanded, his tone eager.

"Sooky baby," Wiri joked. He batted Mac's shoulder with the back of his hand.

"Kiss him again." Mac caught hold of Wiri's fingers and dragged him closer. Wiri tussled with him, tickling Mac's ribs and causing him to slip sideways. Logan's formidable presence filled the room as he stepped through the doorway, holding Hana's phone aloft in his left hand.

"You have a text," he informed her, his tone couched in warning.

Hana swallowed, worry already tightening her chest and scenarios filling her head.

41

Helmet

The text from an unknown number left Hana crippled with angst. Logan dispatched the boys to the kitchen for Wiri to fulfil his promise. He suggested a board game and left Phoenix setting it up in the lounge.

"Doesn't he realise I spent my Saturday afternoon at the morgue?" Hana's voice rose in protest as she held the phone out to Logan. "Doesn't he understand another fireman is dead?"

"I doubt it." Logan sat on the bed next to her and took the phone from her outstretched fingers. He slipped his other arm around her shoulders. "What did you find out from Wiri?" His brow furrowed, and Hana knew his thoughts without him voicing them. The child came from dubious parentage. Kane Du Rose never obeyed the rules and that fact sat at the back of everything.

Hana exhaled and flopped back onto the mattress. She bent her knees and dug her toes into the expensive bedspread. "He got bored in a technology class and set up a Gmail account. He's spoken to Tama once a week for the last while. I suspect he logged on via my phone a couple of times during the summer holidays when he didn't have access to the school computers." She turned her head sideways to meet Logan's raised eyebrow. "I kept having to log into my email, remember? That would happen if Wiri logged me out to get to his own account."

Logan rolled onto his stomach and raised his eyebrows. He winced at the sound of crockery clattering in the kitchen. "Did you see what he used as his password?" He lowered his voice. "If you can keep him busy, I'll have a dig around his email account."

"Okay." Hana pushed herself upright. She rattled off Wiri's email address and then his password.

"Phoenix's birthday?" Logan pushed his fringe away from his eyes. "I thought he'd pick a swearword, seeing as nobody monitored him."

"Well, you thought wrong." Hana planted a kiss on the top of his head as she rose. "He used underscores between each of the numbers and typed the year as four digits. Sounds like something you'd do."

Logan scoffed and reached for the laptop, sliding it across the bedspread. "I wouldn't use anything as obvious as a birthday."

Hana pursed her lips and grinned. "From a man who named his company CircleLine Holdings, I find that hard to believe."

A shout from the lounge forced her to turn her feet towards the door. "Mama!" Edin screeched. Urgency laced her voice. Hana pitied her the nightmares which haunted her without regard for day or night. A wail of rage indicated one of the other children had tried to comfort her and been rejected.

"Coming," Hana called. She sighed as she headed through the doorway and met Mac on his way to find her.

"Edie." He took her hand and pointed towards the other end of the house. He indicated the sign for crying by using his fingers to imitate tears running down his face. "Come," he pleaded. "Come."

Edin sat in the centre of the sofa, her eyes narrowed to slits and her lips pursed into a fearsome line. She growled at Phoenix as her cousin attempted to soothe her. "Oh dear, Horsey fell on the floor, look." Phoenix bent to retrieve him, rewarded by another wail, as Edin held her arms out for him.

"Thanks, sweetheart." Hana squeezed her daughter's shoulder as she passed her. "That's kind of you."

Phoenix tossed her head, causing her ebony curls to cascade over her right shoulder. "She's just impossible!" she chided, sounding much like Leslie.

"Edie want snack!" The child glared at Hana. She lifted the battered horse and its legs dangled over the side of the sofa. "Horsey want snack."

"Soon," Hana replied. She held her hand out, not expecting Edin to take it. "Let's play this game first, then I'll make crackers and cheese for afternoon tea."

"Cheese." Edin's eyes widened and her irises glittered.

42

Trammel

The children played a board game with only minor bouts of heated argument. When Wiri produced a box containing chess pieces, Hana directed the smaller children to a game involving a pair of plastic tweezers and a caricature of a human body.

"Horsey." Edin pointed back to the black knight, which Phoenix moved diagonally across the board. She held out her hand, palm upwards in a silent demand.

"We're playing this game." Hana tapped the rounded stomach of the smiling plastic man as Mac lifted off the face to reveal a brain. "We don't take their pieces." She exhaled as Mac repeated a shortened version of her sentence, wondering when she barked orders instead of explaining.

"Their piece." Mac jerked his head towards the chess game, ruining the severity of his expression with a deep chuckle. Intestines like old telephone cables tumbled free of the belly as he lifted the lid. "This is ours." He blinked and shook his head in an action which gave Hana alarm. She tapped his shoulder.

"Is your ear hurting?" she demanded, signing the action one handed while keeping the other clamped over the hem of Edin's skirt. If the child lurched for the chess players, she wouldn't get far.

Mac shook his head and shrugged. He pointed inside the plastic skull. "Brain," he said, and smiled at her.

"Clever boy." Hana tried to engage Edin's attention. "Look at the tummy," she said. "Take a card and we'll see what the operation is. Would you like to wear the doctor's coat?"

"Tummy hurt." Edin frowned and rubbed Horsey across the space beneath her ribs. Hana caught herself with her mouth open and snapped it closed. The little girl never complained about physical ailments and at first, Hana wondered if she referred to the spiralling intestines attempting to break free from the plastic stomach. She took a deep breath and gathered her thoughts.

"The man's tummy, or your tummy?" She removed any emotional load from the question and forced herself to sound casual.

"Edie's." She winced and pushed herself onto Hana's knee, dragging the knitted Horsey with her.

"Let's have cuddles then." Hana allowed her to settle, gratified by her willingness to share physical space with someone other than Mac. Her mind ran through the stock of child friendly remedies in the medicine box secreted at the back of her walk-in wardrobe.

"Milk." Mac said the word but pronounced it as 'moke' and used extended fingers and thumbs on both hands to make alternate up and down motions. Then he bent to seize the escaping intestines and stuffed them back into the patient.

"You want some?" Hana asked. "Or Edin does?"

Mac signed again but added another set of finger movements to indicate pain. He brushed his fingers up and down his chest. Hana cuddled the little girl closer and collected Horsey's dangling legs into her lap. "Milk hurts Edin's tummy?"

"Yep." He delivered a raucous laugh as the plastic lid for the stomach flipped off and the intestines made a break for it.

Hana shook her head in confusion. "But she drinks so much of it," she murmured.

After disqualifying herself from the game by touching the man's femur instead of his fibula, Hana made a sneaky call to her brother. She remained sitting with the children and smiling at her son's antics. He donned the doctor's coat and cackled like a drain at Edin's clumsy removal of a plastic spleen.

"Well, hullo sister dear," Mark intoned. "How's my nephew doing after his surgery?"

"Great thanks." Hana stuck her finger in her ear as Edin set the lights strobing with a jab at the wrong organ and Mac hooted. "He's noisy for sure."

"Isn't that a good thing?" Whirring sounded in the background of the call, followed by a swearword. "Oops, sorry. We're going for a cycle ride, but my husband is swearing at the puncture he got last weekend and didn't fix." Another expletive spluttered free, as though to make Mark's point. He laughed, sounding a lot like Mac.

"It is a great thing." Hana watched her son's antics. Edin allowed him to guide her hand to a liver shaped plastic object, and she beamed as they placed it in the kidney dish next to the board. Mac held his hand up for a high five and Edin used Horsey to make the contact.

"David Allen just arrived." Logan appeared in the doorway. He held a chocolate cake aloft and jerked his head towards the kitchen. "Leslie sent this."

The chess game forgotten, Wiri and Phoenix bolted towards him. Male voices followed them to the kitchen. The poor man on the operating table lay abandoned, his intestines springing back onto the rug as Mac, Edin and Horsey brought up the rear. Hana exhaled and flopped back on the sofa. She spent the next half an hour engaging her brother in a medical consultation, into which he brought his pediatric surgeon husband.

"I'll visit after this shift rotation," Mark promised. "She likes me. I'll examine her and make some suggestions."

Hana sighed. "We spent half an hour with the doctor last month. I detailed Edin's toilet habits, told her about the rash which comes and goes and explained how obsessed she is with food. She said she'd grow out of it."

She heard her brother-in-law's exaggerated exhale. "Don't get me started on the plight of general practitioners," he growled into the speaker. "They're Jack of All Trades and there's neither money nor time for them to learn all the things. If it's not obvious or they haven't encountered it before, they can't help. But she should have referred you to a specialist. That's what we're here for."

"She said to come back if it continued." Hana's voice trailed off, symptomatic of the futility she felt concerning Edin.

"We'll both come," Mark offered. "Continual hunger may represent a deficiency in her system."

"The doctor did blood tests at the end of last year and found nothing." A tightness entered Hana's voice. "Logan had to come with us and hold her. She wouldn't speak to him for weeks."

"I wonder if it's an intolerance."

Silence greeted Mark's suggestion, and Hana rubbed her eyes. "Perhaps. What should I do then?"

"Nothing yet. Change nothing in the interim. Messing around with her diet won't help without a diagnosis. You'll just confuse things. I'll call you about visiting. We'll come soon."

The phone fell to the cushions as Hana finished the call and collapsed against the back of the sofa. "A food intolerance. Great. Now, she's stuffing her face with chocolate cake." She rose with bones made of lead and followed the sounds of voices and laughter emanating from the kitchen.

43

Farriery

Hana snuggled closer to Logan on the wide bed. She turned on her side and laid her arm across his stomach. "What did David Allen really want?" she demanded.

"He brought the cake up from Leslie." Surprise edged his tone. "You ate some."

Hana released a snort of derision. "I'm not stupid, Logan. You told him about Tama, didn't you?"

"Might have." Logan yawned and his body stiffened until the movement ended with a sigh. "And he might have agreed to check out a few ideas."

"What ideas?" Hana rested her chin on his chest and gazed up at him.

He pressed a kiss against her forehead. "I'll tell you if he turns up anything." His eyes narrowed and his lips formed a tight line. "You're looking tired and I'm worried about you. Please, just leave the Tama thing to me."

Hana opened her mouth to protest, and he placed his index finger over her lips. She sighed and admitted defeat, but with conditions. "Fine!" she grumbled. "But you have to share whatever you learn, otherwise I'll need to poke around for myself."

"Hana?" He added weight to her name with the gravity of his tone. "Do you think your heart might need checking?"

She exhaled. Pushing herself up onto her elbows, she read the fear in her husband's grey irises. "It's not physical," she admitted. "I'm afraid of failing. I persuaded you to take on these extra children and I'm frightened to acknowledge they have needs I can't meet. My father once accused me of rescuing people and he was right, wasn't he? He recognised it in me because I'm a carbon copy of him. But I look at Mark and he's turned out just fine. That's all I want for Tama, Wiri and Edin. Sometimes I track their progress and when I can't see any, I own all the failure." She tapped her breast as the confession rocked a deeper part of her resolve. "I'm lost, Logan."

"It's okay," he whispered. "I see it."

Hana exhaled through pursed lips. The words stuck in the back of her throat. "Thank you," she whispered.

Logan tugged her down against his chest. He kissed the top of her head. "Okay, so in the spirit of honesty, I have a few thoughts about where Tama might have gone to ground. If I find out anything definite, I'll tell you. For the record, you've done an amazing job with all our kids. Tama's turned out fine and Wiri will too if we give him time. Phoe and Mac are amazing. School will help Edin because other adults will reinforce the boundaries we've already shown her. Michael and I ran wild as kids and Angus Blair prevented us from ending up feral, so I know first-hand that routine and structure helps." He paused and released a sigh, which rumbled through his chest wall and into Hana's ear. "I didn't want to take Edin, and I had good reasons for my choice. But I'm sorry for not supporting you more with her. I understand you're scared to ask me for help in case I send her off to her other family. Forgive me, Hana. I'm here now."

She couldn't answer him. Her tears dampened his chest, running down his side and wetting the sheets beneath them. A weight lifted from Hana's shoulders and the ache in her chest loosened. "Sorry for defying you," she whispered once she could speak. "I understood your reasons, but didn't respect them."

"Then, we're all good?" Hope laced Logan's voice as he sought to put their relationship back on an even keel.

Hana nodded. She used the back of her left hand to wipe away her tears. "We're good." She sniffed. "Please, can you tell me what you discovered in Wiri's email account?"

Logan raised his right eyebrow. "It proved interesting. Wiri set up the account last November. He's used it once a week, often on a Monday. He didn't think to open the promotions or social tab, so he missed seeing all the crap. We're fortunate he only spoke to Tama. I'm considering letting him keep the account, but I'll lock it down and supervise, so he only speaks to Tama. The kid sounds lonely. I don't want to remove his outlet for honesty."

"What did he say?" Hana frowned. "I didn't realise he felt lonely."

Logan brushed off her adoption of the personal slight. "Just chit-chat really, but then last month, Tama started asking questions about the fire."

"He showed those emails to me," Hana admitted with a nod. "He doesn't remember much about that time."

Logan nodded, and his hair shuffled against his pillow. "I looked at the ones you mean. But further back, he asked Wiri if he remembered a woman visiting the house on the day of the fire."

"A woman?" Hana's brow furrowed, and she rolled onto her back. Righting her pillow beneath her neck, she stared at the ceiling. "Not Miriam? We both know she visited Reuben that afternoon."

"Not my mother." Logan sighed. "Tama saw this other woman several times in the fortnight before Christmas. On the day of the fire, he said she wore a purple dress. At other times she wore purple shoes or a scarf. Always purple."

"Why would that seem relevant to Tama?" Hana blinked into the glare from her bedside lamp. "A woman in a purple dress," she mused.

Logan twisted his lips. "Nobody visited that house," he replied, his tone severe. "Nev was the only one you could get a sensible conversation out of, even on a good day!"

"They had services though, didn't they? What about representatives from the power company or the council?"

Logan shook his head. "Reuben ran an electricity generator. He fed it diesel. Water came off the mountain and I shudder to think what they did with the waste. Maybe they had a septic tank. I didn't see one in the ruins."

"What about underground?" Hana asked. "Like ours and the one for the hotel?"

"Na." Logan exhaled. "They're both set up with expensive engineering and complicated filters to protect the water table from contamination. Reuben had nothing like that. Perhaps they crapped in a bucket. I'll ask Tama when he shows up again."

Hana wrinkled her nose. "I've learned a heap about Reuben since his death, and he was a clever man. If they had poor sanitation, Wiri would have mentioned it before now. I bet he had something running, maybe a system he invented."

Logan nodded, and the half-light revealed his wistful smile. "Yeah," he agreed. He rolled onto his stomach. "I wondered about the developers, but I dealt with the same lawyer as Reuben. I don't think this woman is linked to them. They wanted my land, not Reuben's, so why torch his house?"

Hana nodded and teased her mind away from the whenua beneath them. It had belonged to Logan since just after his fifth birthday, stolen by his birth father and slated for expensive mountain homes.

Logan continued, "What's sad is that Tama asked Wiri about the woman in the purple dress one time too many. He hinted she had some involvement in the fire. Eventually, the kid bought into his conspiracy and corroborated his version of events. It's heartbreaking." Logan sighed. "He was so eager to please Tama, he's now persuaded himself she exists. Wiri's life changed that day and it went downhill from there. If Tama convinced him that a woman with a purple dress killed his poppa and destroyed his home, we've got bigger problems than we realised."

Hana turned sideways and stared at her husband. "What do you suggest?" she whispered.

Logan winced. "Maybe don't wear your purple dress until we solve the mystery."

44

Loose Box

"Can I help you?" Hana took a step back from the washing line and dropped the damp towel into the laundry basket. A breeze caught the washing and swung the rotary line away from her, a pair of Wiri's underpants flapping against Logan's newest tee shirt. Her gaze moved towards the open gate at the end of the driveway and the utility vehicle blocking the entrance. Mud obscured its number plate, giving it an eerie anonymity.

"Yes." The man took a jerky step towards her, his pecking movements betraying agitation. Dressed in a shabby tan jacket and trousers too big for him, a limp marred his gait. "I just need to know why you met at the golf club with that fire investigator. Tell me that and I'll leave."

Hana pursed her lips to stop herself speaking Melissa's name. She'd been around Logan for long enough to recognise the risk of a bluff. She shrugged. "I haven't met with any fire investigators." Her tone held confidence because she stuck to the truth. Melissa's new job included acting as an agent for an insurance company. Her former name and her original self held no relevance anymore. Hana stuck her chin in the air and eyed the man with calm assurance. "I met with a friend at the golf club yesterday. We organised a hairdressing visit together." Truth. Amy had agreed during a late-night phone call to style Melissa's hair. Hana arranged over text to meet Melissa later in the month and travel to Hamilton with her.

Hana pointed to the ute, realising it still vibrated from the running engine. The man's jerky movements and the general air of tension sent tingles of fear running up her spine. "If that's all you wanted, please leave. Now." Her bare heels found the edge of the concrete slabs, which Logan placed in a neat square around the rotary washing line. The man's fingers opened and closed and she experienced a premonition of him forcing her into the vehicle. Reaching into the pocket of her dress, her shaking fingers found the button on the side of her phone. She pressed it three times in quick succession, hoping Logan saw her SOS in time. Both of her phone cameras would take a snapshot of the inside of her pocket, but he'd call her and if she didn't answer... then what? Her mental wrangling took her no further into the future.

In the split second it took for the man to look back at his idling ute, Hana ran for the open ranch slider leading into the kitchen. He gasped and moved with an ungainly speed to follow her. She held her breath as she hauled the heavy door closed, fumbling with the catch to lock him out on the deck. He rived on the handle, defeated by the sweat on his fingers which stopped him from gaining purchase on the narrow metal ridge.

Hana backed away from the window, her hip contacting the table and sending a chair skittering across the tiles. "Go away!" she shouted. "Help is coming!"

Her phone rang, and she dragged it from her pocket, struggling to focus on the flashing screen. Two jabs of her finger connected the call, and she tried to speak, hearing her own words rambling out of her control.

"Hana!" Logan's voice shouted through the speaker, the sound tinny and faint. She lifted the device to her ear and watched the man casting around on the deck for something. When he bent to seize a heavy terracotta flowerpot, she screamed in fear.

"He's gonna break the window!" she shouted into the phone. "Logan, help me!"

"Where are you?" He rapped out the order, his tone calm and authoritative.

"Kitchen," Hana gasped. The fingers of her right hand strayed to the outline of her pacemaker snuggled beneath her collarbone.

With difficulty, the man hefted the pot and staggered towards the window. He swung his body in a wide arc, aiming for the centre of the glass. Hana had a fleeting sight of the bobbing heads of the marigolds, which Phoenix planted for her as a gift. Rage lit a fire in her heart and instead of running, she stamped towards the danger.

"Don't you dare!" she yelled. "Put it down right now!"

To her surprise, he obeyed. Soil tumbled from the pot as he bent, his body stiff and unyielding. Hana gaped as he stared up at the eaves beneath the roof line. She held her breath and heard an echo of her husband's powerful baritone. It came from the phone in her hand and boomed around the house, seeming to come from every angle. "You can't get away," he stated, his tone cold. "We blocked the driveway and my men are waiting for you. Touch my wife or one more thing on my property and I'll make you sorry."

"The cameras," Hana hissed. She lifted the phone to her ear. Logan's voice sounded louder outside on the deck than through the phone speaker. He'd used the security system to protect her. Nausea rose into her chest as her heartbeat thudded in her ears and throat.

The man slumped onto the deck with a sigh. Dirt stained his fingers as he ran them over his eyes. Thin, mousey hair lay in strands across his head and his shoulders slouched in defeat. Logan's voice continued around him. "I have video footage of you, and a group of angry stockmen are on their way. You'd better hope they get to you before I do." A breathlessness entered his tone, and she sensed him running.

The man rose to his feet and limped out of view. Hana ran to a side window and saw him increase his speed across the lawn. He'd driven the single lane up to the house and believed Logan's threat of a reception committee waiting for him at the bottom. He clambered over the fence with laboured movements and disappeared into the bush, eaten by the canopy.

Hana's knees knocked, and she gripped the edge of the windowsill with shaking fingers. The black-and-white floor tiles moved around in her vision as she sank to the ground and stuck her head between her knees. Scenarios and possibilities rampaged through her mind. If he'd arrived the day before, he'd have found them easy pickings. The children left all the doors unlocked as they moved around the house and garden, leaving through one and entering via another. He'd have encountered Mac on his scooter, Edin digging in the dirt and Wiri kicking his football. Phoenix spent an hour after dinner swinging in the hammock and reading her latest acquisition from the school library. All vulnerable, all at risk.

The panic took hold and forced tears of shock and dismay to fall. Hana lifted the phone to her ear and heard nothing. She laid it on the tiles and covered her head with her hands as the 'what ifs' created even more terrible thoughts.

It took twenty minutes for the first of the diesel engines to arrive at the top of the driveway. Hoof beats vibrated through the bush as Logan requisitioned his stockmen from their various locations. They seemed to arrive at once in a cacophony.

"Hana!" David Allen shielded his eyes and peered through the window, searching for her amid the scattered furniture. He used the side of his fist to hammer on the glass. "Hana!"

She pushed herself to her knees and crawled the first few metres across the kitchen before grabbing the table to haul herself upright. Using her forearm to scratch away the evidence of her weakness speckling her cheeks, she called to him, "I'm okay, Dave. I'm okay."

45

Split-eared Bridle

"They tracked him to the gully at the bottom of Dead Man's Ridge." Logan's lips tightened as he spoke the name. It conjured an image in Hana's mind of a teenager with a broken leg lying at its stony bottom. She dismissed it with a flap of her hand.

"He fell?"

Logan snorted. "No. Unlucky for him. Toby's got him. They're on their way back here."

"Here?" Hana's eyes widened. "You can't bring him here." She glanced at her watch and forced her scrambled brain to count the hours before she'd need to fetch the children from school.

Logan's jaw tightened. "What do you think I'm gonna do to him, Hana?"

She swallowed. "I don't know, but you're angry. It leaves several horrible possibilities."

"Right." He snatched a glass from the cupboard and filled it with water from the tap. He drank before turning to face her.

Water speckled his chin, and he wiped it away with the back of his hand.

"The cops aren't coming, are they?" Dread snaked a tendril around Hana's heart. His raised eyebrow gave her the answer. She ground her teeth in her jaw. "I'm bringing the children home in four hours. They can't know about any of this."

"Trust me." Logan's smile made his lips slide back from his teeth. The expression contained a primeval enjoyment laced with anger. The man had trespassed, compounded his sins by threatening Hana, and then fled. Each action triggered Logan's sense of fair play. Hana fought the desire to climb in her truck and run to Leslie's apartment, but leaving allowed the men to operate without boundaries.

David Allen called from his position by the front door and Logan shot through the house at a run. Hana followed with slower steps, wanting to see and yet desperate to hide.

The man's ute sat idle at the edge of the lawn, company trucks parked bumper to bumper behind it. Four loose horses grazed beyond them, penned into their corner by the vehicles. A strawberry roan turned to face Hana, the orange head of a marigold bobbing from his lips.

Hana gasped as a metallic click echoed around the hallway. David Allen lifted a shotgun to his shoulder, his body stiffening as he took aim at something beyond Hana's view.

Toby trotted his horse along the driveway, shifting onto the lawn to spare the mare's hooves on the gravel. A length of rope tied to the saddle horn led to the wrists of the man he towed behind him. Men followed, some walking and others on horseback. Hana gasped and covered her mouth.

Cowed and frightened, the man's eyes darted left and right. His gaze rested on his abandoned truck and he swallowed. The limp had worsened and the orange clay of the mountain stained his trousers and one side of his face. His ripped jacket exposed a bleeding elbow. Hana no longer saw a potential attacker, but a human being.

"No!" She slid past the gun barrel and through the front door. "Stop this!" she demanded. "This isn't the wild west."

Toby slid from his horse and faced her, one shoulder raised in a shrug of disbelief. He opened his mouth to speak, but the lift of Logan's eyebrows silenced him. "He fell on the way to Dead Man's Ridge," he grumbled. "We used the rope to pull him out of the gully." His horse dropped its muzzle and nosed the grass at his feet. Fast moving lips tugged at the lawn. Toby loosened the knot, keeping the rope secure over the man's wrists, and seized the back of his collar. Muscles bulged through Toby's shirt sleeve as he exerted more pressure than necessary. "Where are we doing this?" he demanded.

Hana exhaled and her shoulders slumped. Their loyalty to Logan trumped any reason she might add to the mix. Wiri had reminded her of the time she hit Kane Du Rose in the face and she quailed against the sense of shame it conjured in her mind. The men had enjoyed her show of force, but it left a nasty residue in her soul. "Kitchen," she barked, not giving Logan time to answer. She smoothed her fingers over David Allen's shoulder as she passed him. "We don't need that yet," she assured him. She'd fired Henri Du Rose's gun once in fear and many times as practice. Watching Logan fire it in anger had squashed any desire to touch it ever again. "Put it away," she advised him, gratified when he dropped it to his side and cracked the barrel open across his forearm.

Dust and mud accompanied the crowd through the hallway and into the kitchen. They removed their shoes but still tracked their mess. Their captive shuffled along in his socks, his head bowed and his shoulders stiff. He entered the kitchen, his eyes still drinking in his surroundings through a series of surreptitious glances.

Hana gasped as he lurched towards her, his hand outstretched. Logan stepped in front of her with a growl, and the man halted. "Sorry," he muttered. He balled his hands together at his chest. "Thought it best if I started again. My name's Colin."

46

Jackaroo

"**C**olin?" Logan repeated. He sounded disappointed, and Hana frowned. She wondered what kind of name justified the fuss he'd caused, and her brain ran off on a mission to find one.

She got to *Hank* before someone snorted and repeated, "Colin?"

Logan tilted his body to glare at them. "Sort out the horses," he barked. "Saddles and bridles off for now." Two of the younger men shuffled from the kitchen with the slumped shoulders of regret.

Colin stepped back and sat in the chair, which Toby pushed towards the backs of his knees. He ran a shaking hand over his hair with extreme gentleness, as though keen not to disturb the fine tendrils disguising his baldness. A patterned weave circled his protruding wrists, evidence of the rope's pressure against his skin.

Hana leaned back against the counter, hiding her trembling hands behind her back. She glanced at the wall clock and then at Logan, not needing to remind him of their time limit. The stockmen gathered around in an arc behind the man's chair. "Well, Colin," she said, sarcasm entering her tone. "I would say it's nice to meet you, but so far you've intimidated me and then attempted to break into my home using a flowerpot." She glanced up at Toby to find him smirking.

"I'm sorry." Colin dipped forward and buried his face in his palms. "But I saw you meet with the fire investigator."

Hana took a step closer, bumping against the back of Logan's hand as he stretched out to stop her. "Are you following Melissa Stratton?"

"Yes." He looked up through red-rimmed eyes. "She broke into my client's home and ransacked it. What we don't know is why."

"Oh." Hana exhaled with a sigh. "Is your client Melissa's ex-wife?"

Colin's feet shifted against the tiles. "I can't give out confidential information." His guarded tone drew a snort from Logan.

"You can if I beat it out of you." He stepped across the distance between them and dragged a chair from beneath the table. Spinning it, he bent his knee and placed his foot on the seat, an intimidation tactic which proved effective against school children. He rested his forearm over his thigh and leaned forward, his fingers bunched into fists.

Colin winced. "I'd hate to involve the cops," he threatened. His eyelashes fluttered as Logan's left hand shot around to retrieve his phone from his back pocket. The device slid into his fingers.

"Be my guest," Logan replied. He unlocked the screen. "I'll call them right now." He raised an eyebrow and spoke to Toby. "What do you think? Trespass, threatening behaviour, criminal damage?" He turned to survey the lopsided marigolds reclining against the side of their pot like collapsed orange dominoes.

Toby cleared his throat. "Attempted home invasion, boss," he suggested. "The local guys get excited over crimes like that." He clapped his hands together. "Better than issuing speeding tickets and investigating roaming sheep. They'll get their teeth stuck right into this."

"Yeah." Logan smiled and lifted the device to his ear.

"Stop!" Colin raised his hand and deep lines furrowed his brow. "I can make an exception." His voice croaked, and he patted his throat. "Please, may I have a drink of water?"

The gathered men leaned against walls and the fridge as Colin slurped the water, which Logan poured for him from the tap. Toby remained behind his seat like a sentry, ready to defend their close knit family from the weedy marauder. "Start anytime soon," he growled, tapping Colin's shoulder with an impatient finger. "Some of us have work to finish."

Logan straddled the chair and rested his chin on his fingers. He raised an eyebrow laced with expectation and Colin spluttered into his glass. "Stop buying time," Logan hissed. "Why are you on my property?"

Colin set his glass on the table with a jerky movement. Water slopped over the side and created a puddle. Toby shoved it back out of reach, removing the stalling tactic and displaying his famed lack of patience. "Let's just shove him back in the gully," he suggested. "He can join the other bodies."

"Yeah, I'm bored now." David Allen inspected the barrel of the gun and blew off imaginary dust.

"Okay, okay!" Colin protested. "My client believes the fire investigator broke into her home and ransacked it while searching for documents."

"What documents?" Logan frowned and leaned forward. "Your time is running out, my friend."

Hana sighed. "Documents relating to a fire here seven years ago. Melissa doesn't have them. She didn't break into your client's house."

Colin shrugged, and his sagging shoulders seemed to slip lower still. "My client is convinced that's what happened."

Hana took a step closer, seeing Logan and Toby both stiffen and map her movements. "The same person broke into Melissa's apartment. She filed a police report. It relates to the fire. Our son is missing."

"Hana!" Logan growled, and she tensed.

"Wiri? Mac?" Toby's eyes widened, and he took a step towards Logan. "Or Tama? Why didn't you say something?" He dug his finger and thumb into the bridge of his nose. "Who's missing, man?"

Hana remained silent, Logan's rebuke stinging her pride. Her husband sighed and folded his arms. "Tama went missing last week. He contacted us, but he doesn't want us looking for him. Hana's right. It's linked to Reuben's fire."

"And a woman in a purple dress." Hana glanced at Logan and swallowed. "Tama thinks she visited Reuben's house in the weeks leading up to the fire and on the day it happened." She appealed to Toby. "Do you remember someone wearing a purple dress visiting this property or Reuben's around that time?"

Toby groaned and spread his hands in front of him. "No!" he snarled. "Why are you asking me?"

Logan exhaled like an irritated stallion as tension hiked in the room. "Because you stayed friends with Nev," he said, his tone tight. "It's not an accusation, mate."

"So did Linc!" Toby snapped. He clasped his fingers at the back of his neck, his shirt riding up to expose defined abdominal muscles honed by hard work.

"Lincoln wasn't here!" Hana protested. She took a step towards him. "I asked you a simple question. They're all dead. What does it matter now, anyway?"

"No one is questioning your loyalty." Logan turned away from his men and reached into a cupboard for coffee. He dumped beans in the grinder and killed all conversation for the next few minutes with the sound of the machine's loud whir.

Colin sat in his chair with his head bowed. His hands still shook, and Hana wondered what terrible thoughts reverberated around his brain. He looked like a man who'd bitten off more than he could chew.

Logan steamed milk and made lattes for his men. If they found the sight of their boss playing at barista strange, they kept their thoughts to themselves. By the time he'd finished delivering hot drinks to the gathered crowd, the tension had dissipated and Toby's body had lost its hard defensive angles.

"Where do we go from here?" Hana demanded. She leaned against the counter and surveyed the gathered testosterone. Logan dumped a mug of coffee on the table next to Colin and shoved a teaspoon and sugar bowl in his direction.

"Dunno," he replied. Exhaustion snaked around him, and Hana frowned. The bumps and bruises from the muster took their toll on his body, the welts lurking beneath his clothes and taking longer to heal than they would on her. He sighed. "Damned if I care anymore." He jerked his head towards Colin. "Drink that and go. Come here again and I'll make sure you don't leave."

Hana's lips parted in surprise. "You're giving up on Tama?"

Logan snorted. A warning tick flickered from a vein in his neck. Toby's mouth flapped like that of a stranded fish and he placed his coffee mug on the table in front of him. "Okay," he said with a sigh. "Truth. Yeah, I stayed friends with Nev. Even after I started working for Jack." He shot a glance towards Hana as he said Jack's name. She forced herself not to react. "Your family picked the fight with Nev's, not mine. This is a small town, and it took your grandmother's side against Reuben. But some of our generation kept out of it. Yeah, I liked Nev. We stayed mates. I visited their place sometimes, even on the day of the fire." He closed his eyes and his eyeballs moved beneath the shutter of his eyelids. "I didn't see any woman wearing a purple dress that day." His jaw tightened and his gaze flicked to Logan. "I only saw your ma."

Logan turned away from him and rested his hands flat on the counter. He gazed through the kitchen window at the Tasman Sea in the distance. High tide dragged the surf closer to the land, only to reject it again in an hour. Hana ached to reach out and touch him, knowing he wouldn't appreciate her coddling him with an audience.

Colin ignored the coffee next to him and rose, his movements careful and performed with intricate slowness. He tensed when one of the other stockmen cleared his throat. His face screwed into an exaggerated wince, as though waiting for one of the men to pounce.

"I saw a woman at Reuben's place." Hana could count on one hand the number of times she'd heard Paulie speak over the last eight years. His voice held a strangled quality, as though he'd dragged his words over grit.

"What?" Logan turned towards him with a frown. Paulie rose from his chair before setting his drained coffee mug on the table.

"I saw a woman in a purple dress," he confirmed, nodding to emphasise his truth. "But not on the day of the fire. She came afterwards. Said she had your permission." He grunted as he tucked his loose shirt into the back of his jeans. Gnarled fingers and craggy joints completed the action. He straightened his spine and set his features into a blank mask as Logan observed him with a frown.

"My permission? After the fire?" Hana's husband cocked his head.

"Yeah, boss." Paulie exhaled with relief as Logan focussed on the facts of his sighting and didn't dwell further on the issue of family loyalty. "I stayed on the site with the excavator crew, if you remember. One time she wore a purple dress, but the other times she wore boots and a hard hat. Seemed like she was searching for something in the rubble."

"Other times?" Hana stared at Paulie in confusion.

"Yeah." He nodded with enthusiasm, his cheeks flushing pink as all eyes turned to him. "She came every day for a week."

47

Stirrup

"What if Tama got it wrong?" Hana turned to face her husband.

Logan shrugged. "And ran off chasing ghosts?" His tone sounded doubtful. "Na." He dismissed the notion with immediate denial. "That kid's a hundred-watt bulb. He had to learn to survive, growing up in that house." He jerked his head towards Paulie. "And someone else saw the woman."

Hana exhaled and her fingers twitched behind her back. Logan's easy dismissal included her. "I'm not doubting the woman exists." Her tone held a bite. "Just her appearance at Reuben's house. He might have got the timing wrong."

"True." Logan dragged out the word and offered a tight smile. He sensed he'd brushed her off without proper consideration, and his eyes sparkled with a silent apology.

"What will you do with me?" Colin's hand shook as he brushed sweat from his forehead. "May I leave now?"

Toby snorted and Hana sensed the testosterone fizzle in the contained space. David Allen raised an eyebrow at Logan, as though seeking permission to take command. Hana saw the faint uplift of Logan's chin.

"We want all your information first," David growled. He'd leaned the shotgun against the wall but his stance suggested he could reach it at a second's notice, crack the barrel and take aim. "We want your client's name and any details you've discovered. Then we'll think about letting you leave."

Hana glanced again at the wall clock. The hour hand slid past the twelve, making her late for her shift at the museum. She imagined Will wearing a hole in the floorboards with his wheelchair and winced. She should text him, but her phone remained in her pocket.

Melissa's ex-wife hadn't just employed Colin Skeldale to investigate a burglary. She'd got a sniff of hard cash in the form of a legacy left to Melissa and wanted her share. He spread his knotty fingers in an expression of placation. "Someone broke into a locked filing cabinet and tipped everything out onto the floor. A family member died in the week leading up to the burglary and my client believes the intruder stole documents relating to that person's estate."

Hana exhaled. "That's extreme, isn't it? Who employs a private detective to follow their ex-partner, hoping to challenge a will?"

Colin's head bobbed from side to side. "Not a will. A divorce settlement. My client kept the house in exchange for agreeing not to go after her ex-husband's pension. The legacy didn't feature in the discussion and it changes things."

"Wait, what?" Toby raised a hand and closed his eyes. "The husband's name is Melissa?" He winced as though his brain struggled to comprehend the details, and Hana glanced at Logan for help.

"Yes." He answered for her. "The husband is now a woman named Melissa. Keep up, Toby."

"Right." Toby blinked and dropped his hand.

David Allen intervened, speaking to the back of Colin's head. "You realise it's not relevant, right? A divorce settlement is a final agreement between the parties. She gets what she gets. If this Melissa inherited anything after the Decree Absolute, it's tough on the ex-wife, but she's entitled to nothing. Are you unscrupulous enough to follow someone's every move and bill a client when you know it's pointless?"

Colin tipped his head from side to side. He swallowed twice before answering. "This is my first case." A collective groan drowned out his excessive throat clearing. "The client is a friend of a friend."

Logan bristled, and his biceps tensed. The moko tattoo peeked from beneath his tee shirt sleeve, bearing Hana's name and those of his children. Except Edin. "On what planet did you think it was okay to drive to someone's home, terrify the owner, and attempt to break and enter?"

"I'm sorry," Colin pleaded. "I just didn't think. She ran from me and I needed to speak to her. If Melissa Stratton has acquired a fortune, it entitles my client to half."

Hana tugged her phone from her pocket and before anyone could stop her, she dialled a number. The call connected after two rings. "Hey Hana," a male voice replied.

"Hi Mel." Hana glowered at Colin. "You have a problem."

***

Hana sat on the low wall surrounding the school playground. She exhaled a giant sigh and closed her eyes. Logan had prevented the men from becoming feral around Colin. David Allen seemed over enthusiastic about the prospect of shooting him and the other men concocted horrifying ways of disposing of his body. Hana left them to it, knowing either way Colin wouldn't still be sitting in her kitchen when she returned with the children.

The sun warmed her stiff spine, and she forced herself to relax. Her phone buzzed in her pocket and she hauled it out and peeked at the screen through one eye.

Melissa had typed, *'Thanks for the info. Sorry you got dragged into this.'*

"Not as sorry as I am," Hana mused.

Wiri emerged first, trailed by his usual troop of adoring girls. He showed no concern, and Hana watched their eager faces with sadness. What strange wiring compelled them to fall in love with someone who wasn't interested? He piled his bags at her feet and ran to kick a ball around with a knot of other boys. The girls shuffled behind him before their parents hijacked their worship session.

Phoenix appeared. She slumped next to Hana on the wall after placing a kiss on her cheek. "I loved my sandwich today, Mama," she said with a smile. Hana cast her mind back a lifetime to the exercise of buttering bread the previous night.

"Good," she said. "I'm pleased. What did you learn today?"

Phoenix waggled her dark eyebrows and dipped forward to watch a ladybird crawl between her sandals. "I learned Macky took the plaster off his stitches at lunchtime. It had blood in it. His teacher came to fetch me because Edin wouldn't let anyone near him. She kept growling." Her eyes widened, and she flapped her hand. "You know that thing she does?"

"Yeah." Hana nodded. She knew the sound first hand. The growl, the hiss, and the snort. She exhaled and braced herself for trouble.

The smaller children appeared at the blue door, their teacher holding the hand of the leading child. She glanced around the playground to identify parents before sending her charges off to their respective adults.

Hana rose as Mac dashed through the door. His backpack bounced behind his thin shoulders. He towed Edin behind him like a pilot boat, tugging an ocean liner into port. His other hand gripped the chubby fingers of a round shaped boy with protruding ears. Hana cocked her head in surprise.

"Hi, Chester." Hana smiled at the extra member of her crowd as he worked to avoid eye contact. He frowned and hid behind Mac.

"Hey, Chester." Phoenix dipped sideways to peer at him and the boy's lips quirked upwards into a tiny smile. Her tone held a bounce as though she'd spoken to a baby.

"Oh, there you are." Chester's mother barrelled across the playground. Flushed pink cheeks wobbled above a bow shaped mouth. She lurched for his wrist and he squawked and kept hold of Mac. His arms and legs flailed as he struggled to maintain his grip.

Then Edin laughed. "Funny," she spat and cackled like a maniac. She imitated him and he paused with a frown. "Cake," she said. She dropped her knees and spoke up and into his face. "Cake?" The second attempt held more of a question.

Chester's mother floundered. She looked in every direction except Hana's, sweat beading on her brow. She spoke to Edin in a high, unnatural voice. "Perhaps not today," she began, wringing her hands and taking another swipe at her son's wrist. He dodged the movement with practice. A circle of mothers turned to face Hana, eyebrows raised amid winces of discomfort.

"Cake!" Edin spoke through gritted teeth. She squeezed her fists into balls of frustration and tensed every muscle in her body hard enough to shake her frame. "Nonie. Cake!"

Hana considered her options, which proved few.

"Look." Mac pointed to the visible scar above his ear. With the surgical plaster off, the skin appeared pale and bare. "All gone," he said, spreading his hands in an attitude of disbelief. He dropped Edin's hand and pointed to Chester. "Found it," he said with a grin.

"He means Chester found his plaster." Phoenix giggled and swung her feet backwards and forwards. "Not that he found Chester."

"Right." Hana considered the hui taking place in her kitchen. The men would have dispatched the private detective, but their method would dictate the level of cleaning required. She hoped Colin had driven away but couldn't take the risk with an unexpected guest in tow. She dug her phone from her handbag. "Let me see if Nonie has any cake before we invite ourselves," she suggested. Activating her screen highlighted a missed text from Leslie.

'The scones are hot. Come and get them.'

Hana cocked her head. "Not quite cake, but how do we all feel about some hot scones with butter?"

A cacophony of noise rose around her as the children expressed their enthusiasm.

48

Bearing Rein

They arrived in the hotel car park twenty minutes later. Hana navigated the winding route with practiced ease but kept her speed lowered to allow Chester's mother to follow them. She wound down her window and pointed at the guest car park before she made the turn into Logan's space. Someone else had parked in hers and she passed the problem onto her husband.

The children disembarked without fuss, used to Hana's lectures about car parks and distracted motorists. But Chester's mother showed no control over her son as he barrelled from the vehicle even before the wheels ceased rolling.

Phoenix gasped. "Om, that's naughty!" She folded Edin's fingers around her hand, bending them against her resistance. "Hold my hand!" she barked. "Or no scones for you!" Edin's lips tightened, but she curled her fingers over Phoenix's.

Chester stopped in a cloud of dust as the gravel settled around him. He stared at the children already paired, and his gaze tracked to Hana's expression of disbelief. "Traffic!" she said to him and pointed at a truck reversing alongside the front of the steps. "You ran right behind it."

"Chester, come back here!" His mother bumbled towards them, shouting over the warning beep of the delivery truck. She followed his path right behind the vehicle. The driver slammed on the brakes and Hana stared open-mouthed at Wiri.

He shrugged and offered her a knowing smile. "You can't legislate against stupid," he hissed.

Hana rolled her eyes as his words encapsulated pure Logan Du Rose. Chester looked up at her and she offered him her hand. "We don't run across roads or car parks." She recited the familiar mantra and waggled her fingers. "Hold my hand or Mummy's. You choose." He gritted his teeth and slid his hands behind his back.

"Fine." Hana glowered at him in the ten seconds it took his mother to apologise to the irate driver and scurry across the car park. "No hand holding. No scone."

With great reluctance, the child offered his hand, his fingers flinching at her touch. His mother arrived and did a double take at her son's instant obedience and shot Hana a look of admiration.

"Bloody hell!" Hana whispered under her breath, after smiling at her. "It works for your son, but not for Edin. Would you like to swap?"

Hilda glanced sideways at the tiny spitfire and her fingers fluttered in a show of hesitation. Edin chose that moment to narrow her eyes and glare at Hilda. "I'm fine, thanks," she replied. She followed behind the orderly troop as they crossed the car park in safety. Chester withdrew his hand metres from the hotel steps. He gave a definitive shake and escaped, breaking into a run as though unable to control himself anymore. A car spun around the turning circle and headed straight for Hana. Gravel spat from behind its wheels. The sun's rays glanced off the windscreen to obscure the driver's face.

Hana gasped and broke into a run, just reaching the bottom step as the car jetted behind her. She clutched her chest in shock, her jaw slack as she reached Hilda and the other children. Grit spattered her calves as the vehicle sped the wrong way around the circle and shot onto the main thoroughfare. Hana wiped a hand over her lips. "That was too close for comfort," she breathed. The children stared back at her wide eyed as though the near calamity had driven home all the warnings about road safety.

"Are you okay?" Hilda shielded her eyes with her hand and squinted at the blue car heading towards the driveway.

Hana nodded. "Yes, thanks." She forced herself to exude a calm she didn't feel. "Nicely across the reception and up the stairs!" she hissed, issuing the command for Edin's benefit. She saw the child's eyelashes flutter as though batting her instruction away from her. But she obeyed, tugging at Phoenix's hand as she walked stiff-backed up the main staircase towards Leslie's promised baking.

"Are you sure this is okay?" Hilda puffed behind her, using the banister rail to haul herself up the steps. "I don't want to intrude." Laughter issued as a burst of noise from the ballroom, drifting up to surround them. Hilda paused and glanced over the balustrade at the receptionist's bowed head as he spoke to someone in front of the counter. "What was that?" she demanded.

Hana shrugged and gripped Chester's hand. "A conference," she replied over her shoulder. "I can't remember what this session is about. We can check the board on the way out, but I believe it's about the release of new gaming software."

"Oh." Hilda paused and her eyes grew round. "My husband loves gaming." She spoke the sentence as though not sure whether Hana would approve of his hobby.

Hana waited for her as the children walked on ahead. They turned at the first level to continue up to Leslie's apartment and the tantalising scent of scones and bread which wafted from the upper floor. "Tama plays computer games," Hana admitted. She gulped as a sharp pain blossomed out from her heart. "He's one of our older boys."

Chester glanced up at her with a frown, his lower lip bulging into one of discomfort as she gripped his fingers too hard. Hana relaxed her hand and offered him a smile of encouragement. Hilda reached the first floor landing and stared along the wide hallway. Rooms branched off on both sides. "This place is enormous." Her eyes bulged in her face and Hana experienced the familiar sadness begin as a tick in the pit of her stomach. She'd gained many new friends over her years with Logan, most curious but few genuine. After a tour of the Du Rose empire, they faded away with superfluous fodder for the gossips. Her shoulders sank, and she pushed a fake smile onto her face.

"I'll give you a tour before you leave," she offered. Lagging out the inevitable wasn't worth it.

Hilda shook her head. "I've seen most of it. Humphrey and I stayed here for our honeymoon." She arrived alongside Hana. An achingly familiar loneliness sparkled behind her hazel irises. "I'm just here for the company."

"Cake!" Chester interjected. "And cake."

"Okay." Hana exhaled and watched Wiri pause at the top of the next level. He glanced down at her and smiled.

"Come on, Ma," he said, his tone cajoling. "Do you need a push?"

"Push!" Edin turned, with her eyes wide in her elfin features. She fought Phoenix's firm grip on her fingers, battling her to escape. "No!" she yelled at the top of her voice. "No push my mama!"

Hana dropped Chester's hand, willing Hilda to take responsibility for her own child. She powered up the next flight of stairs at a run, catching Edin in her arms and squeezing her tight. "No one will push me," she soothed, whispering into the child's hair. A fragment of the hard surface of her heart crumbled, letting Edin into her inner circle just a little more than she'd intended. "It's all okay," she promised, kissing the damp cheek squashed against her neck. "Hana's okay."

Edin's head popped up, tears sparkling in the corners of her eyes. She tilted her chin downwards and glared at Hana from beneath a ledge of furrowed brow. "Not Hana," she said through gritted teeth. "You my Mama."

49

Curry Comb

Chester preceded Hana up the stairs to Alfred and Leslie's apartment. Hana wasn't sure if it was fear of the unknown or of her displeasure, which kept his fingers gripped around hers. The tantalising scent of baking drove them higher, with Hilda puffing behind them.

Leslie threw open the door at the top of the stairs and Mac beamed up at her. He wrapped his arms around her waist and buried his face in her stomach. She grinned and dipped to kiss the top of his head. "Hot scones!" She clapped her hands and sent a cloud of floury dust spinning into the air. Phoenix coughed as she walked past, halting to give Leslie a dignified side hug. "Poppa Alfie is already at the table waiting for yous all." She flapped her hand towards the dining area and the old man frowning towards the oven.

"We brought guests." Hana winced and looked for approval as she introduced Hilda and Chester. Leslie's gaze passed over them and she greeted them as family.

"Come in, whānau," she trilled. "All are welcome here. Leave your shoes there and wash your hands in the kitchen sink."

Hilda kicked off her low court shoes and Chester wriggled out of his chunky sandals. They left them next to Wiri's, the other children padding barefoot towards the sink and forming an orderly line. Even Edin, Hana noticed as she took her place next to Phoenix.

"School is excellent for her." Hana frowned and jerked her head towards the dark, curly head. "I hate to admit when Logan is right."

Leslie wrinkled her nose and enfolded Hana in a floury embrace. "Let's not tell him," she whispered. She reached into the front pocket of her apron. "I picked up these for you at reception earlier today." Her gnarled fingers produced a handful of envelopes. Hana wrinkled her nose and took them, sifting through with disinterest as she kicked off her sandals. Until the last one, a white envelope with a handwritten label. Her shoulders sank and her mood switched to one of foreboding.

"It's them again," she said with a sigh. "I can't take much more of this."

"Who?" Leslie leaned closer, fighting the distraction of five clamoring, hungry children and a grumbling Alfred.

"It doesn't matter." Hana waved her away with a fake smile. "Please, can I use the bathroom real quick?"

As Leslie hauled hot scones from her whirring oven, Hana slunk past and headed to the bathroom. At the bedroom end of the apartment, it doubled as an ensuite. She locked the interconnecting door and sat on the edge of the bath to tear the envelope. Her fingers shook, and she dropped the other mail onto the bath mat. A type-written notice informed Mr and Mrs Du Rose that because of their unwillingness to negotiate with their client, they had begun a custody action via Oranga Tamariki. Hana groaned and let the letter flutter to the floor, where it landed on top of a power bill and a shareholder notification from CircleLine Holdings Ltd. She cocked her head and stared at it as a random thought percolated through her mind. The warning came from Logan's lawyer and not the usual company. She reached for her phone and dialled Logan's number. When he didn't respond, she left a message on his voicemail.

"Hey babe, we've got another letter from that family's lawyer. But it looks as though they're using Liza's old firm. Isn't that a conflict of interest? Anyway, they've involved social services." She exhaled. "We're at Leslie's now. Mac brought a friend." Her tone lifted during the last sentence. "Yeah," she repeated. "Mac has a friend."

Hana flushed the toilet for effect and collected her mail into a pile. The lawyer's letter dampened her spirits, making her feel as though it forced her head under water. She pushed it within the folds of the power bill and smoothed her dress over her thighs.

"Here you go." Leslie set a plate for her on the table, smacking away Edin's fingers as she lurched for Hana's scone.

"Thanks." Hana stuffed the mail into the nearest school bag and padded to the table. She gazed around at the gathered crowd, forcing an inane smile onto her lips. "Nice?" she said to Chester, and he replied with a serious nod.

"You must have a stunning view of the mountains with the French doors open." Hilda nibbled her scone and pressed an index finger over an escaped sultana.

Alfred blinked and opened his mouth to say something, but Leslie jumped in before he could wreak trauma on the children with a tactless reply. "I don't like the flies when I'm baking," she stated, her tone terse. "Or when we're eating."

"Right." Hilda's gaze slid to the sash window in front of the sink. It gaped like a mouth and the flimsy curtains on either side flapped in the breeze.

Hana's stomach roiled as she lifted the scone to her lips. Butter oozed over the sides and dripped onto her plate. Leslie glared at her. "What's wrong with you, kōtiro? You love my scones." Her eyes narrowed, and she jerked her head towards Hana's stomach. "Unless you have something to tell us."

"I do not!" Hana growled. She bit into the scone and coughed on a loose sultana. Wiri frowned at her and in that moment, she hated his inherited Du Rose perception. His grey eyes sparkled, and she pursed her lips and shook her head at him across the table. She imagined telling him she'd lost custody of Edin and anticipated his reaction. He wouldn't care. He'd shown little affection for his half sibling. It occurred to Hana that he might express relief at his world going back to the way it was before Nev dropped from the balcony just metres away from his chair.

Hana's gaze coasted over the bowed heads to Edin, catching her in the act of licking her plate. The child halted, her tongue elongated and dotted with crumbs. Then she grinned, an eye crinkling expression which lit up her face from a pot of gold hidden within her soul. Hana smiled back, a complicit, shared moment of relief amid a frantic existence. Her right hand squeezed the fabric of her dress in a death grip and she made a silent promise to fight for Caroline's daughter. No matter what.

❧❧❧❧❧ ❧❧❧❧❧

The stockman nodded to Hana as he held the hosepipe over his horse's withers. Edin held her breath and clapped her hands. Wonder filled her eyes. She turned to Hana, her lips parted in wonder. "Washing?"

Hana nodded and dropped to a crouch, speaking to her on her level. "Yes. The horses get hot and tired, just like us. Mr Paulie is giving Sheila a shower."

"Sheila shower." Edin cocked her head. "Sheila shower."

Wiri gave an eye roll of dismissal and crossed the stable yard. "Hey Mr Paulie," he said, approaching the man.

"I wonder if Clara's had her foal yet." Phoenix skipped to a nearby stall and peeked over the half door. Her nose wrinkled in disappointment, but she stayed to greet the rounded muzzle, which rose to sniff her open hand. Leslie followed, not interested in the horses but tagging along through boredom.

"Cobbles." Mac pointed at the rugged floor and Chester grimaced.

"Concrete," he whispered from behind his hand.

Mac shook his head and pointed at the floor again. "Cobbles," he repeated.

Hana winced and did the thing Logan hated. She spoke for her son. "He's telling you, this floor used to be created from rounded pebbles. We have photographs in the museum." She swallowed and smiled at Mac. "Clever boy. You remembered."

Hilda turned her head as she surveyed the stable yard. "I loved horses as a girl." She sounded wistful. "I haven't ridden for years."

"You should come up here sometime," Hana said with a smile. "Lincoln set up a riding school last year. You can come for lessons."

Hilda glanced down at her flouncy skirt. "I've got larger since then." She sighed.

Hana touched her forearm with gentle fingers. "It doesn't matter," she soothed. "There are plenty of horses to choose from."

"Thank you." Tears flooded Hilda's eyes, and she walked closer to Paulie's mare, severing the connection as though finding it painful. He greeted her with an upward jerk of his head, his gaze lingering for long enough to pique Hana's interest. She paused a moment before following her across the yard and finding them already in discussion.

"Sheila. That's an unusual name for a horse." Hilda lifted her right hand and smoothed it along the shining white shoulder. "She's beautiful."

"Bred her myself." Paulie's shoulders pushed back with pride. Life oozed from his otherwise dour expression, and Hana stared at him with curiosity. She expected the conversation to dry up as usual, but it didn't. He pulled a pony nut from his front pocket and held it beneath Sheila's nose. Her hairy lips twitched as she sought it out and crunched with her eyes closed. "I worked for old Mr Du Rose and when Mr Logan took over the farm full time, he gave me Sheila."

"Wow!" Hilda stroked chunky fingers over Sheila's neck. The ring on each of her fingers drew the flesh in to create folds. "He just gave you a horse?"

"Na." Paulie shook his head. "Better than that. He gave me Methuselah's latest foal." He tugged at one of Sheila's white ears, rubbing the tufts of hair beneath work coarsened finger and thumb. "Trained her myself. Best horse I ever rode."

Paulie's smile faded as fast as it appeared. He flicked his head towards the dripping hosepipe, glancing at Hana from beneath his bushy brows. "I best get on with this," he said, his tone returning to its customary dismissal.

"Mama, please, can you lift Chester?" A thud echoed around the yard as Chester's knees clattered against the door of the loose box. Phoenix grunted as she tried to inch him higher. "He wants to see Clara's fat belly."

"Oh, don't hurt yourself!" Hilda jogged to assist her, taking Chester's weight. "He's a big boy for his age."

"He is!" Leslie commented. Her voice echoed around the yard. "I tried to lift him but near snapped my spine. His papa must be a giant."

Hana cringed and diverted her attention away from Hilda's reddening cheeks. Her phone buzzed in her pocket and she drew it out to inspect the screen. This time, she recognised the identification number for the prison. Her fingers slid over the icon to reject the call and she pursed her lips. She muted the sound and stuffed it back into her pocket.

Wiri gave her a worried frown before wandering away to stroke a mare in the round pen. She nibbled at grass poking from beneath the layers of sand.

"Colic." Paulie jerked his head in Wiri's direction. "Linc walked her most of the night. Looking better this morning.

Mr Alfred doused her with his special remedy." The hosepipe sputtered as Paulie released the pressure. Sheila sighed as cold water covered her legs and belly. She lifted a back hoof and kicked at it with lazy strokes and Paulie grumbled something unintelligible.

Hana turned towards the knot of children talking and pointing at Clara's belly over the half door. Her feet remained fixed and unmoving. "Paulie," she began, her tone curious. "Can you tell me about the woman in purple?"

He winced and avoided her gaze as he focussed on the mare. Water trickled through her coat, creating channels on its plunge to earth. "I shouldn't have mentioned it." His tone held a warning. "Spoke without thinking."

Hana turned back towards him, her body stiffening. "Why shouldn't you talk about it?" Tension pressed down on her head and caused her spine to bend beneath its weight. "Tama's missing and this woman is linked."

"I can't help you, Miss." He walked behind Sheila's swishing tail and began washing her other flank.

Temper flared inside Hana's breast. Her fists balled by her sides and she stalked around the horse, giving the shifting feet a wide arc. "You're going to tell me!" she demanded, embarrassed by her bratish tone. "Or you'll tell my husband."

Paulie rose, his hazel irises flashing. He drew himself to his full height and his hand gripped the hose pipe hard enough to diminish the flow. The pressure changed to a dribble, and he didn't notice the water trickling over his boot. "I already told Mr Logan what I know," he said, jutting his whiskered chin forward in defiance. "And I sent him to Mr Alfred. He's the one who told me to forget her in the first place." The horse jerked as he aimed the hosepipe at her forelegs and released the pressure. "I should have said nothing. Now, I've got to get on with this."

"Do you know what she was looking for?" Hana persisted. She ground her teeth against the whine in her voice.

"Dunno, but she didn't find it." Paulie splashed water over Sheila's hocks. "But that's maybe because I found it first."

"What? Found what?" Hana edged closer and water sprinkled her toes. "Please, just tell me."

"Ask Mr Alfred." Paulie's tight tone accompanied a wave of his hand. The hose pipe snaked free and spray soaked Hana's skirt and legs. She edged away from him and ground her teeth in her jaw until it hurt.

Leslie frowned at her tight expression when Hana rejoined them at the stable door. The children marvelled over Clara's rounded stomach and the smaller ones demanded lifting to see into the darkened space. Clara obliged by pushing her head over the door and lipping at the girls' ponytails in search of food.

Inwardly, Hana seethed and turned Paulie's words over in her mind. What the hell did the mysterious woman want from the charred remains of Reuben's life? Her phone vibrated again, and she cringed.

50

Dismount

Hilda dragged Chester back to the car after an hour on the play equipment attached to the camp ground. He didn't want to leave and demanded Leslie walk back to the car park with him. "I'm so sorry," Hilda gushed, gripping Hana's fingers as though in solidarity. "People don't understand how hard it is to have troublesome children, do they?"

"No." Hana exhaled, and her gaze flicked to Edin. The child sat on the see-saw in mid-air with her arms folded in front of her. Horsey's knitted legs bunched in her lap. Mac leaned back and spread his weight onto his bottom, refusing to let her down until she held on with both hands. Hana eyed the silent stalemate with a wince.

"Thank you for not judging me." Hilda swallowed and followed Hana's gaze. "The other mothers don't like Chester. I know they think I'm the problem."

Hana gnawed on her lower lip, Hilda's words acting as an unintentional rebuke. She had judged her too when her obedient children filed from her truck like little angels. Before Edin. "Do they say that about me?" she asked, then wished she hadn't. She waved a hand in the air between them. "Don't answer that. I'd rather not know."

"Well, thank you again." Hilda exhaled as Chester gripped Leslie's fingers and trotted along the path towards the hotel. She followed at a run, her long legs swishing beneath her skirt. Hana stepped onto the playground just as Horsey plunged from Edin's lap and she let out an angry squeal.

"Hold on with both hands," Hana demanded. She scooped up the toy and sniffed his rumpled body. "Horsey needs a bath," she said, with a wrinkling of her nose.

"Me, me!" Edin gripped the see-saw one handed and held out the other for Horsey. Hana placed him back in her lap and looped his long legs around her waist.

"Mac wants you to stay safe," Hana told her, smoothing her ruffled fringe away from her forehead. "He loves you." She frowned at her son and he pushed his weight into his feet, springing from the rubber surface like a ball. Edin dropped from Hana's shoulder height with a squeal of delight.

Leslie reappeared at her elbow. "What's going on?" she demanded.

Hana shrugged. "She wouldn't hold the handle, so Mac suspended her in the air. I don't know whether to tell him off."

"Don't," Leslie concluded. "What else did you want him to do? He couldn't keep himself in the air, could he? The person with their feet on the ground is the one with control."

"Yeah. True." Hana exhaled through her nose. "We need to talk." She seized Leslie's elbow and led her away from the children.

"I didn't do it." Leslie's chins wobbled from side to side even before she'd asked her anything. "Wasn't me." Her body convulsed, and she released a groan hedged with reluctance. "Why are you so damn hard to lie to?" She screwed her eyes closed tight and turned away from Hana.

"What did you do?" Hana's brow furrowed. She sensed her body tipping forward and righted herself. Her feet still edged towards Leslie. "Are you okay?"

Leslie slumped onto a nearby bench with a grunt and flapped her hands in front of her. "Will you tell Logan?" she demanded, her tone laden with defeat.

"Tell him what?" Hana sat next to her, hovering on the edge and leaning forward to study Leslie's expression. "You're frightening me!"

"Chocolate pudding." The old woman hissed through the side of her mouth, and Hana looked around her in surprise. A cool breeze moved through the trees to create a gentle shushing. It lowered the temperature to a more bearable level.

"Where?" she demanded. She reached out and grabbed Leslie's writhing fingers. "Oh no! Is it code for something?"

"What?" Twin vertical lines appeared above Leslie's nose and her jaw hung slack. "Code for what?"

"I don't know!" Hana dropped her hand and flung herself back against the bench. It emitted a creak of protest. "I just needed to ask you something about Antoinette Du Rose."

"Oh! Ohhh." Leslie winced. Her shoulders slumped, and she leaned back to match Hana's stance. She crossed her feet at the ankles. "Ask away, kōtiro."

"What did you think I meant?" Hana narrowed her eyes and glanced sideways at Leslie.

She flapped her hand in dismissal. "Doesn't matter. What do you want to know about Antoinette?"

Hana blew out a breath. "Can you remember Caroline's arrival here? She's older than Logan by a few years, so I know from Phoenix Du Rose's diaries that she lived with Reuben at the house before all the upset."

Leslie shrugged. "Antoinette went north for a few months. She took Nev and Kane with her." She cocked her head and closed her eyes. "Or did she? It's such a long time ago, I can't remember. Maybe she left the boys or only took Kane." Her lips pursed into a thin line and she sighed. "Can't ask either of them now, can we?"

"No." Hana shook her head. "We can't."

"Why does it matter?" Leslie slapped her thighs with her palms and squinted to watch Wiri soar high on a swing.

Hana swallowed and prepared her words with care. "We've had another letter from the lawyer relating to Edin. This other family wants her and they're involving social services. But now they've snagged our lawyer, and I think that means we're out in the cold without legal representation. Caroline doesn't want the other family to have Edin, but it seems the word of a convicted murderer won't count for much in court. I need to understand who they are and ascertain how strong their claim is, then perhaps I can thwart it. The only way to do that is to dig into Caroline's history and work out their familial connection, if there is one."

Leslie shaded her eyes with her right hand. "Why don't you just let the girl go to them? She's a lot of trouble."

Hana swallowed. She weighed Caroline's blackmail threat against her growing love for Edin, and her thoughts stalled. "Lots of reasons," she offered, unable to separate her motivations with any clarity.

"I'll tell you what I know and you fill in the blanks," Hana began. "Phoenix Du Rose believed Antoinette went away to give birth to Caroline. She had an affair with the blond drover who disappeared after she fell pregnant." She blew out a pursed breath. "Jack killed him to protect Reuben's reputation." A surge of heat worked its way from her chest to her forehead, and she leaned forward and brushed her wrist across her brow. "Like he tried to protect Logan's by disposing of me and Mac."

Leslie's soft palm landed on her shoulder and stayed there, offering comfort and solidarity. "Mad old man," she said with a sigh. Her hand moved across Hana's back in a wide arc of gentle rubbing. "But we don't know Jack killed anyone before that Sylvia woman."

Hana released a sigh and continued, not liking the painful foray into the seedier moments of her shared history with Logan. She felt grateful that Leslie skirted the issue of Caroline and Kane sharing the same mother. The pressure lessened in her chest with Leslie's touch and the heat faded by degrees. "Phoenix believed Antoinette left Caroline with the family in the north, but fetched her later when they couldn't cope with her behaviour. But she never accounted for her different surname. I assumed Reuben forgave Antoinette and accepted Caroline, but didn't adopt her. I checked some old photos and Caroline resembles the blond drover. No one remembers his name, but it's a fair guess it was Marsh."

"So what?" Leslie's hand stilled. "How can that help?"

Hana released a groan. "I need to keep hold of Edin. I feel I'm getting somewhere with her after all these months. She doesn't even know these other people. I want to fight for her."

"What does your tāne say?"

Hana twisted her lips. "I haven't told him about this latest letter. He wasn't interested before, but he's stepped up with Edin in the last week and it's made a massive difference to her behaviour." Her gaze flicked to the abundance of curls bouncing up and down on the see-saw. Mac threw his head back, and he cackled like a maniac with every bounce. Two of Horsey's knitted legs dangled across Edin's knees, the others still knotted around her waist. If she pushed aside Caroline's threat, she realised she would have fought for Edin, anyway. She sighed.

"Also, Paulie told me he recovered something from the remains of Reuben's house. But he won't tell me what. He said Logan asked him about it and he sent him to Alfred." She tapped her fingers against the wooden slats of the bench. "Can you find out what it was?"

Leslie rolled her eyes. "You're dumping the problem on me? Gee thanks. He hates talking about Reuben and Miriam."

"I know." Hana patted her fingers in a second of shared empathy. "But you're better at getting things out of him."

Leslie glanced down and used both hands to plump her ample breasts. "I have my ways," she said with a grin. "I'll see what I can do."

"Thanks. I think." Hana winced. "I wondered about calling Liza and asking her advice about the legal stuff." She sat up straighter as she considered her sentence. "That's it! Liza and Caroline were friends. She might have the answers I need."

Leslie recoiled, removing her hand as though afraid of contamination. "Liza got a bad run in the media when Caroline's case hit the front page." Leslie formed air quotes with her fingers. "Woman judge friends with convicted murderer. She won't appreciate you bringing it up again. Maybe ask Logan to phone her. She doesn't fry his ass like she does everyone else's."

"No." Hana shook her head. "I need to figure this part out for myself." She exhaled and drew her phone from her pocket.

Leslie spread her hands out before her. "Why don't you just ask Caroline next time you see her?"

"Logan's cancelled all visits for the next few months." Hana patted the air between them with her hand. "I know it sounds cruel but Edin hates the prison. All the clanging makes her distressed. She spoke to Caroline last night over the phone and Logan said it went well. For the first time in ages, she talked about her mother over breakfast." Hana winced and tilted her head. "Although she referred to her as locked-up-mama and I don't know how to fix that." As if in accusation, her phone vibrated in her pocket again and Hana ignored it.

Leslie shrugged and her dress shivered over her breasts. "That's the choice she made when she killed Nev. Too late crying about it now. She's lucky you took in her pēpi and cared for her. Many wouldn't in your shoes, not after the trouble she caused."

"Can you manage the children for five minutes while I leave a message for Liza?" Hana jerked her head towards the gigglers on the see-saw and extracted herself from Leslie's condemnation.

"Just those two. Wiri and Phoe are fine on the swings." She frowned as her daughter held on with one hand, her Kindle gripped in the fingers of the other. The soles of her sandals scraped against the rubber surface of the playground as she lost herself in the story.

"Fine!" Leslie grumbled. "But I want to hear what she says."

***

Hana made the call, expecting to leave a message for the busy judge. But when Liza answered after the second ring, she faltered and shot Leslie a look of alarm.

"What do you want, Hana?" Liza demanded. Her tone softened. "Unless it's one of the children. Who is this? Is it Wiremu?"

"No, it's me," Hana confessed. She exhaled and then replaced it with a deep breath. "Is Wiri using my phone to call you?" She glanced across at the tousle-haired boy and sighed. "No matter. I thought I'd need to leave a message for you. It took me by surprise when you answered."

"Well! What do you want?" Impatience leached through every syllable.

"It's about Caroline," Hana began. She rushed on ahead to prevent Liza ending the call. "I need some help and some history. And then some advice."

Leslie raised both hands and waggled two sets of crossed fingers at Hana. Then she ruined the effect by using one set to draw a line across her throat.

"That bloody woman!" Liza growled. "Do you know how many messages she's left me just this week?"

"I think I know why." Hana gnawed on her lower lip. "It's not about her conviction. She isn't asking for help with another appeal. Someone is challenging our right to custody of Edin. Logan used his lawyer to flick them off but they aren't losing interest. Now, we're getting letters from the same lawyer. What do you suggest?"

Liza's tone altered as Hana presented her with legal fodder for her quick brain. "Logan uses Rob," she stated. "He's from my old firm. I'll call him."

"Thank you." Relief flooded Hana's muscles, causing her hands to shake. Leslie winked at her before lumbering to her feet and walking towards the see-saw. She grunted as she bent to retrieve a fallen Horsey from the rubberised matting. Hana blinked at the sight of lacy bloomers peeking from beneath Leslie's skirt. "I'd appreciate that," she added in haste. "Because we've received a letter from him acting on their behalf."

"Right." Liza dismissed her with a single word. "I need to go now."

"No, please just listen for one more second," Hana begged. "I want to understand more about Caroline so I can parent Edin." She took a deep breath. Although Liza made no sound on the other end of the call, she counted it as a positive sign she didn't terminate it. "Phoenix Du Rose's diaries claim Antoinette was Caroline's mother. Caroline was a Du Rose long before she married Kane. I'm trying to ascertain whether this family have a familial claim to Edin. We can't fight what we don't understand."

"Just leave it with me," Liza bit. The call ended and another kind of silence rang in Hana's ear.

She groaned and dropped the phone into her lap. Leslie returned to the bench, rocking it as she slumped onto the wooden slats. "She hung up on you?"

Hana rolled her eyes at her observation. "Yeah. But she listened and asked me to leave it with her." She shrugged. "I'm stuck now."

"Then do as she says." Leslie humphed. "She has private detectives at her disposal if she uses them. I imagine there's not much she can't find out if she wants to enough."

Hana cocked her head as a thought came to her. She narrowed her eyes and glared at a cloud bobbing past a lower peak of the mountain. "That's right," she whispered. "So, why isn't she looking for Tama?"

"Does she care about the boy?" Leslie frowned and flicked a fallen rose petal from her skirt. "Does the Honourable Judge Du Rose care about anyone other than herself?"

Hana tilted her head in thought. "Yes. I think she has a soft spot for Tama. He missed a meeting with her and she turned up at his house." She fingered her phone screen and winced. "Do you think I should risk calling her back and asking her for more help?"

Leslie's eyes bugged, and she waggled her head from side to side. "Wait until she calls you about Caroline and then slip it into the conversation."

Hana snorted. "Do you think she realises we're all so afraid of her?"

"Oh, yes," Leslie replied with a sigh. "She banks on it."

The children played for a while before Hana corralled them into the truck. Leslie walked around the vehicle, pressing kisses to foreheads through the open doors. Except Edin. The child resisted, turning her face away and squeezing her features into a twisted knot. "Suit yourself," Leslie grumbled and slammed the door. A wail ensued as Edin changed her contrary mind.

"Tell me about the chocolate pudding." Hana turned her back so Mac couldn't read her lips and Leslie matched her pose, leaning against the truck. Edin's wail grew louder, punctuated by a rebuke from Wiri.

Leslie pursed her lips into a line. "Alfie fancied a snack late one night. I let myself into the kitchen and took a chocolate pudding from the chiller."

Hana turned to face her. "You still have a master key?"

"So?" Leslie bridled and her chins wobbled as she bent her elbow and placed her right hand over her hip. "I didn't know there would be an inquisition over a bloody pudding!"

"Right." Hana's eyes widened at a memory of a half absorbed story via Logan. It related to missing food from the kitchen and she'd paid it little attention at the time. "*That* chocolate pudding." She winced. "I'd give Logan the key real fast if it was me. The hotel manager kicked up a big fuss. I think he accused the stockmen of helping themselves after hours." She wagged a finger at Leslie. "But nobody suspected you."

Leslie snuffed out a heavy breath. "I'll think of something." Rapid blinking highlighted her sense of guilt.

Hana stood up straighter. "Does that master key open Logan's office?"

"No!" Leslie raised a bushy eyebrow.

Hana slumped back against the truck. "And you know that because you've tried?" She cackled at the guilty silence and Leslie bristled next to her.

"You have a low opinion of me kōtiro." She turned, her sensible sandals grating against the gravel. Her brown irises glittered. "What do you need from his office?"

Hana shrugged and pursed her lips. "Just stuff." Her mind flicked to the laden shelves and the potential for more inflammatory diaries to have slipped between the accountancy and business books. She swallowed, knowing she had bigger issues in that moment.

Her phone rang, and she jumped. Mac laughed at her reaction and pointed. Edin screwed her head around to watch as Hana fumbled the phone up to her ear. "Hello, Hana Du Rose speaking." She opened her mouth to continue her polite greeting before Liza barked at her.

"I know who you are, you moron. That's why I called you."

Hana winced and rolled her eyes at Leslie. The old woman shifted sideways as though it might distance her from Liza's bile. "Hi," she managed before clamping her teeth down over her bottom lip.

"First," Liza snarled, "Leave Tama alone. He doesn't need your molly-coddling." Hana opened her mouth to speak and

Liza rode right over her ineffectual squeaks. "Second, the family coming after you are called Alderbank. Clive and Lana. Father and daughter actually, so not a couple. I spoke to Caroline, and she asked you to keep hold of her kid. She says the daughter got in touch after her engagement to Logan made the Auckland society pages. They've stayed friends on Faceache and had a few conversations. When Caroline lost name suppression during the court case, Lana wrote to her at the remand centre and asked questions about the child. There's some kind of shit storm brewing. Stay out of it. I've instructed a different lawyer to look into the relationship. He's good but busy for the next few weeks. Rob apologised for the mix up but his clerk agreed he'd advocate for the Alderbanks. Anyway, Oranga Tamariki can't just take the child away from you when you have legal guardianship."

Before Hana could respond, the call ended and her phone screen darkened. She turned to face Leslie with a disgusted expression. The other woman slithered further away from her. "You've got a face like a slapped ass," she muttered.

Hana exhaled a huff and ground her teeth. "Why does she always have to stick the knife in to the hilt?" she spat. Slipping her phone into her pocket, she pushed herself upright and glared at Leslie. "And how come Logan's engagement to Caroline made the Auckland society pages and mine didn't?"

51

Saddle bag

Leslie snorted. "That's all you got from her thirty second rant?" She gave a visible shudder which seemed to rock every mound of spare flesh. "Caroline made the society pages, and you didn't?" She waggled her bushy eyebrows. "You didn't have an engagement and you got married in secret."

"So?" Hana stuck her chin in the air. "Liza had lots more to say. But that particular part offended me the most." Her lips flattened into a snooty line. "And she thinks Facebook is called Faceache."

Leslie shrugged. "Wouldn't know. Don't have it."

Hana turned to watch the children messing around in the back of the truck. Edin leaned sideways to hold Mac's hand across the empty seat between them. Phoenix perched on the pull down seat in the boot with her nose in her story. Wiri slumped in the front, inspecting his eyebrows in the vanity mirror. Hana exhaled. "Have you ever heard the name Alderbank?" She narrowed her eyes and studied Leslie for any sign of recognition.

"No. Yes." Leslie frowned. "Maybe."

"Which is it?" Hana jerked her chin forward.

"It sounds kinda familiar in a distant way." Leslie waved to the children and moved away from the truck. "I'll talk to Alfie. He might remember." She glanced up at the sky and flapped her hand at an ominous cloud gobbling up the sunshine. Grey and foreboding, it promised rain. A heavy drop pinged off the end of Hana's nose and she roused herself.

"Thanks," she called to Leslie.

Hana pulled open the driver's door and settled behind the steering wheel. She fired up the engine and eased the truck up the driveway towards home. The rain grew more enthusiastic with each passing kilometre until Hana's wiper blades formed a blur across the windscreen.

Half way up the mountain, Hana caught a flash of blue ahead of her. The swish of the wipers revealed a small car careening towards them around the worst of the uphill bends. It moved at speed on the steep camber and Hana jammed her foot on the brake. She released a squeak of terror as her seatbelt tightened across her chest and ribs. Wiri yelped as, still fiddling with his left brow in the mirror, he jabbed himself in the eye. Horsey flew forward and hit the back of Hana's seat, his knitted legs flicking over the head rest and whipping her cheek. Edin gave a growl of fury at his desertion from her knee.

The long driveway wasn't wide enough to carry two vehicles side by side, but the blue car showed no sign of giving way to Hana's larger truck. It edged closer, two wheels moving onto the narrow grass verge bordering the asphalt. It headed for them on the wrong side of the lane. Empty space yawned beside Hana's door as the sheer drop threatened them. She jabbed at the switch to lower the passenger window, putting out her hand and shouting a warning. "Stop!" she yelled. "There isn't room!"

She held her breath as the car squeezed past her, the low roof trim brushing her fingers. Its wing mirror collapsed against the other driver's side window with the force of the first impact, but still scraped a groove along Hana's passenger door with its tip. It gouged the paintwork from front to back, trapping Wiri in his seat as metal ground against metal. A crack and a ping betrayed the moment the mirror detached from the vehicle in a shower of reflective glass and shattered plastic. Hana closed her eyes and covered her face with her hands, expecting at any moment to feel her truck sliding over the precipice to her right. The roar of the other car's engine told her it had bounced back onto the driveway behind her and continued its journey.

"Shit!" Wiri exclaimed. "Did you see that?"

"Of course she saw it!" Phoenix shouted from the back of the truck. Hana glanced up to catch sight of her daughter's frightened face in the rear-view mirror. "How did she manage not to push us over the side?"

"I know!" Wiri turned in his seat. "She must have driven on two wheels like one of those trick drivers."

Rain pelted the truck's roof as Hana swallowed and turned to face him. "She? What do you mean? Did you see the driver?"

"I did." Phoenix unclipped her belt and clambered over the back seat. She landed with a plop between Mac and Edin. Her fingers shook as she retrieved Horsey from the foot well where he'd fallen and placed him back into Edin's arms. "A woman driver. Blonde hair. I think I've seen her before today."

"Where?" Hana demanded. "When?"

"At school." Phoenix licked her lips and glanced at Wiri. "Watching us. You invited Hilda and Chester back to Nonie's for scones and she glared at you and stamped away to the car park."

Hana shook her head and blinked. "She's a school mum? What's her child's name?"

Phoenix shrugged and pursed her lips, shock rising as sparkles in her grey irises. She rubbed at her left arm. "I hurt myself when you stopped, Mama. I banged my arm on the back of Edin's seat and dropped my Kindle on my foot."

"I'm sorry," Hana gushed. She peered through the windscreen at the strange angle at which she'd halted their ascent. A steady stream of water trickled along a drainage ditch beneath her driver's side wheels. The emergency stop left her slewed across the driveway and she marvelled at how the other driver had passed them without hitting the jutting bank. She exhaled and examined her shaking hands. "I'll check you out when we get up to the house." She half turned in her seat. "But who's her child, Phoe? Do you know them?"

Phoenix shook her head. "She never has a kid with her."

"You've seen her more than once?" Hana regretted the alarm in her voice as Phoenix recoiled with a silent nod. Her cheek bumped the side of the seat and flared with heat at the welt from Horsey's flying hooves.

"Yes." Phoenix gulped. "I saw her on Friday and today."

Once at the house, Hana didn't begin the usual homework routine, allowing the children to slob in the lounge and watch a Disney movie while eating snacks. Sympathy and an ice pack satisfied Phoenix. She sat at the kitchen table and examined the blue bruise on her left arm.

"Leave the ice on it," Hana ordered. "Stop taking if off to admire the bruise." She stopped in the process of gathering snacks into a bowl for each child and narrowed her eyes. "How did you hurt your arm, anyway? That truck has more safety features than anything else available."

Phoenix studied the ice pack with increased interest, her body stiffening as Hana waited. "Okay, so I might have sat sideways with my legs on the seat," she admitted.

Hana groaned. "Please tell me you still wore your belt?"

"Yes, I promise." Phoenix widened her grey eyes and blinked, perhaps hoping to lessen Hana's ire with an impression of puppy-dog-innocence. She wrinkled her nose. "I hate the back seat. I liked it better when no one had to sit there." Before Edin.

The rebuke carried through the words she didn't say. Hana's shoulders slumped in defeat and she continued loading junk food into the bowls.

"Is Papa coming home early?" Phoenix perked up and the ice pack slipped away from the bruise. "Did you tell him what happened?"

"I don't know and yes, I told him about the accident."

"It wasn't an accident." Phoenix recoiled and her chin disappeared into her shirt collar. "She rammed us."

Hana winced as she fought to down play the incident. "The air bags didn't deploy with such a tiny bump. Perhaps she thought she could squeeze past us."

"What was she doing at our house, anyway? Did you check the post box?" Phoenix rose. "Can I see if she left something for us?"

"No!" The word emerged in a rush and Phoenix frowned, seeing right through Hana's feigned calm. "It's raining too hard." She jerked her head towards the ice pack. "And you're hurt. Go into the lounge and cuddle up on the sofa. I'll bring the snacks."

After a second's hesitation, Phoenix padded from the kitchen. Hana heard the other children demanding to examine her war wounds. A scrap broke out as Edin and Mac both tried to sit next to her and Wiri's voice rose as he adjudicated.

Hana's phone vibrated on the counter and she snatched it up and held it to her ear. A glance at the open kitchen door meant she dismissed the option of activating the speaker. "Hey babe." Her voice wavered as she answered her husband's greeting. "Did you see anything on the house cameras?"

"Yeah." The tightness in Logan's voice sent tension sparking through Hana's spine. "Not enough to warrant calling the cops, but she left her vehicle at the gate and walked around the house on foot. I can't see her registration plate to get an identification but I'll check your dash camera when I get home. Once I have that, I can get an address and start from there. She's blonde, thin and dressed in a business suit. She pressed the bell and knocked on the door for a while before peering through all the windows."

Hana exhaled. "Don't hold out too much hope for my dash cam footage. I had the wiper blades running at full pelt."

Logan sighed and Hana closed her eyes and imagined him wrapping his arms around her. "We'd just got the first mob drenched and out to the lower slopes when the heaven's opened," he said. "I'm wearing my spare clothes from the office because I got drenched. But it filled the creek enough to get us through to the autumn, so I can't complain."

Hana swallowed and resented the weakness in her voice. "Do you think you could leave a bit early tonight?"

"I don't know." His voice seemed louder and Hana jumped as he leaned against the kitchen door frame and continued speaking into his phone. "I guess I could." He killed the call and smiled at her. "I came in through the side door. Can't see anything amiss, but she touched nothing."

Hana laid her phone on the counter and forced herself to take measured steps across the tiles. Logan's muscles tightened as he enfolded her, cradling the back of her head in his left hand. He kissed her forehead as she tilted her face to look up at him. "What about fingerprints from the windows or the front door?"

Logan snuffed out a shallow breath. "What forensics team will be interested, sweetheart? She didn't commit a crime at the house. Let me look at the dash cam footage and see what I can get from that."

Hana nodded and pressed her nose against his tee shirt. Her right hand snaked beneath the hem until her palm coasted over his soft skin. A familiar ridge of scar tissue caught against her fingers and she sighed, knowing each dip and blemish by heart.

"Yey! Papa!" Phoenix strutted through the kitchen doorway and her lips parted into a wide grin. She wrapped her good arm around her father and turned her mouth down into a pout. "I'm injured," she declared, waving her ice pack in the air.

"So, I see."

"Can I check the post box to see if the lady left us something?"

Logan snorted. "She left two dented wings and a shredded bumper." He raised his hand to forestall her objection. "The box is empty, but it's academic. All our post goes to the hotel."

"Academic." Phoenix tasted the unfamiliar word. "What does that mean?"

"Ma's giving us snacks instead of dinner." Wiri appeared, glancing at the bowls and then back at Hana in a silent rebuke for her tardiness. "We're starving."

"Are you?" Logan waggled his eyebrows and grinned at Hana. "How about you give her a hand, then it might come quicker."

As though sensing they might miss out, Mac and Edin barrelled through the kitchen door. Mac made a beeline for his father. "Papa!" He squeezed between Hana and Phoenix and wrapped his arms around one of Logan's legs.

"Papa!" To Hana's surprise, Edin wedged herself into the melee, dragging Horsey with her. His woolly brown hooves trailed along the tiles, his resigned expression peeking from beneath Edin's left armpit. She wound her arms around Logan's other thigh and Hana stepped back in surprise.

Phoenix emitted an impatient huff which dissipated at speed as Wiri carried two bowls of snacks past her nose. She scurried behind him, dumping the dripping ice pack on the kitchen table.

"Oooh!" Edin froze and lifted her index finger. She widened her eyes at Mac and they both listened to something only she registered. But he trusted her enough to follow as she set off at a run towards the rustling of a crisp packet.

"Yours are here," Hana said. She raised her voice to draw them back to her before handing out their respective bowls. Edin frowned as she inspected Mac's and then her own. Satisfied of their equality, she followed him from the room.

Logan sank into a chair and patted his thighs. Hana sat on his knee and draped her arms around his neck. "Aren't you flavour of the month then?" she grumbled. "I'm demoted to cook, chauffeur and chief toilet cleaner."

Logan smiled up at her. His fingers pressed against her spine to draw her closer. "I'm glad you're okay," he said, his tone thoughtful. "I can't face a life without you."

Hana gave a visible shudder. "Can you check the dash cam video?"

"I've got the memory card here." Logan leaned back and dug his fingers in his jeans pocket. I'll download the footage onto my laptop and review it."

Hana frowned. "How did you get into my truck?"

"Because someone didn't lock it." Logan flattened his lips and wrinkled his nose. His expression held no rebuke but Hana mentally kicked herself as she groaned.

"Sorry! What an idiot! A woman followed me to school, snooped around the house and picked a fight with my truck on a mountain track. So, I leave the vehicle unlocked for her to come back and do whatever she likes to it."

"She didn't." Logan grabbed Hana's flapping hands and drew them against his chest. "I checked the house cameras on my phone app when I found your truck unlocked. Stop being so hard on yourself. It looked like chaos just getting all the kids out and through the front door."

Hana sighed. "It was. You're certain the police won't be interested?"

"Positive. Unless I can find something on your dash camera, and then it's just reckless driving on private land. I don't think that's even an offence. But I'd like a good image of her registration number."

Hana frowned. "Okay. Hey, did Paulie tell you any more about the woman he saw at the fire site?"

"He noticed her a couple of times. He said she always wore something purple, a jacket or a scarf. She stood and watched them clearing away the rubble. He thinks the digger driver caught her going through the skip one day and threatened to call the cops. She didn't come back after that." He ran a hand over his face. "Paulie said he told Alfred, but she didn't return, so he forgot about it. I'll talk to Alfie next time I see him. He's unhappy with me for putting Methuselah permanently out to grass."

"And what did you do with Colin the private detective?" She narrowed her eyes and studied his reaction. "Promise me I won't trip over his body when I peg out the washing?" She groaned. "Oh crap, the washing. I need to get it back in before dark."

Logan's grey irises glittered like diamonds and a vein in his cheek twitched. "We let him go, but he won't come back here in a hurry."

"You're very calm." Hana leaned back and stared at him through narrowed eyes. "What aren't you telling me?"

Logan raised his right eyebrow and his lips parted to speak. But a squeak from the lounge heralded an argument over the snack food.

"Yuk!" Phoenix's voice rose over all the rest. "Mama! Edin's hiding her chocolates behind the sofa cushions."

"She's licking them first!" Wiri added, his tone indignant.

Hana's shoulders slumped. "Whatever made me think I'd be a better parent second time around?" she said with a sigh. "You deal with the miscreants, and I'll fetch the washing."

52

Anti-sweat rug

Torrential rain reflecting off the windscreen made the dash cam footage useless. It detected the blue streak of movement amid the trailing drips, followed by Hana's panicked maneuver. Then the rocking of the truck as the other car scraped alongside it.

"It's a Suzuki Swift." Logan frowned and zoomed in on the image of the blue streak. "Look at the body shape."

Hana peered over his shoulder, reliving the pelting of the rain on the truck roof and the taste of danger. "She could have pushed us over the side of the mountain," she said, her tone laden with dread. "If she wanted to see us so badly, why run when she met us on the road? Why not pull over and have a conversation with me?"

"I don't know." Logan's quick fingers pulled up a Google search, and he showed Hana a static image of a Swift. "Did you see a blue car like that in the school car park?"

Hana nodded. "I think so. Phoe definitely did." She tapped her lips with her index finger. "So, she came to school but didn't speak and then drove to the house, walked around it and crashed into me to avoid contact on the way down the mountain. If she followed us home from school, she'd know we went into the hotel." She inhaled with enough force to make Logan jump. "The hotel! Check the cameras there. It's possible she tried to mow me down in the car park. I didn't see the driver's face. But the high camera should get the registration number, shouldn't it? I figured it was an accident but it might have been deliberate."

"Yeah." Logan twisted his lips. "But it also means she drove to the house while knowing you were elsewhere. She's watching you but doesn't want contact. If I get the reggo number, we can find out her name and address. Do you think Bodie might help?"

Hana winced. "Not without a crime number. He won't do anything to jeopardise his career and all their systems are tracked. He's lodged the missing persons forms for Tama, so perhaps he can link the two incidents." She clicked her fingers. "That reminds me, I spoke to Liza today. She said Tama's fine and I should leave him alone."

Logan wrinkled his nose. "Does that mean she knows where he is?" He frowned up at Hana. "Do you need me to call her?"

"No." Hana sighed. "She got cross with me. The Alderbanks have somehow hijacked our lawyer so he can't act for us anymore. Liza said she'd find us someone else. Can we look at the hotel footage now?" She slumped onto the sofa next to her husband. Trying to deal with more than one problem at a time fritzed her mind. "While the children are quiet."

Logan shook his head. He slipped an arm around her shoulders. "I'll need to go down the mountain. It's all run from a server in the administrator's office." He yawned. "I'll drive down after the kids go to bed."

"No, don't." Hana turned sideways on the sofa and rested her cheek against his chest. "You're tired and you're teaching tomorrow. And if she pulls that stunt on the lane again, you'll be the one going over the cliff." She tilted her head to stare up at him. "Do you think we should invest in some crash barriers for those bends? Wiri will learn to drive in a few years' time.

"Maybe." Logan yawned again and stretched. "I'm not at the school this week, remember? The seniors went on their leadership camp yesterday. The Year 12s have a careers week."

"Can I admit to feeling relieved?" Hana exhaled, and the tension left her spine. "Do you have farm work to do?"

"I thought if this rain stops, you might ride with me." He kissed the top of her head. "What do you think?"

"I think a gallop would cheer me up heaps," Hana admitted.

"Mama?" Phoenix appeared in the doorway, Hana's phone gripped in her fingers. "Nonie wants you."

❧❧❧ ❧❧❧

"A box?" Hana held the phone away from her ear as Leslie shouted the words. They echoed around the hallway. "Where are you?"

"On the roof. It's windy." Clattering bisected the sentence as the speaker tried to cut out the background noise. "Moving some plant pots nearer to the stairs. Alfie's struggling with the hose pipe when he waters them."

Hana exhaled with impatience. "Why are you doing it at this time of night? Logan doesn't want another angry phone call from the manager when the guests complain! Wait until tomorrow and I'll move them for you when I come to the museum." She swallowed and pushed aside her guilt. Will sent her a text earlier asking if she still wanted to work there or if he should advertise her role to attract someone who might show up occasionally.

"Almost finished." Leslie grunted and leaned sideways to shout at Alfred. "Put it over there hon. No, not there, over there."

Hana's eyes widened at the sight of her son streaking across the doorway. His pink buttocks wobbled as he ran. Phoenix's voice lifted alongside a snort of laughter from Wiri. "Mama! Mac's nakey again! Tell him! I don't want to see all his low hanging fruit!"

"Hahaha!" Wiri's side-splitting guffaw distracted Hana, and she moved towards the doorway. "Low hanging fruit," he chortled.

"Put some clothes on, son." Logan's baritone rumbled from along the hallway and Hana halted and turned away from the trouble. Footsteps followed Mac to his bedroom, and the one sided discussion continued. "Not everyone wants to see that, mate."

"Why did you mention a box?" Hana sank onto the sofa and winced as a Lego train driver dug into her left hip. She retrieved it and waited for Leslie to stop berating Alfred for his abuse of her marigolds.

"You asked me to check with Alfie about the fire site!" Indignation filtered through Leslie's voice. "So, I asked him. Paulie found a charred metal box where the shed used to be and he took it to Alfie. He mentioned a woman turning up to the site each day and compromising their health and safety protocols."

"Health and safety protocols." Hana repeated the sentence with a snort. Only Logan cared about the legalities of the business, herding his employees into some semblance of order while knowing they ignored him as soon as he stopped watching them. Miriam's death and Phoenix's birth had sidelined him from much of the demolition process. Alfred dealt with it.

"Yes," Leslie continued, sounding indignant on her husband's behalf. "They wore hard hats and steel toe caps because they pulled a lot of the remains down by hand. Alfie installed a chain across the bottom of the driveway and padlocked it. Paulie said the woman walked up the mountain once after that but they'd levelled everything and trucked out the remnants. He threatened to call the cops if she came back, but she didn't."

"Charred metal box." Hana mused over the words and stared at a blank spot on the ceiling. "Does Alfie know where it went?"

"Alfie!" Leslie didn't pull the phone away from her ear. "Where'd the box go after Paulie gave it to you?"

Hana strained to hear his reply but couldn't quite make out the sentence. Leslie huffed into the device, creating the effect of white noise in Hana's ear. "He said they couldn't open it. The lid twisted in the fire and they figured everything inside melted, anyway. Alfie moved to Jack's." Leslie paused and Hana's chest tightened. "Sorry, but he did. And then he came back here, so it's lost in transit."

An overhead clap of thunder shook Hana's house and reverberated through the phone as it echoed over the hotel. "Ooh," Leslie remarked. "Talk tomorrow."

Hana let the phone drop into her lap and narrowed her eyes at the rain pelting against the darkened lounge windows. Lightning flickered over the black outline of the Tasman Sea in the distance. She closed her eyes and remembered where she'd seen the box, without knowing how she'd liberate it from its hiding place in plain sight.

53

Bar

At the first opportunity the next morning, Hana used the laptop to research the Alderbank family. She hid in the bathroom in her underwear; the door locked to ensure a few moments of peace.

"Mama! I need you!" Phoenix called from behind the door. The handle jiggled beneath her frenzied grappling. "I can't find my sports kit. Mr Whitehead will give me a detention."

"Garage. Already in your bag." Hana tensed and listened to her daughter's feet padding away. She exhaled and performed another Google search. Alderbank appeared to be an Auckland name, but the online telephone directory contained four pages of relevant searches. Hana switched to social media instead, scrolling through the various profile images attached to anyone with that surname. "Why do so many people use cats as their pictures?" she grumbled.

A Google search with keywords suggested by the algorithm threw up a news article from ten years earlier. A smiling grey-haired man posed with the prime minister of the time. Hana frowned as she read the headline. *"Free trade agreement with Beijing,"* she read. She scrolled further into the article. *"Successful salvage magnate, Clive Alderbank assisted with the modernisation of the 2008 bilateral free trade treaty provision."* Hana growled in her throat. "Well, it can't be anything to do with the same people then, can it?"

"Hana?" A sharp rap on the door made her jump. "Are you almost ready? The children are getting edgy."

"Yeah, I'm coming." She logged out of the laptop and closed the lid. "Please, can you make sure Wiri has his sandwiches today? He keeps forgetting on purpose so he can get cooked lunches. It's costing me a fortune when they bill at the end of the term. I've told his teacher he needs to go hungry next time."

"Yep." Logan's steps moved away from the door, and Hana left the bathroom. She slipped the laptop beneath the bed and put her investigation on hold.

Her phone buzzed on the nightstand and she tensed. The prisoner identification number bloomed on the screen and she held her breath. Caroline had gone to great lengths to call her each time and guilt blossomed as heat in Hana's chest as she sent her to voicemail again. An alert popped up on the screen, but she doubted the inmate had left a message. She hadn't the other ten times either.

The threat against Isobel had played in her mind and caused her to lose sleep. The last thing she wanted was another conversation with a woman who used blackmail as a weapon against someone who'd shown her kindness. "Narcissist!" Hana spat and turned her phone face down on the mattress. The force of the action nudged an abandoned cup of tea on the nightstand as she flapped her hand. Liquid dribbled down the side of the mug to leave a wet ring on the wood.

She groaned as the phone vibrated again, the floral bedspread muting its pitiful whir for attention. Hana grabbed a tissue and mopped up the spill, grinding her teeth and ruing the moment Caroline took her generosity and wrapped it around her neck with a threat.

***

"I don't want to be late! Ooh, Mama!" Phoenix halted in the open doorway to the bedroom, her brother hot on her heels. She gasped and pointed at Hana's underwear. "You're showing your kuruhope!" As Mac tried to peek around her, she clapped her hands over his eyes. "No, Macky!" She pushed him backwards out of the room. "Mama's got her booty out." His pink feet crossed over each other and he listed backwards at a dangerous angle.

Hana grunted as she hauled her jeans over the uncomfortable black thong. She'd wiggled into the lacy thing with difficulty, putting it on backwards at the first attempt. Squatting a few times, she tested her ability to sit without sending the flimsy crotch into all the wrong places. "It's fine!" she called, snatching up the delicate blouse she'd selected from her wardrobe. "He can come back in. What's the matter?" She swore as her head became stuck in the neck of the flouncy fabric. Wide cuffs flowed from a nipped wrist and hindered her as she twirled on the spot.

"What are you doing?" Phoenix demanded. Her brother escaped her protection and bounced onto the bed. He cocked his head and pointed at Hana with a frown before spreading his hands in confusion.

"I didn't factor in the push-up-bra," Hana grumbled from within the white folds. "My boobs have ended up higher than I anticipated."

Cool fingers touched her spine as Phoenix tugged on the hem of the blouse. A moment later, Hana's head popped free, and she gave her daughter a grateful smile. "Thanks. I knew you'd come in handy." She straightened the bottom of the blouse and assessed her cleavage with a critical eye.

"Where did you get that strange boobie holder?" Phoenix pointed to her own chest in a delicate stabbing action with her index finger.

"I've owned it for years." Hana peered at her dishevelled hair in the mirror and winced. "When I worked at the school."

"Ohhhhh." Phoenix sank onto the mattress next to her brother. "Before your boobies looked like spaniel's ears."

Hana's jaw dropped open, and she hurt her neck, staring down at the perky breasts bulging from inside the bra's scaffolding. "Rude!" she sighed.

Mac signed something to Phoenix in her peripheral vision and his sister shrugged. "I'll ask," she signed back. "Mama?" Her tone became wheedling and Hana tensed. "Did you say Edin could have five chocolate bars in her packed lunch?"

"No!" Hana loosened another button on her blouse to display a little of her newly acquired cleavage. "Five things, which include sandwiches, fruit and crisps. Tell her to put them back in the fridge."

"Okay." Phoenix's grey irises glittered with a dangerous heat. She held her chin rigid as she flounced from the mattress on extra light steps. She fluttered her left hand towards her mother. "I can see your undies through your shirt."

"Yes, thanks for that." Hana didn't add that was her intention. She squatted in the jeans and thong again and Mac giggled. He bounced from the bed and copied her, bunny hopping across the room and into the hall. Screams emitted from the kitchen as Phoenix raided Edin's lunch box.

The fray delayed Hana's exit as she confiscated the extra chocolate and hid it on the top shelf of the pantry. They got half way down the mountain before Wiri remembered his sandals. "I got told off for bare feet yesterday," he grumbled. "Mr Duggan said we need to wear shoes or sandals in the junior classes."

"I always wear mine." Phoenix stuck her left foot between the front seats and dangled it in Wiri's face. "I'm ready for juniors."

She cocked her head and wiggled the errant foot again. "Kiss my foot." She giggled.

Wiri gave a visible shudder and shoved it away with a frown. "No," he protested. "Kiss my..." A sideways glance from Hana halted the alternative on his lips.

"Tiss mine." Edin pushed her bare foot on top of Phoenix's and another set of pink toes belonging to Mac twinkled against her knee. Phoenix giggled and dropped her leg, taking the others with her like a complicated game of toe-Jenga.

"Behave." Hana sighed at herself in the rear-view mirror. Her anticipated ride with Logan had left her rattled. She craved time with her husband, hoping for long conversations and romance. But a voice in her head counselled against disappointment should she find herself digging holes for fence posts or galloping across country at a break neck speed to admire a new track.

She frowned at her daughter's reflected face, her lips raised in a grin. A yellow glow from the already high sun cut a swathe of light across Phoenix's left eye to make her squint. "Why are you sitting between those two?" Hana demanded. She did a double-take at Wiri, slouching in the passenger seat. "Hang on, it's your turn in the back today, isn't it?"

"I don't mind." Phoenix's expression softened as Wiri turned his head to smile at her. "The little ones don't fight with me in the middle. And I wanted to give you this." She lifted a ratty woollen object from her lap and dangled it between the seats. "Here you go, Mama." Wiri took it from her as she leaned forward and pushed it into his hand.

Hana slowed on the steep downward and glanced sideways at the old blue cardigan as he held it across to her. "I don't need that, thanks." She shoved it out of the way as she changed down the gears for a sharp bend. "The forecast is for another hot day."

Wiri's lips flattened into a line of uncertainty. His eyes widened, and he jerked his head at Hana's torso. "I think you should take it," he said, his voice wavering. "It might stop your thingies from escaping."

Hana switched on the VHF radio as they neared the bottom of the driveway and male voices filled the truck.

"What's wrong?" Wiri frowned across at her. He dropped the cardigan into his lap and his long fingers rested over it. "Why are you listening to the stock hands' sitreps?"

Hana shrugged. "I'm trying to work out where everyone is."

"Why?"

Voices crackled as the workers checked in for their eight o'clock situation reports. Hana counted the men off in her head as they gave their locations. They kept their conversations short.

"Toby went to Auckland." Phoenix pursed her lips. "So, at least he won't see your boobies." She rolled her eyes at Hana in the mirror. "I hope you're not seeing Pastor Sam dressed like that, young lady." She mimicked Leslie's tone to perfection.

"I'm riding with your father today." Hana's stomach gave a skip of excitement and she tamped down her enthusiasm. The radio conversation told her the men were already out, which meant she'd get Logan to herself.

"Ouch." Phoenix winced. She reached into the school bag at her feet, knocking Mac's legs aside to fumble in its depths. "I thought of that too." She raised her hand and a pair of Hana's most raggedy grey knickers dangled from her fingers. The breeze from Hana's open window caused them to rise like a sail. "I don't want a call from the hospital when you split your difference."

"Put those away!" Hana squeaked. She steered onto the grass verge and stopped as a campervan lumbered alongside her. A man lowered his window and thanked her in cheery German.

"Bitte sehr," she replied, her tone strangled. She snatched the knickers from Phoenix's outstretched fingers and jammed them behind her spine. Her foot slipped on the clutch and the truck stalled. The man frowned, and the camper rolled away towards the hotel.

"They're not supposed to go that way," Wiri commented. He screwed his head around to peer through the back window.

"They missed the sign for the camp ground entrance. We should tell them."

"Nope." Hana restarted the truck and bumped it back into the lane. "Nope, nope, and nope." She picked up speed and made it to town in record time.

The school car park buzzed with traffic and pedestrians as parents spat their children from moving vehicles. A hatchback blocked the exit as a mother screamed at her child in a high-pitched wail over an unknown infraction. Hana tapped on the steering wheel and frowned. "I might have to abandon the truck and we'll run in real quick." She tugged on the handbrake and seatbelts clicked as an echo in the resulting silence.

"I don't think you should run anywhere today." Phoenix bugged her eyes and shuffled aside as Edin bounced from her seat without permission. "You should walk. Very slowly and carefully."

Wiri glanced at her chest and swallowed. He shoved the cardigan over her blouse buttons and waited until she caught hold of it. His name hailed from a nearby vehicle as a blond boy emerged and slammed the rear door. A ball rolled between his legs as he headed towards them. "Come on! We need a goalie."

"Please, don't get out." Wiri struggled to maintain eye contact as his gaze drifted to her shirt and up again. "Phoenix can take the little ones into school." He turned in the seat and his eyes emitted a silent plea. "Can't you?"

"Okay." Phoenix pushed the door next to Mac and hopped down first. She held out her arms to him and he filed into her capable hands.

"Oh." Hana felt the rejection as the stab of a slender blade. "What about kisses? And I need to see your teachers about that lady in the blue car. She's not allowed to hang around the school if she doesn't have children there. You mustn't speak to her. She tried to hurt us."

"I'll tell the teachers everything." Wiri pointed to Hana's cleavage. "You keep your rude parts inside the vehicle."

Edin rammed her head between the seats, and Hana pressed her lips to her forehead. On the ground, Mac turned to enable Phoenix to settle his lunch bag on his back. Hana kissed Edin's head again. "Pass that on to Mac?" she asked her.

"Kay." Edin withdrew her face and clambered onto the runner board and then onto the asphalt. She clasped Mac's cheeks in both her hands and administered Hana's second-hand kiss. They both waved through the open door, their faces disappearing as Wiri slammed it closed hard enough to rock the truck.

"Bye then. Remember to call Nonie if you need something. I might not have a signal. and don't go near that lady." Hana waved through the windscreen as the group trooped towards the school gate. The other boy and his rolling football followed them like a tributary joining a rushing river. Their heads disappeared amid the throng of children and adults, and Hana watched until another influx of bodies obscured them all. A car honked behind her and she discovered the hatchback had left her to take the blame for the blockage.

She sighed and set off for the hotel, her thong already feeling like a piece of cheese wire beneath the rough fabric of her jeans.

54

Barde

Hana parked her truck next to Logan's in the staff car park and hurried towards the museum. She found Will already in the office, the wheels of his chair squeaking across the tiles.

"Kia ora, can I help you?" His formal tone sent a flare of guilt up her spine. He held out his gnarled right hand. "I'm Will. Nice to meet you."

"I know, I know." Hana dodged his outstretched fingers and ignored his sarcasm. "I'm sorry." She slumped into an office chair and stared at a stack of papers piled on the desk. "Edin seems to like school." She ran a hand over her lips. "I'm hoping to come back to help you soon."

Will smirked. He rolled his wheelchair near enough to bump his knees against hers. "It's okay, kōtiro," he soothed. "Your tāne pays that university student to help me out with tours. She's not as pretty as you, but she doesn't talk so much." He patted his left ear. "Gives me a bit of a break."

"Oh." Hana's head shot back as she absorbed the impact of his news. "What university student? Logan never mentioned her."

Will wagged a finger under her nose. "Probably because of that face right there. He didn't want to make you feel like a failure."

Hana's shoulders slumped, and she wished she hadn't sat down with such force. She wriggled in the seat. "Not as pretty as me, you say?" She fished for the compliment and glanced at him from beneath her lashes. A blob of mascara drew her attention, and she didn't realise she'd gone boss-eyed until Will snorted at her.

"Well, not right now." He frowned and lifted his glasses from the top of his tufty head before seating them over his nose. Blinking, he cocked his face until peering at her through the strongest part of the bifocal lenses. He blew out a calculated breath and pursed his lips. "You seem to have a costume malfunction," he said, flapping his left hand at her chest.

Hana peered down at her breasts protruding over the edges of the inadequate bra. She tutted and battled them back beneath the black lace as Will spun his wheelchair in the other direction. "Sorry. Wooing my husband takes more effort than I remembered. Everything keeps popping out." She shimmied in the seat and grimaced. "Or up."

"Too much information." Will waved his hand and turned the wheelchair with the faint hiss of rubber on tile. He snatched a sheet of paper from the towering pile. "Your husband worships the ground you walk on. Only person who can't see it is you."

"Yeah." Hana sighed and considered Logan's forbearance over the last year and a half. "He's amazing. I just don't want him to run out of patience with me." She peered at Will from beneath her lashes. "Or my decisions."

Will waggled his bushy eyebrows. "Right. Well, I'm glad we got that sorted. Can you leave please if we're done talking? I feel a heart attack coming on any second now." He used the paper to flap air towards his face.

"Rude." Hana rose and yanked the thong's slender thread from its hiding place, finishing with an undignified wiggle. She turned towards the door and then stopped. "Hey, Logan has a box in his office. I think it came from the fire up at Reuben's old place." Her eyes glazed as she ran through scenarios. "It looks warped. If I bring it here, could you open it for me?"

Will emitted a low growl from deep in his throat. "That has disaster written all over it."

Hana nodded with sincerity. "It was. People died and we're still suffering from the effects of it now, even years later. Things crop up and trace right back to that night."

Will lifted a gnarled index finger and jabbed it towards Hana. "Not the fire, you clown! The box." He wedged his hands over his hips and lifted his chin. "I'm doing nothing without Logan's permission. We've been here before."

Hana suppressed her inner groan. "He won't mind."

Will's bark of laughter echoed around the narrow office. It reverberated off the plaster walls to condemn her. She lifted a shoulder in dismissal. "I'll sort it out." She set off across the museum's parquet floor without looking back, her boot heels clicking against the hard surface.

"There you are." Logan strode across the reception area to greet her. He clasped his battered Jackaroo hat in his left hand. The force of his aura reached Hana before him, shrouding her in his familiar authority. Foregoing responsibility for the running of the hotel had removed a weight from his shoulders, and the return to teaching added a permanent smile. "I saw the truck and assumed you'd come here first." He jerked his head towards the museum door. "Everything okay?"

"Yep." Hana shrugged her shoulders and saw her husband blink. His long lashes swished as her cleavage nodded to him from between her straining shirt buttons. His pupils dilated and Hana prayed her uncomfortable underwear wouldn't ruin her precious time with him. She slipped the fingers of her left hand through his elbow and half turned away from him to deal with the thong again. "I'm so looking forward to this," she gushed.

"Yeah." Logan ran a palm across his chin and bumped the hat brim against his nose. "I figured when I saw your knickers in the truck."

Hana groaned. "I need the cardigan, don't I?" She used her right hand to wrestle her breasts back into the bra. "I'll get the cardigan." The receptionist frowned from behind the desk, his brows knitting into a solid line of perplexity.

"You'll get too hot." Logan spoke the sentence and then reran it in his mind. His lips curved upwards into a grin. "You're gonna get very hot, actually."

❧❧❧❧❧❧ ❦❦❦❦❦❦

Logan slipped his arm around Hana's shoulders as they walked to the stable yard. "I've tacked Polly for you," he said, lifting his arm to seat his hat on his head.

Hana missed her footing and stumbled, shooting a sideways glance towards the mountain. The roof of the bunkhouse showed on the first of many ridges, obscured by lush manuka trees. Logan halted and offered her his hand, keeping hold of her fingers as they navigated a gathered crowd of conference delegates. "She's David Allen's horse." Her lips flattened into a line. "He won't approve."

"It's fine." Logan brushed off Hana's observation, distracting her with a kiss, which left her breathless. "Come on, I've a surprise for you."

Hana grinned and raised her shoulders to her ears in excitement. She'd sampled a vast array of her husband's surprises and teased herself with thoughts of a few romantic hours in solitude. When Tama's image moved across her inner vision, she batted it away with the smallest flicker of guilt. She'd given until she'd emptied her well and sensed herself running on a deficit. A day riding with Logan promised to refill her energy bucket and allow them to connect without constant interruptions.

Polly lifted her head as Hana approached. She accepted the stroke to her muzzle as Hana shifted to ensure she'd seen her through each of her gentle brown eyes. "Where's David Allen today?" Hana kissed the horse's long cheek and checked the bridle with practiced fingers. "Why isn't he riding you?"

"Ready?" Logan rounded the dappled gelding to face her. He'd vaulted into the saddle and his long legs mastered the grey horse within seconds. Lowering the reins to tap its withers, he moved towards her. Mahogany leather wither bags rested in front of the saddle horn. They sat snugly over the base of the horse's wide neck, and Hana hoped they contained alcohol.

"I'll use the mounting block." She released the rope from the wall bracket and trailed it behind her as she slipped the reins over Polly's head. "Do we need lead ropes?" she asked.

"Na." Logan leaned forward and held out his arm. He took it from her and called to the man, passing with a wheelbarrow. "Here ya go, Rawiri," he called. "Special delivery." The rope flew through the air and the man caught it with a smile.

"I'd rather have cash," he joked. He looped the rope around his neck and continued walking, straw and dung trickling over the sides of the barrow in a steady leak.

Hana mounted from the block at the end of the stable yard. Polly flicked a fluffy white ear back to acknowledge her presence and waited with infinite patience as she altered David's stirrups to fit her shorter legs. "Where is he?" she demanded, as Logan edged alongside her.

Leaning down, he checked her girth and tapped her thigh to indicate he wanted to tighten it. Hana pushed her left leg forward, and he lifted the saddle's tan skirt and hauled on the buckle. Polly's ears shot back, and she turned her head as though to bite. The other horse snorted in protest and Logan poked Polly's muscular shoulder. "Sorry, girl. Precious load."

He grinned up at Hana as she glared at him. He made no reference to her horror at his swinging girth and too long stirrup leathers.

She pursed her lips and satiated herself with the scent of his aftershave. It shrouded her as he clicked his tongue to signal to the horses to move. A fire ignited in her soul at his nearness. She ached to touch him and a million endearments tore through her brain, spilling over one another in their need for expression. Her lips parted, but Rawiri's loud swearing caused her jaw to clamp shut over her words of love.

Logan's nose wrinkled, and he leaned towards her as he gathered his reins into his left hand. "He's tipped the barrow again." He jerked his head towards the gate leading into a lush paddock at the end of the stable yard. "Let's get moving before he throws a tantrum."

"Shouldn't we help him?" Hana wavered as Logan's horse moved ahead of her.

"No." He frowned back at her. "He just needs to pump up the front wheel, but he's too lazy. Linc told him to do it three weeks ago." His lips turned up on one side and his perfect teeth shone between them. "I'm so glad I don't deal with this crap anymore." His gelding flicked its tail in a perfect circle as Logan pushed him on towards the gate.

Hana's phone buzzed as she waited for Logan to lean over his horse's neck to close the gate. She groaned and dipped her head to peer through the clear plastic of the holder fastened to her left arm.

"Just leave it," Logan urged. He clicked to his gelding, his movements effortless as the horse danced on the spot beneath him. "You told the kids they need to call Leslie today, didn't you?"

"Yeah." Hana frowned. "It's a private number." It continued to ring, the icon showing up as a strobing image of a telephone. She sighed with relief at not seeing the familiar identity number which flagged Caroline's calls. "I should answer it." Her index finger jabbed at the button, but it failed to connect the call through the plastic. Logan shook his head as it stopped.

"They got bored with waiting," he commented. A glance at his watch gave Hana fair warning of his growing impatience. "If it's important, they'll call back."

"But what if it's Tama?" A dark cloud settled over her shoulders and the day's promise drifted away from her.

"It's not." Logan tapped the gelding's neck with his reins and the dancing hooves dug into the turf.

Polly whirled in response, flattening her ears back against her mane at the thrill of the chase. Hana tutted and held her seat as the horses powered across the paddock. They scattered the cream Charolais herd in their wake like speed boats cutting through the Tasman's unpredictable surf. A bold heifer kept pace with them for a few hundred metres, enjoying the unexpected excitement. She peeled away with a tired grunt and trotted back to her sisters, her tail flicking in agitation.

Hana settled into the steady, uphill gait, relaxing her stomach muscles and sensing the tension rolling from her shoulders. Logan rode ahead of her, melded to the stocky Western saddle and his body rocking to the motion of the horse beneath him. His left hand controlled the reins, his right arm free, and his fingers relaxed against his thigh. Hana edged Polly closer to the gelding's heels, and they rode in companionable silence.

❧❧❧❧❧ ❦❦❦❦❦

Dust kicked up beneath the horses' hooves as they halted at the first gate. Logan dipped to release the catch and edged the gelding backwards as he hauled the aluminum gate open enough for Polly to pass through the gap. He repeated the exercise in reverse on the other side. The bush rose above them, birds and insects creating a cacophonous white noise.

Hana exhaled and smiled at Logan as he drew alongside her. She reached out and stroked the gelding's dappled ears.

"What's his name?" She cocked her head to inspect the regal brow and arced Roman nose. "He looks part Cob."

"Yep." Logan slapped the sweating neck with affection and the horse flicked his ear back and forth in acknowledgement. "And Kaimanawa." Gentle curls escaped the slickness to create a spiked appearance. "His name is Son of Dove. He's a five-year-old. Lincoln picked him up yesterday, and I'm trying him out for a few weeks." His ready frown betrayed the hole in his heart left by the wily Sacha.

"Do you call him Sonny?" Hana ruffled the curled hair at the horse's poll and he blew out a breath filled with warm air and grass seed.

Logan wrinkled his nose. "Haven't called him anything yet. This is his first real run out on the mountain. I didn't want to name him if he wasn't staying."

The horse shook his head and his bridle tinkled with the edifying sound of metal on leather. Hana smiled up at her husband's furrowed brow and covered his fingers with hers. "I like him," she said. "He suits you somehow."

Logan shrugged and turned his attention towards the well-used track through the bush. "I thought I could breed something suitable again, but maybe Sacha was a fluke. Linc turned up with this dude to put me out of my misery." His lips lifted on one side. "Said he's sick of listening to me complaining."

Hana dipped forward to peer into the nearest of the gelding's brown eyes. "Hello, Sonny," she said, her tone soft. He blew out again and his stomach swelled and released. Hana sat up and winked at her husband. "I like him. You need something reliable. Much as we both loved Sacha, that mare had her own agenda for every situation." Hana pursed her lips and frowned. "At least Sonny won't get evicted from the stables for inappropriate behaviour. What does Rawiri think of him?"

"Likes him." He flipped a clump of stray mane over Sonny's neck to match the rest. It rebelled, rising by small degrees until it settled on the wrong side again. Logan glanced up to find Hana watching and shivered as he gave himself a mental shake. He raised his eyebrows and forced a smile onto his lips. "Right, Mrs Du Rose. We should get going or we won't make it back in time to meet the kids."

Hana edged Polly sideways on the track, using her reins and heels, making room for Sonny to pass them. He swished his grey streaked tail as Logan lowered his reins and urged him into a trot. Hana patted Polly's white neck and grinned at Logan's retreating back. "Think someone's secretly pleased," she whispered to the mare.

55

Check Rein

The ride up the mountain took over an hour as Logan led Hana across trickling creeks and alongside towering ridges. They circled enough for her to become confused and disoriented, but her husband kept moving with no sign of doubt.

"You still okay?" He turned in the saddle to face her. His brow furrowed, and she forced a smile onto her lips.

"Yeah. Just out of practice. Is it much further?"

"Nope." He waited for her on the edge of a clearing. The wide trunks of kauri trees snaked towards the light above the canopy, ferns and undergrowth spreading in a carpet at their feet. Logan dipped sideways to kiss Hana, his lips warm and his eyes ablaze with pleasure. Polly snorted and crunched her bit in protest at Sonny's proximity, and Hana smiled into Logan's kiss.

"I've missed this," she whispered. "I let life get too busy."

"We're both guilty of that." He lifted his right hand and brushed her fringe from her eyes. Cocking his head, he studied her unruly auburn curls. "Where's Mama's hat?"

Hana shrugged and dismissed his question with an excuse. "I got distracted in the museum and forgot to grab it from the tack room." She cleared her throat and avoided his gaze, not wanting to admit she hadn't seen it for months.

Logan studied her with his usual intensity, stilling her beneath his gaze like a lepidopterist adding a rare butterfly to his collection. He reached up and clasped her chin between fingers and thumb. Hana blinked and pursed her lips, the instinctive swallow escaping her throat as a gulp. Smiling, he pressed a kiss to her forehead. "I can always tell when you're lying." He winked at her. "Phoe wore it to the muster. I bet it's at the bottom of her wardrobe." He dropped his hand with a smirk which lifted his lips only on the left side. "She wore the same expression when I asked if you knew she had it."

Hana gritted her teeth together to avoid releasing the snappy reply, which bounced onto her tongue. The children had promised to wear hard hats. But she knew better than to try to win against her husband. He outclassed her in every arena, and the knowledge provided as much irritation as relief.

Logan edged Sonny forward, and they skirted the tender roots of a towering kauri. He touched his forehead in respect to the age and provenance of the tree before continuing downhill.

Polly followed without Hana's encouragement, used to trail riding and keen to avoid separation. Hana shifted in the saddle and wished she'd lengthened her stirrup leathers earlier. "Where is David Allen?" Her question reverberated through the bush, overlaid by the buzz of cicadas enjoying their last weeks above ground.

"Doing a job for me," Logan replied, calling over his shoulder. "Why? You missing him?"

Hana shrugged and loosened her reins to give Polly room to stretch her neck on the slope. "Kinda. I wanted to thank him for rescuing me from Colin the other day."

Logan twisted in the saddle to face her, and his eyes narrowed. "You didn't thank me and I sent him." Indignation laced his tone, but his eyes twinkled. "Na, he's good. Don't worry about it."

"What job is he doing for you?" Hana tightened her stomach muscles as Polly slid down the rest of the slope on her rump and lurched upright to stand square in a narrow dip. They passed Logan on the way to the bottom and Sonny blinked and shook his head, unused to the ease with which the stock horses covered the mountain. Polly waited, giving a shake which started at the nose and finished at the tip of her tail. Hana held her breath as her muscles ached and her bones rattled. Sonny picked his way to the bottom with care, taking time over every step. Logan frowned as he came alongside Hana.

"Just a job," he replied, his tone terse. "Don't worry about it."

Hana's lips pursed. "He's looking for Tama, isn't he?" Logan's right eyebrow quirked enough to give her confirmation. She exhaled with relief and tilted her head back on her shoulders. "Thank you," she sighed.

Logan's head jerked back, and confusion covered his face. His long lashes shuttered his sparkling irises. "I thought you'd be mad," he replied. "I told you to leave it alone."

Hana shook her head and contemplated the steep ridge to her right. She waited for Logan to filter past her, hoping he didn't intend to clamber up the ragged slope. "I'm just glad someone is looking out for him. Wherever he is, he's in a mess."

Logan clicked his tongue, and Sonny picked up his hooves and trotted along the bed of the dry creek. Hana watched the soft frogs in their centres appear and disappear as his fetlocks bent beneath him. She dropped her reins to Polly's neck and encouraged her to move with a gentle press of her heels against the hairy stomach.

They caught up to Logan, and a heavy sense of oppression laid itself over Hana's shoulders. The bush canopy blocked the overhead sun to create long shadows in the undergrowth. Thirst burned the back of her throat and she cursed herself for not thinking ahead. Logan turned as she released a deep sigh.

"What's wrong?" he demanded.

"Just tired." The gully seemed to sap her energy. Even Polly's hoof beats slowed, laden by an added, unseen weight. "Thirsty. I should have brought a drink." Hana shook her head. "I leave the house with enough snacks, drinks and changes of kids' underwear to survive an apocalypse, and then forget the basics for myself." She frowned. "I assumed I'd be better at this parenting thing second time around, but I'm not."

She glanced up to find Logan holding out a water bottle. An open flap on the saddle blanket revealed its hiding place below the leather rigging guard. She edged Polly closer and accepted it from his outstretched hand with a sigh of gratitude. Logan's fingers touched hers as she took it. "You look after us and I look after you." He lifted his hand and his thumb caressed her cheek. Water shot from the nozzle of the bottle and Hana choked on it. Her eyes watered, but not just from the shock. Logan's words unlocked a vault in her heart and she knew he spoke the truth.

"I feel so alone," she confessed. Her hand shook as she wiped it across her upper lip.

Logan nodded. He accepted the bottle and tilted it, drinking in long draughts. "Sucks, doesn't it?" he replied. Hana loved him more in that moment than if he'd offered trite platitudes or unrealistic solutions. He just joined her in her bunker-of-doom and sat with her there. She reached out and laid her hand across his thigh. Her fingers caressed his firm muscle through the hard jeans fabric, and she kept her head bowed.

"Come on." He slipped the bottle back into the pocket and closed the flap. "Not far now. It's worth it, I promise." His smile parted his lips to reveal perfect teeth marred only by a tiny chip to the front tooth. His irises sparkled with promise, diamonds in his tanned face. Hana nodded, knowing she'd follow him anywhere.

The gully gave way to a wider mouth as it converged on another. Water trickled from the second, gushing over the horses' hooves and forcing them to pick their footing with more care. Polly stumbled over a hidden rock, and Hana gasped. Frowning, Logan turned Sonny in a circle and jerked his head towards the left. "Can you go first?" he asked. "Polly's been up here before, so she knows what she's doing. It's all new to this guy." He patted Sonny's wide neck, and the horse flicked his left ear back and forth in response.

Hana nodded and skirted them to face the growing mouth ahead. Logan called directions from behind her. "Keep left and follow the tracks."

"What tracks?" Hana peered at the ground, unable to distinguish anything but the lazy ferns sweeping beneath Polly's hooves.

"Just let her take her head and she'll show you." Logan spun Sonny in a circle, sensing the gelding's growing agitation. "I need you out of the way before I take him up there. As soon as you reach the top, veer sharp left and don't look down."

"Oh great!" Hana muttered. She relaxed her reins and clamped the fingers of her right hand over the saddle horn. "On you go," she told the horse, pushing Polly onto the slope.

Nothing mentally prepared her for Polly's uphill bound or the sight which met her at the top. A cliff edge yawned beneath her, the toes of her right boot backed by nothing but air. Polly extended her neck and veered left, ignoring Hana's gasp of terror. Her powerful shoulders flexed and her hooves dug into the baked earth, carrying Hana to safety.

Hana pressed her heels into Polly's stomach to encourage her away from the edge, driving her far enough away to give Logan room to maneuver. An angry snort from Sonny preceded the brim of Logan's hat appearing through the narrow gap. The horse's eyes rolled in terror as blue sky and crashing waves appeared in his peripheral vision. He reared on his back feet in protest, his eyes not yet adjusted to the brightness of the sunshine.

"Get up!" Logan shouted at him, using his heels and reins to drive him through the narrow entrance. Hana held her breath as Sonny panicked, a vision playing in her mind's eye of Logan pitching sideways over the cliff to his death. It replayed over and over like a film reel as he struggled against the horse and she sat there, powerless to help.

The battle ended as quickly as it began. Sonny popped over the final ledge in a flying leap from a standstill, veering left in the last seconds. His eyes rolled back in his grey face and Logan's torso dipped as he went with him.

Every muscle trembled in the dappled grey shoulders, the skin crawling over them like a wave. Sonny trotted towards Polly, bumping her without care as he sought the comfort of her nearness. Hana's chest ached, and she restarted her breathing with a ragged gasp. "I thought you'd go over," she said. Her teeth chattered as she spoke.

Logan grinned. "Me too," he admitted. He slapped Sonny's powerful neck and shook his head. "But we didn't."

Hana blew out a breath in an effort to control her fear. Her gaze fell on Sonny's front hooves and the open nail holes where Logan had stripped off his metal shoes. She shook her head and glared at her husband. "You'd already decided to keep him," she said with a bite in her tone.

Logan's nose wrinkled, and he turned Sonny to face the panoramic view stretching out before them. "Maybe," he replied.

56

Breeching

Hana dismounted, releasing Polly from her heavy saddle and bridle. Dark sweat lines peppered the horse's solid body, collecting in the furry pit between her chest muscles and trailing in a line where the girth had hugged her stomach. Hana called to Logan over her shoulder. "Are you sure they won't run?"

"They won't." His voice held an element of certainty, and Hana dumped the saddle so its gullet and pommel lay in the pale grass. She gathered the bridle and reins together, draping them over the cantle.

Polly strolled away, her muzzle already buried in the coarse blades poking from the dry soil. She moved towards the edge of the clearing where the trees cast the ground into shade and the grass looked greener. Sonny grunted in a half-hearted whinny of protest, his head lifting to track her movements.

"Can you trust him?" Hana laid a hand over Sonny's bridle, hearing the clank of metal as Logan loosened his girth.

"We'll find out, won't we?" His head popped up level with the horse's withers and he smiled at her as he slipped the saddle and blanket off together. "I imagine he'll stick near to Polly." He set the saddle down and Hana released the throatlash and gathered the reins and bridle together. She tugged it off, waiting until Sonny's silky ears slid through the gap.

"There you go," she told him as the bit clanked free from behind his tongue. "That's better, isn't it?"

Sonny stretched his neck and opened his mouth wide, snaking his tongue and shaking his head. He arched his neck and rubbed his cheek against her thigh hard enough to knock her over. Hana laughed and moved out of range. "Find Polly," she told him and patted his muscular shoulder. The horse moved away, tossing his head and blowing out warm breaths. He inspected the scrubby grass at his feet before joining Polly beneath the trees. They grazed side by side, doing their own thing in companionable silence.

Hana glanced down to find Logan laying Sonny's blanket on the ground. Two plastic bottles containing a heavy red liquid listed on the uneven camber next to two packets of sandwiches. She bit her lower lip and smiled. "This reminds me of our very first ride together.

Logan squinted up at her. The sun's rays cast him into shafts of light and shadow as his fingers stood the bottles upright, only to have them fall like skittles on the uneven ground. "I thought you'd enjoy it." He rose and straightened the hem of his tee shirt. Awkwardness shrouded him as he surveyed his imperfect picnic. His boots scraped against the hard earth and churned up puffs of dust.

"I love it." Hana stepped to the edge of the blanket and eased herself into a sitting position. She tugged off her boots and crossed her legs. Her fingers fluttered over the space next to her as she patted it flat.

"Is it too damp?" Logan knelt up next to her with a frown. "He got up a bit of a sweat on the ridge."

"It's better than the ground." Hana twisted to observe the clearing, the stunning vista sweeping in front of her. She unwound her legs and leaned back, stabilising herself with rigid arms. The sun kissed her cheeks and forehead and she sighed. "It's beautiful up here."

"Yeah." Logan sank down next to her. He jerked his head towards the horses on their left. "My kuia cleared this land in the 1950s. She grazed it quite hard back then, but I've been letting the bush reclaim it." Crinkles appeared at the corners of his eyes as he smiled at Hana. "It feels good to give back to the mountain after all this time. We've taken enough from her."

Hana closed her eyes and tuned in to the peace surrounding her. A light breeze took the edge off the heat and brought light relief. Bees buzzed nearby as they made use of the last blooms of white clover. The horses flicked their tails in a steady beat, which added to the laziness of the moment, and she released a little of the tension held in her chest. "Thank you," she whispered. "I needed this."

Plastic crackled as Logan released the lid on a bottle and handed it to her. "A toast to us," he said with a smile. A frown strode across his forehead and disappeared. "I apologise for the lack of culture, but I couldn't risk glass bottles with that gelding." He exhaled. "Sacha was different."

"I'm happy with this." Hana tapped her drink against his. "It's perfect." She sipped and the heady merlot hit the back of her tongue in a blast of flavour, causing her to cough. "Gosh!" She laughed and covered her mouth with her hand. A dimple appeared in Logan's right cheek and he shook his head.

They drank in silence, shoulder to shoulder at the apex of the mountain which had seen so much. The sun slipped further to its northernmost point and blazed down on them, scorching the grass and casting long shadows at the edge of the bush canopy. Hana glanced across to see Sonny rolling in the dust, all four hooves waving in the air like bobbing flower heads. "I like him," she said. Her words broke the silence.

Logan inhaled and snuffed out a laugh at his crazy mount. "Yeah," he agreed, his tone soft. "Me too."

Hana screwed the lid back onto her drink and reached for a packet of sandwiches. "Did you see Sacha's foal in the news last night? Du Rose Future. He's jumping at 1.25m and won his class." The heat stole her appetite, and she dropped the packet back onto the blanket.

Logan shook his head. "I haven't followed him lately."

"Do you wish you'd kept him here?" Hana slipped her right arm around his shoulders and touched her temple to the brim of his hat.

"Na." Logan sighed. "He's better where he is. I had nothing to offer a horse like him." He lifted his hat and dropped it onto the blanket between his knees. "He'll come back here at the end of his career and I'll see if I can breed with him. I'm glad he's doing well."

Hana kissed her husband's exposed cheek and laid her head on his shoulder. "Did you check the hotel cameras for that car?"

"Yep." He turned his head and his warm breath stirred her hair. "I also spoke to your son this morning before we left."

"Bo?" Hana jerked up straight. "Wow. Who called who?"

"I called him." Logan's pupils shrank as he surveyed the ocean beyond the precipice. He wrapped his arms around his shins and sighed. "He paid me back that grand I lent him. I rang to thank him."

Hana swallowed. Any suitable words escaped her, and she found herself with nothing to offer. She realised she hadn't expected Bodie to honour his agreement after all. She managed a weak nod.

Logan scraped his chin across his bent knee and licked his lips. "He's opened a case file on Tama and added the other incidents to it. I told him about the accident and the woman snooping around the house. He asked me to put the video files into a Dropbox and he'll see what he can discover." Logan turned to face Hana, and he frowned. "You walked right in front of the car at the hotel, but probably didn't notice. That means she knew you weren't at home and drove up there."

Hana shrugged. "Only if she knew I lived there. We were just a rag-taggle group of people walking into the hotel."

"True." Logan tilted his head before nodding. "I got her registration number, anyway. Bodie has it now. Installers are coming next week to put a gate at the bottom of the driveway."

Hana groaned. "Great. I'll get wet twice now when it's raining."

"It's electric." Logan chewed his lower lip. "And once it's in, you can leave the top gate open."

"Yey!" Hana punched the air with her right fist. "That's awesome!"

Logan snorted. "You won't say that when you're constantly getting buzzed by tourists who took a wrong turn."

Hana quirked an eyebrow. "Yeah, but at least I won't find a campervan smoking outside the front door like last time. The poor guy needed a cuppa and a bathroom break after his terrifying ride up the mountain." She flapped her hand between them. "Although I have no idea how he missed the giant hotel just beyond our turn or the signs declaring the driveway private."

Logan exhaled and lay back, using his stomach muscles. His tee shirt rode up to expose defined muscle bisected by white scars. He squinted up at Hana. "Happy birthday for tomorrow, Mrs Du Rose."

Hana groaned and flopped down next to him. "Don't remind me," she grumbled. "I feel at least a hundred."

57

Bridoon

"**Y**ou're not bad for a hundred-year-old woman." Logan flopped back onto the blanket. His head and shoulders reached beyond its boundary, and he bent his arm and rested his neck on it. "I put your knickers in the glove box, by the way. Why were they on the front seat of your truck?"

Hana groaned and snuggled against him, her head fitting into the nook of his armpit. "Phoenix. And don't ask."

"Does that mean you're not wearing any?" His tone became sultry, and he turned to his side, capturing her with his other arm.

"Believe me when I say I wish I'd thought of that." Hana exhaled and gazed into his stormy irises. Flecks of black and green danced around his dilated pupils. She reached up and grazed her lips across his. "Remember that set you bought me in Paris?"

Logan's lips rose in a wide arc. "Hell yeah. One word. Mac."

Hana snorted. "Yes, Mac."

Logan's fingers slipped beneath the waistband of her jeans and his thumb coasted over the seamless back of the thong. A low growl issued from his chest and his legs wrapped around hers, pinning her in position. Hana clamped her teeth over her lower lip as she battled with the buttons at the front of his jeans, his arousal pushing against her fingers.

Hana groaned with relief as Logan liberated her from the painful underwear. They didn't speak, the bush adding the musical crescendos as they loved each other. Afterwards, they lay together in the scratchy grass, savouring the peace of the rare interlude from life.

"Fancy a nudey dip in the stream?" Logan kissed the side of her head and relaxed his arm muscles.

"Yeah, I do." Hana sighed. "As long as you're sure we're safe."

"From what?" Logan's brow furrowed as he leaned back to peer at her expression. "It's not fast enough this time of year to wash us over the edge. We'll stay well back from it."

Hana traced the outline of his tattoo and sighed. "I meant from stockmen riding up here unexpectedly to eat their lunch."

Logan offered a sultry wink. "I know where they all are and they're far away from here. Didn't you hear me keep checking the radio on the way up the mountain?"

Hana's hair swished against the hard ground as she shook her head. "Sneaky." She yawned and blinked beneath the harsh midday sun, not wanting to admit she'd checked their sitreps from her truck. "I need to move. There are more parts of me exposed than I expected, and I can feel my skin burning."

Sonny blew out a breath from nearby, his casual air masking his need to stay close to Polly. He grazed behind her, trailing in her wake like a needy foal. She swished her tail in irritation, dusting his muzzle with the coarse hairs. Oblivious, he nosed the grass near Hana's head and covered her with moist air.

They collected their discarded clothes and laid them out to warm on the rocks jutting from the gully's steep sides. Logan lay down in the shallow water, whooping as its iciness covered his body. Hana sat next to him, grimacing as loose grit dug into her buttocks. She wrapped her arms around her shins and rested her chin on her knees.

"Can I ask you something?" She shivered with a mixture of pleasure and pain as the excited water danced across her toes. It carried the scent of fern and manuka, earthy and bitter sweet.

"Yep." Logan pushed himself up and ran his hands through his hair. The dappled sunlight sneaking through the overhead canopy highlighted the grey streaks in his fringe. "Spit it out, Hana."

She blinked at him before shuttering her eyes behind her lashes. Feigning innocence, she spoke with exaggerated softness. "Please, can I have that box in your office?"

"Kuia's blanket box?" Logan's nose wrinkled across the bridge as he peered at her. "Yeah, if you want it. There's nothing inside. Is it for the house?"

"No, not the big wooden one." Hana balanced her chin on her knees and studied the vista before her. The water trickled over the edge of the cliff, joining the Tasman somewhere below it. "The other one. It's metal. I saw it on the shelf."

"Oh." Logan shrugged, and his muscular arm brushed her shoulder as he stretched. "Yeah. I think it's Alfred's. I asked him about it yesterday and he acted real vague. Paulie found it up at the site of Reuben's fire. The lock got knackered somewhere in its lifetime. I tried to open it yesterday and bent the whole thing even more. Alfred remembers Antoinette having something similar when they all lived together in the hotel." He yawned and covered his mouth with his hand, good manners prevailing despite his nakedness and their isolation. "Ask one of the lads to grind off the hinges. It's heavy, so there's something inside, but I don't know what."

"Thanks." Hana studied her fingers in the dappled light. She stopped her mind from dwelling on his parents' hideous end.

Logan looked up at the sky and released a sigh. "We should head home now. Let's tack up the horses and lead them down here to mount."

"Okay." Hana agreed with enthusiasm. "But you can lead them down one at a time, and I'll hold the first while you walk back for the other one."

"Coward." Logan smirked, but didn't disagree.

He dressed with more speed than Hana. She struggled to pull her jeans over her cold skin. Her damp foot got stuck in the left leg and her breasts threatened to spill from her bra as she hopped around in the shadow of the bank. She pulled her blouse over her head and retrieved her right boot as Logan appeared, towing Polly behind him. "Wait, wait!" She held up her hand in warning, not wanting them to spring down on top of her. "I'm still getting dressed." She grimaced at the realisation Logan had already tacked both horses as Sonny's muzzle appeared over Polly's rump.

"You're just too slow." Logan grinned at her from the bank and flapped his free hand. "Shift to your left and I'll lead her down. I think the boy will just follow." He switched to the horse's off side to avoid her shoving him over the ledge.

Hana picked her way towards the rocks and jammed her foot into her sock. Logan hopped down and Polly followed, her ears flicking back and forth as she landed with a splash in the stream. Water filled Hana's stray left boot as she reached for it, too slow to avoid Sonny's death-defying leap down behind her. She cursed under her breath and imagined her uncomfortable descent trapped in the unforgiving underwear and a wet boot. Sonny stood in the stream, lowering his muzzle to drink the cool water in satisfying gulps.

Hana finished dressing and waited for Logan to grab her bent left knee and boost her into the saddle. The ice water had inoculated her against the chafe from the thong, but water dripped from her boot to darken the leather housing the stirrup iron. "What was the surprise?" she asked.

"What?" Logan frowned up at her as he tightened Polly's girth. Crow's feet appeared at the corners of his eyes as he dropped the saddle skirt and took a step back. "Me." He curved his body and pointed at his pectorals. "I'm the surprise."

"Liar!" Hana grinned down at him. "I can get that any time. What was the surprise?"

Logan walked to Sonny and leaned against his shoulder as the horse took another draught of fresh water. "I knew you'd freak out if I said I needed to talk to you."

Hana's spine stiffened, and she sensed herself following a well-worn pattern of behaviour. "Okay." She dragged out her response.

"See." Logan shook his head and squinted up at her from beneath the brim of his Jackaroo. "Told ya."

"Just tell me the surprise!" She gritted her teeth. Polly tensed beneath her and tried to turn away from the source of Hana's anxiety.

Sonny lifted his head, water cascading from his hairy lips. "I want to build a bush hut up here. A couple of schools have approached me about running camps. What do you think? We just need an ablutions block and somewhere under cover for them to gather. They can sleep in tents."

"Oh. Right." Hana pursed her lips and brushed leaf fragments from the saddle horn. "How will you get the building materials for a bush hut up here?"

"Helicopter. Like our house." A line appeared on Logan's brow.

"Expensive." Hana cocked her head and studied him from beneath her lashes. "Will it pay for itself or just tie up manpower and time while running at a loss?" Logan loved teaching. His proven gift with wayward teenage boys made him gravitate towards them. Hana imagined more lonely nights and weekends at home with the children, and it polluted her reaction. She tilted her head sideways. "Are you bored, Logan? Why diversify again when you just got rid of running the hotel?"

His bottom lip protruded, and he exhaled. "Fair questions. I'll give it more thought."

"My phone!" Hana gasped and pointed to the dark holder laying across a nearby rock. "I forgot it."

Logan bent and retrieved it, frowning at something through the protective plastic screen. "You missed a couple of calls," he said, handing it up to her. "Try phoning them now. As soon as we head into the bush, you'll lose your signal."

Hana loosened Polly's reins so she could put her head down and drink from the bubbling water. She dug her phone free of the holder and unlocked the screen. A text from Bodie blinked alongside four missed calls. Logan waited for Sonny to finish before springing into the saddle with the ease of years of practice. He patted the sturdy neck, and the horse flicked his ears in response. "Bodie texted." Hana frowned. "But the missed calls don't give a number." She glanced up at Logan. "Can you remember if the school shows up as private?" Her finger shook as she scrolled through the list. Nothing from Caroline.

"I'm not sure." Logan twisted his lips and lifted the radio from its holster on his belt. It crackled to life as he tuned into the frequency of the hotel. Hana read the text and the happiness of the last few hours trickled over the edge of the precipice with the glee of the stream. Logan's voice paled into the background as a series of faint words.

Hana dialled Bodie's mobile number and lifted the phone to her ear. She winced as she got his voicemail, electing not to leave a message. She shoved the phone back into its holder and strapped it to her upper arm. "We need to go," she said, her tone tight.

"No one from the school has phoned the hotel." Logan pushed the radio back into its clasp. "Margaret on the reception desk just rang Leslie in the apartment. She's heard nothing. It's not the school."

Hana flapped her hand in front of her face to deter a cloud of gnats, eagerly descending to sample her blood. "I think it's Bo. He's texted me about that fireman who died, so he might have called from the police station. He wants to speak to me about him."

"Hey." Logan drew alongside her and covered her scrabbling fingers with his hand. He dragged them onto his thigh and teased them flat against his jeans. "Don't lose this morning in all the rubble." He leaned over and kissed her, his lips warmer than hers. "Take the good stuff when it comes and then just roll with the punches." He dipped his head to study her face, and she nodded.

"I'll try," she promised in a whisper.

58

Cantle

Logan led the descent at a steady pace, letting Sonny find his own footing. Hana fidgeted behind him, communicating her angst to Polly and causing her to stumble. Logan looked around as she gasped and clung to the horn. She lost her reins, and they dangled along Polly's shoulder.

"Steady!" Logan shifted on the narrow track, driving Sonny into the waving ferns. He caught Hana's reins and held them as she righted her seat. "Try him again." He jerked his head towards the phone strapped to Hana's arm. "You should get a signal." His lips curved upwards, but Hana sensed his irritation blooming between them.

"Okay." She wrestled her phone free. Bodie picked up after the second ring and she jabbed the screen to put him on speaker.

"Hey, Mum."

"I'm in the bush, Bo." Hana raised her voice and a kereru's wings stirred the musty air in the undergrowth as it rose in irritation. "I might lose you."

Static surrounded his voice, and Hana darted a frightened glance at Logan. "Did you hear what he said?"

"Morgue." Bodie's voice gained a disjointed quality before clearing. "Yeah?"

"Say it again, please?" Hana held the phone almost to her lips, her brow knitted in concern.

"The guy in the morgue," Bodie repeated. "Remember his hat? You said it was fire service issue."

"Oh. Yep. I remember." Hana held her breath. "Do you know who he is now?"

Bodie's voice crackled again and Hana jerked in frustration. Logan touched her hand. "He said yes." He cocked his head. "Brother. Yeah, he said brother."

Hana swallowed. "I can't hear you very well, Bo. Did you say he's the brother of a fireman?"

"Yes." Her son's voice became crystal clear and Hana kept her hand still to avoid losing the signal. "Got drunk with mates in Mercer and ended up in the river." Interference distorted his voice and Hana frowned up at Logan.

"Reggo plate." He took the phone from her and spoke into it, his baritone carrying with more clarity. "We're out of range, Bo. We'll call you back at the hotel."

A word crackled before the connection died. Hana didn't protest when Logan pushed her phone into the bag across Sonny's withers. The carefree mood of the bush left her in a rush, reminiscent of the water plunging with abandon over the ledge. A rock wedged itself in her chest and her shoulders folded around it. Sonny shook his head and crunched his rear teeth over the bit, eager to get moving. Time froze around them as Hana prepared to face the world, waiting for her at the bottom of the mountain. "You should do it," she said, her voice soft.

"Do what?" Logan frowned, his lips drawing back from his teeth.

"The bush hut." Hana gathered Polly's reins into her left hand and turned her back towards the downhill slope. "It's peaceful up there. Kids can get away from their troubles for a night or two. Just make sure it's financially viable and that the health and safety stuff is covered. Maybe Linc could run it for you?"

"Thanks." Logan pushed Sonny onto the track and overtook her as she waited. "But not Linc. I'll check it all out and come back to you." His right hand rested over his thigh as he guided Sonny with his heels.

Polly followed without needing Hana's input or direction. Her heavy plodding echoed in the bush like the tick of a clock. A need to uncover the truth caused Hana conflict, her heart both eager and recoiling from the fate of the poor boy in the morgue. The brother of a fireman lay on a slab, gaining his identity while losing everything else.

But it wasn't Tama. It had never been Tama.

A tear pushed from the corner of her left eye and she brushed it away with an angry movement. Polly jerked as she lifted the reins, confused by the signal to halt. "Sorry," Hana whispered, dropping the reins and patting the muscular neck with her right hand.

Sunlight dappled the bush, and the birds made the most of the heat to sun themselves in the higher levels of the canopy. They cawed and cackled, their cacophony both a distraction and a hum which staved off Hana's fretting.

They cantered across the lower slopes of the mountain towards the hotel, a peaceable silence stretching between them.

Conference delegates occupied the stable yard. Women in unsuitable riding gear busied Rawiri in a steady stream of demands. Evidently, their male counterparts were hitting the bar between sessions.

"You can't ride in trainers." Rawiri's hair stuck up at the front as he faced off with a woman who stood with her hands on her hips. A black vest displayed his muscles to their full effect, sun kissed olive adding to the effect of youth and health.

"But this is all I brought!" she protested. "I want to ride." She turned as Logan and Hana clattered into the yard. Rawiri gave an upward jerk of his head to Logan, but the subtle tightening of his lips communicated his exasperation. Horses milled around, testing inexperienced riders and adding to the sense of chaos.

Logan tutted and dismounted in a single fluid motion. "Where's Linc?" He looked around the stable yard, but Hana sensed more worry than irritation. The dark, foreboding air which circled permanently above Logan's head seemed to still the activity. Attracted to his magnetism, the riders turned to face him and the horses lost their advantage.

A familiar knot of jealousy and fear budded in Hana's heart, and she fought it back with the benefit of experience. Despite a lifetime of opportunity, Logan didn't cheat.

As though sensing her unease, he looped Sonny's reins through a metal ring in the stable wall. He stepped to Polly's near side and, in full view of the rapt audience, held out his arms to Hana. She cocked her right leg over the horn until she sat side saddle before sliding into his arms. "Thank you, Mr Du Rose," she whispered as he leaned down and kissed her.

"You're welcome, Mrs Du Rose." He touched his lips to the end of her nose and smiled, his grey eyes twinkling with humour.

"Excuse me?" The woman wearing the trainers approached them, dodging Polly's front teeth as the horse stretched out her neck and opened her mouth in a wide yawn. "Are you the manager here?"

Logan raised an eyebrow at Hana and turned to face the woman. "No, sorry," he said. He jerked his head towards Rawiri. "He is." Deft fingers retrieved the rubbish from their lunch and he strode off to dump it into a wheelie bin.

The woman shrugged and turned her attention to Hana. "He won't let me ride in trainers. It's ridiculous."

Hana pressed a kiss to Polly's cheek and reached beneath her stomach to loosen her girth. The metal buckles chattered as they swung away and hung from the other side. "What size shoe do you take?"

"Pardon?" The woman drew closer. Returning from the dustbin, Logan stayed away from her and shot Hana a telling wince. He busied himself with Sonny, removing his tack and pulling a hoof pick from his back pocket.

"What size are you?" Hana grunted as she pulled Polly's saddle free, taking the blanket with it and resting it over the half door of the stall beside her. "We have spares in the tack room."

"Oh." Met with kindness, the woman faltered. "I thought I'd be okay with these." She pointed to the toe of her left trainer and stared at it as though hoping it morphed into something more suitable.

"You should have got a leaflet in your pack when you signed up for the conference." Hana slipped a head collar around Polly's neck before loosening the throat lash of her bridle. "You need a sturdy shoe or boot with a heel. If you fall off, there's a risk of getting dragged."

Disappointment showed in the woman's blue irises as she glanced at Logan over her shoulder. "I didn't see that. Can't you make an exception? Can he?"

"No!" Logan's growl of irritation made her edge closer to Hana. Polly flicked her ears back and forth and lifted her chin to rest on Sonny's withers with a sigh.

"I'll find you some boots in the tack room." Hana jerked her head towards Polly. She eased the bridle over the horse's ears and let the bit slide from her soft mouth. "Just let me finish here."

"I'll take care of the horses." Logan spoke while letting Sonny's giant near front hoof drop to the concrete. He dipped beneath Polly's neck and patted her shoulder. "You go. Rawiri is getting them mounted up now."

The woman's eyes widened as she saw her fellow conference goers boosting into their saddles. Rawiri's Jackaroo perched on his head and the casual stable boy stood holding the reins of his Appaloosa mare.

"Thanks babe." Hana smiled up at her husband. "Back in a sec." She led the woman around Sonny's rounded flanks, keeping her hand against the dappled skin so he knew she was there. "I'll get this lady some boots," she called to Rawiri, and he gave her a nod of acknowledgement.

"Okay. But we're leaving in five," he shouted over his shoulder. He bent to cup a blonde woman's knee in his left hand while clasping her ankle with his right. She flew through the air and clattered into the saddle with a bump.

Hana opened a cupboard at the back of the tack room and pulled out a selection of the family's old riding boots. The woman selected a pair of jodhpur boots and hurried into them, leaving her trainers on top of the cupboard. She thanked Hana and ran outside to resume her ride. Not content with having delayed the activity, she tried to engage Logan in conversation. Hana leaned against the balustrade and watched her husband resist her efforts.

"Could you help me up?" she asked, ignorance or stealth directing her to lead the white mare behind Sonny. Hana smiled as she sensed her husband's teeth grinding against each other. He lurched for the reins as Sonny lifted his rear hock as though to kick.

"Don't!" Logan slapped his flank and led the mare to safety. Not interested in getting any closer to the woman than he needed to, Logan crossed to the horse's off side and leaned on the stirrup iron. Instead of boosting her as Rawiri had done, he let her bounce around on her right leg until she got enough momentum to spring into the saddle. She arrived in the seat, puffing.

"Thanks, boss." Rawiri appeared next to him and dealt with the girth and stirrup leathers while the woman frowned down at him.

Logan's fringe flicked against his eyelashes as he used the hoof pick on Polly's enormous feet. Hana joined him as he selected a body brush from a nearby box. She smirked up at him and picked up a curry comb to run it over Polly's lithe body. "You really don't like people, do you?"

"You noticed?" He smiled at her and sent a cloud of dust rising from the short fur covering Sonny's ribcage.

"What's the deal with Lincoln?" She peered at him over the gentle dip of Polly's spine.

Logan wrinkled his nose and winced. "It's not my story to tell," he said. He turned away from her frown of curiosity and pulled the hosepipe from its hook. Water rushed over Sonny's body and the horse closed his eyes with a sigh of pleasure.

59

Cavesson

"You won't tell me what David Allen's up to in any detail, will you?" Hana leaned on the paddock gate and rested her chin on her forearms. Sonny and Polly took off at a gallop to the other side of the open space. The mare gave a kick of exhilaration, her coat still wet from her shower. "Is that not your story to tell, either?"

Logan slipped an arm around her shoulders and didn't answer. His gaze followed the line of riders through the last gate into the bush. Rawiri stayed at a steady walk, allowing for the cross section of experience among the riders. Raising his hand to shield his eyes, Logan nodded in satisfaction as the stable boy leaned down to close the gate. "He's a good kid. Responsible. I'll check with Linc if we can give him more hours."

Hana exhaled and rested her cheek against his shirt. She closed her eyes and savoured the moment of peace before the onslaught. "I'll phone Bo back," she said with a sigh. "And grab that box from your office."

"Okay." Distraction entered Logan's tone as he turned his mind back to his work. "Take it first if you want it. I need to make some calls this afternoon." He lifted his wrist to check his watch, and Hana sensed herself losing his attention. She slipped her fingers around his and accompanied him back to the hotel entrance.

"Are you calling him Sonny?" she asked, waiting for him to hold the front door open for her. A blast of freezing, conditioned air hit them like a wall.

"Yeah. Thanks." Logan nodded and let the door bang behind them. He raised a hand towards the receptionist and took the corridor leading past the kitchen. "It suits him."

Once in his office, he strode across the rug towards his desk and examined a diary on its wooden surface. His sloping handwriting covered the pages he lifted. He reached for his desk phone, studying a number on the page while dialling.

"I'll just take this." Hana's fingers closed around the box and she cradled it against her chest. It felt much heavier than she remembered, but nothing moved inside when she jiggled it. She turned to leave, stilling as Logan set the phone in the cradle after pressing the speaker.

"Hana?" He beckoned her with the fingers of his left hand as a male voice greeted him through the phone. She fought the irrational urge to push the box behind her back before approaching him. Her breath caught in her chest, but Logan dug his fingers into his back pocket and pulled out her phone. He smiled at her as she stumbled towards him.

"You there, Du Rose?" The speaker rumbled with a good natured voice and Hana smiled and thanked Logan for her phone. She took it and escaped his office with the box under her arm.

Returning to the stables, Hana sought Lincoln in his office. He glanced up at her as she entered after knocking and dropped a sheaf of papers onto the desk. "Mrs Du Rose." He addressed her with formality, maintaining the uncomfortable truce between them. "How can I help you?" He rose and leaned on the desk, his knuckles taking the weight of his bent body.

"Please, can you open this?" Hana hoisted the box in front of her, excitement driving away animosity. "Logan said he bent it trying to break it open, but I wondered if any of your blacksmithing tools might work."

A flicker passed across Lincoln's face, and he swallowed before shaking his head. "Logan trims all the hooves now." He cleared his throat. "We're keeping the trail horses barefoot like the stock mounts."

"Oh." With her enthusiasm doused, Hana backed towards the door. Logan told her not to ask Linc, and she'd discovered the reason. Lincoln had dropped his role as the property's blacksmith. They stared at each other for a long moment, awkwardness swirling like a mist. She realised as his long lashes brushed his cheek that she was tired. Angst and hostility sapped the little energy she had left each night. She'd presented the box as an olive branch, but he couldn't help her. Or wouldn't. She couldn't decide which of the two governed his reply.

The office still belonged to Jacob D'Arcy, the faint scent of his marijuana laced tobacco ingrained in the concrete walls. Smashing out the interior and adding a fresh coat of paint hadn't eradicated his memory or the crawling sensation which caused Hana to shiver with an ethereal chill. His hatred for her during his last months seemed to darken the room and create an oppressive atmosphere.

"I can't be here," Hana blurted. She grappled behind her for the door handle. She twisted and pulled, but it didn't budge. Her lips parted in a grimace of terror and she heard herself make a series of gasps. The handle rattled beneath her fingers and she dropped the box to the floor with a crash. Jacob D'Arcy's spirit dive bombed her, producing the same effect as a bucket of cold water. She became blind as she fought the brass knob, her fingers slipping but the door not budging.

"Hana." A soft voice spoke from behind her and strong fingers grasped her shoulders. Pine scented aftershave surrounded her to block out the sweet tang of illegal tobacco.

She gulped as her chest locked and Lincoln spun her around to face him. "It's okay. You're safe." He enfolded her, protecting her from Jack's misguided spectre as it circled overhead. Linc pressed her face against his shoulder, his arms providing a fortress. The discarded box shifted as he moved his feet, its metallic surface grating against the loose grit and straw walked into the office over time. "You're okay," he promised. He rested his chin on the top of her head, his left hand stroking her shoulder as though trying to press safety through her blouse and into her skin.

The fear released her as quickly as it had claimed her heart, leaving Hana with the sensation of dirtiness. She drew away with enough suddenness to hit her back against the door. Pain blossomed through her spine and into her neck. "Logan will kill you." The words spluttered free, and she squirmed against the wood, the handle digging into her hip.

She jerked at Linc's bark of laughter. "You think?" He turned away from her, moving back behind the safety of his desk. "A mercy killing." He wagged an index finger at her. "I like it."

The withdrawal of adrenaline left Hana shaking. She pressed herself against the door and eyed the box laying on its side on the floor. One edge touched the tassels of a worn rug which ran in front of two chairs. Placed there for occasional visitors, they hadn't moved in the eighteen months since Lincoln took over management of the stables. Nobody ever sat to discuss business. They walked around the stables, peering into loose boxes or retired to the hotel bar.

Hana blew out a breath and scrubbed her eyes with her knuckles. "Sorry for bothering you," she managed. She ducked and retrieved the box, clasping it hard enough for her knuckles to show through the skin. "Logan said not to ask."

"Did he?" Lincoln raised a blond eyebrow and dipped his chin. "Did he say why?"

Hana shook her head and reached for the door handle, finding it turned on the first attempt. She hissed out her irritation at having twisted it the wrong way and made a fool of herself.

"Parkinson's."

"Pardon?" Hana half turned, closing her eyes and gulping in the warm air which sneaked through the gap between the door and the frame. The perfumed scent of horse flesh drifted across her face. Horses, dry grass and summer.

"I have Parkinson's disease."

She whipped around to find Lincoln watching her. His handsome face contained defiance. And fear. Hana licked her lips, but no helpful words filtered into her brain to dig herself out of the mess she'd made. Linc's smile also held sadness.

"Turns out taking a bullet for your man led to my diagnosis. I'm not sure if it was a happy accident or a curse." He frowned and lines dug deep furrows into his brow.

"I don't know what to say," Hana whispered. She clasped the box to her chest like a lifeline, the jagged edges poking through her blouse.

"Say you still hate me." Linc swallowed, the sound strangled in his throat. "Change nothing out of pity."

"I won't." Hana turned towards the door, resting her forehead against the knotty edge. Roughness grazed her skin. "But I don't think I ever hated you, Linc. You did some mean things to me, but I didn't hate you."

She glanced back to find he'd flattened his lips into a thin line. As he lifted the pen in front of him, she saw the subtlest shaking of his hand. "Strangling, threatening and blackmail? Don't dismiss it yet. That was some of my finest work," he said, feigning joviality through a light-hearted tone. The pen bounced in his fingers and Hana slid through the widening gap with her prize, closing the door behind her.

60

Chamfron

"Hey, Hana. What do you need?" A roar preceded Toby's appearance on a bright red quad bike. The safety helmet perched on top of his head, the chin strap dangling alongside his jaw.

Hana groaned. "I've seen you now!" She slapped her thigh with her spare hand. "So, I'm legally responsible." She jabbed a finger at his incorrectly worn helmet.

Toby snorted. He killed the engine and dismounted from the bike, his long legs bending and flexing as he stood. He dangled the helmet from the handlebar. "Someone took the health and safety talks to heart, didn't they?" He grinned at her. "After your stunt with my truck, I should report you for the hell of it." He slapped the side of his head with the heel of his hand and affected a high, squeaky voice. "Ouch! It really hurts. You should have made me wear my hat, you being a director and all." His irises sparkled with mischief. He punched her left shoulder with his fist, the contact minimal and aiming for camaraderie. "I won't tell if you won't." He glanced up at the sun and judged the time without checking his watch. "What do you want, anyway?"

Hana blinked and gaped at him. Her encounter with Lincoln had robbed her of sense and direction. Toby snatched the box from beneath her arm. "Linc said you want this open." He spun on his heel and jerked his head towards the equipment shed. New roll doors kept out opportunist thieves, and he headed for a locked door around the side.

Hana forced herself to follow him, curiosity budding to life beneath the other swirling emotions. "Linc called you?" Her voice wavered as Toby used a numbered code on the locking mechanism.

"Yeah. Just then." Toby frowned. "What's wrong with you? Didn't you enjoy looking at Logan's latest scheme?"

"I did." Hana followed him into the darkness of the vast shed. Skylights created pools of sunshine in long strips of yellow heat in the centre of the room. A sleeping tractor and several quad bikes stood in a neat line. Toby flicked a switch and overhead bulbs bloomed to fill the space with white light. He headed for a workbench towards the back and dumped the box in the centre.

The shuffle of footsteps sounded behind them. A woman stood in the doorway, a pair of riding boots in her hand. "Hey, what should I do with these?"

"Oh." Hana recognised her from the group who'd headed up the mountain with Rawhiti. She frowned. "Are they back already? What happened?"

The woman wrinkled her nose. Her gaze moved from Toby to Hana and back again. "Riding isn't for me," she said with a dramatic sigh. "I got off at the end of the first paddock. The guy at the back untacked my horse and left it there. He said he'd pick up the gear later. Thanks for the loan of the boots."

Hana shrugged. "No worries. Just leave them there and I'll put them away again." She turned back to Toby, waiting for the sound of the woman's footsteps to fade.

"Didn't Logan try to open this yesterday?" Toby prodded it with his finger and frowned. "Didn't it come from Rueben's place?"

Hana nodded. "Yeah. He said he bent it by accident."

Toby wrinkled his nose and shrugged. "Not like him to admit defeat," he mused. Lifting the box he peered at marks along the slim gap between the lid and base. "Look." He held it towards Hana, his index finger tapping the metal and causing a dull thud to echo inside it. "The clown tried to grind it along the opening. That was never gonna work."

"Do you know how to do it?" Hana drew closer so that her hand bumped his hip. She glanced up at him. "Sorry for taking your truck the other day." She offered the apology by way of consolation. "I needed to meet Melissa without Logan. I hoped she'd tell me where Tama had gone."

"But she didn't." Toby raised a blond eyebrow and Hana shook her head.

"She didn't know." She sighed and drew back enough to lean against the seat of a nearby quad bike. "We know he met with her about Reuben's fire and the documentation was never filed. Then his house got burgled and then Melissa's apartment, and her ex-wife's place." The tale tumbled free, surprising Hana with the catharsis of sharing it. "Then Bodie took me to the morgue to see a boy he thought was Tama."

Toby's eyelashes fluttered, and he shook his head. "Shit, Hana."

"It wasn't him." Her eyes glittered with unshed tears. A flush of embarrassment worked its way up her throat and into her cheeks. She'd told him nothing he didn't already know after the private detective's appearance at her house. She floundered, watching his fingers brush the pitted surface of the box. "Sorry, you know all this. But Bo phoned me earlier, and it seems a fire officer's brother got drunk and fell in the river. He had a service hat, but it wasn't his." Her nostrils tingled with the remembered scent of the morgue. Overpowering disinfectant fumes infused her with the need to gag. She cleared her throat to dispel it and licked her lips. "I promised to call him back but I'm distracting myself. Sorry I took your truck, but I filled it with diesel."

Toby turned back to the bench and used a handle to open a clamp. He slotted the cash box into it sideways and tightened the teeth. Then he reached to plug in the drill he snatched from an organised shadow board. Hana recognised her husband's freakish need for neatness in the angular outlines of the tools hand drawn onto the board. She covered her ears with her hands as the shriek of metal on metal filled the space. Orange sparks scattered onto the bench and the floor, flaring before they died.

The drill bit whirred slower before stopping. "See, easy." Toby placed the tool on its side. Hana edged closer, wrinkling her nose against the scent of heated metal. Silver shards dotted the surface of the bench like glittering snowflakes. Toby released the box from the clamp and sat it on its warped bottom panel. "We might need to prise this off the front," he said, tapping the remains of the lock. "Or maybe not." The lid lifted in response to his first gentle tug.

Hana peered inside as a hush descended over them both. Their heads bumped in their eagerness to view the box's contents.

"Well, that's disappointing," Toby said finally, reaching in to poke the aged pieces of paper and the frayed cloth bag. "I was hoping for a lottery win."

※※※ ※※※

"Careful!" Hana shoved Toby's fingers aside as he reached for the fragile paper at the top of the box. "It looks old. I need to take this to Will and get him to decant it."

"Can I open that?" Toby's index finger strayed towards a pale cloth bag nestled below it. The frayed tassels of a drawstring poked from beneath the paper item.

"No." The end of Hana's ponytail tapped Toby's powerful left biceps as she shook her head. "Will should do it in case it's precious or something." She pursed her lips and wondered about the *or something*. Her hands trembled as she reached for the box, lifting it with care from the silver shavings remaining of the lock.

A spark of an ethereal flame coursed up her spine, and she shivered in response. The charred and bent box took on new meaning in its open state. It contained the power to wreak absolute destruction on the Du Rose family, something it hadn't possessed while closed.

Toby flattened his lips into a narrow arc of sympathy as Hana lifted it free. She closed the lid over the contents and cradled it against her blouse.

"You look nice today." He jerked his head towards the flared sleeves and blinked. Hana watched his pupils dilate and observed his mental struggle as he tried not to stare at her exposed cleavage. Then he sighed and rescued himself from the terrible path his mind caused him to stray onto. Hana lifted the box to cover more of her chest and thanked him for his help. She sensed him staring at her as she dipped to collect the discarded boots and left the shed.

Will greeted her with a grunt as she reached the entrance to the museum. He raised a bushy eyebrow towards the box cradled in her arms. "Oh, bugger!" he breathed, turning his chair and wheeling after her. "What disaster have you dug up now, wahine?"

Hana walked into their shared office and laid her prize on the table, standing back to wipe her hands on her jeans. She dropped the boots under the desk. "It's the box I told you about. From Reuben's fire." She frowned and pursed her lips before leaning down to kiss Will's bristly cheek. "Toby drilled it open for me. We touched nothing inside but we should."

"Oh, should we?" Will's eyebrows danced on his forehead as he wheeled closer to the table. Curiosity crackled over his head like electricity loosed from a transmitter and Hana caught his excitement and stepped next to him.

"Yes. I'll get gloves for us both."

"Got mine." He tugged a pair of cotton gloves from the top pocket of his waistcoat. He slipped them over his gnarled fingers and waved Hana away from him. "You don't need any because you won't be touching anything."

Hana narrowed her eyes and placed her hands on her hips. She jutted out her chin and lifted her shoulders. "You can't tell me what to do!" she snapped.

Will glanced back at her and his eyes bugged. "I can and I will! Cover up those uma before I go blind!"

Grumbling, Hana tugged an apron from a hook on the wall and slipped it over her head. "Wait!" she demanded. "I found it."

Will leaned an elbow on the desk and turned to face her. "Does your tāne know you have this?"

Hana nodded her head hard enough to give her a pain in her neck. "Yes. I promise," she replied with emphasis. "He said I could take it. He even told me he'd tried to open it yesterday. Someone else already tried though. I looked at it a few days ago and it was already bent out of shape."

Will lifted the box, keeping the two halves closed as he examined the melted paint on its battered surface. The welts from Logan's efforts scarred the opening on one side and he shook his head. "It's from the 1960s," he said, his tone soft. He turned it over in his fingers and studied the lid, tapping a gloved index finger in the centre. "It should have a handle welded on here. I'm guessing it wore a nice coat of forest green gloss paint at the time of manufacture. It melted in the fire." The fibres of his glove caught against the rough surface. Hana held her breath, desperate for him to work faster. "Logan added the fresh scratches, but these are older." Hana noticed a tremor in his hand as he lifted the box to examine the side of the lid.

"There's a paper inside it and a rectangular cloth bag." She edged closer and sought Will's approval. "It's why the contents don't rattle. They fill the whole box. I stopped Toby from removing them."

Will grunted low in his throat and his fingers coasted across the sharp lip at the junction of the lid and base. He wrinkled his nose and after his painstaking examination, he set it on the desk. "Take photos," he said.

Hana exhaled and let her head fall back onto her shoulders. She stared at an array of mysterious marks on the ceiling. "You can do that later," she protested. "I want to look at that paper."

"Tough. Fetch the camera."

Like a crime scene examiner, Will forced her to photograph the box from every angle, and document each scratch and dent they discovered. Hana scribbled notes onto a pad in her looped handwriting, hoping Will didn't make her type them into their cataloguing system before opening the box. As the clock ticked without mercy towards the end of school, Hana fidgeted and tapped the pen on the lined surface of the pad. The curve of Will's lips communicated his enjoyment of her discomfort. So, she accepted the delay as punishment for her abandonment of their joint project and held her breath in expectation of the treat which lay just beneath the battered lid.

The hinges creaked as Will lifted the twisted lid. Hana swallowed and stilled the urge to shove him out of the way and snatch up the contents. He forced her to photograph the items in their situation before picking up the folded paper. Hana ground her teeth and craved knowledge like a burning brand against her forehead.

"There you are!" The loud greeting caused Will to drop the paper, and he swore with enough viciousness to send Leslie backwards a few paces.

Hana exhaled and gave her a feckless wave. The camera strap dangled from her other hand and she winced in apology. A glance at the clock showed she'd run out of time. "Damn!" Her voice rose into a wail. "I need to go to school!" She nudged Will's shoulder with the camera. "You did that on purpose!"

"What are you looking at, you grumpy old man?" Leslie entered the office and her breasts jostled Hana out of position as she stared into the box. "Oh." Her eyes widened, and she screwed her neck around to look at Hana. "You found it."

"This is a birth certificate." Will used tweezers to spread the paper open on the desk. Fragile and yellowed, age had decayed its surface. Tiny flecks of fluff speckled the desk as Will put the folds under pressure by opening it. Faded typeface scrolled above faint pink lines and Hana read the name over his shoulder.

"Catherine Finlaggan." She wrinkled her nose. "Is that what it says?" She exhaled in disappointment. "It's the short birth certificate. Pity it doesn't show the parents and their occupations."

Will nodded and lifted a magnifying glass from a nearby pot. Pens and pencils clanked in its wake as he removed it. He peered at the faint brown ink of the registrar's name. "I can't read this." Turquoise print appeared smudged and distorted. "This would have told us which office registered the birth. Never mind. See here, the date is the twenty-third of February."

"1969." Leslie finished the date for him and curled back her upper lip into a snarl. "That's the year I married that no good idiot from Kawhia." Her expression softened. "But he was a fine looker back in those days. Every girl in the township fancied him." Her exaggerated breath moved the delicate paper in Will's fingers. "I didn't realise he'd shagged most of them too."

"Hush, woman!" he barked. "I don't want your sexual history again, thanks." He jerked his head towards Hana. "It's bad enough having this girl smacking the back of my head with her push-up boobies. It contravenes all kinds of work place regulations."

"Push-up bra," Hana corrected, "although I guess it creates push-up boobies." She took a step back, pulled the apron away from her blouse and peered down her cleavage. "Do you think I'm too old for push-ups?"

"They look good. Do you think one of them pushy-uppies might work on my babies?" Leslie collected her voluptuous breasts in both cupped hands and shifted them up towards her chin. "What did your tāne say, anyway?" She pushed Hana's face aside and inserted her own into the apron. "They look very upright. My nipples haven't faced the same way since 1986."

Hana grinned. "Logan said little. I think he liked them though." Her shoulders twitched, and she giggled. Leslie caught her inference and cackled loud enough to make Will wince.

"Ow! You go girl. You did the nasty in the wild, didn't you," she squawked. She slapped Hana's arm, and the camera swung and bumped against Will's head.

"Bugger off!" he yelled. "Both of youse. Get out!"

"But it's my box!" Hana dumped the camera into Leslie's arms and lurched towards the table. Will shoved it out of her way and she hung over his shoulder, her hands grappling in mid-air.

"Get your push-ups off my head!" he shouted, his voice muffled. "I'm calling WorkSafe!" His wheelchair shifted forward under their combined weight and Hana's gaze fell on the birth certificate as Will engaged the brake.

Her phone vibrated in her back pocket and dread snaked its way through her sense of competition. Caroline's persistence bordered on harassment and she acknowledged the sickening fear. The inmate held her in a vice, forcing her to keep Edin while maintaining the right to take her away at a moment's notice. It was a double whammy of the worst kind.

"Oh!" Hana stood and took a few laboured steps back, her breath catching in her chest. The fight left her but another hideous thought budded into a filthy taste on her tongue. "Alfred remembered Antoinette owning a similar box." She stared from Leslie to Will, seeking confirmation or denial. "What if Caroline is Catherine Finlaggan?"

61

Terret

Will released a groan and tore the gloves from his fingers. "Bloody hell!" he growled. "Here she goes again. The Caroline obsession. She goes from A to Z and misses out all the letters in between."

Hana waved her hands in front of her. "No, listen to me for a minute. Why did Antoinette keep a child's birth certificate hidden in a cash box?"

Leslie shrugged. "Maybe they lost a baby."

"That makes no sense." The idea caught fire and Hana burned with its intensity, frustrated at her audience's lack of enthusiasm. "Why would the child have a different last name?"

"Caroline had a different surname until she married Kane, remember?" Leslie's eyes narrowed, her unkempt eyebrows creating a frill over her hazel irises. "It convinced you last year that Kane and Caroline committed incest."

Hana pressed her fingers over her heart. "No one would be happier than me to prove otherwise," she said, her voice lowering. "Don't forget I'm raising their daughter."

"We're not likely to forget it," Leslie grumbled.

"Go get your tamariki," Will ordered. He glanced up at the clock above the door. "Don't be late."

"I want to see what's in the bag." Hana bent her legs and pressed her knees together, frustration making her spine rigid. "Open it and then I'll leave."

"I'll fetch the babies." Leslie's expression darkened with distaste as she drew back her lips. She edged away from the box and held out her hand for Hana's truck keys. "I want nothing to do with this. I'll bring the tamariki back here for some cake."

"No!" Will shoved Hana's thigh with his gnarled hand. "She's trouble. Take her with you."

"Open the bag." Hana glanced at the clock again and ground her teeth in her jaw. "And in the future, I'll do my own investigations before I bring you anything I find on my husband's property."

Leslie blinked at the fury in Hana's eyes and pursed her lips into a line. She nudged Will's shoulder. "Just do what she says," she advised. "She's got that look in her eye."

He turned back to the desk with a grunt and tugged the gloves over his fingers. Hana closed her eyes against the painstaking movements intended to cause her frustration. A dull thud sent her skittering forward to peer over Will's shoulder. "What's that?" she demanded.

"Give me room." He flapped his hand behind his head and Hana took a reluctant step backwards, clattering with Leslie.

He worked with care, lifting the box and tipping the cloth bag into his hand. It held a rectangular item and his wrist bent enough to indicate its heaviness. "Help me weigh it," he ordered and Hana opened a cupboard behind her and pulled out a flat scale. She activated the digital display and set it next to Will on the desk. He laid the bag onto it with a delicate sleight of hand. "Four hundred and fifty three grammes," he said, squinting at the display. "Or a pound in Imperial measurement."

"But what is it?"

Leslie bumped her shoulder. "Even he can't see through bags!"

Will released the drawstring and Hana held her breath. Thin tissue paper covered the item which slid into his gloved palm. He used the tweezers to prise apart the tattered folds, and the women gasped as something yellow winked beneath the office lights.

"A gold bar?" Leslie wrinkled her nose and shrugged. "Reuben didn't have a dollar to his name when he died. Why would he keep a gold bar in a box and starve?"

"It's not a bar." Will leaned back and stretched his arms. "It's gold leaf."

"For cakes?" Leslie cheered up and her eyes glazed as she imagined herself serving Alfie gold edged muffins. She held out her hand and Will nudged it aside with a shake of his head.

"No. This looks expensive. It might be twenty-two carat gold." He tilted his head sideways to inspect dents around the edges which showed the bending of the delicate pages. "We need to engage an expert. It looks old to me, and we found it with a birth certificate from the late sixties." He glared sideways at Leslie. "You can't just slap it onto muffins."

Hana exhaled. "What is it worth? The expert might cost more than the value of the find."

Will shook his head. "Fifteen thousand dollars is a conservative estimate. I'll study it some more and make a phone call."

"Please can I take the birth certificate?" Hana held out her hand, unsurprised when he shook his head.

"No. It stays together for now." His eyebrows drew together in a line. "You can take a picture on your phone if you must. I'll make some proper digital scans if I ever get an assistant."

Hana snapped a picture using her phone camera and glared at Will as she walked towards the door. Her fingers grappled behind her at the apron strings.

"Just keep it on," he advised, a low chuckle in his throat. "Spare the little children."

62

Rosette

Hana parted company with Leslie in the hotel car park as they debated which of them would fetch the children from school.

Leslie settled her hands over her hips. "They love it when I get them," she protested. "Give me your keys and I'll bring them back here."

Hana pursed her lips and pondered how many household chores she could get done in the half an hour it took Leslie to fetch the children and drive home. She tapped her foot on the floor. "Okay. Thanks. But I can't decide whether to visit with Alfie or whack a load of washing into the machine at home. And I still need to call Bo."

"Do both. Call him at the same time." Leslie held out her hand, the keys to her rusting Toyota already dangling from her index finger. "Swap."

Hana handed over her keys with reluctance. "Add no more dings to the side then please. I think Logan booked it into the panel beater's tomorrow."

Leslie drew back with indignation marching across her features. She tossed her greying hair and straightened her shoulders. "As if!" she protested. "Not with my mokopuna looking."

Hana watched her drive the truck out of her parking space in the staff car park. She trudged towards Leslie's car parked in the shade of a totara tree and wrinkled her nose as she opened the driver's door. The heavy scent of dog wafted out, despite the fact her and Alfred had never owned one. Hana paused a moment for the smell to dissipate. She used the creaking handle below the window and cranked it open enough to create ventilation.

She'd remembered Tama's washing half way down the mountain and recalled abandoning the task after Caroline's call. Poking her nose into the car, she realised she'd need to brave it and just set off if she intended to meet the children at Alfie's apartment. Her phone vibrated in her pocket as she sank into the driver's seat.

"Hey, Bo." The fingers of her other hand closed around the steering wheel and she recoiled as something sticky transferred to her thumb. "Yuk!" she hissed and wiped it on her apron.

"I had a missed call," he said, his voice clearer than before. "Was it you?"

"No." Hana leaned her head against the rest and then thought better of it, bouncing forward and hearing her neck crack. "I'm nipping up to the house to do some washing. I intended to call you there."

"All good." Bodie cleared his throat. "Jas says hi." Wet sounds issued from the speaker and doused Hana's ear.

"Say hi back," she replied. "I miss him. We'll come down soon, or maybe you could visit here?"

"Sounds great. The kids love your place. Hope doesn't stop talking about that riding lesson you gave her last time Amy drove them to see you."

Hana exhaled and jabbed the key in the ignition. "We had the best day," she said with a smile. The car started with a shuddering reluctance and backfired a cloud of dark exhaust fumes. "Sorry, I've borrowed Leslie's car to get home. I'm not sure it'll carry me up the hill." She set her phone between her legs on the seat. "I've got you on speaker because there's no Bluetooth. You can't arrest me because I'm on private property."

Bodie snorted. "The law is there to protect you, Mum, because driving while speaking on the phone is dangerous. But no, I can't arrest you. The lawmakers realised long ago that they couldn't legislate against stupid."

"But they keep trying." Hana released the hand brake and the car bunny hopped out of the car park. "Tell me about that registration plate for the car I clattered with the other night." She paused to let a food delivery truck rumble past, the brakes squealing in protest. "Who do I send the bill to for the panel beating?"

"Is the car you're driving now roadworthy?" Bodie huffed out a breath at a horrible clunk. "No, don't answer that. I hope you're at least wearing your seatbelt."

"Yeah, I'm wearing my belt but let's not go there with the state of the car," Hana replied. "Alfie still consults on the beef herd, so Logan offered him and Leslie a fleet truck because she does all the driving. She said no because this car apparently has sentimental value. I think it's just because she doesn't want to accept anything else from Logan."

Bodie made no response and Hana winced. Grateful for his uneasy truce with her husband, she turned onto their driveway and pushed the gear lever into second. The engine wailed.

"The plate is registered to an address in Auckland," Bodie said. His voice rose as Hana navigated the first of many hairpin bends. "Jas! Don't make your sister do that! Hope, you don't have to, honey. She's not your sergeant, mate, she's your sister."

Hana bit her lip and smiled. "Am I allowed the address for the registration plate? We need to put in a claim."

Bodie blew out a breath. "You don't want it, Mum. Just forget it. Claim on your insurance and put it behind you."

"What? Why?" Hana stopped on the steep incline to allow a family of pukeko to traipse across in front of the vehicle. The sticky foot brake made a grinding sound, and the car rolled back enough for her to panic and yank on the hand brake. The birds took their time, stalking on their ungainly legs and unafraid of the revving engine. "Damn, I'm stuck," Hana breathed.

"What do you mean? Stuck where?"

Hana tutted. "I stopped for some birds and the foot brake wouldn't hold." She pumped the gas and switched her left foot from the brake to the clutch. The car lurched backwards, and she fought to find clutch-bite. "How does she drive up this hill?" she marvelled. "Leslie must just slam her foot down at the bottom and not stop for anything." The clutch caught, and she released a sigh of relief as the engine revved and the vehicle rolled forward. "I'm confiscating this car," she said with a shake of her head. "It can't be roadworthy. No wonder she borrows mine when she transports the children anywhere. The woman must secretly be Lewis Hamilton." The car coasted around another bend and the phone slipped from between Hana's thighs, landing on the floor at her feet. She swore. "Don't say '*I told you so*,' but you're on the floor now, Bo. Please don't slip under the brake pedal. I'm almost at the top of the hill." A clunk revealed the phone sliding beneath her seat and hitting the array of wires dangling there. Hana didn't understand Bodie's muffled reply.

"Why do I always think I know best?" she hissed through gritted teeth. A bang sounded from somewhere underneath the vehicle, followed by a hideous, teeth-aching grinding. Hana glanced in her side mirror and saw sparks flying out from beneath the chassis at a point below the rear seats. Knowing that neither brake would hold the car in place if she stopped, she pushed on the gas pedal and forced it up the steepest incline of the mountain. Her rear-view mirror showed grooves in the gravel as the sparks increased. The engine boomed, the sound echoing off the side of the rocky ridge and hurling itself onto the paddocks far below her.

The grinding stopped as the exhaust pipe detached itself from the baffle. It bounced away behind her. Hana groaned. She'd need to alert Logan before he drove over it and damaged his truck. The boom continued, and she rounded the last bend, sensing the camber of the narrow road change as it dipped downhill. The car picked up speed and Hana pressed the brake, gasping when her momentum didn't change.

She only noticed the vehicle parked outside her gate as she ploughed straight into it.

63

Trace

Pain blossomed outwards from a point above Hana's nose. She gasped and her lungs restarted as though she'd held her breath for far too long. Her fingers scrabbled at her face, smearing aside the blood which coursed from the injury. Steam rose in a haze from a space beneath the crumpled bonnet, curling and hissing as it dissipated into the azure sky.

Hana tugged at the seatbelt, wincing as it cut into her shoulder and formed a tight band across her chest. She followed the webbing down to its junction in the socket next to her left hip, depressing the button three times before it released. The buckle flew up and slapped her chin as it recoiled back into its housing. The rear-view mirror displayed the back seats of the car and the empty road behind. Hana leaned up to stare into it, shocked at the amount of blood coating her cheeks and forehead. It originated from a cut across the bridge of her nose where her face hit the steering wheel on impact. "No air bags," she murmured, patting the bulge beneath her collar bone where the pacemaker lay. "No heart attack."

The crumpled bonnet obscured the view ahead, and she tugged on the door handle, desperate to escape. Meeting resistance, she panicked. "Bloody car!" she wailed. "Let me out!"

The door gave way beneath her weight and she tumbled out and onto the gravel. Grit dug into her elbows as her legs remained in the foot well.

"Steady, steady! Oh, crap!" A woman's voice spoke near her left ear and brawny arms slipped beneath Hana's armpits. She felt herself hoisted into the air and set on her feet. "Lean against the car," the voice continued. "Well, what's left of it, anyway."

Hot metal bore through Hana's jeans as she rested her hip against the chassis of Leslie's car. Steam billowed from a puncture in the radiator, turning back to water and trickling beneath Hana's boots. She bent at the waist and clasped her knees, aware of a sickening sensation rising into her throat. The apron billowed at the neck and her plump breasts waved to her from inside the push-up bra. The left one attempted to escape and Hana sighed.

"Stay upright." The voice held the command born of experience. "You're bleeding."

Hana rubbed blood from her eyelids and peered up at the speaker. She blinked at the familiar woman. "Jordan?" She groaned. "I'm sorry about your car. The brakes failed and I couldn't stop. And I dropped my phone under the seat." She gulped. "I hope Bo didn't hear any of that."

Jordan's face screwed up into a sneer. "You were driving while speaking on the phone?"

"Not exactly." Hana shook her head. "The exhaust pipe dropped off half way up the mountain and the brakes are dodgy so I couldn't stop. I came around the corner and they failed completely."

Jordan tugged a tissue from her pocket and handed it to Hana. "It's clean," she said with enough conviction to assure she told the truth. "But that's the least of your problems. You just wrote off two cars and a gate."

Hana rested her hands on her knees and bent double. Blood rushed to her head and pulsed at the cut across her nose. "Please can you get my phone?" she asked Jordan. "It's under the seat. My son's probably already on his way here."

Jordan retrieved the device from the back seat of the vehicle. Hana blinked at how far the impact had flung it, grateful for the seatbelt which left a welt across her right shoulder and stopped her following it. "She's fine. Just a cut across her forehead. Yeah, I'll stay with her. Don't worry. No, I don't think she needs an ambulance." Jordan's reassuring tones continued as Hana stumbled in the general direction of her house. The boot of the other car had curled like a scorpion's tail towards the roof. Hana groaned as she patted the twisted bumper, jerking her hand away as a chunk of plastic tumbled onto the gravel.

"Tama," she hissed. "Oh, no. I'm so sorry. You love this car."

"Where are you going?" Jordan demanded. "I need to check your head."

Hana waved a hand towards the house. "Tama's here. And I want to sit down and drink a cup of sugary tea." Shock caused her to channel her mother's old wives' tale about sugar and blood and other things she couldn't remember. With the front half of Tama's car mangled with the metal gate, she weaved her way over the wooden fence to the left of it. Arriving at the front door, she recalled her house keys and turned to stumble back to the wreck.

"Looking for these?" Jordan strode behind her, dangling the fob from her index finger. Hana nodded and sank onto the edge of a wooden planter by the front door. The spines of a miniature lemon tree dug into her left buttock in protest at her uninvited proximity.

Jordan unlocked the front door with deft fingers but halted on the mat at the sound of the burglar alarm beeping a warning. Hana groaned and hauled herself upright, pausing with her fingers over the keypad. For a moment, the code evaded her, the numbers swirling in front of her face. "Logan's birthday," she breathed as the speed of the beeps increased as though hurrying her. She pressed the buttons until the sound stopped and then turned to survey her hallway.

"I might revise that ambulance decision." Jordan winced. "You don't look so good."

"I'm okay." Hana used the flapping cuff of her sleeve to dab blood from her eyebrows. "We have a first aid kit in the kitchen. I need to see Tama first. Why didn't he turn off the burglar alarm?"

Jordan cocked her head, her ponytail swinging either side of her neck like a pendulum. "You might need more than sugary tea and a plaster," she cautioned. "I'm a fire officer, not a paramedic."

Hana retrieved the ice cream tub containing medical supplies from the pantry. Jordan confiscated it as she fumbled with the bendy lid. "Sit." She pointed to a dining chair and Hana sank into it with a sigh of gratitude.

"Where's my son?" she demanded.

Jordan flattened her lips. She dug through the supplies for long enough to delay her reply. "I thought you might know the answer to that," she said. "I don't know where he is."

"Then why are you driving Tama's car?" Hana asked. "He loves that car. Nobody drives it except him."

Jordan tugged a packet of antiseptic wipes from the box and extracted one. She winced at the mess on Hana's face and tugged free two more. "He left me the keys," she replied. Pausing with the wipe above Hana's nose, she rolled her shoulders and cracked her neck.

"Do you have whiplash?" Hana quailed in her seat as guilt set up a warning sound in her brain. It bore a horrible similarity to the burglar alarm.

"No." Jordan mopped at the cut, her nose wrinkling in concentration. "I got out to open the gate, thank goodness. You came around the bend and I realised you weren't stopping.

"I'm so sorry." Hana closed her eyes to facilitate Jordan's gentle mopping action to coast across her eyelids. She exhaled. "Tama loves that car."

"Loved. Past tense." Jordan's shoulders lowered as though a remembered sadness consumed her.

"He's not dead!" Hana spat the words and her body stiffened.

Jordan stopped mopping and dropped the bloodied wipe onto the table. "No, but the car is," she mused.

"Why are you here?" Hana peered out from beneath a fresh wipe. Its pristine white surface muddied quickly beneath scarlet streaks.

Jordan exhaled but her fingers continued to move across Hana's face. "I came to see Tama." She collected another wipe, the plastic packet crinkling beneath her ministrations. "I need to see him."

"He's not here!" Hana reached up and clasped her wrist. Jordan's hand stilled. "He's still missing."

Jordan winced. "That's bad. I didn't realise." She darted a glance at the ceiling as though considering an internal issue. "I guess I should probably tell you the truth then."

"What about?" Hana demanded. "Do you know something?" A steady vibration issued from her mobile phone. It moved a few millimetres with every buzz and Hana saw Caroline's identity number flash across the screen. "Leave it!" she commanded as Jordan dropped the wipe and reached for it. "Tell me about Tama."

A bang sounded at the front of the house and a gust of warm air moved the childish scribbles taped to the fridge. Heavy footsteps pounded along the hallway and Hana tensed as Logan exploded into the kitchen. "What the hell?" he shouted. His gaze took in Jordan, her hand half raised and a bloodied wipe still clasped in her fingers.

Logan lifted the mobile phone in his hand and pressed it against his ear. "She's here," he said to the person on the other end of the call. "She's upright but bleeding. I'll let you know more once I know what happened." He frowned, his demeanour dark and foreboding. "Yeah, she's totalled both cars and the gate." Deft fingers pushed the phone back into his jeans pocket and Logan reached Hana's side in three giant strides. "What did you do?" he demanded.

A spark flared in Hana's heart and ignited the waiting inferno in her chest. "What did I do?" Her voice rose high enough to send Logan back two paces. "What do you think I did?" Guilt and shame mingled like oil and water, smearing her usual good sense with a muddiness which stuck to every syllable. "I stole a car, talked on an unsecured phone, ram raided my own house and almost killed a woman! Just for kicks, Logan! What can I say, boredom is a thing."

"Wait, what?" Logan blinked and his right hand rose to sift his fringe. "I didn't suggest you did it on purpose." He glanced across at Jordan and he swallowed his next sentence. "Are you okay?" He moderated his tone in response to the indignation flaring behind Hana's pupils. "At least you didn't hit the kauri tree." The attempt at humour bombed as tears prickled against her irises.

"Congratulations," she snarled. "At least your heritage is safe."

Wrong footed, Logan looked to Jordan for inspiration. She rifled in the first aid box and offered him neither assistance nor information. He cleared his throat. "I'll start again. Are you okay? Bodie phoned me in a panic and I've got half of someone's exhaust pipe in the back of the truck."

Guilt tore at Hana's insides at the enormity of her wrecking spree. Her boot pressed against the tiles as she relived the moment of engaging the foot brake and realising her speed hadn't diminished. Logan's instant assumption of her recklessness fuelled her misery and sent her brain recycling to find a different ending.

If only Jordan hadn't parked outside the gate.

If only she'd gone for the children in her own truck.

If only she hadn't defied Logan by accepting care for Edin.

If only Caroline would stop hounding her.

Hana rose on shaking legs and ran from the room, travelling by muscle memory of where the kitchen ended and the hallway began. The recriminations began in the silence of her bedroom and she sank onto the bed and gave in to them.

What if the children had been in the car with her?

What if Jordan hadn't already walked through the gate?

"Hey." Logan's strong fingers closed around her shoulder and she gasped as though inhaling water. "I didn't mean to make it your fault."

64

Liverpool Bit

"**S**top!" Hana's heart pounded as she picked a fight with her husband. She dabbed at the cut on her forehead while sinking onto the mattress. She assumed Jordan had extracted herself from their heated spat when she didn't follow Logan into the bedroom. "Don't lecture me. I'm not a child."

"Then stop behaving like one." The quiet strength in Logan's tone should have served as a warning.

Hana snorted and stepped over the precipice and into emotional danger. "How else do you think I'll get my choices heard over the clamour of your decision making? What do you recommend?" The fingers of her right hand strayed to the outline of the pacemaker and she willed herself towards calm, knowing she'd left it too late to rescue herself.

Logan's hands settled over his hips, and he dipped his head to study her. "I make excellent decisions for my family. That's not what this is about. You just had a car accident, Hana. What's going on with you?" No hint of self-doubt peppered his confidence. Hana ached for even a part share of his self-assurance, condemned to a life of second guessing and running alternative scenarios which always ended in doom. The remains of her energy headed south, treating her to the proverbial two-fingered salute before exiting through her toes. Her body sagged.

"Why are you raging about my decisions suddenly? Are you still upset because I didn't want Edin in the first place?" His gaze drilled a hole in the side of Hana's head and she closed her eyes to avoid meeting its intensity. "Or because I sent her to school?" He tutted and his analytical mind sifted the data, listing more of his choices for her approval. "Or about leasing the hotel? We discussed it and it's worked out well for us." When Hana still didn't reply, he ventured further along the time line of recent changes hoping to placate her temporary insanity. "Is it the part time teaching role?" Impatience leaked through his voice and she sensed him reaching his limit. Then he seized upon his latest scheme with enthusiasm. "I asked you about the hut in the bush. You thought it was a good idea."

Hana's breath exhaled with a whoosh. She tipped backwards and let her body sink into the mattress. A rib ached before settling with a pop, sending a dart of pain into her spine and snaking up the back of her neck. "Don't treat me like an idiot!" she breathed. "You already cleared the space for the bush hut and planned it in your head. The events management company approached you about leasing the venue weeks before you mentioned it to me. The new hotel manager had worked here for a whole month before I met him. You asked me if I thought you should work at the school but I'd already seen the contract arrive in the post. And I thought you wanted to try Sonny out today but you'd removed his shoes which meant you'd decided to keep him. My opinion counted for nothing. You probably won't even keep the name I gave him. It's easy to include me in your decision-making process when the only answer available to me is yes."

The push-up bra dug into her fifth rib and she experienced the urge to rip it off and burn it. She turned onto her side and pushed herself upright. "Go to the children please. Give them some reassurance while I get rid of the blood and make myself presentable." Her gaze fell on Logan at the same instant his lip curled back in a grimace. "Grow up, Logan!" she snarled. "Make nice with Leslie for five bloody minutes, please. It won't kill you." She staggered as she locked her knees and managed some semblance of uprightness. Logan's brow furrowed, and he lifted his left hand as though to support her. Hana waved him aside, though her heart screamed at her to make the rift she'd caused between them right. His hand dropped to his side, the fingers curling into a fist.

"Fine." Logan turned and strode from the bedroom, his heels clicking against the wooden floor. He spun in a complete circle in the doorway and winced as he stared back at her. "I don't think I should leave you." Uncertainty clouded his usual assurance, and he winced. At the glare Hana shot in his direction, he ran his tongue over his upper lip. "Okay," he concluded. He tapped the frame with his index finger and left.

Hana made it as far as the ensuite bathroom and braced her palms against the smooth surface of the sink. She exhaled and bowed her head as the front door slammed at the other end of the house. Curiosity urged her to raise her gaze and admire the mess she'd made of her face, but she delayed the inevitable reality check.

"Hana?" Jordan's soft voice accompanied her tap on the door. "Your husband asked me to check on you." She edged into the room and placed a gentle hand on Hana's shoulder. "He said you're vitriolic, not that I know what it means."

Hana exhaled and met her gaze in the mirror. "It's the original name for sulphuric acid. It means bitter." She snorted and winced at the same time. "Can you tell he teaches English?"

"Right." Jordan's lips formed an upside down arc which caused her chin to flatten. Dimples formed in her cheeks. She stared at a point on Hana's forehead, disinterested in accompanying her down a linguistic rabbit hole. "Let's get you cleaned up and I can assess the damage." She leaned closer and squinted. "You should see a doctor with a head injury like that."

Hana shook her head, and the action sent an unhealthy vibration through her spine. "You'll do for now. Tama's first aid skills are always handy in a crisis." She flapped her hand towards the door. "I'll grab a shower and meet you in the kitchen. Help yourself to drinks or food."

Jordan rolled her eyes. "I'll stay here, thanks. Call me if you feel faint or if your head bleeds again." She pointed towards the bedroom. "I'll be right outside the door."

Hana extracted herself from her blouse with less difficulty than her jeans. She pursed her lips to prevent her grunts escaping and summoning Jordan as she pushed them off inside out and stepped on the legs to release herself. "Ridiculous!" she berated, catching sight of her torso stuffed into the unsuitable underwear. "Whatever were you thinking?"

The heat from the shower eased the aching in her muscles, both from the horse ride and the accident. She washed her hair, causing the cut on her forehead to sting beneath the floral conditioner. A dressing gown and a ponytail later and she felt able to face Jordan and apologise again for rendering her without transport. They sat on the bed while Jordan taped tiny fabric stitches over the cut.

"I could have killed you." The full weight of responsibility bowed Hana's shoulders. "Thank goodness you weren't in the car."

Jordan dropped her hands into her lap. "I almost came yesterday," she admitted. "And the day before and the day before that." She sighed and scrubbed at her eyes with the back of her left hand.

"What didn't you tell me about Tama?" Hana's heart ached with the weight of his disappearance. "Why is he avoiding me?"

Jordan exhaled and rested her chin on her fist. Her body bent into an elegant arc as she balanced her elbow on her knee. "He wouldn't avoid you." She snuffed out a breath. "He adores you. I think it's me he's avoiding. I'm the reason he went into hiding."

"You?" Hana breathed out the word and clasped the other woman's slender wrist. "Do you know where he is?"

The shake of Jordan's head collapsed the fragile tower of hope in Hana's mind. "We agreed it was just sex between us, but then I caught feelings for him. Everyone knows he's in love with the section chief but she's not interested. I thought I could win him over and things seemed okay for a while. But then last month my section had this fire where a man and his wife died. They had this old pair of twinkly lights in their lounge and they left them switched on when they went to bed. The house had illegal wiring, and we assumed when the lights shorted, they melted the rubber coated wire and everything ignited like a tinder box." She exhaled and shook her head. Her ponytail sagged over her shoulder like a loaded washing line.

"This is where it gets weird. I told Tama about the fire because we chat about our shifts. And he started asking all these questions and wanting to know who'd been assigned to the investigation and what they'd concluded." She flapped her hand between them. "He seemed frustrated that I saw it as just another job. He kept saying I didn't understand. One of the other seniors on his rotation got fed up with him poking around at work and told him to leave it. Apparently he just lost it with him. The deputy fire officer sent him home early. I was sleeping off a night shift, and I woke up to find him pacing his room."

Jordan rose and walked to the dressing table. She fingered a china backed hair brush which had belonged to Hana's mother. "Three weeks ago, we had a massive fight, and he went out drinking. He arrived home with lipstick on his shirt and a love bite on his neck. A crew member picked him up for work the next day but I stayed home sick." She focused her attention on the hairbrush, stroking the hand painted sprigs of lavender with a crooked index finger. "I took a week's leave and followed him."

She swallowed. "He met a woman in a cafe twice and then again in a bar. I figured I'd caught him cheating."

Hana groaned. "What did the woman look like?"

Jordan didn't turn to face her. "Tall. Always well dressed. Quite puffy blonde hair." She lifted her hands to her head and waggled them as though for effect.

"Bright lipstick?" Hana shook her head. "Quite angular? Possibly wearing a wig?"

"Yeah." Jordan turned, her complexion pale. "Do you know her?"

"Yes!" Hana dipped forward with a groan and blood pounded behind her tender forehead. "Melissa Stratton is a former fire investigator. Tama's grandfather died in a fire caused by faulty Christmas lights."

"He never said!" Jordan's eyes widened as though in accusation. Her fists balled by her sides and she took a step towards Hana. "How am I supposed to know that? The only person Tama ever talks about is you. I thought you were his mother when you turned up at the house."

"Well, I'm not." Hana rose and tugged her dressing gown cord tighter. Time sped away from her and she turned her energy towards her children. Logan would last about five minutes in Leslie's company before extracting them all. It gave her little time to prepare for their arrival home and the shock of seeing the remnants of Leslie's vehicle mounted on the rear of Tama's. "I should get ready." She bent to dig comfortable underwear from the drawer next to her bedside. She shimmied into the knickers but used Jordan's distraction to shrug from the robe and wriggle into the cloth bra. The wardrobe disgorged a set of lilac lounge-wear she'd purchased on a whim and never worn. She considered a litany of kind phrases to soothe Jordan's jealousy. Tama hadn't slept with Melissa, but a love bite and a lipstick stained shirt suggested he'd cheated with someone. She considered the lipstick stain on the shirt she'd brought home from his bedroom.

Hana eyed the bathroom and weighed her skill with make-up hoping to disguise her injury for her children's benefit. But Jordan's gasp of desperation halted her half way across the room.

"I did it." Jordan bent double and her voice cracked. "I ransacked his room a week ago looking for evidence." A sob caught in her throat. "And the more I thought about it, the angrier I got. I wrecked his room and threw stuff around downstairs. He arrived back sooner than I expected and I didn't have time to clear up after myself." She stared at Hana, a muted plea in her vivid irises. "He called the cops and left me no choice. I let them think I forgot to lock the back door and someone came in and burgled the house while I slept. That's what I came to tell Tama, that I'm sorry. But if he's still missing, then it's all my fault."

❧❧❧❧❧ ❦❦❦❦❦

"Y̶ou're not serious?" Hana's voice rose into a wail of anger. "You did that?"

"I know, I know." Jordan sank onto the mattress and covered her eyes with her hands. "I got scared when you turned up looking for him. Is it my fault he's disappeared?"

"It certainly didn't help!" Hana grimaced but discovered too late that frowning tugged at the cut on her forehead. She steadied herself and steered towards a calmer expression, relaxing her balled fingers by a sheer act of will. "When did you trash the house?"

"The week before he went missing. I finished my shift at eleven o'clock and showed up at the snooker hall where his team plays. He'd already left. One of the other guys said he'd gone to meet a woman at the Thai restaurant on Quay Street so I drove there. I ordered a take away on my phone and nipped inside, just to catch him cheating." The hand she raised to her eyes shook.

"I picked up my order and bought a drink so I could watch him. They looked cosy with their heads together whispering. I wanted to approach them both and demand an explanation, but public incidents attract the attention of the station chief. An argument with my last boyfriend led to a disciplinary after I tipped a drink over his head at the cinema." She swallowed. "I drove home and wrecked his room looking for the woman's name. When I didn't find it, I trashed the kitchen and lounge. Then he arrived back before I could put everything away where I found it."

"What happened next?"

Jordan exhaled. "We argued when the cops left. I asked him where he disappeared to after the snooker match and he lied. Said he went for a beer with a mate. I called him out and he lost his temper with me. He stayed in his room crashing around until after I left for work. I spent the week waiting for him to ask me to leave. Then he disappeared."

"Okay." Hana slumped into an armchair on the other side of the room. She studied Jordan through narrowed eyes. "So, who gave you the love bite I noticed when we visited on Friday?"

Jordan twisted her lips into a pout. "We slept together on Sunday. But then I followed him to meet that woman again on Monday night after the awards ceremony." She pressed her fingers flat against the mattress. "Sex means nothing to him, does it?"

"No." Hana's shoulders softened. "It's not how you reach Tama. History has taught him to treat it as a throwaway commodity, a weapon or an enticement. I'm sorry for how that makes you feel."

"I just wanted him to love me." Jordan hung her head and Hana pitied her more than she would ever acknowledge. Her answer held too much harshness.

"I don't think he knows how. Let him go." She pursed her lips. "Does he know you have his car?"

Jordan shook her head. "No. Mine failed its Warrant of Fitness the day after I met you and is stuck in the mechanic's yard waiting for a part. Tama left his keys, and I figured he owed me, so I borrowed it."

Hana rolled her eyes. "This is a big mess, Jordan. You need to tell the police there was no burglary."

"No!" The woman rose, the buttons of her jacket clicking as she pulled the lapels closed. "It's not relevant."

"Of course it is!" Hana bit. "It's been falsely linked to two other burglaries. I had a private detective here the other day trying to tie them all together."

A line appeared in Jordan's forehead. "Colin something? Yes, he came to the house a few times. Once before Tama disappeared and again afterwards. He's the husband of the woman Tama meets. He said Tama's only involved with her for the money."

Hana's shoulders slumped, and a leadenness entered her bones. "I'm too old for this," she said with a sigh. "And he lied. Melissa isn't married to anyone. Her ex-wife is the person who hired Colin." She flapped her hand. "This is all too hard."

"How do I get home now?" Jordan's features puckered into an entitled wince. "You've wrecked my transport."

Hana ground her teeth and then regretted the action. She squeezed the end of her nose to stave off the pain. "I don't know and I don't care. My husband might give you a lift to the hotel, but don't bank on it." Hana snapped her fingers. "Also, in the spirit of truthfulness, my son is a detective. He needs to know that you burgled Tama's house." She paused as a thought trailed across her mind. "Did you give the detective this address?"

Jordan flattened her lips into a line. "Not exactly. I thought Tama might have come here, but I only had the name of the hotel and the rough location. Colin promised to let me know if he found him here."

Hana snorted. "Well, obviously he didn't. Instead, he found ten angry men facing him with a shotgun."

"He could have told me Tama wasn't here," Jordan griped. "It would have saved me a trip."

Hana blinked and pursed her lips. Logan hadn't mentioned the private detective's whereabouts, and she hadn't inquired after the man's health. She didn't want to know anything about it. She moved the subject away from the skinny man's encounter with the stockmen. "Did Tama say anything else about the fire which sparked his interest?" She glanced at the clock over the hearth and winced. "My children will be home in a few minutes."

Jordan walked to the window and stared across the vast expanse of bush visible from the ridge. The Tasman lay like a turquoise blanket in the distance. "Not to me. But he pestered the fire investigator daily until she reported him to the deputy." She turned with a sigh. "The investigators discovered the lights didn't cause the fire. They found an accelerant poured underneath a rear window. Turpentine, I think. The plug socket for the lights was situated underneath the same window, so it initially caused confusion."

"So, the lights didn't cause the fire?" Hana whispered. An ugly notion wormed its innocuous way through her mind, refusing to allow her to push it aside in favour of logic and reason. And evidence.

Jordan shook her head. "No. The police arrested the son for arson on the day of the awards night."

"Arson." A memory flooded Hana's inner vision. Its intensity tightened her chest with the acrid tang of smoke, flames crackling with elation as they chewed up the cedar house and spread to the bush nudging its boundary. Her throat locked as she tried to swallow and a sentence died on her lips. A woman screamed like a ghoul from the past, her hair escaping the loose bun and streaming out behind her as she ran.

Into the flames.

Into death with Reuben.

And out of Logan's life without a backward glance.

65

Dandy Brush

The children displayed horror at the vehicle pile-up in their driveway. Phoenix conveyed her fear as tears when she saw the state of Hana's face.

"You have black eyes," she sobbed, pressing her cheek against Hana's shoulder and cutting off her airway with tightly wrapped arms around her neck. "Pansy's mother died last week. I can't cope if you die."

Wiri watched with interest, his body still and his mind racing. "You'll just be like me," he said, his tone flat. "Every time I get a parent, they die or go to prison." He exhaled. "Edin's the same. We're like parent jinxes."

Hana gasped, but Logan saved the situation. He walked through the doorway in time to hear Wiri's statement and swept him off his feet into a bear hug. "You'll never get rid of me, buddy. I'm your worst nightmare." He lowered his voice to a growl and tossed Wiri over his shoulder. Then he tickled the backs of his knees until he shrieked.

"Me! Me!" Edin and Mac gravitated to the furore like moths to a flame, raising their arms and shrieking for a turn. Logan chased them all into the lounge, leaving Hana to reassure her daughter.

Hana sighed and kissed the top of Phoenix's head. "I had a stupid, stupid accident," she said. "But I'll hurt even more when Nonie gets hold of me for wrecking her car."

Phoenix wiped her nose on the sleeve of her pullover. "Poppa Alfie hates that car. He says it's a deaf trap."

"Death trap. Really?" Hana raised an eyebrow which creased the skin on either side of the cut. "Ouch."

"Where's Tama?" Phoenix sat upright and peered into Hana's face. "Is he hiding?"

Hana swallowed, and her body stiffened. "What do you mean?"

"His car is here, silly. You squashed it. Is he in his room?" Her eyes widened and bulged like marbles. She clapped a hand over her mouth. "Oh no! You didn't squash him too, did you?"

"No, no! He isn't here. He lent the car to a friend."

"The lady who Toby drove to meet the taxi?" Phoenix's shoulders lost their tension, and she slumped backwards on the bed and clutched her ankles. "Do you want to see my rolly-pollys what I learned in gym class today?"

Hana watched her daughter flip over onto her face and smiled with indulgence. She scrabbled for the hem of her school skirt before Phoenix rolled off the side of the mattress. "Very nice. Papa said Nonie gave you dinner, so rolly-polly through to the bathroom and grab a shower before bed."

She groaned as Phoenix took her literally and tumbled like a ball from the bed to the doorway. Clattering with the frame, she righted herself before continuing her precarious journey along the hallway.

Logan had placed Hana's phone on the nightstand to charge, and it vibrated itself across the wooden surface. Hana stood, every bone and muscle in her body raising a silent protest. She activated the screen and peered at the number before answering the call. "Hey Bo," she said with a sigh. "I'm fine. Sorry for frightening you."

Bodie grunted. "I phoned Logan when I heard the crash. He said you'd cut your head."

"Just a wee scratch." Hana caught sight of the bruise spreading beneath her eyes and winced at the lie. She licked her lips and glanced at the open door before lowering her voice. "I have a different problem at the moment. Remember Caroline Marsh? Well, Du Rose after she married Kane."

"Yeah."

Hana breathed out through her nose in a snort of festering anger. "She's threatening to tell Izzie about Vic's affair. Says she has friends in Invercargill who can get to her."

"How does she know about that?" Bodie growled. "Who did you tell?"

"Nobody!" Hana swallowed. She didn't want to admit she'd revealed the damaging secret to Logan at the start of their marriage, knowing Bodie would jump to a wrong conclusion. Logan wouldn't tell Caroline the time, let alone something so personal to his wife. She pressed the toes of her right foot against the floor as though stamping on her doubt.

"She worked at the school, right?"

"Yeah, years ago. Are you thinking perhaps Anka gossiped about me?"

"Who else? Ivan knew, and they were married. Maybe it became common knowledge without you realising."

Hana shivered against the hideous thought that her colleagues might have pitied her more after Vik's death for her inadequacy as a wife. She disconnected the phone cord and sank onto the bed. "That makes me feel sick," she admitted.

"Cut ties with her," Bodie advised. "She's toxic. I know you're attached to the little girl, but there must be someone else who can take her."

A giggle erupted from the lounge as Logan's play included Edin. Mac released a belly laugh and Wiri's voice rose above the others.

Hana frowned. "Why did you tell me to just claim on my insurance for the collision with the blue car? Why won't you give me the name of the driver?"

Bodie groaned and Hana sensed his mind working at a premium to avoid telling her the truth. To her surprise, he relented. "The car is registered to Lara Alderbank, Mum. She's a nasty piece of work. Her husband is Clive Alderbank, owner of a merchant shipping and salvage company back in the day. He was also a cabinet minister during the late 1960s and part of some big free trade agreement with China in later years. Odering worked for ages on a racketeering case involving that family and he almost had a nervous breakdown. Evidence disappeared, witnesses turned hostile in court and it became a real mess. That's when he turned his interest to Laval and went after him instead."

"Ah, yes, Detective Sergeant Odering." Hana sighed and flattened her lips into a grimace. She bent the phone connector back on itself along the cord before correcting herself and letting it fall to the floor.

"Detective Chief Inspector Odering," Bodie corrected her. "Remarried, moved to Wellington and rose high and fast through the ranks."

"Lucky him." Hana released a groan. "You've actually just made my problem much worse. Liza told me the family coming after Edin were Clive and Lana Alderbank. She said they weren't a couple, so now I'm confused. Also, if she's the woman in the vehicle I clattered with, did she plan to just take Edin from me? I need to tell Logan." Her voice rose. "She can't just take her, can she?"

Bodie hissed. "No, but I wouldn't put anything past that crowd. It's not like them to do their own dirty work, though, so that's unusual."

"I'll tell Logan," Hana promised. She reiterated the invitation to her son and his family before ending the call. The pain in her forehead swelled to a crescendo as she listened to Logan rough house with the children. She'd wait until later to spoil his evening.

66

Afterwale

Hana tugged her laptop free from beneath the bed and tucked her legs under her as she opened a Google search browser. She researched Lana Alderbank, discovering she owned a boutique near the wharf in Auckland. Her fingers stilled on the keyboard at an image of the store frontage. "Purple Primp," she breathed. "Purple. Woman in purple." She pressed a finger over her lips. Whatever Lana Alderbank had searched for in the rubble of Reuben's house couldn't have been Edin. "But it could have been the box," she whispered to herself. "Which means the box is somehow linked to Edin and Caroline." She searched again and discovered another article. More pieces slotted into place. "Ah, the daughter is also Lana Alderbank," she sighed to herself. The younger woman in an accompanying photograph linked arms with her mother. The article said she'd taken over the running of Purple Primp as the older woman retired.

Finding herself in a mental cul-de-sac, Hana switched her search to newspaper articles from the archives of the New Zealand Herald. She skimmed through the many iterations of

Logan's name in connection to mentions of the hotel and added Caroline to the field. It pained her to see their names snuggled together in the search bar. Her finger hovered over the mouse pad before she forced herself to activate the algorithm, which might reveal the answers she sought.

"There you are," she whispered with a sigh. A younger Logan posed for the coloured photograph, no hint of grey in his dark hair. His half smile conveyed sex appeal to the general populace, but Hana saw only reticence and resignation. Caroline clung to his arm, her short blonde hair immaculate against her tanned face. She smiled like a woman who possessed everything her heart desired and for a while, that had been the truth. A couture skirt lifted in the breeze to show her perfect knees and the elegant curve of her calves. Sunlight kissed her hair with highlights, as though approving of her evident happiness.

The reporter hadn't known Logan owned the hotel in the mountains, or that he could have bought and sold the property he'd graced with his presence. Logan stood next to Mr and Mrs Che, the genuine celebrities of the moment. Hana zoomed in to connect with the dead eyes in Mrs Che's face before jerking backwards in distaste. She blinked at the headline.

'Big business! Yichén Che opens his eleventh restaurant in Auckland during the election campaign.'

Hana scrolled down through the article. *'Millionaire Che is excited to represent the minorities of Auckland in his recent bid for parliament. If successful, he is determined to spearhead calls for a bigger slice of the Chinese market for New Zealand exports. His good friend, Logan Henri Du Rose of Rangiriri, joined Che in the restaurant opening. Du Rose is considered as family by the Ches after his heroic medical intervention when Che collapsed during a business meeting. He brought him back from a near fatal heart attack. Accompanying Du Rose was his new wife, Caroline Du Rose. Caroline is the daughter of 1960s Waikato beauty queen, Antoinette Du Rose.'*

Hana's head jerked back with such ferocity, she released a gasp.

"Would you like more pain killers?" Logan's soft voice cut through her horror. "You shouldn't use a screen with a head injury. Give it here."

"Why does this article say you were married to Caroline?" she snapped. "What haven't you told me?"

Logan sank onto the mattress next to her and tried to take the laptop. He frowned at the newspaper article and shook his head. "I didn't speak to the reporter. She did." He exhaled. "Why doesn't it surprise me she lied? We were there for Che's restaurant opening, not to blab our lives to strangers." He relinquished his hold on the laptop as Hana tugged it hard enough to slide it across her thighs. His teeth clamped down over his bottom lip. "Jealous, babe? Or worried about bigamy?"

"I'm not jealous," Hana grumbled. "Well, maybe a little. Did Mr Che get into parliament?"

"No." Logan shook his head. "Thank goodness."

"Right. But did you know Antoinette was a beauty queen?"

Logan shrugged. "I think my mother won some contests too, but they never progressed beyond the rural ones. White girls always won the major competitions because old white men decided." He leaned sideways and stretched out his arm, causing Hana to dump the laptop on the bed next to her with a squeak. "No, scroll down," Logan urged. "I saw a picture of Whaea Antoinette at the bottom of the article."

Hana turned her body and tapped the mouse pad. She skim read the scanned document until it ended with a black-and-white photograph of a tall woman posing in a long dress and high heels. "Wow!" she whispered. "She was stunning!"

Logan leaned back against the pillows. He slipped his arm around Hana's shoulders. "She looked like my mother, but I never met her. Died before I was born." He blinked. "Did you see they listed Antoinette as Caroline's mother?" He waggled his eyebrows. "Be careful what you wish for, hey?"

Hana left the laptop on the mattress next to her and turned towards his chest. She rested her cheek against his tee shirt with a sigh. "My head hurts," she declared. "And I have lots to tell you."

"Okay." Logan gave her a gentle squeeze before releasing her and rising. "There's a recovery truck coming for Leslie's crap heap in the morning. He'll have to come back for Tama's. They're both totalled."

Hana exhaled with a groan. "I am sorry. It wasn't because I was driving and talking to Bodie. The phone fell under the seat ages before the brakes failed." She swallowed and pursed her lips. "Will Remi from the township drive the recovery truck?"

"Probably, why?"

Hana took a deep breath. "Can you ask him to look at the brakes on all our fleet vehicles? Just in case."

Logan exhaled. "Our trucks are fine, Hana. Leslie's car is a rust bucket and an accident waiting to happen. Let me put these kids to bed and then we'll talk. Yeah? I'll grab the booster seats from your truck and stick them in mine before it gets dark. They might as well drive yours in for panel beating when they take the wrecks." He left the room and Hana sighed with relief, grateful for his calm in the face of a crisis. She heard him moving around the house, directing the children in their routine. When it grew quiet, she imagined him reading their communal bedtime story in one of their bedrooms. She yearned to join in, but her legs refused to budge from the comfy mattress.

Instead, she lifted the laptop onto her thighs and performed another Google search. This time, she sent the algorithms seeking the name Catherine Finlaggan.

"Logan, this is bad." Hana sat in the bed with the laptop balanced on her knees. He shook his head at her as the children trooped into the room to say goodnight.

"Ouchie!" Edin tried to touch the tape on Hana's forehead, her eyes widening as she jerked aside with a wince. "Rongoā," she said, twinkling her fingers. "Nonie?"

"We'll see if she has any cream in the morning," Hana promised. She dipped for a kiss, gratified when Edin put gentle lips over hers. "You can ask her advice tomorrow," she added.

"I don't want a kiss. We can shake hands." Wiri held out his long fingers and Hana took them in hers with a sigh, unwilling to argue about silly things, when a hammer pounded inside her skull.

Mac wrapped his arms around her neck and pointed to his implant. "Mended," he said and gave her a thumb up gesture.

"He wants to wear the processing unit to school tomorrow. I said we'd ask you." Logan smiled as Mac turned his sunny face towards him.

"We'll look at it in the morning," Hana promised, speaking and signing with her hands. Mac twisted his lips but didn't argue.

Logan dispatched the children to their bedrooms and returned with a mug of hot chocolate for Hana. He settled himself on the bed next to her. "I think you can have more paracetamol in an hour," he said, glancing over her shoulder.

Hana rose on her knees and dumped the laptop onto his thighs, before grasping the drink in shaking fingers. "Look at the tab I already opened. It's an article from 1969 about a baby called Catherine Finlaggan."

Logan heaved out a sigh and squinted at the screen. He scrolled down, speed reading the awful story about a baby snatched from outside a corner store in Auckland. "What am I looking at?" he asked when he'd finished. "It's sad that a baby went missing, but I don't understand."

Hana shook her head and regretted it. She winced and touched a finger to the butterfly stitches Jordan had fixed over the cut. Unable to contain her angst and afraid of spilling the drink, she set it on the nightstand. "Okay, I need to back up a little. Toby helped me to open that box I took from your office. Will and I found a parcel containing gold leaf and a birth certificate."

"Weird." Logan leaned back against the pillows, raising his arms above his head and closing his eyes. "Why would Reuben keep a box with gold in it when he couldn't afford to fix up his house?" He exhaled and rolled his eyes. "Apart from the fact he was an alcoholic. I guess that used up his disposable income."

"No, no!" Hana flapped her right hand and let it land on his chest. "I don't think he knew about the box. And it's gold leaf, not a gold bar. Apparently, it has a unique value. That's not what I've discovered. The birth certificate in the box belongs to Catherine Finlaggan." The sharp exhale caused an accidental whistle to escape her lips.

"Oh." Logan sat up and scrolled to the top of the article. The person who'd scanned the original newspaper to create a digital copy had place it at an angle, and he frowned at the blatant disregard for symmetry. "So, that box contained the birth certificate for the baby missing in this story?"

Hana's head bounced on her neck and she groaned again at the pain it caused in her forehead. With quick fingers, she forwarded the article to Bodie in the hope he had access to more in depth information. "Yes," she hissed. "I think Antoinette stole a baby."

"Wait! What? No!" Logan released all three words in succession, like bullets from a machine gun. "Hell, no!" He pushed the laptop off his thighs and bounced to his feet. "Don't say that!" His eyes widened, and he glanced at the open bedroom door. "My family did some dumb stuff, Hana, but stealing a baby is a step too far." Anger consumed him and his shoulders rose to meet his ears as his body hunched. He funnelled his fear as disappointment and directed it towards her. "No more, Hana! It stops right here, right now! You seem determined to pull my whānau to pieces in front of my eyes. Isn't it bad enough as it is?"

The top of his head caught the green voile surrounding the four poster bed, and it cascaded down as a filmy sheet, cutting him off from Hana. A lump grew in her chest as she watched his translucent outline stalk across the bedroom. The door closed behind him with a click.

Hana sank onto her bottom and pushed her hip against the pillow. Her shaking fingers picked up the mug, and she sipped the hot liquid, using the burn against her lips to banish the numbness in her heart. She'd hurt her husband without meaning to, cutting deep into his tenuous hold on his whakapapa and branding more of his family as criminals. He didn't deserve the blackening of his name for the crimes of others, but he'd taken each painful blemish to heart.

Adulterers and murderers.

And she'd just added kidnapping to the growing list.

67

Curb Chain

"Ma! Ma!" The hysterical voice burst from the phone as Hana lifted the device to her ear. She paused and released the white shirt into the laundry basket. Logan drove the children to school, but they still hadn't spoken since the argument the previous night.

"Tama?" She gushed his name as a rush of gratitude. "Tama. Thank goodness you're okay." She paused and waited for his reply, alarmed to hear the frantic gulping on the other end of the line. "You are okay, aren't you?"

"No," he rasped. His voice sounded hoarse and his tone uneven. The words returned as an echo of his environment. A door banged somewhere in the distance. "He's dead, Ma. Ari is dead. They told me what would happen. I stayed away from you, but I didn't even think about him."

"Who's Ari." Hana registered the clunk of the washing machine as it took her weight. Her hip complained against the pressure as she leaned against the metal. "Tama, who's Ari?"

"My friend." He gulped again and her heart broke at the sound of him sobbing. "I just saw it on the news. He's dead."

The hitching of his chest truncated his words. "What have I done, Ma? What have I done?"

"It's okay," Hana soothed. The fingers holding the phone trembled. She lowered her voice and picked through a litany of alternative sentences, seeking the right one for the moment. She licked her lips. "Come home, Tama. Come home, sweetheart. Logan can sort everything out. You know he can."

"Not this!" Tama's voice rose to a screech. "Not this time. He's dead, and it's all my fault." His frantic exhale whooshed through the phone and into Hana's ear. She ached to hold him, to comfort him and make promises.

"It's not your fault, baby," she said, keeping her tone even. "Tell me what happened."

"I can't. I must move again." Impatience clipped his voice as he spoke through his teeth. "I can't believe he's dead."

Hana opened her mouth to speak but contemplated static as Tama disconnected the call. She stared at the black screen for a moment before trying to phone Logan. She went straight to voicemail and checked the time, realising he'd probably just arrived at school with the children. "I can't leave a message," she breathed. "What would I say?"

She slid down the washing machine until her bottom reached the tiled floor. The metal flexed against her spine and she bowed her head until her forehead touched her knees. It proved a mistake as her eyes watered and the migraine headache she'd suffered since the accident intensified. The cut over her nose pulsed.

Tilting her head back, she let her phone slide down to rest on her stomach. The combination of the washing machine's cool metal surface and the tiles helped to salve the ache in her spine. She marked time until she could contact Logan. "He'll fix this," she murmured to herself. "He'll fix everything."

When her phone rang, she jumped. Her stomach muffled its cry, and she lowered her knees to the floor and retrieved it. "Logan?" she said, her tone urgent.

"It's Bo, Mum." Her son's baritone cut across the kilometres between them. "How are you feeling this morning?"

Hana exhaled. "Like I stepped into a boxing ring with my hands tied behind my back." She squeezed her eyes closed, and it seemed to help. "I'm glad you phoned," she began.

"That's nice." He didn't wait for her to launch into a recount of Tama's woes. When his throat cleared, she tensed, tuning into the sound of voices in the background. Distant sirens wailed, and she realised he'd called her from work. Bodie cleared his throat again, as though he disliked the task he'd called to discharge. "We have a problem," he said, lowering his voice. "We suspected that kid fell in the river while drinking." He waited a beat and Hana struggled to switch subjects and catch up with him. "The medical examiner found evidence of a struggle and colleagues searched his home address." When he paused to swallow, Hana knew it was bad. "Mum, we found a hoodie in his bedroom and Tama's driving licence in the pocket. DNA on the cap matches that on the hoodie. My colleagues think it's Tama's and they're launching a manhunt for him. They believe he killed the kid."

68

Forewale

Logan arrived home to find Hana sobbing on the laundry floor. She watched through her tears as his expression morphed from irritation to guilt. "What the hell happened now?" he demanded.

"They think Tama killed the boy at the morgue." Every hitch of her chest caused her forehead to pound. She reached sideways and seized her phone. "Tama called me. Ari was his friend. Someone threatened us. That's why Tama stayed away. But they killed his friend."

Logan squeezed the bridge of his nose between his finger and thumb. "What else did Tama say?"

Hana closed her eyes and leaned her crown against the washing machine. The cool metal contrasted with her warm, thudding head. "I don't know. I don't know." She lifted her right hand and scrubbed at her eyes. Her phone flipped onto the tiles as she tucked her feet beneath her. Tama's shirt lay on the floor like an allegory of his defeat. Hana picked it up and pressed it against her face. "What can we do?" she breathed.

"I don't know." Logan blew out a ragged breath. "I haven't heard from David since yesterday." He pursed his lips together.

"Are you tracking his truck, too?" Hana peered at her husband from behind the folds of Tama's shirt. Hope budded in her soul. "Maybe he found Tama and they're together. Find one, find them both."

Logan wrinkled his nose. "Sorry. All our vehicles have the company branding. We thought it best if he borrowed Paulie's private ute."

The glass in the front door rattled with the sound of heavy knocking. Hana froze, but Logan waved away her concern. "It's the guys with the pickup. They already took Leslie's car but came back for Tama's." He lifted his index finger and pointed at her. "Stay there, Hana. Let me deal with the wreck, and then we'll talk."

Hana's fingers shook as she pushed Tama's shirt into the washing machine. She added the other light coloured garments from the laundry basket and held the carton of powder in her right hand. It tipped and a sprinkling of white dust feathered the clothes. "No," she hissed. She dumped the carton on the side and hauled Tama's shirt free, lifting it to her nose and inhaling his familiar scent. She couldn't bear the thought of cleansing it and removing all traces of him. Fear and grief mingled in her brain.

Tangled metal screeched across the mountain as the men winched Tama's vehicle onto the truck. Unable to separate it from the gate, they took that as well. Hana set the washing machine running, listening to the gurgling of the water as the motor sucked it through the pipes. She watched through the laundry window as Tama's pride and joy set off down the mountain, bouncing on the back of the truck. Shards of plastic showered the road behind it until it moved out of sight.

Logan's truck parked beneath the kauri tree. He'd squeezed it into the narrow space to allow the wreckers access to the crumpled mess she'd made. The rahui pole stood at an angle and she took the guilt for its disturbance onto her slender shoulders, adding it to the growing pile.

Her phone buzzed on the floor and she glanced at the number. Caroline again. "Leave me alone," she hissed. She buried her face in the shirt and held her breath, replaying her conversation with Tama. He'd threatened to move. What difference did it make if she couldn't find him in the first place? She picked through his hysterical declarations, tuning into his sobs of despair. His voice had echoed off a hard surface, and he'd whispered as though afraid of someone overhearing. "Where are you Tama?" Hana breathed.

Logan disappeared around the side of the house. His long stride took him beyond the boundary and she imagined him checking the bubbling stream which fed the water tanks. She sank onto the stray camping chair, which no one had yet put away. Closing her eyes, she sniffed the shirt and played over the conversation. "He's going to move," she whispered, her lips shifting against the soft white fabric. "Find him before someone else does."

The police wanted him.

But someone else searched for him too.

And David Allen had also disappeared.

Hana played through the conversation again, perplexed by her obsession with it. Was it Tama's hysteria or his desperation which drove her?

Or that elusive other thing which called to her subconscious?

Hana exhaled and rose. The chair flew backwards and hit the wall.

Something else had bothered her, a familiar resonance in the conversation which tugged at a buried memory.

She kept Tama's shirt clutched in her fingers and ran along the hallway in search of her husband. Snatching up his truck keys from the hall table, she shouted his name before flying through the open front door. He didn't answer her, and she spun on the gravel, grit spitting from beneath her fluffy slippers. A breeze picked up the hem of the shirt and flapped it against her thighs.

"I know where Tama is!" she shouted.

Guessing the sound of the stream had dulled her voice, she ran towards Logan's truck and hoped he'd heard her. She fired the engine and performed a hazardous, jerky reverse from beneath the unlucky kauri tree. The missing gate left the driveway gaping, and she gunned the gas pedal and pushed the vehicle through the gap.

Still no Logan.

Gravel sprayed on every side as she yanked the steering wheel into a hard circle and crossed the lawn. The heavy tyre grips gouged tracks in the grass as she headed back out through the gate and powered far too fast down the perilous mountain.

69

A Mullen Mouth

Hana perched on the edge of the driver's seat, struggling to keep her feet on the pedals. She regretted not making time to alter the settings from Logan's long legs to her much shorter ones. She didn't fasten her seatbelt, unable to bear the constriction across her bruised torso. It wasn't in her nature to dice with death, so she pushed away the misgivings as the truck lurched around the second of eleven hairpin bends.

Unwilling to waste time slowing at the blind turns, Hana sounded the horn loud and long as she approached to warn any oncoming vehicle. The sole of her slipper became glued to the gas pedal, and she kept her nerve.

The gabled end of the hotel's west wing rose from the landscape as the road curved into the valley. Hana slewed the truck right at the end of the driveway, almost tangling with a campervan lumbering up from the hotel entrance. The driver stood on his brakes. Hana avoided eye contact with him, aware of the chaos the sudden stop would have caused to the crockery housed inside the van's cupboards. She pushed the truck through the iron gates and drove the wrong way around the turning circle. Gravel spat in every direction as she skidded to a halt at the bottom of the main steps.

Hana abandoned the truck and exited at speed. She snatched the keys from the cup holder but left the driver's door open as she flew into the hotel.

"Mrs Du Rose?" The receptionist rose, a frown on his forehead as her fluffy slippers tore past him. He gaped at the black bruises circling her eyes and the weeping cut across her forehead. Dipping sideways, he reached for the phone and dialled a number.

Hana ignored the curiosity of the receptionist and the knot of people browsing leaflets on an information stand. She used the main staircase, slipping at the first dogleg and saving herself by gripping the banister rail with scrambling fingers. Two more flights took her to the floor she needed.

Logan's old room gazed out over the driveway, and Hana ran along the corridor until she reached it. Her breath came in heaves and she bent for a second with her hands on her knees. A remembered snippet about the room being occupied told her to knock first before entering. But her fingers acted of their own volition, pressing the code into the keypad with enough haste to get it wrong the first time.

An empty bedroom greeted her, the sheets stripped from the mattress and the room lifeless. Net curtains billowed inward from the ranch slider left ajar to air the room. "No!" she groaned, gripping the door frame and covering her mouth with her right hand. Tama's shirt dangled from her fingers. "I was so sure I'd find him here."

The pieces had fallen into place with such certainty. The unavailability of Logan's private room and the familiar sound of slamming doors in the background of Tama's call. An echo backing his voice convinced her he'd called from the tiled ensuite bathroom. And a panoramic view of the front of the hotel would have given him access to her movements. He'd watched her con Toby and understood she was going somewhere important. Maybe he'd even seen Lana Alderbank visit the property in search of Edin, or the box, or both.

Hana walked to the ranch slider and parted the net curtains with her fingers. She stepped out onto the balcony and sank into the ornate iron chair which had once belonged to Miriam Du Rose. Its pair sat next to it, dust and grass seed blown from the mountainside to cover the tiled surface beneath it. Hana frowned and peered between her feet. The chair had moved recently, leaving four dirty circles on the tiles.

"He's been here," she whispered to herself. Her mind wouldn't let go of her theory that Tama had hidden in plain sight. She reached in her dress pocket for her phone, her lips parting in a grimace. "Idiot!" she groaned. A memory of her phone still lying on the laundry floor returned to punish her. It seemed with every attempt to help Tama, Hana made the situation a thousand times worse. Now, she'd abandoned her already irritated husband at the top of the mountain and stolen his truck. She peered over the balcony rail at the vehicle blocking the turning circle. A car honked as it tried to reverse. The receptionist appeared in front of it. He slammed the driver's door and looked up while speaking into a handheld radio. Hana ducked back in time to avoid his scrutiny. "Face the music," she breathed to herself while scrunching her body further back in the chair.

Voices sounded from below as the receptionist attempted to sort out the gridlock. Hana rose and edged back into the bedroom, closing and locking the ranch slider behind her. It would surprise the housekeeper when she returned to do it later. Hana gazed around the familiar room, recognising every part of the decor she'd helped to create. Her brother had stayed here last and her father before him. Logan insisted they kept the room for family visits, writing it into the contract with the events company. They rarely asked Logan's permission to house conference guests in it.

Hana walked into the bathroom, smelling the lemon and lavender scent of the cleaning products used by the housekeepers. She ran her finger over a damp line on the sink and estimated they'd just finished servicing the room after the mysterious visitor's exit. She knew how long each hotel task took, having done most of them through necessity. Ten minutes to strip sheets, dust, hoover the floor, and clean the bathroom. The lack of towels or replacement bedding meant they expected the room to remain empty. A heavy weight pressed against her heart, accompanied by the bitter taste of failure. She'd wanted Tama to be there. Just to hold him and promise everything would be okay, but without knowing how.

Sudden voices in the bedroom caused her to jump. She clasped her right hand over her heart as the tinny sound continued in an even tone. She stepped from the bathroom to find the TV playing, a news channel lighting up the wall mounted screen. A timer flashed in the bottom righthand corner. The last person to use the remote had accidentally set it to standby instead of powering it off. An image of a young man filled the screen, before a talking head of an Auckland police officer asked the public for more information. The man's name scrolled across the bottom of the image, a white font encased in a blue banner. '*Chief Inspector Lampard of NZ Police.*'

"We're currently seeking a person of interest and ask for the public's assistance." The sunshine glinted off his uniform buttons as he paused for effect. He stood on the steps of the main police station, a lectern supporting his notes. Disinterested, Hana turned away.

"The death of Aria White has shocked the Auckland community. We want information on this man." She whipped around as the screen halved and Tama's face slid into place. A grainy picture of him posing with a woman saw him grinning like a maniac. He held a beer bottle in his right hand and poked his tongue at the photographer. The news broadcaster had blurred the woman's face, but Hana recognised her distinctive hair and the way it frizzed around her.

"Bitch!" she hissed. Jordan had furnished the investigating officers with the most unflattering image she could find. She'd finished putting the boot in by making sure the public saw Tama's irresponsibility instead of the fireman who regularly put his own life on the line for others. Hana ground her teeth until her forehead ached. She gripped the truck keys in her left hand and glared down at her slippers. "Do I need shoes to evict you?" she asked. "No, I don't." She ran a mental calculation, figuring she could get to Auckland and back, throw Jordan out of Tama's house and still make it to school in time to fetch her charges. The police officer continued speaking.

"The suspect is Tama Hohaia. He also goes by the name of Tama Du Rose. Anyone sighting him should call the number on the screen. New Zealand police consider Hohaia dangerous and not to be approached."

Fury rose into Hana's chest and a pink film descended over her vision. "He doesn't go by the name of Tama Du Rose!" she shouted. "It is his bloody name!"

She realised now why Bodie had called her. They'd got it all so wrong. Her slippers made a whipping sound across the rug as she barrelled towards the door. The air disappeared from her lungs as she ran into a rock-hard chest, bouncing off it like a stray rubber ball. Tama's shirt fluttered to the ground after her, muffling the clank of the fallen truck keys.

70

Girth

Hana expected words, but Logan didn't waste his breath. He went straight for the man with his fingers still gripping her shoulder, not caring about the obstacles in his way. Like his prized Charolais bull, he charged, his gaze fixed on his wife's grimace of pain.

Her captor tried to defend himself, raising his fists and protecting his head. The action proved futile as Logan landed a spiteful left handed punch to his ribs and another to his face as he flailed towards the carpet. Then he kicked him in the stomach as he rolled on the floor. He stayed down, his hands fluttering over his smashed nose.

The other man's defence showed more flair as he dodged three sharp punches and folded his body in half. His head hit Logan square in the groin and shoved him backwards into the bathroom.

Hana scrabbled at the cable tie trapping her ankle to the chair, glancing up in panic as ceramic smashed in the small ensuite. Logan's grunt heralded a crash against the shower cubicle and the grinding of metal twisting out of shape.

She tried kicking off the lower spindle to release herself from the chair, but it didn't budge. Instead, she hurt her heel, and the pain ricocheted up her ankle and through her shin. The sound of splintering glass set her heart thudding faster, and she shuffled towards the ensuite door, dragging the chair along the floorboards. When it tangled in the corner of the bedspread, she lifted it and spun it round, carrying it in front of her and leaning forward to grip each side of the seat. It helped her move faster, although the wooden legs bruised her shins and left painful welts on her thighs.

"Stop!" she yelled at the top of her voice, slamming the back of the chair through the half-open door. It bounced off the remains of the shower cubicle and caught on the edge of the glass panel, which had tipped sideways. "Get off him!" Hana waded into the tangle of arms and torsos, using the chair as a battering ram. A gash to Logan's cheek flowed like a creek, spreading his blood over the other man's arms and hands until they became slick. As they wrestled back and forth, Logan aimed a swift head-butt at the other man's nose and struck gold. He swore, and Logan used his momentary distraction to kick at his bent knee. He missed, hitting the wall heater between the man's legs and roaring in temper.

Logan's attacker drove him into the tiny space between the toilet and the wall, making it impossible for him to use his legs. Hana tipped the seat forward, so the curved wooden top rail created a blunt edge. She couldn't get it as high as she needed, but she waddled forward, still bound to the chair leg.

She hit the man in the small of his back, jerking the chair upwards as it landed against his spine. It did minor damage but provided enough of a distraction to divide his attention between both fronts. Logan freed his left hand as the man glanced sideways and hit him on the cheek, driving his body through a ninety-degree turn. The man fell backwards against the chair, losing his balance as his arms flailed in the air. He took the sleeve of Logan's tee shirt with him, clattering with the chair as he tumbled. The loose fabric fluttered down after him.

The impact sent a sharp pain through Hana's ankle, and she sensed herself falling as the world tipped. With her hands around the chair, she couldn't save herself. The back of her head cracked against the door frame and the broken ensuite disappeared from her vision. And Logan's opponent landed on top of her, crushing her beneath the knotty spindles of the wooden chair.

71

Hoof Pick

Hana expected words, but Logan didn't waste his breath. He went straight for the man with his fingers still gripping her shoulder, not caring about the obstacles in his way. Like his prized Charolais bull, he charged, his gaze fixed on his wife's grimace of pain.

Her captor tried to defend himself, raising his fists and protecting his head. The action proved futile as Logan landed a spiteful left handed punch to his ribs and another to his face as he flailed towards the carpet. Then he kicked him in the stomach as he rolled on the floor. He stayed down, his hands fluttering over his smashed nose.

The other man's defence showed more flair as he dodged three sharp punches and folded his body in half. His head hit Logan square in the groin and shoved him backwards into the bathroom.

Hana scrabbled at the cable tie trapping her ankle to the chair, glancing up in panic as ceramic smashed in the small ensuite. Logan's grunt heralded a crash against the shower cubicle and the grinding of metal twisting out of shape.

She tried kicking off the lower spindle to release herself from the chair, but it didn't budge. Instead, she hurt her heel, and the pain ricocheted up her ankle and through her shin. The sound of splintering glass set her heart thudding faster, and she shuffled towards the ensuite door, dragging the chair along the floorboards. When it tangled in the corner of the bedspread, she lifted it and spun it round, carrying it in front of her and leaning forward to grip each side of the seat. It helped her move faster, although the wooden legs bruised her shins and left painful welts on her thighs.

"Stop!" she yelled at the top of her voice, slamming the back of the chair through the half-open door. It bounced off the remains of the shower cubicle and caught on the edge of the glass panel, which had tipped sideways. "Get off him!" Hana waded into the tangle of arms and torsos, using the chair as a battering ram. A gash to Logan's cheek flowed like a creek, spreading his blood over the other man's arms and hands until they became slick. As they wrestled back and forth, Logan aimed a swift head-butt at the other man's nose and struck gold. He swore, and Logan used his momentary distraction to kick at his bent knee. He missed, hitting the wall heater between the man's legs and roaring in temper.

Logan's attacker drove him into the tiny space between the toilet and the wall, making it impossible for him to use his legs. Hana tipped the seat forward, so the curved wooden top rail created a blunt edge. She couldn't get it as high as she needed, but she waddled forward, still bound to the chair leg.

She hit the man in the small of his back, jerking the chair upwards as it landed against his spine. It did minor damage but provided enough of a distraction to divide his attention between both fronts. Logan freed his left hand as the man glanced sideways and hit him on the cheek, driving his body through a ninety-degree turn. The man fell backwards against the chair, losing his balance as his arms flailed in the air. He took the sleeve of Logan's tee shirt with him, clattering with the chair as he tumbled. The loose fabric fluttered down after him.

The impact sent a sharp pain through Hana's ankle, and she sensed herself falling as the world tipped. With her hands around the chair, she couldn't save herself. The back of her head cracked against the door frame and the broken ensuite disappeared from her vision. And Logan's opponent landed on top of her, crushing her beneath the knotty spindles of the wooden chair.

72

Overcheck

"Hana! Hana!"

She roused with a floating sensation, which lowered her into a mire of confusion. Then pain.

"Owww!" She reached a hand up to her head and her fingers found hard wooden edges. "Get this chair off me!" she whined, her voice wavering as she fought the welcome hands of sleep.

Keys jangled and someone gave a muted groan. "Got his phone." The familiar voice held a breathless quality and Hana forced her left eye open, squinting into the light. Her legs ached as a weight lifted off them with an uneven lurch and a grunt. Logan ducked as eager hands lifted his attacker off Hana, his shoes missing her head by mere centimetres as he disappeared behind her. A pitiful groan sounded alongside the thud of arms and legs hitting the floor.

"Stay there!" David Allen ordered, his tone hoarse and uncompromising. He spoke through gritted teeth.

Hana's ankle rocked as the weight of the chair lifted. The cable tie clicked open and the tension on her Achilles' heel diminished. Logan hefted the chair from across her chest and stomach, his face streaming blood and his tattered shirt covered. Hana held up a hand and spread her fingers over his uninjured cheek. "You just did everything you tell me not to do," she croaked. "Wading in with both feet without assessing the situation. They could have killed you."

Reaching forward, he pressed his forehead to hers and closed his eyes. His precious plasma dripped onto her hair and slithered along her neck. "You're my weakness, Hana Du Rose," he whispered. "Always and forever."

"My head hurts." Hana reached her free hand backwards and touched a sore spot on her crown. Her fingers came away sticky and her eyes widened. "Is it bad?" Her gaze tracked to the door frame in her peripheral vision, noticing a shard missing and a streak of red blood. She looked back at her husband. "Please tell me there isn't a massive piece of wood sticking out from the back of my head?"

"Nope." He blinked and wiped his hand across his eye. The gash oozed, and his fingers spread the mess further around his face. "But between us we wrecked the room."

"What happened?" The hotel manager appeared in Hana's peripheral vision. "This is intolerable! We could hear the ruckus from downstairs!"

"Can she sit up?" David Allen's boots appeared next to Hana's face. He ignored the slender man strutting around the room and inspecting the damage. She squinted through her left eye to witness David fighting with the packaging from a gauze bandage. A bottle of brown fluid nestled beneath his right arm.

"I can hear you," she bit. "And I can see up your nostrils."

"Lucky you." He replied without missing a beat. "Maybe I'll charge you extra for that." He squatted next to her, the bandage unrolling in his fingers. He lifted a pair of angle bladed scissors from his back pocket.

"I'm fine." Hana pushed herself up, using her elbows. "I don't trust you with those." She leaned sideways on one hip and pressed her hand against her wound. "It's stopping now. Deal with Logan first."

"You lost consciousness." David raised a bushy blond eyebrow and frowned down at her.

Hana sighed. "But my husband is hemorrhaging. Can you help him first, please?"

"Do you have any medication on you?" David's boots scrunched up the rug as he spun his bent knees towards Logan.

"Yeah." He exhaled, rising to scrabble in his jeans pocket.

"I have a bottle of his nose spray in my handbag." Hana pushed herself onto her knees. She searched the floor for her bag, swallowing against the heady nausea which blurred her vision. Her fingers closed over her stray slipper and she stuffed her foot into it.

"I have an emergency pill somewhere." Logan continued to fumble in his pocket, his gash still dripping blood onto his soaked shirt.

Hana used the door frame to rise to her feet, groaning as the room shifted on its keel around her. She muttered to herself, blinking and shaking her head to clear the fog.

"Ice." A whoosh of air sent her listing sideways as the familiar voice returned. He wedged himself between David and Logan, pressing an ice pack to Logan's cheek. "You have some factor at home, don't you? I can jab you." Hana's brother narrowed his eyes at her and shrugged. "I drove up to check on Edin. Found carnage instead."

Hana nodded her thanks and leaned against the wall. She surveyed the room, spying her handbag lying in the middle of the rug. Two men lay on their stomachs at right angles next to it, forming a two-sided human triangle alongside the tan leather bag. Their foreheads almost touched as they glared at each other in defeat. A hotel security guard leaned on one man's back while Toby placed a cable tie around the other man's wrists. The hotel manager hopped from foot to foot, muttering to himself.

"Cops are on their way." David moved next to Hana and held up a wad of gauze. He spread iodine over its surface. "Lean forward."

She resisted at first, her efforts wasted against his determination. "It stings!" she complained as he cleaned blood from the back of her head.

"Good," he replied, his tone more jovial. "That means you're alive."

"I bet you were popular in the Air Force," she grumbled.

"Yeah, as a fireman." His lips stretched into a wide grin and then a laugh as Hana slapped his hand away from her.

"Then keep your scissors to yourself!" she snarled. She ducked out of range and winced at the pain. As Toby appeared in her peripheral vision, she called to him. "Please, could you fetch my bag for me? I have Logan's spare meds in it."

Toby leaned down and snagged the handbag strap. It dangled from his fingers as his long stride carried him across the room.

"Suits you," David Allen said. He chuckled after blowing Toby a kiss. Hana dug her fingers into the bag's interior as Logan produced a foil wrapped tablet from his back pocket.

"Found it," he remarked to himself and set about popping the pill loose.

"Where is he?" Hana dropped her bag to the floor between her feet. She leaned sideways to see past the men. "I know he's here. Where's he gone?"

Toby stepped backwards, shaking his head and waving his hands in front of him. "That's not my circus, thanks. I'll help the guys get these clowns downstairs for the cops. They'll need to check the room, maybe take some photos." He spun on his worn leather boots and headed towards the knot of bodies.

"Well?" Hana fixed her hands over her hips. "Don't make me beat the truth out of you!"

David glanced at Logan with a smirk. "Is she for real?"

Logan swallowed his tablet with a gulp. His Adam's apple bobbed in response and he pressed the ice pack harder against his wound. "Never underestimate a redhead," he replied. "They have ways and means."

"Fine." Hana gritted her teeth and stared at each of them. "I'll find him myself."

Logan heaved out a sigh and righted the chair next to him. He sat in it and stared down at his feet.

Irritation carried Hana into the wide hallway of the hotel, following Toby and the security guard as they drove her attackers before them. Cable ties cinched the men's wrists together. One of them glared at her through narrowed eyes. "She won't stop," he hissed. "There's too much at stake."

"Shut your face!" Toby hissed. He bent the man's elbow into a tighter angle and forced it upwards, causing him to hiss in pain as the cable ties dragged his wrists higher. The right-hand side of his body listed as he limped to the end of the hallway. They disappeared into an open room to wait for the police officers.

"Right!" Hana snapped. She spun in a wide arc before cocking her head and narrowing her eyes. "Where are you, you little git!" She motioned to the shocked hotel manager to follow her and stalked along the familiar hallway. The event management company had retained the decor of the family's former bedrooms, but moved the furniture into a cookie cutter formation for ease with cleaning. Each vacant room had lost its personality and sense of life. Clean towels nestled on starched sheets ready for a fresh round of visitors, the doors wide open in welcome.

Hana shivered. Apart from the stairs to Alfred and Leslie's loft apartment, she rarely visited her old home.

One door remained closed in the wide corridor. and she paused for a moment outside it. Hana lifted her hand and hammered, offering a warning more than a request for entry. Then she jerked her head towards the hotel manager. "Open it!" she commanded.

"This is not acceptable," he growled. "We need to amend the contract and deny your family access to the hotel. I'll speak to the company chairman today." He used his master keycard on the electronic lock. "I'm not comfortable about this!" he snarled.

Hana lowered her chin and glared at him. "You're right," she agreed. "It's not acceptable. I'll speak to my husband about terminating your contract." Her green irises flashed like gems and he took a step backwards out of range of the threat in her eyes. He watched as she pushed open the door of Liza Du Rose's old bedroom.

73

Crupper

Tama turned to face her, wringing his fingers in front of his chest. Hana glared at him through the open doorway.

But the hotel manager pushed past her and began apologising. "I'm so sorry, sir. This is a complete misunderstanding. Sorry to bother you. This lady thought she recognised you. We'll leave you to it. Is there anything I can get you?"

Tama blinked and stared at him, frowning as the man went into a well-practiced groveling routine. "Hi, Ma," he said, directing his greeting to Hana. "You found me."

The hotel manager's lips slammed shut. He glared from Tama to Hana and back again. Then he left the room in long strides, muttering obscenities under his breath.

As soon as the door clicked shut behind him, Tama rushed to inspect Hana's injuries. "What happened?" he gushed. "And what was all that noise a few minutes ago?"

A loud honking issued from the front car park and Tama turned to listen. "What's going on?" he asked again.

"Your mates came for Edin," Hana began. She halted and her expression morphed into one of fear. Her lips turned down and her eyes widened. "Logan. I need to speak to Logan." She turned and left Tama's room at a run. The hotel manager darted to the side as she pattered around him. "Logan!" she shouted, her tone urgent. He appeared within seconds, still holding the ice pack to his bleeding cheek. He stood in the hallway and dripped blood onto the floorboards. The hotel manager pursed his lips but kept moving. Two police officers lumbered up the main staircase and stopped to speak to him.

"What's wrong?" Logan's irises darkened to storm clouds. He glanced up to see Tama and his lips twitched.

"Those men tried to take Edin from school. They said she's not there!" Hana pointed her feet towards the stairs and dropped her arms to run. Logan stepped in front of her.

"She's with Leslie." He cocked his head and frowned. "She tripped on her way into school and skinned her knees. We couldn't console her and she kept crying for Nonie's rongoā." He narrowed his eyes at Hana. "If you'd hung around long enough, I'd have told you."

"Sorry." She covered her face with her hands. A steamroller had moved into her head and begun pounding her skull.

"Can I look at you?" Her brother touched her right shoulder, and she nodded.

"Okay. But please, can someone phone the school and tell them not to let our children outside the building? They need to know about the threat."

"I'll do it." David dragged a mobile phone from his jeans pocket. Blood stained his fingers as he Googled the number for the school.

Mark held three fingers in front of Hana's face and she batted them away. Impatience dogged her as the police officers finished bemoaning the trouble which followed the Du Roses. Slightly mollified, the hotel manager strutted down the stairs. Hana watched him go and pushed Mark's fingers away again. "Three fingers, Mark!" she snapped. "Logan!" She dipped sideways to locate her husband behind her brother. "Raymond works for the Alderbanks. He's been spying on us all this time! Lana Alderbank sent those men after Edin."

"Who? What?" Logan's pained expression frustrated her. "Isn't that the family who want to adopt Edin?" She lacked the energy to catch him up on the intrigue. Snatching Tama's wrist, she set off after the hotel manager, faltering at the top of the stairs.

"I think I'm concussed," she declared as the banister rail wiggled like a snake beneath her gaze. Tama slipped his arm through her elbow and offered support as they descended the main staircase in time to collide with the new crowd of conference attendees. The hotel manager bustled around, barking orders at the receptionist. "Raymond!" Hana growled. She strode behind the reception desk, enjoying how he started at her proximity.

"Ah, Mrs Du Rose." He gulped and pressed his lips together as though collecting his thoughts. "Can I trouble you to move the truck from in front of the hotel steps?" He processed a guest's details at speed and issued them with an electronic card for their room. "Third floor, second room on the right." Leaning forward, he offered a polite smile. "There's an information pack in your room. Any questions, just dial zero."

"I'll dial zero." Hana shook off Tama's steadying hand. "And then I'll shove the phone where the sun doesn't shine."

"Excuse me, excuse me!" The hotel manager elbowed Tama aside to get to Hana. "Sorry, sorry," he said to the curious guests queuing to collect their room information. He yanked on her elbow and she shucked him off and slapped his hand. "So sorry about this," he continued, speaking through the side of his mouth.

"Arrest this man!" Hana shouted.

Tama jumped into action, seizing Raymond's shoulder in a painful grip. "Where are those cops?" he replied.

"Still upstairs." Hana edged from the narrow space to allow Tama to wrestle with Raymond. The receptionist made a grab for something in his jacket pocket and fished out his mobile phone. Hana snatched it from his fingers. "No, you don't!" she snarled.

"This is too much!" The hotel manager dabbed at his forehead with a handkerchief in between apologising to the silent crowd. They gathered between the reception desk and the door, some edging backwards in alarm.

"Hey everyone!" Logan's voice boomed out from the bottom step of the main staircase, and he waved his arms for attention. "Your rooms are ready and we appreciate some of you had a long journey to get here. If you'd like to head into the restaurant, staff can provide you with a complimentary tea or coffee while you wait for the backlog to clear here. We'll fetch you in groups of four. It saves you waiting around in the heat."

Despite the blood staining his shirt and the ice pack in his hand, Logan commanded enough authority for the guests to obey. The hotel manager went with them, springing ahead to lead the way. He narrowed his eyes at Logan as if to suggest he picked up the bill for the complimentary drinks. Logan's face creased into a sardonic smile.

As the guests filtered along the corridor to the restaurant, the police officers clumped down the stairs with Hana's attackers. Hand cuffs replaced the cable ties.

"There's another one here!" Hana called. She reached around Tama and grabbed Raymond's sleeve. "He's in on it too."

Raymond squirmed. "I don't know what she's talking about," he stuttered. "I've worked here for years."

"Yeah. Since just after the fire," Hana snarled.

Tama took a horrified step back, his complexion paling. His grey irises glittered like diamonds. "That's right," he breathed. "And I let myself into Uncle Logan's room when I arrived last week, but he found me a new one earlier when I heard about

Ari." He swallowed and his Adam's apple bobbed in his throat. "You called those guys, didn't you?"

Logan's eyes bugged in his tanned face. His lips parted back from his teeth. "Is that true? Did you set these clowns on my wife?"

Raymond diminished in the face of Logan's might. He began babbling and making no sense. The police officers clutched their prisoners before one of them radioed for back up. Hana held Raymond's phone in front of his face. "Code!" she demanded, her forehead heating with pain but her voice as cold as ice.

74

Poll Guard

Hana recovered Lara Alderbank's number from Raymond's phone. She sat in Logan's office and called it as the police officers led the receptionist away with the two thugs he'd let into the hotel. Logan sat next to her on the sofa, his phone balanced between them on the cushion. A line of fabric plasters created a hashtag on his cheek.

"My name is Hana Du Rose." She didn't give Lana the opportunity to ask questions as she pressed ahead. "The police have Raymond and your two hired idiots. I'm guessing they'll start talking soon."

An irritated huff echoed against the wooden panelled walls of the office. With a nod from Logan, Hana continued. "You almost ran me off the road the other night after running your car at me in the car park. And the school is on high alert after you sent those clowns to abduct Edin. We need to talk."

Lana's voice sounded lower than Hana imagined. Its gruffness reverberated through the phone. "What do you suggest? I already snagged your fancy lawyer. You're running out of options. I'll get what I want in the end. I always do."

Hana exhaled. "I'm tired and bruised. Let's meet like adults. Somewhere neutral."

"Okay." Lana capitulated. She suggested somewhere they could meet, and Hana paused before answering. She looked to Logan for agreement, and he nodded. He ended the call with the prod of his index finger and laid back against the sofa with a groan.

"What now?" Hana demanded. She squinted from beneath the pain in her eye sockets.

"Sleep," Logan said with a sigh. "Sleep, for a week." He closed his eyes and rested his right hand against his chest. Hana peered at her watch before leaning her head on his shoulder and allowing herself a few precious moments of peace.

"Half an hour," she murmured. "Leslie said she'd fetch the other children from school."

The impromptu nap did little for either of them. Mark interrupted with a gentle knock on the office door. He strode across the rug, giving the couple enough time to uncurl themselves before sitting in the visitor's chair and spinning it to face them. Hana's brother smiled. "You both look terrible," he concluded. He raised a hand against Hana's protest. "I'm heading off home soon. But I thought you'd like to know my conclusion about Edin's health."

"Sorry." Hana rubbed her eyes, wincing as she caught the cut across her nose. "You drove up here to see us and spent the morning patching everyone back together." Her gaze drifted to the healed wound across her left wrist and she turned her hand over to hide it. She'd had need of her brother's surgical skills before and the memories threatened to slip free.

Mark waved away her apology. "I believe Edin has Coeliac disease. Her obsession with floury products indicates her body craving what she mustn't have. I palpated her stomach, and it's tender. She visited the bathroom twice over a half an hour period and both times encountered diarrhoea." He shrugged. "She's in pain. All the time. She exhibits short temperedness because she depletes her energy with the effort of just getting through each day."

Hana's jaw dropped. Her lips parted, but no sound escaped. She pressed her right hand over her chest and her eyes swam with tears. Logan reached across and tugged her fingers into his lap. "Don't do that," he murmured. "You're an exceptional mother, Hana. I won't allow you to blame yourself for this."

Mark nodded in agreement. He dropped his chin to observe Hana from over the top of his spectacles. "Your local GP visits should have thrown this into the spotlight. But you've described some tense standoffs there. Bring her down to see Tris in pediatrics next week. He'll get his clinician to send you an appointment. She'll let him take blood, won't she?"

Hana shrugged and shook her head. "Yes. No. Maybe."

Mark rose and his face creased into tender lines. He held his arms out to Hana. "She loves my husband. I'm sure she'll succumb to his charms. We'll work it all out." She pressed her cheek against his chest and wrapped her arms around his slender frame. He stroked her hair and kissed the top of her head. Hana released him and waited while Logan rose to shake his hand. Mark waggled his eyebrows. "I'll see you both soon." His face lit with a smile. "And in better condition."

"Yeah." Logan wrinkled his nose. "Grateful to have a surgeon in the family."

"You betcha." Mark left, and Hana frowned as the door closed behind him.

She sighed. "Are you coming home now, or do you still have work to do?"

"Home." Logan smoothed her fringe away from the dressing across her nose. "I'll leave Leslie my truck so she can get the children from school. We'll use the spare ute from the equipment shed. I'm guessing Tama is still hiding behind Leslie's apron?"

Hana shook her head. The earlier conversation with their resident fire fighter hadn't gone well. Hana wanted to call

Bodie and iron out the murder accusation, but Tama had run upstairs to the apartment and locked himself in the bathroom. Fortunately for him, the police officers who arrested Hana's attackers didn't recognise him from the hourly broadcast as New Zealand's most wanted felon.

Logan turned off his computer and locked his desk drawer. His gaze drifted to the shelves and the gap left by the box. "Do you want to see Will before we meet with Lana Alderbank?"

Hana nodded. "Yeah. We can go there now."

They parted company as Logan took a call on his desk phone. He stuck his index finger in the air to indicate he wouldn't take long. Hana smiled and left the room, heading to the museum. She found it locked up, and no sign of Will.

The hotel manager glared at her from behind the reception desk. "He's gone out with his son," he growled. the pen in his right hand scratching notes on a pad. Hana paused to read his scribblings upside down, finding only gibberish written there in his attempt to appear busy.

"I'm sorry about Raymond," she said, her tone sincere. "Nobody imagined he'd become involved in kidnapping and an assault." She bit her lower lip as thoughts of the dead fireman intruded, fighting not to add murder to the list of Raymond's crimes.

The man shrugged and stared at his pad. "My employers don't wish to change the terms of the contract," he grumbled. "Perhaps you could refrain from such public dramas in the future."

Hana gritted her teeth hard enough to send a dart of fire into her forehead. "Absolutely," she replied, her tone sickly sweet.

She unlocked Logan's truck and retrieved her phone from the glove box where David put it after moving the vehicle off the main thoroughfare. The screen showed two missed calls from Melissa and a text. *'Call me!'* Her fingers shook as she dialled and waited for the call to connect.

"Bit of news for you," Melissa began, not pausing for a greeting. "I discovered my neighbour has security cameras, and we identified the burglar. The cops picked him up last night and you'll never guess what?"

Hana's head ached and her tired brain wouldn't make the links. She sighed. "What?"

"He looked just like your description of the private detective who turned up at your place. The one my ex denies employing."

"Oh." Hana winced. "Are you sure it's the same man? Skinny, balding, with a limp. Colin?"

Melissa sighed. "The cops won't give me his name. They've arrested him. The security camera picked up his registration number, and that's how they found him. Your description fits him, though."

Hana frowned and sank into the driver's seat of the truck. She watched a tui skipping through the branches of an alder tree and gnawed her lower lip. If the police had Colin, it was evidence that Logan hadn't killed him and disposed of his body on the mountain somewhere. Either Logan was slipping, or he'd decided the idiot would slip his own neck into another noose sometime soon. And he had.

"You still there?" Melissa cleared her throat and waited.

"Yeah." Hana toyed with the new idea spiralling through her mind. "Are you sure your ex-wife suffered a burglary?"

Static occupied the connection as Melissa picked up the fragile thread. "I think I see where you're going with this. But why would she lie? And Tama's house suffered a break-in too."

Hana touched tentative fingers to the bump at the back of her head. "Tama's house wasn't burgled. His flat mate went on a wrecking spree when he upset her. If Colin committed your break-in and your ex employed him, then perhaps hers was a smokescreen. That means it's not about Tama. It's all about you."

"Nice." Melissa's disparaging tone matched Tama's when she'd told him. "So, what do you suggest?"

"Your situation is about money." Hana blinked as the tui dive bombed the truck. It rose on powerful wings and disappeared into the oak tree shrouding Miriam's rose garden. "Your ex-wife feels entitled to your inheritance. The private detective definitely visited Tama's house because his flat mate verified it. But it's because he's tracking the money. Just like he said, your former wife doesn't want you to go into a new relationship and take the cash with you. She thought your meetings with Tama were a sign of dating."

Melissa blew out a breath. "That makes sense in light of the other thing I found." She cleared her throat again. "I've also discovered something else."

Hana tensed. Her muscles ached, and she prepared herself for the news. Melissa paused before telling her. "Okay." She drew out the word, buying time and joining the conspiracy to put off the dreaded moment.

"I'll just come out and say it." Melissa tapped something against her phone, creating an annoying pulse beat in Hana's ear. "The fire was an accident."

"Reuben's fire?" The words caught in Hana's throat. They never got easier to say.

"Yes. I stand by my investigation at the time. The paperwork has surfaced. It got lost during the updating of the records. This file and several others didn't get scanned onto the new system. I escalated my formal request at the beginning of the week and the records are now viewable."

"Right." Hana closed her eyes and covered her mouth with her hand. "So, what is this all about?"

"I don't know." Melissa yawned. "Sorry. Hard week. But it's not about the fire. The original cause still stands. There's no doubt Tama dislodged something with his poking, but not arson."

75

Sweat Scraper

"It's been the longest week of my life." After surviving a hectic dinner and putting the children to bed, Hana rested her sore head on the pillow with a sigh of relief.

Logan turned on his side and smiled at her. His fingers strayed to touch the red curls splayed between them. He sifted them through gentle fingers, admiring their likeness to a waterfall. "It's not over yet," he murmured.

Hana groaned and turned away from him. "Let's pretend," she whispered, closing her eyes.

Edin woke numerous times in the night, her skinned knees prickling in the warm air. Hana laid on the lounge sofa with her until day break, her knees bent and Edin's thin calves resting across her thighs. She woke to a shadow passing across her eyelids, wincing in expectation of a slap. But a kiss brushed her hairline.

Hana opened her eyes. "Hey," she said, her voice croaky.

"Hi Mama." The child beamed at her. "Look." She waggled her dark eyebrows and pointed towards her knees. "Nonie's rongoā. All better now." She stroked a gentle finger along

Hana's forehead, stopping short of the dressing. "Want some? Edie's rongoā for your sore?" She cocked her head, her grey irises sparkling with an open sincerity.

Hana nodded, noticing the crick in her neck. "Yes, please." She yawned and buried her face against Edin's soft cheek. "Snuggle for a minute more."

"Minute more." Edin cackled. "Nonie's coming for knees." She tensed and lifted her index finger, her body as still as a statue. "She coming!" she hissed.

Hana groaned. "It's too early for Nonie. I think we're meeting her at the apartment before school."

"No." A frown bisected the elfin features. "Here. She coming now." She leapt from the sofa like a spring lamb and bounded along the hallway to the front door.

"Okay." Hana covered another yawn with her hand and tried to stretch. Every muscle ached, and the action ended in a moan of discomfort. She shifted her feet onto the rug and arched her spine to tease out the kinks.

"She here!" Edin bellowed. Hana rose at the sound of the chain sliding back and the lock clicking on the front door. She'd made it as far as the hall table when Edin blinded her with light and yanked open the door. A thousand moths followed Leslie into the house. "Told ya!" Edin sang, lifting her voice to ensure the rest of the family enjoyed her elation.

Only they didn't.

Wiri stumbled from his bedroom with his hair coiffed on one side. Tama followed him, sporting a pair of boxer shorts too small to have ever belonged to him. Phoenix poked her head around her door and then retreated. A thud echoed as she pitched back into bed.

Logan appeared from the kitchen with a mug of coffee in his left hand. He ground to a halt at the sight of Leslie with her fluttering hat of live creatures. His lips curled back from his teeth in disdain. Dried blood had turned the hashtag of plaster into something more gruesome.

"I hope that's for me." Hana held out her hand for the coffee and fixed her most pitiful expression on her face.

"Yeah." Logan eyed Leslie with a wince. His pyjama shorts failed to hide his defined pectoral muscles or the scar which looped his body from armpit to hip. For once, Leslie kept her opinions to herself. She skirted him on her way to the kitchen, taking her swarm with her. A flax kete hung from its woven strap over her forearm and the scent of hot crossed buns wafted past Hana's nose.

"I brought breakfast," she sang, passing into the kitchen. "Who wants it?"

They all wanted it, joining the trailing moths in their adoration. Hana scoffed her bun with lashings of butter and used the distraction of her children to join Logan in the shower.

Water pounded the back of her head as she rested her cheek against his chest. His work calloused fingers spread soap across her spine and shoulders, massaging away the tumult of the last few days. When he lifted her chin for a kiss, water from the overhead jets filled her mouth and blinded her. Logan laughed and blocked the spray with his shoulders. "I love you, Mrs Du Rose," he whispered.

"Me too," Hana replied. She squeezed her eyes closed and shook her head. "I love you, not me."

Logan shielded her from the spray, his kisses turning her knees to jelly. Her stomach looped as though she rode a playground swing. Hammering on the bathroom door made them both jump. "Mama!" Edin yelled. "Want you."

Logan snuffed and wrinkled his nose. "She's not the only one," he breathed.

"I'm coming!" Hana called, adding a false brightness to her tone. Logan shot her a sideways glance. Hana shook her head and pressed an index finger over his full lips. "Don't say it," she whispered. "I can read your mind."

She shoved conditioner through her red curls and drew a comb through their length. Edin continued to shout at her as she speed washed and exited the shower. She drew a fluffy towel around herself and closed the bathroom door behind her. The entire household occupied her bedroom, and she gulped, grateful for Edin's interruption.

"Family meeting," Tama drawled. He lay sprawled on her bed with a pillow over his face.

Edin balanced Horsey on his stomach and chatted to her knitted toy. She wore her cardigan backwards to match the school skirt, which looked odd with the pleats at the front. Hana tamped down her exhale of frustration, grateful the child had dressed herself.

"What you want to do about that?" Leslie jerked her head towards Edin's attire and waggled her eyebrows.

"Honestly? Nothing." Hana blew out a breath and shrugged. "That's the least of my problems. She dressed herself. It's an improvement on chasing her around the house." Hana's gaze slid to the bedroom doorway where her son sat cross legged on the threshold. She frowned. "That, on the other hand, is a different issue." Mac rolled a yellow tractor up the door frame. Not a stitch of clothing covered his nakedness.

"His pa used to run around like that." Leslie offered her pearl of wisdom and Hana tensed, not wanting her to finish with a lascivious inference about Logan repeating the habit as an adult. "Always buck naked that boy."

Hana opened her mouth and widened her eyes, the frantic head shake making her brain feel as though it dislodged. Too late.

"Buck naked!" Edin yelled at the top of her lungs. "Papa buck naked!"

Hana heard Logan swear from the bathroom. Wiri released a peal of laughter and covered his mouth with his hand. He continued to snigger behind his fingers. "Let's all meet in the lounge," Hana suggested. "Give us five minutes to get dressed."

"This is all my fault." Tama had progressed through grief and disbelief to sullenness and self-recrimination. "Ari was my best friend. He was moving out of his mother's house and taking my spare room. He borrowed the hat and hoodie after a big night out when he puked on his own. Why would I kill him and leave my clothes as evidence?"

"Poor baby." Phoenix patted his forehead. Her gaze slid to her brother and she cocked her head. "Mac could be a good murderer then. He's always nudey dudey. He wouldn't need to leave clothes as evidence." She fumbled the technical word.

"They don't have my DNA," Tama grumbled.

"Once they catch you, they'll get a warrant and take it." Leslie's eyeballs grew round and white in her face.

Phoenix uttered a whimper of concern and increased the patting of Tama's head.

"Let's stop this," Hana urged through gritted teeth. "Lounge. Five minutes."

The group filtered out, although Tama needed persuasion. The promise of coffee acted as leverage because he hated Leslie's insipid brew and bolted to make his own. Hana closed the door with a sigh and leaned against it. Edin continued, yelling her new favourite words at the top of her lungs. Her voice echoed in the hallway.

Hana pulled on underwear and yanked a dress over her head. Logan emerged from the bathroom, droplets scattering from his hair. A towel hugged his hips, leaving his stomach exposed. Hana pursed her lips at the sight of the tantalising line of hair which ran from his navel and into the towel's sumptuous folds. She turned away with a sigh and slapped lipstick and mascara onto her face. "Do you think I could risk taking off this dressing?" she mused, inspecting the damp fabric in the mirror.

Logan dropped the towel to the floor between his feet, and Hana watched his reflection. The curve of his strong buttocks reminded her of what the intrusion had robbed her of enjoying. "Dunno," he replied, his back turned as he dipped to choose clean underwear from a drawer. "I'll look at it before we leave."

"Thanks." She stalked towards the bed and sat down, running her fingers along the nearest post and straightening the voile curtain nestled in its delicate tie. "The hotel manager isn't happy with the Du Roses, is he?"

Logan frowned as she distanced herself from the family by using their surname instead of a pronoun, which included her. "No," he replied. "He wants us to have limited access to the main building. He cites food theft and disruption as the reason."

Hana wrinkled her nose. "He has a point."

"Yup." Logan peered at his shirt as he fastened the buttons. "They already get free accommodation, but can't resist stealing food as well."

"Ah." Hana peered at her fingernails and debated slapping on a coat of polish. "You heard about the chocolate pudding?"

Logan snorted. "And the rest, Hana. I'm at my wit's end with their antics. They're like geriatric terrorists."

Hana giggled. She pictured Leslie as a chunky ninja conducting dessert raids on a darkened kitchen.

"It's not funny." Logan's tone held enough pique to wipe the smile from her lips. "I don't want to run the hotel. I like it this way. Maybe I'll renege the bedroom and that will stop the company from nullifying the contract."

"They won't." Hana shook her head. "The manager confirmed it yesterday. I kinda threatened him with you pulling the plug when he raised his voice and shouted the odds." She chanced a covert glance at her husband from beneath her lashes. "Sorry."

"Risky." Logan dragged grey jeans over his long legs. "What would you have done if he'd said okay?"

Hana stared at the rug between her bare toes. "Expected you to sort out my mess." She pursed her lips and ignored his snort, not sure if annoyance or humour precipitated it. Something flashed through her memory and she grabbed it as it shot past. "Oh, Leslie's master key doesn't open your office door." She turned to face him. "Which means no one else can get in there either."

"I changed the lock when I took the business over from Alfred. Too many people had the key." Logan fastened a belt around his waist. "I have the only set now."

Hana nodded. "How many times do you think Raymond attempted to get hold of that box?" She cocked her head in thought. "Unless he didn't know what Lana Alderbank wanted." She shrugged and rose from the mattress, straightening her skirt with her hand. "I guess we'll find out today, won't we?"

76

Fulmer Snaffle

The family meeting proved a non-starter.

"I don't like this idea." Tama shook his head and gnawed at his lower lip. "My legs are too long."

"I saw Tama's face on the telly." Wiri dug his thumbs into the rear pockets of his shorts and swung his hips. "The news man wants him captured." He spun his body in a frantic circle until his bare toes found a lost Lego piece and he switched to hopping on the spot. "I can help him swim to Grandpa in England. I'm a wonderful swimmer." He stopped hopping and performed windmill actions with his arms. The Lego piece spun off towards the skirting board.

Mac released a heady peal of laughter. Still naked, he continued rolling his tractor across the arm of the sofa. Hana waved at him until she snagged his attention and then signed for him to get dressed. His eyes widened, and he dropped his gaze, the action as close as Mac got to disobedience. Hana hissed in a breath and closed her eyes, waiting for her husband to speak sanity into the chaos.

"You would have fitted in the boot of my old car." Leslie glared at Hana. "But it's wrecked now."

"I'm not hiding in a car!" Tama rose, six feet and three inches of pure muscle. He appealed to Hana. "I've changed my mind. Please, can you call Bodie?"

Hana's lips parted, but Logan halted her reply. "Not yet. Spend the day here. We have a meeting which might change everything." He pointed at Mac. "Get dressed, son." Mac couldn't ignore the command because he signed at the same time as he spoke. The child rose and sloped off to his bedroom, bending to retrieve the discarded rectangle of Lego. Popping it into the bucket of his yellow tractor, he trotted into the hall.

Tama and the younger children filtered away. As soon as they were out of earshot, Logan rounded on Leslie. "Stop putting stupid ideas into their heads!" he hissed. "Hide him in the boot and drive him to the South Island! What's wrong with you?"

Leslie bristled. She perched on the arm of the sofa, performing the banned activity to rile him on purpose. Her breasts spilled from between the buttons of her shirt, constricted by her folded arms. "I'd love to see the South Island," she declared. "I've always wanted to visit the Maldives."

Logan made a whimpering sound and turned away from her belligerence. Hana smiled at Leslie's geographical incompetence and assumed she meant Marlborough Sounds. A glance at Logan's rigid shoulders halted the gentle correction on her lips.

"Anyway," Logan continued as though the moment hadn't happened, "Please can you take the children to school and possibly fetch them? Hana and I have an appointment in Auckland."

Leslie pushed her lower lip high enough to tap the underside of her nose. Logan's jaw moved from side to side as though the effort of waiting for her acquiescence might kill him. Hana observed the familiar standoff through shuttered lashes, knowing how it always played out and just waiting for Leslie to decide she couldn't win this time, either. After lasting longer than usual, she dropped her arms and nodded. "Fine!" She ground the words through gritted teeth.

"Thank you." Logan left the room before the apology landed, perhaps afraid his bunched fingers might stray towards Leslie's florid neck and squeeze.

Hana released a sigh and rose with as much dignity as her aches and pains allowed. "You can take Logan's truck. We're using the old ute."

Leslie waggled her eyebrows. "You can't. It's not roadworthy. The boys run it around the property like Jack's old red Jeep." She winced as she said the man's name and covered her guilt with a toss of her grey curls. "You can't take it on the public highway."

Exasperation lit a fire in Hana's chest. She forced a smile onto her lips and aimed for benevolence, hoping to fall somewhere at least near tolerance. "Logan will sort it. He always does." A wave of gratitude washed away the brewing irritation. Tama wasn't missing, and she had her family around her. No one solutioned the hell out of a problem quite like Logan Du Rose. It offered her a fleeting sense of relief.

***

Logan switched the battered ute for Toby's truck and they reached the outskirts of Auckland at the tail end of the rush hour. Hana sat up straighter in the passenger seat and tugged down the sun visor. She peered at her forehead in the vanity mirror. "Does this look terrible?" she asked her husband. "I hid the black eyes with makeup."

Sunglasses masked any sense of a lie as he shook his head. A fresh batch of Steri-strips created an outline resembling a butterfly across his cheek. "No. Yours looks better without the dressing. Just like a cut. We both resemble boxers the day after a fight."

Hana nodded and flipped the visor closed with a sigh. "Good job I'm not naked. The seatbelt bruise looks awful."

Logan pursed his lips to avoid dwelling on her nudity. Hana spied the pulsing vein in his neck and smiled to herself. She turned her mind to the forthcoming meeting with Lana Alderbank and her heart rate picked up speed. "What will you say to her?" She pulled her legs beneath her on the seat and shifted to view her husband's expression.

Logan shrugged. "I don't plan conversations in my head, babe. Let's see what she has to say first, shall we?"

Hana nodded, but his rationale foxed her. Their differences amazed her. An internal monologue chattered in her mind on a continual loop. It sifted information and rehearsed whole dialogues, which rarely ever happened. Blissful silence occupied the strategic channels of Logan's brain. She sighed as they passed the sign for the prison and the internal voices went into overdrive. She wanted to ask him if he'd imagined their conversation once she discovered he knew exactly where Tama had hidden. Experience told her not to bother. They'd all learned it at some point. Logan, Toby and David.

"This is such a weird place to meet." Hana jumped from the vehicle and slammed the door behind her. She surveyed the wide car park and waited for Logan to lock the truck. Then she reached for his hand and walked towards the open front doors of the residential care home.

77

Saddle Blanket

Hana recognised Lana Alderbank from the news article as she rose from an armchair opposite the reception desk. An angular jaw gave her a masculine appearance which contrasted with the flowing white skirt which swished at her calves. She moved towards them with the stealth of a lynx. "Did you bring the box?" she demanded, her tone harsh. She'd swept her blonde hair into a bun which helped to iron out the creases in her face.

"Logan and Hana Du Rose. Nice to meet you." Logan's sarcasm made a giggle bubble in Hana's throat, and she turned it into a cough.

The woman's blue eyes flashed. "Lana Alderbank. I need that box. And I want my niece."

Hana groaned and sank into the comfy folds of the nearest armchair. Exhaustion nipped at her patience. "I thought you wanted to discuss things."

"And I thought you'd seen reason." Lana's jaw worked in a circular motion, creating the illusion of a rolling tide beneath her cheek. She clasped her hands in front of her, the knuckles knotted and distorted. "I already took your lawyer. I'm in this fight for the long haul."

Logan tutted. "Then we've had a wasted journey. We owe you nothing, lady. But I'm surprised the cops haven't already paid you a visit."

Her shoulders relaxed, and she gave a nonchalant shrug. "They'll find nothing to connect me to any of your troubles."

"Really?" Logan cocked his head and lowered his chin. His narrowed eyes bored into Lana's face like twin drills. "I have security footage of you visiting my home, plus dashcam footage of you side swiping my wife's vehicle. The hotel camera shows you almost hitting her on the driveway."

Her mouth slid into an attractive smile, which revealed an unexpected level of confidence. "The dashcam footage is inconclusive, and I think you'll find your security tapes suffered a minor fault."

Logan's teeth snapped together with a snarl. Hana sighed and buried her face in her palms. Raymond. The fly in their ointment.

"We're leaving." Logan whirled on the spot and ended the standoff. He held his hand out to Hana as she dug her soles into the sumptuous carpet and rose. Fury flashed in his stormy irises, and Hana winced against the vengeful thoughts he sent in Raymond's direction.

"Wait!" Lana Alderbank held her palm up as though taking an oath. Her lips flattened into a line. "I need you to understand," she said, command in her tone. An aura of unease shrouded the receptionist who observed the altercation from behind a wide desk. Fear sparkled in her eyes. Logan glanced at Hana, and she gave a slight uplift of her chin. Curiosity claimed the upper hand over common sense.

"Okay." He glanced at his watch. "Five minutes."

Hana followed her husband into the bowels of the home. Disinfectant overlaid the tang of decay. It filled her nostrils, sending her back in time to another home and an elderly priest who'd held her heart in his calloused palm. Father Sinbad's ghost whispered to her from the successive open doorways, placing a mantle of calm over her shoulders. Logan towed her behind him, his fingers firm around hers. She sensed the pent up aggression building in the set of his shoulders and the stiffness of his gait.

Lana strode before them, her steps confident as though she knew the route without needing to look. She halted by an open door and turned to wait for them, her lips twisting into a determined knot. Hana blinked at the sheet of white paper pinned to the door. *My name is Lana Alderbank*, it said in a typed, cursive font.

Giving them a second to orient themselves, Lana stepped over the threshold. Her voice became light and forced as she spoke to a sunken woman lying in a hospital bed. "Hi, Mum. I've brought visitors," she said. Her hand flapped towards the door, but she didn't invite them into the room. Hana rested her weight on her left foot, lifting the other so her sandal balanced on the toe. She gripped Logan's fingers as confusion shrouded them.

"Box." The voice croaked from beneath starched white sheets, its sound almost inaudible.

The blonde woman gulped and pursed her lips, choosing her words with great care. "Not yet, Mum." She dipped her head nearer to the face flattened against the pillow. Wisps of grey curls hung around it like a cloud. "Soon. I'll bring you the box and your granddaughter." A gnarled hand rose from the mattress, slipping free of the sheets like a cobra escaped from its hiding place. Lana's head bobbed as crabbed fingers snatched a hank of her hair and yanked her head lower. She cried out in pain, and Logan jerked in shock. He shoved Hana backwards and shielded her with his solid torso.

Hana peeked under his armpit as Lana's cheeks flamed red and she extracted her hair from the fingers with difficulty. Humiliation's army stormed across her features, contorting them into a grimace. Hana's breath caught in her chest and she closed her eyes to concentrate on the surging pulse pounding blood through her ears. She pressed her cheek against Logan's powerful arm. The scene held a sickness she hadn't expected.

"Back in a minute, Mum." Lana's steady tone suppressed a vault of buried emotion. Hana tensed as she stepped back towards the door and the shocked Du Roses. A clump of loosened hair floated down to catch against the buttons of her blouse. She paused to let them stand aside and then indicated they should follow her along the corridor.

A nurse smiled as she passed them. Hana gripped Logan's fingers, her head darting left and right as she anticipated unnamed hidden dangers. Lana entered an open doorway with *Meeting Room* inscribed on a metal plate and mounted next to the frame. She sank into an armchair beneath the window and nondescript curtains. Logan slid into the room and towed Hana with him. He didn't release her fingers even after they claimed armchairs nearest the door.

"Let's have it," he commanded, his tone terse and businesslike. "Your mother is Lana Alderbank, and she wants the box."

The woman nodded. A pink tongue massaged her upper lip and her shoulders sagged. "She was never an amiable woman, even whilst in good physical shape." She sighed. "My father managed her for all their married life, mitigating for her and smoothing over any upsets." She swallowed after the last word as though the minimising of the turbulence cost her. "Dementia claimed Dad's faculties piece by piece over the last decade. He'd been a powerful man, and he became just a rambling shadow." Lana paused, her blue irises sparkling with unshed tears. "But he started talking about things nobody knew. Hidden stories dredged from a dark pit in his soul."

She rose and Logan stiffened. He dropped Hana's fingers and his left arm shot out as though to shield her. Hana studied the side of his handsome face and yearned to kiss the dark stubble prickling through his cheek. She wished them anywhere but here, with the scent of decaying humanity and lost memories swirling around their heads. Lana turned towards the window and became silent. A man wearing overalls shoved a petrol mower around the flowerbeds. Its guttural rumbling provided a backdrop to Lana's sad sigh. She continued to speak as though keeping her face hidden provided her with dignity. "I had a sister." She spat the words. "The nanny stole her and it broke my mother. She just took the child and disappeared." She turned and her eyes blazed in her hardened features. Blunt angles cast severe shadows over her body as the light silhouetted her. "My mother couldn't find her, but it seems Dad always knew where she was."

Hana gulped. "Caroline Du Rose?" she whispered.

Lana cocked her head and nodded. She turned back to face them, gathering her features into a mask of indifference. "Yes. Dad said nothing, not even when Mum spent years trying to find her. She followed a lead to a house in the mountains, but the man told her the child died. He even showed her a death certificate. Then nine years ago, a newspaper article mentioned Antoinette Du Rose in context with a daughter. It's not a common first name, and it sparked Mum's fury. She recognised the bitch's photograph." Lana's face contorted as though she'd swallowed something distasteful. "My mother isn't tech savvy, so she employed the help of cousins to make contact through social media. But my sister wasn't interested." Her jaw twisted as she ground her teeth. "Fast forward to my father rambling all his secrets. That's when Mum discovered he'd helped the nanny leave with the child and even given her a gift." Sarcasm infused her tone. "She heard the engagement fell through and tried to see my sister. Again, she rejected her. So, Mum set out to retrieve the box. Spite motivated her more than anything else. But she failed. Antoinette's husband knew nothing about it. He sent her away countless times. She'd lost her daughter *and* the thing my father gave the nanny for safekeeping. Then a fire destroyed the last piece of the puzzle. My father hoped it was finished for good."

Hana cocked her head and frowned. "Your mother owned Purple Primp? She's the woman who visited Reuben's house and, later, the fire site. You share a first name."

Lana sank back into her seat. The cushions hissed as they reshaped around her. She exhaled. "I saw a news broadcast about eighteen months ago, which claimed my sister murdered her brother-in-law. It mentioned a child. My niece." She sighed and shook her head. "Why must you be so difficult? We'll give her a privileged life. She'll have everything my sister didn't."

Hana shrank back into the chair. "I love her. And she has a half-brother. We won't separate them." She stuck her chin in the air and clenched her teeth. Logan glanced sideways at her, his fleeting gaze containing a smile.

She loved Edin. She'd said it. A flower burst to life in her heart and warmed her from the inside as the emotion took hold and blossomed and blossomed.

She. Loved. Edin.

"What about Raymond?" Hana frowned and cocked her head. "Why keep him in place all these years?"

"Coincidence. Familial loyalty. He's my cousin. My mother's nephew." Lana didn't sound certain of his motivations. "I don't think it's that complicated. We hadn't spoken to him for years until recently when Mum got sick. He overheard gossip about the fire. And whispers about something found in the rubble." Her shoulders slumped, and she sank into the armchair. It seemed to swallow her, leaving only her face and hands revealed. The fingers wound through each other like a surging sea, constantly in motion. "Mum suffered a stroke and we made an unspoken pact to give her whatever she wants.

"What about our son?" Hana edged forward, driven by the need to free Tama from his burden. "Why did you go after him?"

Lana shrugged. "I didn't. My mother started this. I'm trying to finish it. For her."

Logan rose with fluidity. Hana blinked at the suddenness of his movement. She gazed up at the hard set of his jaw and felt grateful she wasn't on Lana's end of his angry glare. "A man died," he hissed. "And my son is in the frame for it. Did those two guys at my hotel kill him? Why? What's so important about this box?"

Lana pursed her lips. She held Logan's gaze, but her eyelashes fluttered as though trying to mitigate the force it contained. "It's bigger than just the contents of the box." She waved her hand towards Hana. "We didn't know what my father gave her until last month. Just before he stopped speaking altogether, he confessed." She exhaled and her hand shook as she ran her fingers over her eyes. "My father ran a salvage company. It's how he made his money." She cocked her head and shifted her attention to Hana. "You own a museum. Have you ever heard of the General Grant?"

"I have." Logan watched Lana through narrowed eyes. "It went missing in the 1800s after striking the Auckland Islands. It carried the largest shipment of gold ever lost at sea."

"Gold?" Hana swallowed. Her heart sank, landing like a lead weight in her stomach.

"Yes." Lana's gaze flicked to the open doorway and back to Logan. She lowered her voice. "My father found it in 1969. He stripped what he could but left the wreck on the seabed."

Logan's sarcastic snort echoed around the room. "Riiiight." He drew out the word as though a string hauled it from the depths of his powerful chest. "And he gave Antoinette something for the child."

"Something from the wreck. Gold." Hana shook her head. She rested her chin on the heel of her hand, bracing her elbow against her knee. "But why would your father allow the nanny to kidnap his own daughter?" She searched Lana's face for the clues she couldn't see. The answer appeared as a wince of pain, fleeting enough to miss notice. But Hana had worked in a high school. She'd witnessed all manner of parental cruelty and its outworking in the minds and behaviour of teenagers. "Caroline wasn't safe, was she? Your mother is cruel."

Lana pursed her lips. A mixture of anger and grief drove tears to sparkle against her blue irises. She looked at that moment as though she hated Hana for calling attention to her pain. Her lips rolled back from her teeth. "I wish he'd sent me away with a nanny." Her tone sounded brittle. "Perhaps I would have learned to enjoy life."

Hana groaned and leaned back in her seat. The bruising to the back of her head sent out a flare of heat as it hit the cushion. "Caroline's life wasn't all hearts and roses. She's in prison for manslaughter."

"Let's go." Logan turned his feet towards the doorway and waggled his fingers at Hana.

Lana rose at speed, tripping over her own feet as she tried to block their exit. "But what about the box? If that gold hits the open market, everyone will know where it came from. They'll know what my father did."

Logan exhaled. His fingers closed around Hana's as he helped her to stand. "You can't hide the truth forever." His tone conveyed a casualness he didn't feel. "Tell the cops what you know about the kid's murder and let our boy off the hook."

Lana's teeth ground in her jaw. Her gaze darted left and right. For an awful moment, Hana imagined her attempting to prevent them from leaving. "Wait!" She lifted her hands and bobbed them. "Mum's guys killed the boy, but they said it was an accident. I'll tell the police what I know, but only in exchange for the gold and my niece."

Logan's fingers clamped around Hana's hand hard enough to crush her slender bones. She suppressed a hiss of pain which rose onto her tongue. His voice cracked like shattered glass. "You want us to exchange one child's freedom for another's?"

Lana shrugged, straightening her spine and planting her feet with more confidence. "It's fair. And I'll pay for the damage to your vehicle." Her gaze slid to meet Hana's. "It's the last thing I can do for my mother. I don't care what it costs." She tilted her head and an emotion akin to pride and satisfaction raised the corners of her lips. Hana ached for her need to satisfy the spiteful old woman in the bed.

"Okay." Logan's definitive nod caused a stabbing sensation in the back of Hana's brain. She stared up at him, her lips parted and her heart breaking in waves of agony in her chest.

"No!" She tugged on his wrist, but his grip only tightened. The set of his jaw and the sideways glare silenced her. She kidded herself that he didn't mean it. It was a bluff. A ruse. A confidence trick.

"We'll be in touch," he said, his tone businesslike.

"No." Hana twisted her wrist and used the weaker connection of his thumb to snap her hand free. "Get a DNA test." She tilted her chin upwards and faced Lana with fire in her eyes. "Prove she's your niece and I'll give you visiting rights." Her heart thudded in her chest. The fingers of her right hand fluttered to connect with the outline of the pacemaker beneath her left collarbone. A stress reaction. A reflex. She'd die before she let Lana Alderbank near Edin.

"Easy." A wicked smile lit Lana's lips, their thin rails parting to reveal even teeth. "Supervised. I'll say where and when. And once I've proved it, I'll take her."

The acridity of the atmosphere made it difficult for Hana to catch her breath. She slid around Lana and into the wide corridor, finding no relief there. Running her hand along a wooden rail fixed to the wall, she stumbled towards the reception area and the automatic front doors.

My name is Clive Alderbank.

The printed sheet on another door caught her attention as she crossed the gap. Her fingers fumbled for the wooden rail beyond it. A shrunken man sat in an armchair, a tartan blanket wrapped around his knees. The TV played, but he showed no recognition of the images passing across his vision. Hana pitied Lana for a fraction of a second. Circumstance had left her circling the residential home, visiting her ghoulish parents and clearing up their mess. And now Logan had condemned Edin to the same routine. Her Edin.

"Come on." His hand rested on her shoulder and she writhed away from his touch. A glance at his expression showed no emotion at all. He'd discarded the little girl without a fight.

Hana jerked away from him and strode ahead, forcing herself not to run. They passed the room containing Lana's mother, and she paused, dodging Logan's outstretched hand as he failed to stop in time. A nurse appeared in the doorway and smiled at her. "Can I help you?" she asked.

The white face on the pillow turned to observe and Hana baulked at the violence in the elderly woman's sparkling blue eyes. She held her breath and shook her head at the nurse. "I'm just leaving," she whispered.

The woman nodded, her smile genuine and her eyes bright in her tanned face. She glanced at Logan's combative stance as he glared at his wife.

"Wait!" Hana glanced behind her to ensure safety from Lana. She lowered her voice and pointed back towards the doorway containing Edin's alleged grandmother. "What's wrong with her?"

The nurse wrinkled her nose and winced. "Stroke. Two months ago." she replied. She pursed her lips. "Patient confidentiality means I can't tell you anything else." She glanced towards the reception area in the distance, the corner of the desk just visible. Turning her shoulder towards Logan and leaning closer to Hana, she confided, "She's a bitch. I wouldn't bother going in there."

"Thanks." Hana's head wobbled on her neck as she acknowledged the nurse's advice. The old lady's stroke coincided with her family's need to finish her hideous work.

Without glancing at her husband, she stalked past him and aimed her gaze at the automatic doors sliding apart in the distance.

78

Hana reached the truck before Logan. She leaned against it, both palms flat against the metal. The sun's rays super-heated it and it burned her fingers, grounding her internal agony in a blistering rage. Logan took his time walking across the car park. He stopped to speak into his phone, and Hana ground her teeth in fury. She nudged the heavy tread tyre to her right, the pain in her toes reminding her of the bruised caused by kicking Logan's assailant. A barrage of pre-planned arguments soared past her inner vision, taunting her to collect one from the ready conveyor belt and use it against him. He turned his back on her as he spoke to the caller, daring to release a low, rumbling laugh against the backdrop of her utter misery. Her fists balled by her sides and she turned towards the gated exit to the site.

A click sounded as Logan deactivated the central locking. He strode towards her, slipping his phone into his jeans pocket. "You can get in," he said, his tone casual.

Hana backed away from the truck. She shook her head in disbelief at his nonchalance. "No." Her voice wavered. Sadness flared in her chest. She'd go nowhere with him again.

The heel of her sandal clattered with the curb surrounding the car park. She righted herself and continued backing.

"Hana!" Logan's tone conveyed a warning. He sensed the turmoil building in her eyes and took a step towards her. "Get in the truck."

"You get in the truck." She repeated his words as a hiss, but like a kettle rising to the boil, the next time her lips parted brought a louder version. "You get in the truck!" Hysteria laced her tone. She continued backing away from him, the collapse of her world imminent. Logan glanced around him at the empty car park. Determination lit his grey eyes like an oil slick spreading across a lake.

He strode towards her and she couldn't turn fast enough. She hadn't factored in the tree to her left and ran straight into it. The air left her lungs in a whoosh. Logan's firm hands righted her, his chest a wall against her bunched fists. A squeal of pure rage exploded from her lips after her next inhale, and he released a sigh of resignation. "Truck! Now!" he growled. Dipping his body, he collected her over his shoulder in an undignified fireman's lift. He kept her left hand gripped in his fingers and her right arm trapped against him. Not bothering to walk around the truck, he fumbled with the rear door and held it open with his hip. A breeze caused Hana's dress to flutter across his cheek. She piled onto the seat backwards like a bag of groceries, screaming threats and obscenities as he slammed the door on her.

Her aches and pains from a wicked week prevented her from sitting up fast enough. Logan shot into the driver's seat and locked the doors before she spun onto her backside. He activated the child locks to prevent her escape. She rose like a leviathan in his rear-view mirror and saw him wince at her reflection. Scrabbling at the door handle proved futile.

"You can't get out." He fired up the engine, and the truck tore from the parking space with the squeal of tyres on asphalt. Hana lurched back against the seat and her left knee contacted the hard plastic of the centre console. "Get your seatbelt fastened."

"Let me out of this car!" Hana waved her arm between the front seats and whacked his muscular shoulder. "Right now!"

"No!" He turned onto a busy road and braked for a red traffic light. Hana bumped her nose on the back of his seat. She released a grunt of pain and rage, her fingers covering the partially healed cut over the bridge of her nose. Logan hauled on the handbrake and turned to face her. "Please, Hana. Just trust me." His tone held desperation. "Don't lose it with me, yeah?" He sighed and narrowed his eyes. "Your forehead's bleeding. Fasten your seatbelt and sit tight for a few minutes. We're meeting Bodie, I promise."

Hot tears coursed down Hana's cheeks. The fear of losing Edin consumed all rational thought. She could no longer distinguish where one emotional ache started and a physical one ended. Her fingers slipped in the blood oozing from the bridge of her nose. Obedience replaced the rebellion she no longer had the energy to maintain. Logan would take her to see Bodie. He'd said he promised, and he never broke his promises, even if satisfying their conditions almost killed him.

She'd left her phone and purse in the glove box, giving her no choice but to trust her husband. Sickness roiled in her stomach, angst churning the remains of the hot crossed bun she'd enjoyed hours earlier. He never promised they'd keep Edin. She'd done that for both of them.

"I need coffee," she said with a sniff. She used the hem of her dress to wipe away her tears, wincing at the stain of the bloodied foundation which spread across the sunny yellow fabric.

"We'll get coffee." Relief accompanied the sigh Logan released. "Coffee and explanations. I promise."

There it was again. The Logan Du Rose promise.

Despite the tumult in her heart, Hana forced her seatbelt into its buckle with a click.

79

Tail Bandage

Hana tumbled from the rear seat, and Bodie blinked in shock. He shot an accusing glare at Logan. "What happened?" He spread his palms in question and took a step towards Hana. The driver's door of his patrol car drifted closed behind him, but a warning alarm on the dashboard continued to trill. "Why is she bleeding?"

Logan cleared his throat and slammed the truck door. His fingers twitched against the handle. "Meltdown." The single word condemned Hana to the rank of a foolish child. Her cheeks pinked with injustice.

"I thought he gave Edin away." Her chest hitched with emotion. "She can have the box and the gold, but she's not taking Edin." Her irises sparkled with the fire of accusation.

"Why did you ask for a DNA test?" Bodie ran a hand through his glossy hair and leaned against the driver's door of his car. The sun beat down on them like a judgement. "I didn't understand that part."

Hana frowned. Logan retrieved a clean handkerchief from his jeans pocket and thrust it towards her. She dabbed at the ooze on her forehead. "How do you know about that?"

"I listened to the conversation." Bodie tapped the lapel of his jacket and grinned at Logan. "We opened a call as you went inside and I recorded it."

"Oh." Shame robbed Hana of the vestiges of her energy, and she sank onto the curb next to Logan's truck. She closed her eyes and rested her chin on her knees. "What now?"

"That's what we're here to discuss." Logan's voice held no recrimination. No disappointment or rage. He kept it all inside, circling the vault containing other unexpressed emotions. "She wants the gold and Edin. I want the evidence that Tama didn't kill his friend." He jerked his head towards Bodie. "How do we do this?"

Hana's son blew out a ragged breath. "I need to escalate this higher up the food chain. If the father raided the General Grant, he's in big trouble."

Hana turned her head and pressed her cheek against her knee. She wrapped her arms around her shins. "Clive Alderbank is in the residential home. I saw him. Good luck with getting him to court."

Bodie made a sound low in his throat. "The mother sounds poisonous." He tutted. "A lot of this makes no sense, especially the part about giving the daughter away to the nanny. Who does that?"

Hana blinked beneath the sun's glare. It cast the two men into silhouette. "A man with a violent, unpredictable wife. He feared for her. It makes perfect sense."

"Okay." Bodie released a sigh. "I'll take this recording to the office and see what I can dig up in terms of offences and further action." He winced at the sight of Hana. "I don't think you should go in there." He jerked his head towards the fast-food restaurant beyond the car park. "You look like you just fought a wall and lost."

"Yeah." Logan nodded. He held out his hand towards his son-in-law. "We'll get take aways from the drive through."

Bodie's fingers clasped his, and he jerked his chin down in a nod. "I should go." He patted his smart black trousers and keys jangled in his pocket. He extracted a fob and turned back to his vehicle. The soles of his shoes ground against loose grit as he spun to face Hana. "Hug, Mum," he said and held out his arms.

Hana hauled herself upright. She wrapped her arms around his waist and laid her cheek against his chest. A disgusting sniff ruined the moment, and she turned her face to avoid staining his white shirt with blood and makeup. When she dropped her arms and backed away, he stooped to kiss her temple. Hana spied Logan fiddling with the truck key in her peripheral vision. Public displays of emotion weren't something he favoured, but he didn't deny her rare moment of connection with Bodie. Her son smiled at her, creases forming at the corners of his eyes. "You didn't answer my question." He lifted a brown index finger and familiar lines deepened in his brow. "Why ask for a DNA test? I'm curious."

Hana shrugged. "I assumed she'd refuse. The birth certificate we found with the gold doesn't belong to anyone with the surname of Alderbank. I'd hoped Caroline wasn't her sister, which would show in any DNA test with Edin." A sigh escaped her lips. "But she didn't falter. And I don't know what to do if it now returns a positive result." Her mind filled with the ramifications of attempting to take a sample from a furious Edin. Perhaps Mark's partner could include it in his testing regime.

Logan shook his head. "We'll deal with it when it comes to it." He held out his hand to her. "Caroline gave us guardianship over Edin. No court will award custody to a stranger against the mother's will."

"A mother in prison for manslaughter." Hana murmured her contrary statement, not wanting to frustrate Logan with her negativity.

Bodie winced, and his expression contained sympathy for Hana's dilemma. "Let's see where this information goes first," he said. "It's inadmissible because of the way I acquired it, but it may open up lines of enquiry which will satisfy the prosecutors." His steps held an uncharacteristic bounce as he walked towards his car. Hana studied his deft movements and sensed the hunter having caught a scent. She hoped so at that moment. More than anything. Incriminating Lana Alderbank would help the Du Roses keep Edin.

80

Trail Ride

Hana sat back in the office chair with a sigh. The words on the screen before her merged into a blurred pattern.

"What's eating you, kōtiro?" Will turned his head to peer at her, his spectacles perched on the end of his pointed nose. "You're huffing and puffing like a train. I can't think straight." He set his tweezers on the desk in front of him and removed the cotton gloves from his gnarled fingers.

Hana shivered beneath the cool air, which maintained archival conditions in the museum and workroom. She wrapped her arms around herself and closed her eyes. Thoughts paraded before her inner vision in a confusing jumble, and she frowned. "Ouch!" She hissed and sat up straight, pressing her fingers over the cut across the bridge of her nose.

"Talk to me." Will turned his wheelchair to face her and dipped forward, his hazel irises sparkling with interest. He cocked his head like a wise bird. "What are you looking for?"

"Answers," Hana replied with a sigh. She shoved at the pencil lying on the pad next to the keyboard. She'd written the heading, *Catherine Finlaggan*, over an hour earlier after returning from the meeting with Lana Alderbank. Then nothing else. A coffee mug stain marred the lined paper beneath it. "Okay." She turned her body towards the old man and pursed her lips. Her hands waved before her as though drawing thoughts from her chest on a hidden strand. "You're Lana Alderbank. The mother." Will blinked, but made no comment. "Someone kidnaps your daughter. At some point, you track her to a house on a mountain but the homeowner tells you the child died. He shows you a death certificate." Her hands waved with increased speed, jerky movements punctuating each word. "Where did Reuben get a death certificate for Caroline? Is she the child or was there another?" She shook her head and seized the pencil in frustrated fingers. "Anyway, you can't call the police because it's your word against his." She paused and stared at the ceiling. "And why isn't there a record of the nanny taking the child? That's weird in itself, isn't it?" She flapped her hand and continued. "Later, when your husband has dementia, you discover he not only let the nanny kidnap your child, but gave her something to keep. A gift." She jerked her head towards the box lying open next to Will. He'd separated the delicate leaves of gold and placed each one between sheets of archival tissue paper. "You read about your potential daughter in the newspapers with her fiancé. Or husband." Hana huffed, a breath loaded with exasperation. "You realise she's alive and well, but she rejects your effort to contact her."

"Go back to your question about the death certificate." Will used the button on the chair's arm to wheel himself closer to Hana. "There's no record of another female child in Reuben's family. Phoenix Du Rose mentioned Caroline in her diaries."

Hana nodded. "Yeah. Mixed up and terrifying. That's a perfect description of Caroline."

Will dipped his chin to peer at her over his spectacles. "Or mixed up and terrified. What if Antoinette liberated her from the Alderbank woman like the daughter told you? She hid her with the family in the north until she felt safe. It's possible she brought Caroline back here after Reuben convinced the mother her child died."

Hana groaned and laid her head against the chair. "Then why doesn't the birth certificate name her as Caroline Alderbank? And why didn't Lana break stride when I suggested a DNA test? She must genuinely believe Caroline is her sister and Edin is her niece." She glanced at the clock above the door and sighed. "Why aren't there more hours in a day?"

Will smiled and his expression softened into one of pure indulgence. He mocked and chastised Hana, but his tough exterior vied with a gentle adoration which he kept hidden. Reaching forward, he laid his cragged fingers over her writhing hands. The pencil rolled to the floor and Hana jumped. She dipped to retrieve it. "You're forgetting the nature of Reuben Du Rose," he said, his tone soft. "If he wanted something, he found a way to get it."

Hana stared at the cork notice board behind Will's head. Her voice took on a faraway quality. "A fake birth certificate." She pursed her lips and her thoughts went to Logan. He called it the *Ways and Means Act* as though it existed in time and space as a genuine piece of legislation. It made him appear Machiavellian, but he used it as a rite of passage.

Often.

The Law of Du Rose.

She nodded, the action slow and deliberate. "I can see Logan doing that," she agreed. Her gaze returned to Will's. "But then what? Caroline's their daughter. Reuben knew why Antoinette took her, and that's the reason he kept her after his wife died?"

"Is that enough reason for the woman to scratch through the debris of a tragic fire?"

"No." Hana's curls slithered over her shoulder to bounce against her shirt buttons. "Caroline rejected her. Twice. Why search for a birth certificate for your lost child when the adult didn't want to know you?"

"The gold?" Will's tongue clicked against his false teeth. He answered his own question with a shake of his head. "No. A cursory valuation puts it around twenty thousand dollars. Even a decade ago, it wasn't worth the effort she put in to retrieve it."

Hana's shoulders slumped. "And we're back at the start again." She slid the pencil between her lips sideways and glanced at the clock. "What if it came from the General Grant? What's the value then?"

Will's sudden cackle made her jerk, and the pencil tumbled to the floor again. She winced and left it there, disconcerted that in her distraction she'd already put it into her mouth. "What's funny?" she demanded. Rising, she retrieved her handbag from the floorboards by her chair. "I need to get the children from school."

Will jabbed his finger at the gold leaf. It appeared so vulnerable scattered across his desk in its tissue shroud. "That's never from the General Grant!" he scoffed. "Where did you get that idea?"

"Lana Alderbank told us yesterday." Her lips turned down at the corners. Will's doubt caused offence. "Her father found the wreck and stripped it. They don't want the gold discovered and made public."

Will rocked with laughter in his chair. His body deflated, and he flapped his right hand in front of his face as though to dispel the notion. "You think submerged gold leaf would survive in salt water?"

Hana's lips moved, but she swallowed her words of denial. She stared at the old man as though he'd shone a torch on her soul. Will scratched his sparse hair with lined fingernails. Hana sat in her chair with a bump. The force on the wheels carried her backwards a few centimetres. "It would disintegrate and become a lumpy mess."

"Yup." Will gave a nod of acknowledgement. He held out his hand palm upwards to encompass the fragile artifact. "This never saw a drop of water. Especially not salt water."

"Then what?" Frustration seized Hana in its vice and shook her. "Lana believed it. I looked into her eyes. She told me the truth. Why would her mother tell her such a lie? If it's not about the gold, then it must be about the birth certificate, but why?" Shaking her head, she rose from the chair and pushed it beneath the desk. Its wheels squeaked across the wooden floor.

"Hey." Will called to her as she closed her fingers around the door handle. Hana turned to face him. His lips parted, and she shook her head and hauled open the door.

"Don't say it," she whispered. "Leave it alone, Hana."

"Na." He wrinkled his brow and pushed his spectacles upwards to meet the bridge of his nose. His lips lifted at the corners. "No point saying that to someone as hard headed as you, girl. We've been here before, haven't we?" He dangled her keys in his other hand. "I thought you might need these."

"Thanks." Hana strode across the room and seized the fob and its jangling companions from his open palm. On an impulse, she dipped and kissed his wrinkled forehead. "See you tomorrow," she promised.

"Sure you will," he replied with a grin.

81

Hoof Oil

Tama flagged Hana down as she backed Logan's truck from his parking space. He masked his serious expression with an air of boredom. "I'll come with you," he said, yanking the booster from the front and hurling it over the head rest. He settled himself in the passenger seat.

"Bodie told you to lie low." Hana stared at him before pushing the lever into first gear. "You're like catnip to the school mums."

Tama shrugged and fastened his seatbelt. "I can stay in the truck if you think they can't cope with my awesomeness."

Hana snorted. "That's not the reason. You've spent the last few weeks in hiding. Why risk your safety now?"

Tama ignored her. He leaned forward to fiddle with the seat position before shifting his attention to the air conditioning. He recoiled with a grunt as Hana slapped his fingers. "You'll need to sit in the middle seat on the way home. I can't remember whose turn it is in the front."

"Mine." Tama grinned at her. "Big brother privilege."

Hana sighed and decided she'd leave him to fight that battle alone. "I can't sort out this puzzle," she mused. The truck wheels rumbled along the winding driveway as the hotel diminished in the rear-view mirror. "What did you do that triggered the Alderbanks coming after you?"

"Alderbank?" Tama flipped his fringe backwards and turned to stare at her. "How do you know him?"

"Who? Clive?"

Tama's expression clouded. "No. Sid."

Hana gritted her teeth as a campervan slid past her on the narrow road. She pushed the truck as close to the rocks as she dared and held her breath. Tama leaned forward to watch the van's perilous journey alongside the sheer cliff edge. "Don't they realise they're meant to use the easier route through the township?" he asked. "Shouldn't we tell them?"

"I don't have the energy." Hana pulled back onto the road and took the next bend with exaggerated care. She clicked her fingers to regain Tama's attention. "Who is Sid Alderbank?"

He snuffed. "He sent me home a few weeks ago. I asked questions about a house fire because it reminded me of Poppa Reuben's. He got antsy. Said it wasn't my business."

"You work with him?" Hana's lips parted in surprise. "He's a fireman?"

"Not anymore. He serves in a supervisory role. Swapped his asbestos for a pinstriped suit years ago. Idiot!"

Hana squirmed in her seat. "Did you tell him you were looking into Reuben's fire?"

Tama shrugged. "Yeah. I asked the girls in the administration office to help me."

She blew out a breath and her heart rate soared. "I think this is it, Tama. This is the link."

"Okay." He didn't sound certain. "Nah." His dark curls wobbled as he shook his head with increased emphasis. "It's an unlucky coincidence. The two things might not even be related."

"Of course, they're related!" Hana snapped. "This is New Zealand, the home of two degrees of separation. I bet he and Lana enjoyed lunch last Sunday. They probably had the same dad, and he got around using a push-bike." She groaned and slapped the steering wheel.

"The guy is still a jerk." Tama shifted in the seat and stretched his knees out in front of him. Even the cavernous foot well of the truck couldn't accommodate his long legs. "I don't understand. He must have seen a billion house fires across his service. Why would Poppa's have any relevance for him?"

"Because perhaps he suppressed the records." Hana's lips parted into a grin. "As a favour for a rich and politically connected family member."

Tama ran a hand across the bristles covering his chin. "That's a long shot, Ma," he conceded.

Hana shrugged. "It's all I've got."

Traffic buzzed around the school like ants drawn to a tasty treat. Hana parked along the street and walked the rest of the way. Contrary to their agreement, Tama loped alongside, producing one stride to three of hers. "I'm catnip," he said with a lazy grin. "I like that." His gaze wandered around the amassed women, his lips curved upwards like a child in a sweetshop. Hana dug her elbow into his ribs as they slumped on the low wall in her usual place.

"Stop it!" she chided. "Aren't you in enough trouble? What will you do about Jordan?"

He exhaled, and the wind tossed his fringe into his eyes and hid any emotion. "Dunno," he admitted. "Did you see that disgusting photo she gave to the cops?"

Hana turned to observe him, searching his blank expression for clues. "Who put lipstick on your collar?" she demanded. "Jordan said you had a hickey, too."

His grin revealed a dazzling display of straight white teeth. He clamped them over his lower lip to suppress his inappropriate surge of pride. "Yeah. About that." He didn't attempt to hide his enjoyment. "I don't know if it'll happen again."

"So, you cheated on Jordan?"

Tama squirmed on the wall as he picked through a potential semantic minefield. "Sorta. And sorta not."

Hana groaned and flapped her hand between them. "Then you get what you get, Tama," she said, her tone filled with resignation. "Don't expect sympathy from me."

"But I think I'm in love." His grin broadened despite his efforts to constrain it. "Remember when I broke my arm?"

Hana nodded. "Yes." Her eyes widened as her thoughts collected to form a conclusion. "Oh. The girl in the office?"

Tama reached around her and pressed his palm over her mouth. He didn't confirm or deny her conclusion"Don't jinx it, Ma!" he pleaded. "I'm getting a transfer to a different station. Then I can see her properly. Like boyfriend and girlfriend." His eyes glazed. "Husband and wife."

Hana pushed his hand away. "What about Jordan? You can't just use and abuse people when it suits you. Next time the vet visits to neuter the steers, I'm adding you to the list."

Tama wagged his finger between them. "She agreed there were no strings. It's not my fault she caught feelings."

Hana closed her eyes and pressed her index fingers over her eyelids. No suitable reply rose to the surface of her mind. They'd revisit this particular argument until Tama settled on one woman. And maybe even after that.

The children arrived like a swarm of bees, shrouding Tama with excited hugs and kisses. Edin and Phoenix fought to sit on his knee. Mac trailed Chester, who rebuffed Hilda's efforts at corralling him. "I'm so sorry," Hilda gushed. She maintained eye contact with Hana and showed no interest in Tama's antics as he threw schoolchildren into the air and pretended to fumble the catch. Mac's entire year group formed an excited queue and Hana forced herself not to notice. She rose and turned her back on the entertainment.

"It's fine," she said. "We can have a playdate another day if you like?"

Hilda nodded and bent to placate her son. "Mrs Du Rose says you can visit another day," she hissed. He frowned and glared at Hana as though holding her responsible for thwarting his outing. A low keening left his throat, reminiscent of Edin's frustrated growl. Hana's heart softened towards Hilda, understanding what she went through behind closed doors.

"I promise," she told him. She dragged her phone from her skirt pocket and logged into her calendar app. "Let's pick a day."

They agreed on the following Monday and Hana promised cake. She waited until Chester shoved his way to the front of the queue for Tama's precarious treatment before lowering her voice and leaning closer to Hilda. "Would you like to ride with me soon? We can go during the day and stay in the arena for your first time back in the saddle. Until you feel more confident and then we can trek through the bush."

Hilda's cheeks flushed pink, and she clasped her hands over her heart. "Really? I'll love that." Her irises sparkled with excitement, and she grinned. "I've done nothing for my own enjoyment for years. Not since I left work on maternity leave. Just name the day and I'll be there."

"Okay. Let's aim for next Monday before we fetch the children." Hana absorbed vicarious pleasure from Hilda's reaction. Curiosity drove her next question. "Where did you work before you had Chester?"

Sadness enveloped Hilda as though a hidden hand had cast her into shadow. She exhaled and her shoulders rounded. "I worked at the Hilton in Auckland. But Chester had a lot of health problems and we moved away from the city to help with his allergies. I'd like to return to work now he's at school, but I need something local."

Hana bit back the empty platitude knowing it served no purpose. She knew how it felt to give things up for her family. Before she'd formulated anything more suitable, a concerned parent put a stop to Tama's dangerous brand of child-minding. A collective sigh of disappointment filtered through to the tail of the eager queue. Phoenix and Edin held his hands as they skipped along the street to the truck.

"You can take the front seat." Wiri patted Tama's forearm and stared up at him, his expression hungry for approval.

Hana looked around at the other children, confused about the offer. She had an inkling it was Edin's turn in the front. But when nobody complained, she let her objection pass. As she waited for seatbelts to click and complaints to lessen, she leaned against the side of the truck and closed her eyes. Her phone buzzed in her pocket as someone tried to reach her. Dreading seeing the number for the prison again, Hana tugged it free and shielded the screen with her hand. Bodie's image strobed as he cancelled the call.

"Sorry." She gushed her apology after calling him back and hearing the click of connection before the first ring. "School pick up time." A shriek sounded from the truck's interior as Tama reached behind him and tickled the occupants of the middle row of seats. Phoenix perched on the seat in the boot, her head bowed over a library book. Hana took a step away from the vehicle and stuck a finger in her other ear. "Everything okay?"

"Finlaggan." Bodie's voice sounded distant, backed by traffic noises and birdsong. "I checked that article you forwarded to me. The child never turned up again. A little girl. Catherine Finlaggan."

"I remember." Hana pursed her lips and tapped on the rear window as Edin unbuckled her seatbelt. "Sorry. I need to get these children home."

"Okay, well, I've found the child's father and older sister. I've called the number I have for her and left a message. I'm planning to speak to her, so I'll let you know what I find out once that's happened."

Hana exhaled with relief. "That's fantastic Bo. I'm so grateful. How did you find them?"

Bodie gave a gentle laugh. "I'm a cop, Mum. It's what we do."

"Awesome. I know Lana didn't miss a stride when I suggested the DNA test, but that missing baby is somehow linked to all this."

"All good. I need to run, Mum. I'm due at the temple in ten minutes." Silence greeted Hana's goodbye, and she wrinkled her nose. Wiri's face appeared at the side window and he banged on the glass. His brow scrunched as Edin kicked him and opened her mouth to squeal in protest.

"Okay, we're leaving!" Hana yanked open the door and settled into the driver's seat. She glared at Tama. "Thanks for winding them up, I really appreciate it."

"No worries." He actually looked pleased with himself. As Hana activated the engine, he leaned forward to fiddle with the radio. A news station sparked to life, offering the hourly update.

'The funeral takes place tomorrow for Ari White, the man found murdered last week on the banks of the Waikato River. Police are still seeking information on the whereabouts of a man wanted in connection with his death. Tama Hohaia also goes under the name of Tama Du Rose and we advise the public not to approach him.'

Hana knocked Tama's rigid fingers aside and switched off the radio. But it was too late. Mac smiled at her through the rear-view mirror and Edin whispered endearments to Horsey. But Phoenix and Wiri met her gaze with terror in their grey eyes.

82

Anvil

"They're scared." Hana sat on the edge of the four poster bed and swung her legs against the floral green bedspread. Her heels tapped against a storage box hidden beneath the frame. "I didn't mean for them to hear the news."

Logan nodded and stripped his tee shirt over his head. "Is that why Phoe let Edin sleep with her?"

Hana groaned. "Probably. She usually kicks her out again."

She peered down at the chipped nail polish on her toes and covered one foot with the other. Squinting didn't negate the picture of self-neglect. "What's Tama doing?"

"Last seen in the hotel bar with the boys. I asked them to monitor him. We don't want a repeat of the last time he got drunk there."

"No!" Hana waggled her eyebrows. "He slept with that entire party of bridesmaids and they paid him. Can you imagine the manager's face if he did that?"

"I don't want to think about it." Logan slid his jeans over his hips and wriggled them down his thighs. "The last thing I need right now is the events company holding us in breach of contract. I don't want to run the hotel. I'd sell the bloody thing."

"Would you?" Hana cocked her head and tried to imagine Logan parting with the legacy. His family had owned the house and land since the early 1800s when the Frenchman allied himself with a local rangatira. Alfred's mismanagement had forced Logan to bail it out from bankruptcy, but she sensed he often wished he'd just let it go.

As she watched her gorgeous husband move around the bedroom in his boxer shorts, Hana released her musing into the ether. A low rumble sounded from the motor feeding water into the house as he set the shower running. Hana slipped from the bed and stripped naked, dropping her clothes onto the bedside rug. She stepped into the ensuite and locked the door behind her. Logan's skin felt soft beneath her fingers as she walked them up his spine. He smiled at her reflection in the bathroom mirror, toothpaste foaming around his lips.

The slapping of the spray hitting the shower tray muted the other sounds they made. Logan clasped Hana around her lower back and pressed her against the cool tiles. Her lips slipped over his as the spray pounded the sore spot on her crown. When he used his tongue to part the seam of her lips, her mouth filled with warm water and she choked. But the thought of stopping seemed worse than the inconvenience and difficulty of sex in the cramped shower cubicle. Afterwards, he used his masculine shower gel to coat her body in a white foam. His scent shrouded the small space, wrapping around her head like a hedge of protection.

Hana sighed with pleasure and returned the favour, running her palms over his strong muscular shoulders. "I missed a pill," she whispered. "Do you think it matters?"

"Not to me." His deep baritone echoed against the tiled walls and he lowered his voice. "What will be will be."

Hana nodded, but the threat of another late pregnancy filled her chest with a prickling fear. She'd thought herself past childbearing aged forty-five but at almost fifty-three, it consumed her with misgiving. Her periods had become spotty and irregular and she hoped it heralded the end of a constant cycle of anxiety. She kept her worries to herself and concentrated on stroking the foamy white soap across her husband's powerful chest. Kisses interspersed each stripe of soapy fingers over his skin.

"Do you think Sonny would prove reliable enough for Hilda to ride?" She leaned her cheek against Logan's left shoulder, swaying with the motion of his fingers scrubbing shampoo through his salt and pepper curls. "I'd like someone steady to ride with and she seems keen."

"Yeah." Logan glanced sideways at her and nodded. "Just let me know when." He dipped forward and plunged his head beneath the shower, turning up the spray to rinse the shampoo from his hair. Hana stepped back and leaned against the tiles.

"Next Monday? I kinda already offered."

"Put it in my calendar with a time and I'll make sure he's tacked and ready." He didn't question or criticise. Just solved a problem with the ease of practice. "Who will you take?"

"I don't know yet." Hana closed her eyes and imagined the ease of having Sacha at her beck and call. She missed the feisty white mare with all her being. "I don't know," she repeated with a sigh. "I'll ask Rawhiti if I can borrow one of the trekking horses."

She left the bathroom in a towel and entered the bedroom in time to hear her phone vibrating on her nightstand. She unplugged the charger cable and lifted the device to her ear. "Hey Bo." The grandfather clock in the hall gave a dull chime to mark another hour of darkness. Logan had rescued his grandmother's pride and joy from the hotel lobby when the event company took over. "It's late. Is everything okay?"

"Yeah." His clipped tone suggested he didn't wish to turn the quick call into a lengthy conversation. "I thought you'd like to know that I've heard from Jennifer Doughty, nee Finlaggan. I'm meeting her tomorrow morning at ten o'clock."

Hana swallowed and sank onto the bed. "Ari's funeral is at the same time." She gnawed on her lower lip. "Tama wants to go, and I tried to persuade him not to risk it. Did you see the news earlier? Why do the media still think you're searching for him?"

Bodie hissed a breath of exasperation. "Because the detective in charge of the case won't listen to my suggestions. Please tell me Tama hasn't been wandering around in public?"

Hana bit the inside of her cheek until it hurt, reactivating a coordinating pain in her forehead and awakening the bruising on her torso. She pictured Tama's adoring crowd of school children and the side eyes of appreciation from the gathered mothers. "No. Yes. No," she replied.

"Bloody hell!" Bodie hissed. "I asked him to do one thing."

"I know." Hana squeezed her eyes closed. "I'll set Logan on him. We'll make sure he doesn't attend the funeral tomorrow."

"Good." Bodie's reply didn't match his tone. He didn't believe in her or Logan's ability to control Tama's activities. "Because you're coming with me. I've spent the week working in Auckland, so I'll fetch you around nine o'clock. We're meeting Jennifer in Hamilton. I'll drop you home afterwards."

Hana only just managed to reply as Bodie killed the call. She stared at the black screen and sifted through a catalogue of concerns in her mind. All hope of sleep fled and Logan narrowed his eyes as he emerged from the ensuite in a cloud of steam. "Think we used all the hot water." A lascivious smile curved his lips. Hana nodded and winced, dropping her phone onto the bedspread.

83

Hoof Knife

"You know Antoinette couldn't read, don't you?" Logan sighed and leaned back in his office chair. He ran a hand over his forehead and observed Hana as she perched on the edge of his desk. Leaning forward, he flicked her bottom with his index finger. "Don't put your nono where you put your kai," he said, his tone gentle.

Hana shifted to the sofa and accepted the rebuke. Māori kawa objected to backsides on tables. "I knew that. Sorry." She draped her arms over her knees and leaned forward. "Bo texted. He's almost here. And no, it never occurred to me she couldn't read."

Logan nodded. "Nor could my mother."

"Wow." Hana blinked in surprise. "I never knew that. She ran a hotel. That's crazy."

He shrugged in dismissal. "But it means perhaps Antoinette didn't know what she had in the box. She couldn't read the birth certificate."

"Reuben could though."

"If he knew about it."

The toilet flushed in the bathroom attached to Logan's office, and he smirked. "Tama's riding with me today. Make a run for it before he comes out. He's got a face like a slapped ass and I've hidden all the truck keys."

"Okay." Hana rose and navigated the corner of the desk to wrap her arms around her husband's neck. She pressed a kiss to his temple. "I've got my phone. The children know to call you today. Or Leslie. But there shouldn't be a problem."

"Famous last words." Logan smiled up at her. "Good luck. Stay in touch."

A painful ache gripped her stomach as she closed his office door behind her. A period had surfaced in the early hours, bringing with it relief and physical discomfort. She wasn't pregnant, but she was grouchy and in pain.

Bodie's private vehicle drew alongside the hotel steps as Hana emerged from the reception lobby. Chaos reigned as the hotel manager struggled to contend with a group of departing guests. Despite acting as a spy for the Alderbanks, Raymond's cool efficiency made him great at his job. A coach load of people newly arrived for a biomolecular conference hung around with their suitcases, creating a tripping hazard. The manager shot Hana a glance of mute appeal and she ignored him. She'd assisted many times before without thanks or appreciation. He'd forgotten about that when he'd made demands of the events company directors about excluding the family from the premises.

"Hey." She slumped into the passenger seat of the smart Mercedes and fastened her seatbelt. The walnut detail on the dashboard gleamed beneath the mid-morning sunshine. She ached to compliment her son on his achievements, but the timing sucked. And besides, she valued his personal growth far above his financial accumulations. Bodie appeared edgy as he pressed on the gas and spat gravel behind his wheels. Hana settled in for an awkward journey south.

"Where does Jennifer Doughty live?" She didn't speak until they reached Rangiriri and Bodie made the series of turns onto the expressway.

"Flagstaff." He kept his gaze on the windscreen, using his wipers to scrape away dust billowing from a gravel truck up ahead. "How's Tama?" His question surprised her and Hana tensed.

"Sulking. Logan has him bailed up at the farm. They're riding across the mountain to fetch more of the loose steers in the further reaches of the property. We keep them in the valley over winter."

Bodie nodded. His smile masked a wince. "I know he didn't kill Ari White." He narrowed his eyes before checking his mirrors and overtaking the massive truck. "I'm sorry they let the media run the news clip again. It wasn't my decision."

Hana sighed with relief. "I get it. He doesn't understand, but I trust you and he knows that."

"You do?" Bodie blinked in surprise. He glanced at her for long enough to let the steering wheel follow the camber of the road. The car drifted too far to the left and the truck driver honked his horn. "You trust me?"

"Yes." Hana turned in her seat and bent her right knee beneath her. "You're the police officer."

Bodie's nod appeared slow and racked with indecision. "I wonder sometimes," he said with a sigh. "I swear I try so hard to do the right thing and then watch other people climb the greasy pole ahead of me without a lost second of self-reflection."

Sympathy filled Hana's heart. "You got overlooked for promotion again?" She spoke softly, asking while already knowing the answer. It seemed important not to force him to say the words.

"Yep." Bodie's jaw tightened. "It makes me question everything."

"Do you think it's because of what happened with Laval?" Hana winced and her cheeks flushed. "I know you got reprimanded because Logan called you when he found Boris all beaten up. Did that stick to your record?"

"No." Bodie shook his head. "Odering got it expunged before he moved south. I might call him and see what he thinks. It's possible I'm not moving around enough to attract a promotion. He achieved his by station hopping."

"But you have Amy and the children." Hana studied the sun's rays glittering across the black asphalt of the highway. "The same thing happened to Vic in England. He got stuck in one place and the company thought him inflexible. It's why we emigrated here. And why he worked away such a lot." Hana clamped her teeth over her lower lip and held it, unable to trust herself to speak. Time away from home wasn't the reason Vic cheated. Unless there were more affairs than the one with the office administrator. That relationship had tipped the balance for her late husband.

Hana forced her muscles to relax one at a time, using a mindfulness technique to alleviate her tension. Her phone buzzed in her handbag in the foot-well and anxiety flooded back like a tide. She sighed before leaning forward and retrieving it. The prison number strobed on the screen. She imagined the automated voice requesting she accept the pre-paid call from an inmate. "Caroline." She sighed and dropped her phone back into her bag. "It's mean not talking to her when she goes to such an effort to call me." She tugged a red curl forward and inspected the split ends, ready for Amy's scissors.

"But she's blackmailing you." Bodie raised a dark brow and dipped his chin. "I wouldn't speak to her either."

"She's Edin's mother." Hana dropped the curl and pictured the little girl skipping into her class. School had given her a zest for life and an eagerness to learn. She'd gripped Mac's fingers and not Hana's, frowning with impatience when she'd asked for a kiss. "Caroline must feel I hold all the cards."

"You don't blackmail someone who's helping you." Bodie's firm tone held no doubt. "Look at all the injuries you've sustained this week because of her. The box is linked to her childhood and you're protecting her daughter from a crazy. Yet she wants to tell Izzie about an affair which happened years ago and ruin our relationship with her because we kept it secret."

Hana nodded. She straightened her legs and changed the subject. It occurred to her that the longer she evaded Caroline, the more inclined she'd be to follow through on her threat. She resolved to take her next call. Whenever it came.

"Will is adamant the gold didn't come from the General Grant. The box wasn't airtight. Even if Clive Alderbank transferred the gold from another container and added the birth certificate, the leaves would show signs of damage. Will says few things are impervious to salt water, especially the wooden packing cases used to ship items overseas in the 1800s. He expected to see evidence of seepage if it survived underwater for over a hundred years. It sank in May 1866, and Lana claims her father salvaged from the wreck in 1969. Gold leaf is fragile. Will's using a microscope and tweezers just to look at it."

Bodie wrinkled his nose. "I'll need to take it as evidence if I ever get my superiors interested." He glanced sideways at her. "You know that, don't you?"

Hana nodded. "Yes. I've taken a scan of the birth certificate and photographs of the gold and the box. Will had me take pictures of the entire examination process. You can have copies of those, too." She imagined prising the valuable find from the curator's fingers and figured she'd let Bodie do that. With a seizure warrant. "I still feel this complete debacle relates to that poor stolen baby."

"I agree with you." Bodie's tight smile induced a dart of fear in Hana's chest.

"This isn't an official visit, is it?"

"No." He inhaled and his chest strained against his seatbelt. "No one involved with the case is interested. The two men arrested at the hotel are on remand for other warrants. The detective in charge sees no links between any of the incidents.

Unless Lana Alderbank gives you the evidence against her mother's men and lets Tama off the hook, we've got nothing. We're on our own, Mum."

The drive to Hamilton seemed faster than usual, and Hana's muscles tightened as they neared Jennifer Doughty's house in the suburbs. Her mind raced with her dilemma. She loved Tama, but couldn't swap his freedom for Edin's captivity.

Hana stood behind Bodie as he made their introductions at the front door of a smart two storey townhouse.

A slender, grey haired man invited them inside. His gentle handshake offered Hana more confidence than she expected. Fine boned and delicate, his calm manner thwarted any awkwardness. "Go through," he said, waving his hand towards an open plan lounge and dining room. "Jen's expecting you."

Hana kicked off her sandals, hovering next to Bodie as he bent to untie his shoelaces. The man turned towards her with a smile and tapped his chest. "Sorry. I'm John Doughty. I'm Jen's husband."

"Nice to meet you." Hana gripped her handbag in white-knuckled fingers. The visit seemed mawkish and inappropriate. The cut on her forehead prickled as her heart rate increased and self-consciousness consumed her dwindling energy.

"Thanks for seeing us." Bodie stood up straight and followed John into the sitting area. He perched on the edge of a sofa cushion, his businesslike manner providing comfort. Hana sat next to him, eager to see her son use his police training to still the crackling energy in the room. She pursed her lips, recognising most of the anxiety originated from her.

"Is this an official police enquiry?" John cocked his head. His grey eyebrows drew into a line. "My wife's sister was never discovered. Is there a reason for you examining the case after fifty years?"

Bodie rested his forearms against his knees and dipped forward. "We're making initial enquiries. I can't guarantee my superiors will reopen the investigation, but something has come to light, and it's become personal."

Bodie glanced at Hana and she met his gaze. All useful thoughts abandoned her, and she floundered, wide eyed and useless. She felt like an accessory just occupying a seat on his train ride of truth. He turned back to John. Self-recrimination for her stupidity followed hard on the heels of Hana's relief. Her hands trembled in her lap.

"I'm happy to discuss everything we've found," Bodie promised. "It's best if we wait for your wife."

Hana turned her head at the skitter of light footsteps descending a staircase. Jennifer Finlaggan-Doughty entered the room, dominating it from the second her feet crossed the threshold. Hana's audible gasp caused Bodie to sit up straighter. His left hand swung towards Hana as though making a silent offer of support. But she pressed her fingers over her lips to prevent the nonsensical babble threatening to emerge.

Jennifer smiled at her, an open expression couched by a latent fear of emotional pain. Blue irises sparkled from within almond-shaped eyes, her sharp features giving her an ethereal fragility. Short blonde hair rose in spikes from a double crown, gelled into obedience by careful fingers. Hana closed her eyes and shook her head, unable to verbally account for her extreme reaction.

Jennifer stared at her, lines appearing across her forehead. "Would you like coffee?" she asked in a voice as soft as a gentle wind.

84

Tack

"I'm so sorry." Hana emerged from the bathroom, uttering effusive apologies which tumbled from her as though falling from a tall shelf. She sank onto the sofa next to Bodie, smiling her thanks for the steaming mug of coffee on the stout table placed before her. Her fingers shook too much for her to risk lifting it to her lips. She sat on her hands and collected her thoughts.

"You've found my sister's body, haven't you?" Jennifer turned away from the window and faced Hana. A carbon copy of Caroline sent waves of apprehension through her. She dropped her gaze to avoid the tumult of emotions beating a path from her heart to her brain.

Determination lit a fire behind Jennifer's irises, though she batted away unwanted tears. "I've spent fifty years blaming myself for her disappearance." She glanced at her husband and then back at Bodie. "They left me outside the shop with the pram. I got distracted by a butterfly." A shudder rent from her thin chest, shaking her body on its way through her. "Catherine was a cute baby. Lots of people stopped to admire her. It got boring for a four-year-old and I wandered away. It proved just long enough for someone to snatch her." Her eyes glistened, and she stared at the ceiling before drawing a rumpled tissue from her sleeve.

Hana's heart ached, and she fought the tears which prickled against her lids. "You say it," she whispered to Bodie, unable to break the wonderful and terrible news. He pursed his lips before setting his mug of coffee on a coaster with exaggerated care. "A box surfaced recently at my mother's property." He inclined his head towards Hana, and she gave a jerky nod. "It contained a birth certificate for Catherine Finlaggan. She began investigating and discovered the news article relating to your sister's abduction." He snuffed through his nose, a sign of his exasperation. "How could someone access your sister's birth certificate? And why? I've archived the police file, but there's no mention of it."

"Is it a copy?" Jennifer sank onto the arm of her husband's chair and he reached a supportive arm around her.

"No." Hana cleared her throat before continuing. "It's an original. But it's the short one, not the one which lists the parents and their occupations. I work at a museum and the curator has confirmed its provenance. He's trying to identify the registrar through their signature."

Jennifer groaned and bent double. Hana pitied her as she clutched her stomach. Scratchy and painful, her voice conveyed her agony. "Back then, you had six weeks to register a birth. We walked to the registry office when Mum felt well enough to go. We almost missed the deadline." Her hand shook as she ran her fingers over her eyes. "My mother had difficulty giving birth and needed emergency surgery. She wasn't well enough to leave the house for a few weeks afterwards. My father took the day off work and made it into an outing. We all went to the courthouse together." Her gaze softened as she stared into the past. "He always turned things towards the positive end of the spectrum. He promised us a cake and sent my mother into the bakery to choose her favourite. The shopkeeper called to him when she felt unwell and needed to sit down on a chair near the counter. She'd left her bag at the end of the pram because Dad handed her the cash to buy the cake. I remember the grey check in the pram's fabric and the sound of the poppers snapping closed." She gulped. "But I don't remember who took my sister." Emotion rocked her words. "Whoever stole Catherine grabbed Mum's bag. It contained the new birth certificates." A wail left her, bone numbing and eerie. "She's dead, isn't she? My sister's dead."

"No!" Hana half rose, hindered by Bodie tugging at her hand. He shook his head in warning.

"It's possible we know where she is," he said, drawing out the sentence. "A DNA test will verify it for certain."

The colour drained from Jennifer's cheeks, leaving a waxy hue in its wake. Her husband patted her shoulder with his palm, a gentle, calming stroke of solidarity. "Does she know?" Jennifer whispered. "Does she know about us?"

Hana sat on the cushion next to Bodie with a bump. She winced at the raw hunger in Jennifer's expression. A sparkle lit her blue irises like azure gems, the dormant flame of lost hope roaring to life in her soul. She shook her head. "I don't think so." She glanced at Bodie sideways. "It's complicated."

"How?" John leaned forward in his seat, his brows drawn into a line. He turned his body towards his wife as though shielding her from further harm.

Hana exhaled. She rubbed at her right eye with the backs of her fingers. The fragile scab across the bridge of her nose tightened with the action and she dropped her hand into her lap. "We didn't know what the birth certificate meant until now. It's all that remained of a house fire on the property over seven years ago. It was hidden inside a cash box which was salvaged from the rubble and stored on a shelf in my husband's office. Someone tried to open it and failed, so it just stayed there. The homeowners possessed nothing of value, so nobody worried about what it contained. Recent events threw it into the spotlight and we drilled the lock."

"And found Catherine's birth certificate." Jennifer clenched her jaw and her lips flattened. "So, you know the person who stole her? You're related to them." Accusation laced her tone, and she rose. A faltering step took her towards Hana. The dangerous glint in her eye showed she held Hana responsible for a lifetime of guilt and grief. Her husband rose and clamped his fingers around her forearm to halt her ill considered journey to hurt the messenger. He held tight despite her attempts to flick off his grip.

"She didn't die in the fire?" John cocked his head and glanced from Hana to Bodie. "But she'd been at that property?"

Bodie exhaled. The situation had become messy much quicker than he anticipated. He rose and patted the air between them. "We believe she grew up there, raised by kind people who loved her." He twisted the truth for Jennifer's benefit. The Du Roses had tolerated Caroline Marsh. Perhaps Reuben felt affection for her. No one remained to tell the story.

"Kind people?" Hysteria entered Jennifer's voice, creating a high, unpredictable quality. "Kind people who stole my sister?" Droplets of spit left her lips as she ground out the sentence. The rage in her eyes caused Hana's heart to clench. She sensed Jennifer wanting to hit her, to purge herself of the torturous anger in her soul. She also knew she wouldn't fight back. Not this time.

Bodie shook his head. "We don't believe they stole Catherine. We think they rescued her."

Jennifer stopped. She blinked twice and her jaw worked as she struggled to process their words. The leaden atmosphere weighed on their heads and nausea threatened as acid in Hana's gut. Bodie rose and held out his hand to her. "This was a fact finding mission," he said, his tone soft. "I want my superiors to reopen the case, but I don't have enough evidence yet to persuade them. There are other factors." He sighed and dug his fingers into his back pocket. "This is my business card. Call me if you remember something. It doesn't matter if you think it's meaningless. Call me." He held it for Jennifer, but she just stared at it. John reached out and took it from him.

Hana mulled over the sentence in her head and considered the potential damage it might unleash. She stole a glance at Jennifer's ashen face as the stricken woman unravelled before her. So she took a deep breath and said it, despite Bodie's look of pure horror and the vigorous shake of his head. "You look like her," she said. Her fingers shook, and she shoved them behind her back. There were many things she could say about Caroline, but kindness prevented her from airing any of them. She forced her lips into a gentle, wavering smile. "We'll do our best to sort this out. I promise." She laid her hand over her pacemaker, the covenant containing more sincerity than perhaps Jennifer realised. "Stay in touch with us and we'll do our best for you. And for your sister."

"I want to know where she is." Jennifer ground the words through her teeth. Her husband still clung to her wrist.

Bodie winced. "Not yet. It's unfair. She knows nothing about this." He pointed to his chest. "I need more evidence. And time."

"My mother died." Jennifer's chin shuddered. She'd morphed into a woman clinging to a ledge on the precipice of sanity. Their visit had released fifty years of agony. Hana swallowed. She'd done many things she'd regretted in her life. But nothing more awful than this.

"I'm sorry," she murmured, the words futile and empty but the first to spring from her tongue.

"You're sorry." Jennifer's chest hitched.

Bodie reached the front door and dipped to recover his shoes. He didn't stop to put them on, clutching them against his chest and snatching up Hana's sandals by the straps. The front door handle clanked against his wedding band as he hauled the door open. "Mum!" he snapped, his tone urgent. Hana followed him, her head bobbing in jerky, awkward movements. She retrieved her handbag from the carpet and escaped behind her son, closing the front door behind them. Jennifer's agonised wail followed them up the driveway to Bodie's car.

"Shit!" he hissed. He opened the rear door and flung their shoes onto the carpeted floor. Hana padded to the passenger side and sank into the seat. The belt locked as Bodie fired the engine and cranked the gear shift into drive. She rived on it, unable to stretch it around her. Glancing sideways, she realised he wasn't wearing his.

"Stop!" she begged as the end of the street and a give-way sign hurtled towards them. "Pull over here."

Bodie swerved his vehicle alongside the curb and the expensive brakes squealed at the sharpness of the stop. The engine purred as he leaned forward and covered his face with his hands. "I'm in so much trouble," he whispered. His eyes glittered as he lifted his head and stared at a lone cloud bobbing across the bright blue sky overhead. "That couldn't have gone any worse."

Hana nodded and used the pause to release her seatbelt and begin the process of fastening it again. It locked into place with a click and she leaned sideways and clasped her son's sweating fingers in her cool hand. "It'll be okay," she promised, infusing her words with more certainty than she felt. "Fasten your belt and let's get going." She glanced behind her, the gable end of the Doughtys' house still in view. "Find a cafe and we'll decompress."

Despite his misery, Bodie snorted. "Debrief, Mum." He sighed and checked the road behind him before pulling back into the traffic. "Mind you, right now either would work."

85

Double Noseband

Bodie couldn't face sitting in a cafe while Jennifer Doughty complained to his superiors about his lack of professionalism. He drove them to Culver's Cottage in the Hakarimata Ranges. Hana walked around her old home, caressing the features she'd loved about the property.

"I like these new curtains," she said, running her fingers over the soft fabric. "Did Amy make them?"

Bodie shook his head and slumped onto the lounge sofa. He winced and pulled a contorted Action Man from between the cushions. "No, she bought them already made." He stared at the mug of strong coffee steaming on the table level with his knees. "I think I just lost my job," he said, his tone flat. He'd passed through the stages of terror, anger, and misery. Hana sensed he'd come full circle to terror again.

"I don't think so." She forced herself to perch in an adjacent armchair, though she'd rather keep moving to burn off the excess nervous energy. Her elbows dug into her knees. "You're trying to help them. Why would they complain to your bosses about someone willing to investigate a cold case after all these years? I'd be grateful. Give Jennifer time to calm down and she'll see it differently. It's pointless for her calling the police, anyway. You made it clear there's no official investigation yet."

Bodie bounced his forehead against the heels of his hands. He didn't reply. Hana rose and snagged his phone from the coffee table. The screen remained active where he'd checked his emails for news of a prospective reprimand. He'd looked every five minutes since he stopped driving. She pulled up his list of calls and selected a number with a 07 prefix. "Is this Jennifer's number?" she asked, spinning the screen to face him.

His lips parted in a grimace. "Yes. Why?"

Too late. Hana added the number to her contacts and pressed the call button. He rose, panic in his eyes. "Don't Mum!" he growled. "I'm not five! You don't need to advocate for me! And I accessed that number through a confidential system." He silenced as the call connected.

John's voice rumbled through the device as Hana activated the speaker. "This is Jennifer's phone. She's busy now. Can I take a message?"

"Hi John," she said, her tone level. "Hana Du Rose here. I'm calling to see how Jennifer is coping."

"Oh." He sounded surprised and faltered for a moment. "She's shocked. Sad. Angry."

"That's understandable." Hana glanced sideways at her furious son and turned her back on him. "I hope she knows we're trying to help." The sympathy she infused into her words held a genuineness which translated across the ether. "It must be unbearable for her."

"She just wants to know," he began, a plea entering his voice as a whine. "You could have told her more."

"Sorry." Hana lifted her chin and spoke as though bracing herself for a verbal jousting match with one of Wiri's apoplectic teachers. The boy made an art form out of disobedience and left her to clean up his mess. Just like Bodie, almost three decades earlier. "It's not appropriate. My son is putting his job on the line for Jennifer. No one wants to listen to him. Once we get more evidence, we'll contact you. I promise."

"Right. Yes." John's conciliatory tone indicated he'd considered calling Bodie's superiors. Or Jennifer had proposed it to assuage her fury. "We'll wait," he agreed. Hana heard the cushions sag behind her as Bodie slumped onto the sofa.

"Thank you. We have a few more doors to push before we can tell you everything." Hana paused and considered her words with care. "I need you to understand that another of my sons is in danger and a man has died over this."

"What?" A hiss accompanied John's doubt. "You said nothing about any of this."

Hana exhaled. "We didn't get the opportunity. I'll explain everything, but not now. Please just trust us. I realise it's difficult, but it's important you don't discuss what we told you with anyone else. Not yet."

"Okay." He swallowed, and Hana sensed they'd reached a consensus.

"Please give my regards to your wife. Assure her we understand her rage and grief. I'll be in touch." Hana killed the call and glanced back at her son, a wry smile lifting her lips at the corners. "Goodness me!" she said with a sigh. "That reminded me of all the times Angus dragged me into his office because of something you or Marcus had done." Her shoulders relaxed, and she shoved her phone back into her pocket. "Remember Whoopi-cushion-gate?"

Despite his anxiety, Bodie smirked. "Yeah. Never heard such a big fart come from such a small man. Not since then either."

Hana nodded and stared through the bay window at a view which had once belonged to her. "Yeah," she mused. "It didn't help when Marcus yelled, *'Would you like some toilet paper for that?'* I thought poor Angus might have heart failure.

Bodie laughed, the sound genuine and hearty. The atmosphere lightened, and Hana turned to face her son. Her heart tingled with the tug of the indefinable maternal cord which existed despite tragedy, circumstance, conspiracy, and relationship fractures. She sighed. "And for the record, my darling, you are five-years-old in my eyes and always will be. Make sure I never get the phone number for the man or woman suppressing your career."

Bodie blew out a ragged breath and leaned forward to collect his cooling drink. He took a decent slurp and smiled at Hana. "That's what I love about you, Mum. I can always rely on you to help me hide the body."

86

Pastern Wrap

The weekend promised Hana time to recover from her injuries. Logan took Tama and the older children on another muster in the ritual preparation for a forecasted, harsh winter. Wiri worried about redeeming himself, although Logan promised the stock men had already forgotten his earlier humiliation. "They've slept since then," he told him, as Hana waved them off at the front door.

Mac buried his face in a new computer game and Edin buzzed with the promise of making more rongōa with Leslie in the apartment. She tensed her body in something akin to apoplexy, gritting her teeth and shaking on the spot. "Rongōa!" she hissed through tight lips. "Nonie!"

"Okay, shoes on, let's go." Hana forced away her misgivings, recognising the sign of extreme excitement in the child's behaviour. It gave her a flicker of comfort that what had once appeared as a tantrum was now discernable as a positive emotion. She smiled at Edin. "Exciting, isn't it? What a wonderful thing to do."

"Yeeessss!" Edin's grey irises sparkled and flickered. She continued to speak through gritted teeth, but walked her stiff body towards the front door. Mac followed, his attention glued to the screen in his hands. He wore no shoes and had abandoned his speech processors. Hana groaned and chose the path of least resistance.

"Okay then. No shoes." She unlocked Logan's truck and slammed the front door behind her. Edin bounced into her booster seat with glee, but Mac walked into the pillar supporting the porch and then the truck bumper. He gave a whimper of discomfort and rubbed his forehead. Hana locked the front door and turned, lifting him beneath his armpits. She carted him around the truck and dumped him into his booster. "You guys are driving me nuts!" she murmured under her breath.

Edin dipped her chin and her brow furrowed into a line. Thunder threatened in her clouded irises. "Say sick, be sick!" she growled. "Say nuts, be nuts."

Hana exhaled and fought the sardonic smile sliding onto her lips. "Thank you, Leslie," she replied.

Edin gave a slow blink. "Welcome, kōtiro," she countered.

Hana sank into Logan's driver's seat and released an agonised groan beneath her breath. Circumstance conspired to back her into fights she couldn't win. Edin's face glared at her through the rear-view mirror and she shook her head and wagged a tiny index finger at Hana. "Don't poo on Papa's chair!" she shouted at the top of her voice.

Hana started the engine and turned her mirror to reflect on the ceiling. "God help me," she whispered, making sure the prayer remained inaudible to keen ears. She heard Mac grunt behind her and turned in time to witness Edin whacking his forearm.

"Mama nuts," she whispered to him. "I want nuts."

The hotel car park rumbled with coach engines as another conference welcomed its day guests for a morning session led by a plumbing trade organisation. The manager glared at Hana from his position on the front steps as she swung the truck into Logan's parking space. She texted Leslie to let her know they'd arrived. By the time Hana pried Edin and Mac from the truck and wove them through the throng of bodies, Leslie waited for her at the entrance to the private corridor on the far side of the reception desk.

"I'll take them up the spiral staircase." She lifted her voice over the surrounding chatter. "The main stairs are too busy."

"Without me?" Hana faltered, a frown bisecting her forehead. The healing cut over the bridge of her nose twinged. "I thought you invited all of us."

"No." Leslie placed her hand on the top of Mac's head and steered him away from the crowd. Her voice echoed in the empty corridor. Edin clung to her other hand and bounced next to her. She turned her body to deliver a cheerful wave to Hana. "You can spend time in the museum. Or something." Leslie shrugged, her attention already on the children.

"Oh." A sense of loss engulfed Hana. It descended over her head like a cool sheet on a winter night. "Right then." She'd spent eighteen months desperate to disconnect from Edin's smothering need, and without it, she was lost. The children didn't look back as Leslie herded them towards the private spiral staircase leading to the upper levels of the house. Edin's lips parted in an excited babble and Hana held her breath as Mac walked into the wall. He didn't raise his gaze from the cavorting digital puppies occupying every spare moment of screen time.

"I'm sorry for the delay." The raised voice of the hotel manager cut across the melee, and Hana turned to watch as he drew the surrounding crowd. Sweat formed a dark patch beneath each armpit and continued in a stripe down his spine. His hair stuck to his head, the usual smartness abandoned in Raymond's absence. No one had seen him since he'd gone with the two police officers to assist with their enquiries. Hana blew out a breath and reasoned he'd cut his losses. Logan's reputation made it unsafe for Raymond to return to his post behind the reception desk. Not if he fancied keeping his face intact.

Mindful of Logan's desire to maintain an amicable relationship with the events management company, she swallowed her pride and picked her way through the grumbling group. Slipping behind the reception desk, she smiled at the man at the front of the queue. She pressed the space bar on the keyboard and the screen bloomed to life. After a cursory glance at the wording, she amended her greeting. "Welcome to the conference for members of the Master Plumbers Association. Let me take your name and we'll get you sorted right away." She accompanied her words with a fake smile worthy of an actress. The man leaned over the counter and she entered his surname into the system. As Hana processed the queue with practiced efficiency, the impatient chatter lessened to a gentle conversation. The hotel manager shot behind the counter to assist.

As the last of the guests dispersed to the conference room, he sank into Raymond's empty seat and wiped his brow with his sleeve. "Don't suppose you fancy a job?" he asked, his tone serious. "I don't think Ray's coming back."

Hana flattened her lips and finished inputting dietary information for the last guest she'd processed. She saved it and turned to face him. "Not if he knows what's good for him," she mused. Her gaze softened as he tugged a tissue from the box on the counter and mopped the dampness from beneath his shirt collar. White flecks dotted his skin when he'd finished. "I'm sorry," she conceded. "I understand why you're cross with our family after this week. My life is too chaotic to offer any guaranteed assistance at the moment, but leave it with me for a few hours. I have an idea." She peered at the name badge hanging askew across his shirt pocket. "Karl. Leave it with me, Karl."

His smile appeared genuine. It altered his features from being sharp and disapproving to stressed and overworked.

"Thanks." He blew out a long breath and gazed through the open front doors towards Miriam's rose garden. "I love it here," he admitted.

Hana blinked in surprise and nodded. She bit back the comment about his brain perhaps letting his face know that sometimes, and excused herself. "I'll come back to you soon," she promised.

The museum door creaked as she pushed it open and she paused on the threshold. "Will?" Her voice held a frightened urgency. He never left the door unlocked. "Will, are you there?"

"I'm here." His chair tyres squeaked across the floorboards as he appeared from the workroom at the back of the cavernous space. The whir of his wheelchair's motor preceded him. "Came in to take another look at that birth certificate. Why are you here? Couldn't you sleep?"

"Haha." Her reply held no humour. Hana closed the door behind her and turned to survey the room. Glass cabinets lined every wall, displaying artifacts from the lives of generations of Du Roses. Each item held relevance, its provenance lovingly detailed in the descriptions she'd spent hours typing. She closed her eyes and savoured the peace of the dim paradise.

Her phone buzzed in the handbag slung across her torso, and she jumped. Her hand patted the pocket and then fell to her side. Will cocked his head and surveyed her over his tortoiseshell spectacles. They perched on the end of his pointed nose as though contemplating suicide. "Trouble?" he demanded.

"Yeah." Hana relented and withdrew the device from its pocket. She peered at the screen. "Three missed calls and two ranting texts."

"Logan?" Will answered his own question with a shake of his head. "Nah. Scrub that. Not his style. Who then?"

"Edin's mother." Hana's lips shrank back from her teeth as though she'd sucked a lemon. "I started dodging her calls because she's blackmailing me. I'd decided to answer the next one but then it came while I drove down the mountain. It's not a good idea for Edin to hear her yelling at me." Will's eyes bugged in horror, and Hana continued. "And the other two calls and one text are from a woman named Jennifer who I'm wishing I'd never met. The last text is from Lana Alderbank with the address of a laboratory willing to perform a DNA test on Edin." Her chest tightened at the end of Lana's text. '*Tick tok*,' she'd typed.

Will barked a laugh worthy of a walrus' approval. "Has she met the kid? She won't let you wipe crumbs off her face. I can't imagine that little vixen letting anyone fiddle with her."

Hana shrugged. "Just another day in my wonderful life." She winced against the taste of her own ingratitude. Her mood brightened. "And now I intend to make a nice phone call to someone I like very much." She activated her phone screen again and navigated the freestanding cabinets towards the office. Will followed in her wake, stopping to wipe the smudges from a glass surface with the edge of his sleeve.

The gold leaf rested on the workroom bench, decanted once again from its box. Hana slumped into her office chair and dialled Hilda's number. Disappointment filtered through the phone as she answered. Hana set the device on her desk and Hilda's voice echoed off the walls of the workroom. "Hi Hana. Do you need to cancel Monday?"

Hana took a deep breath. She'd been here once before, allying with a needy woman who tried to steal her husband. It took willpower to push aside the resistance and state the reason for her call. "You told me you worked at the Hilton," she said. Will guided his chair through the widened doorway and raised a bushy eyebrow. Hana pursed her lips and persevered. "What did you do there?"

Hilda listed some obscure role, which meant nothing to Hana. She winced and almost abandoned her plan. "This is probably not relevant then," she said, gnawing on her lower lip. "But the receptionist quit last week and the hotel manager is struggling. He's desperate for a receptionist, but they'll need to drop into almost every role when he's short staffed. He might negotiate around school hours, but I can't guarantee it." She stopped gushing in time to hear Hilda's squeak of delight. "Anyway." Hana ground to a halt. "He's here now if you're interested. Pop to the reception with your CV and ask for Karl. I don't foresee him getting away from the desk much today."

"That's wonderful," Hilda chirped. Hana sensed her mind whirring with possibility and clamped her teeth shut as Hilda worried about after school care for Chester. She nudged the phone with her index finger and glared at Will as he snorted. "I'll pop along today," Hilda said. "My husband has already gone to print off my CV. Should I text you? Will you be there too?"

"No." Hana shook her head and her curls shuffled across the back of her dress in an autumnal dance. "The hotel is independent from the farm. I heard about the job in passing. Good luck. Let me know how you get on." She made polite exit noises and ended the call.

Will cackled and sat back in his wheelchair. He raised his crabbed hands in a mock round of applause. "Who are you again?" he demanded, tilting his head to peer down his nose at her. His spectacles admitted defeat and plunged into his lap. Undeterred, he spread his arms. "That's not like you, Mrs Du Rose. Don't you want to mind her child after school and make dinner for her family? Why aren't you meeting her on the front steps and guiding her in like a pilot boat?"

"Are you calling me a tug?" Hana's jaw hung low, and she closed her mouth with a snap. "How rude."

"I'm just surprised, is all." Will exhaled and the tissue paper encasing the gold leaf fluttered in front of him. "I thought you fixed everything for everyone." His shoulders heaved with a chuckle. "Did you bite your tongue to stop yourself from offering?"

"Yes." Hana pushed her phone aside and dipped her forehead to touch the desk. "But I'm tired. I can't do it anymore, Will. It's the very worst part of my nature and I hate it."

Will's wheels squeaked as he edged his chair closer. He reached his arm around her shoulders and leaned his head against hers. "The very best and the very worst," he whispered. "Without that restorative thread of the Hana I love, I'd have stayed a broken old man in a state house. No legs and no purpose. You gave me a home, a job, a cause and this wonderful electric wheelchair. I don't tell you often enough how much I appreciate you. And my boy too. Our lives are different because of you." He pressed a tentative kiss against her temple.

"Thanks."

He dropped his arm and Hana snagged his fingers, pulling them to her lips and kissing the swollen joints. "You're a good man, Will. But I think I've come to the tassel at the end of my rope. I'm in a terrible mess now and I can't see a way out of it."

His brown eyes softened, and a dimple appeared in his left cheek as he smiled. "How do you eat an elephant, Hana?" he whispered. "One bite at a time."

87

Horse Sox

Hana answered Caroline's next call on speakerphone as she searched the internet for archived news articles relating to Catherine Alderbank. "Don't test me, Caroline," she bit, her tone harsh. "You have much more to lose than me."

"Why are you ignoring me?" A thread of hysteria backed Caroline's response.

Hana sighed. "Because I can. What do you want?" She continued sifting through scanned images of newspapers with the search term *Alderbank* highlighted in yellow. The mouse squeaked as her fingers used it to scroll past the articles about Clive's political career. A pile of printed sheets about the General Grant slid sideways as she knocked them with her elbow.

A sob halted her activity, and she frowned at the phone. Will set his magnifying glass on the desk before him and turned to face Hana. "I'm sorry," Caroline whispered. "I'm sorry. Please don't let that woman take Edin." Her voice held the uncustomary thickness of distress. "The daughter keeps trying to see me and I've refused a visiting order. I want nothing to do with them." Her chest hitched. "They're not good people. Protect my daughter. Please, I'm begging you."

Hana swallowed. Her fingers twitched over the phone before she snatched it up and pressed it against her left ear. Experience told her Caroline would use any tactic to manipulate her. Tears might be part of her newest trick. "What about my daughter?" she demanded. "What about your threats against Izzie?"

"I won't do it," Caroline hissed. "I promise. Don't let them take Edin, and I'll call off my friends. Look, I met the older woman years ago, and she isn't nice. She threatened me and wouldn't leave me alone. I blocked her on social media."

"Lana Alderbank. The woman in purple." Hana's gaze flicked to the computer screen and the list of search items relating to the surname. Some were relevant, but most weren't.

"Yes." Caroline groaned as voices rose nearby. "I didn't realise there were two women with the same name. Now, the younger one is harassing me through the system. Every time I refuse a visit, she just applies again. Wait!" she snapped at someone in her periphery. Her tone became urgent and rushed. "Reuben made me promise to stay away from all of them."

"Reuben? Why?" Hana straightened. The new information sent a prickle of alarm along her spine. "What did he say about Lana Alderbank?"

Caroline huffed, and her speech pattern became too fast for Hana to process. "Dangerous. His wife."

"Whose wife? What?" Hana caught hold of the random words as Caroline's breath sounded heavier against her ear. "Antoinette?"

"Promise!" Caroline snapped.

"Okay," Hana began, but the call ended with a click and the hiss of static.

"Wow," Will breathed as she laid her phone on the desk. Her hands trembled, and she shoved them beneath her thighs. "And we're back to Reuben Du Rose." He shook his head. "Ain't that always how it goes in this family?"

"Yeah." Hana leaned back in the chair and stretched her arms over her head. The bruising from the seatbelt ached across her right shoulder and collarbone. "But if Reuben told Caroline to stay away from the Alderbanks, he had good reason. I only met him once, but I've learned to trust his wisdom from what people have said and written about him." Hana dropped forward and shook her arms on either side of her. She steepled her fingers and laid them over the keyboard with the effortless skill of a touch typist. "Now, I need more evidence."

Her phone vibrated again on the desk and she released a groan of frustration.

"Just ignore it," Will urged. He retrieved his tweezers in his left hand and fitted them between the crabbed fingers of his right.

"It's Lana Alderbank," Hana sighed. "The daughter. Speak of the devil and she will appear."

Will's bushy eyebrows shimmied up and down before he bent to his task. The fragile birth certificate shivered against his breath.

Hana gritted her teeth and connected the call. "What?" she demanded, her tone without energy.

"I sent the address of a laboratory willing to carry out the DNA test," Lana said. "I want it supervised because I don't trust you."

Hana paused, allowing the accusation of dishonesty to aggrieve her. It added the necessary bite to her tone. "No. If you knew Edin at all, you'd understand she detests strangers. She won't allow anyone near her unless she trusts them."

"You suggested this!" Lana snarled. "And now you're reneging. Typical! Let's see how your other son likes prison."

"I'm not reneging," Hana countered. "Edin's been unwell. She's due to see a pediatrician next week. It's possible she'll allow him to take a mouth swab at the same time. She likes him. Send the kit to Mr Dean McIntyre at Waikato Hospital Pediatrics. I'll call ahead and make sure he's fine with it."

"Right." Lana sounded unsure. She waited a beat. "What's wrong with her?"

Hana shot a glance at Will before continuing. His left eyebrow twitched, but he made no comment. "Chronic diarrhoea." Hana pursed her lips and prayed God would forgive her descent into exaggeration. A dreadful sickness emanated in her gut as she offered the worse case scenario, treating Edin like a puppy she didn't want to sell. "Yeah," she continued. "They think she might have a disease. She isn't thriving. Her mother wanted me to homeschool her, as she didn't speak much. I might have to do that if she continues to have such violent tantrums."

"Oh." Lana paused, and Hana imagined Edin losing her shine in the battle for possession. She wasted time picturing Lana's futile, dutiful daughter routine in her efforts to impress her mother. Will's brows drew together into a line of incredulity, and Hana twisted her lips. She shook her head to tell him she had no plans to relinquish Edin. But he didn't understand. He blinked back at her through irises clouded with disbelief. Lana clicked her tongue inside her cheek. The reverberation through the speaker made Hana wrinkle her nose. "Fine!" she snapped. "I've noted his name. I'll contact the lab. But once I have proof, I'll take the kid and you won't fight me. My mother wants this and I'm not failing her."

"I need the statement about the two men who killed Ari White." Hana's jaw ached with the effort of controlling her anxiety. "Names, addresses, times and details. And you'll speak to the police about what you know."

"Okay." Lana's sigh held defeat. "After the DNA result comes back."

"No. Before."

"You're not in a position to bargain."

"Wrong." Hana leaned forward and raised her voice. It caused a hiss of feedback from the microphone. "You're the one in no position to bargain, and don't you forget it. No statement. No cooperation. Phone the police and make an appointment to see Beaudain Singh Johal. Do that today or forget it. Let me know when you're done." Hana's index finger trembled as she killed the call. It prevented her from begging and pleading. She'd wanted to do that more than anything.

Will stared at her in astonishment. He'd dropped his tweezers long ago, and they lay redundant on the blotting pad in front of him. His jaw slackened and he ran his hands down both cheeks without removing his gaze from her face. "I will not mess with you again, kōtiro," he whispered. "You're scary."

"I need to step outside for a moment." Hana shoved her chair back with her calves and it spun away from the desk. The phone slipped into her pocket. Her fingers shook as she clasped the handle and yanked the door open. Trembling legs took her past the reception desk and along the narrow corridor towards the spiral staircase. The hotel manager spoke to her, but she didn't hear him, her ears deaf to all but the pounding of her blood.

Hana gripped the curved banister rail of the staircase and paused. Nausea roiled in her stomach and she sensed herself teetering on the precipice of a dangerous game. It sickened her to play the fate of one child off against another's. It ached like a ball of filth in her gut. The darkened corridor offered no comfort and she couldn't face climbing the stairs to Leslie and Alfred's apartment. Mac would crawl onto her knee with his game, and Edin would condemn her with a look.

Unable to bear it, Hana staggered to the end of the hall and let herself out through the private entrance she often used on her return from the stables. The aluminum handle felt cool beneath her fingers and fresh air filled her lungs. Three tall steps urged her downwards and pointed her toward simple clarity. Aching for the honesty of the powerful beasts which lodged in the loose boxes, Hana set her course for the interconnecting gate. She slipped through and closed it behind her, the jarring song of metal against metal hurting her ears. Silence greeted her in the empty courtyard.

Most of the half doors stood open, a bale of straw leaning against each. Ochre strands escaped from beneath the orange twine and swirled about her feet, dancing to the call of the gentle breeze sliding off the mountain. Hana checked her phone before slipping it back into her pocket, cringing against the vibration which signalled Jennifer's new attempt to mine her for information. She spun on the spot, dust grinding beneath the soles of her sandals. Loneliness shrouded her like a shawl, not because she sought human company but because the open doors signified no equine comfort. That's why she'd come, to kiss a fuzzy nose and feel the warm, steadying breath against her cheek.

The scrape of metal against concrete caused her to swirl around, seeking its origin. A majestic white head appeared over the only closed half door, a bucket dangling from sharp yellow teeth. The head jerked, and the bucket fell, hitting the stable yard with a deafening clang. The walls picked up the sound and threw it around as a toe-curling echo. Hana held her breath. One hazel iris and one blue disappeared in unison with the force of the blink.

"Sacha?" Hana covered her mouth with her hand, her chest heaving, but no air moving into her lungs.

88

Rope Noseband

Hana tripped as she took a step forward, her arms already outstretched and her fingers seeking. The horse snorted, tossing her head from side to side and clattering the wooden door with her knees. Before Hana could reach her, she'd spun until her backside faced the stable yard and the first of her powerful kicks shook the door on its hinges.

"Stop!" Hana cried. She fumbled the bolt, finding it already undone. All that kept the horse contained was her inability to reach the extra latch at ground level. Logan had reinforced it, riveting metal brackets across the whole door. Only one escape artist ever required its fastening. Hana dipped and yanked it back, throwing the door open to the yard. Sacha whirled again, her irises flashing and her power bunched into her hindquarters.

"No!" Rawhiti's terrified yell accompanied the thud of the wheelbarrow pitching over sideways. "Don't let her out!" he cried. He covered his head with his forearms as though Hana had unleashed something dreadful. She had.

Sacha snorted, her giant nostrils fluttering as air sped through them. She launched herself, almost felling the woman with the impact of her wide chest against Hana's slender body. Hana rocked back on her heels before stretching her arms around the furry neck and burrowing her face into Sacha's mane. She breathed in the scent of volcanic clay and the heady tang of silver fern sap. An undertone of saltwater covered her skin, telling of adventures beyond the extensive Du Rose property. Hana clung to her, grateful for the mare's solidity and smiling at the gentle tugging sensation as Sacha nuzzled the back of her dress. Wide lips smacked as she pulled Hana's curls with her teeth. She arched her neck and crushed her closer in a familiar equine embrace.

A scraping sound issued from behind Hana as Rawhiti recovered the fallen wheelbarrow. She kissed the side of Sacha's muzzle and turned to face him, her green irises dancing with delight. "Did Logan find her?" she called. She closed her eyes and let her fingers coast over the familiar arched nose. "Did he put her in the stable?"

"No!" Rawhiti dumped his pitchfork into the empty barrow. "She turned up with a trail horse about ten minutes before you. After having a crack at me, she put herself in there so I locked the door. I tried to put a bucket of water over the door, but she kicked it and it spilled. She bit me when I lifted over a slice of a hay bale." He touched the flapping fabric of his vest. It opened like a mouth across his left nipple.

"Weird." Hana turned her face and sniffed the coarse fur covering Sacha's hairy muzzle. "She smells funny."

Rawhiti edged towards the far gate and the muck heap beyond it. "Get rid of her," he grumbled. "Please?"

Hana twisted her lips in a silent refusal. She gripped the knotty cartilage between Sacha's nostrils and led her across the stable yard to the hose pipe. "You need a wash," she told her. A cursory glance at the clay-stained legs showed a streak of blood. "Then I'll check you over for injury." Sacha walked next to her, as meek as an obedient child. Rawhiti glared at her dangerous flank from far enough away to glean courage from the distance between them. He shook his head and grumbled to himself.

Hana ran the hosepipe over Sacha's body and the mare closed her eyes and enjoyed the sensations caused by the trickling water. She sent her weight into her off hindquarters and rested her nearside back hoof on its ragged front tip. Hana didn't bother to tie her to the metal ring fixed on the wall. Sacha stayed because she wanted to and no rope or bolt would hold her if she rebelled. The mare didn't object when Hana used a bottle of equine shampoo to foam away the streaks of orange clay and bush debris from her coat.

"That's better." Hana stood back to admire her work. Filth covered the floral fabric of her pretty dress and her curls had become frizz in her lopsided ponytail. She'd abandoned her sandals and stood barefoot on the warm concrete. The scraper dripped water onto her left shin. Sacha sighed and shook her head, causing her matted mane to shudder like a mohawk. Hana had tried and failed to remove the knots and debris from the tufted white hair. She dipped to run water over the scraper before hanging it on its hook next to the tap. She jabbed an index finger at Sacha's head. "Hair and then injuries," she said with a sigh, not looking forward to inspecting the ragged cut over Sacha's nearside rear cannon bone.

Logan would have persevered with a mane comb until Sacha's forelock lay flat against her head. But Hana's fingers ached with the effort and she quit long before meeting his exacting standards. Sacha didn't object to the scissors waving around her eyes or the wonky fringe. But when Hana stood back to inspect the odd hairdo, she winced. "I'm relieved you can't see yourself in a mirror," she told her. "I've given you a get-me-the-manager haircut." But the burs lay scattered around Sacha's shiny hooves along with twigs, ferns, and the stains of the strange orange clay. Her tail held an uncharacteristic bluntness assisted by the scissors and a whole can of aerosol silicon. Hana had rasped away the ragged edges of her hooves and cleared muck and tiny stones from around the delicate frogs. The mare looked show ready, apart from the unfortunate bowl cut.

She tolerated Hana dressing the wound on her leg with manuka honey from the tack room. But she didn't appreciate the bandage she wrapped around it. "It's stopping the flies!" Hana protested as Sacha lifted her leg for the fifth time and jerked it away from her. "Just let me finish."

Her phone tipped from her pocket and landed on the damp concrete as Hana abandoned the sticky tape and knotted the frayed ends together. "Damn!" she exclaimed as it landed face down. She lurched for it, relieved to find the screen undamaged. But wiping it on her dress revealed two missed calls. From Jas.

Hana rose and called her grandson. She didn't wait for him to speak before gushing her apology. "Sorry, darling, I didn't hear you call."

"Got a message, Hanny." Jas' tone held an official timbre. "I need to say '*incoming*' to you. He promised you'd understand."

"Sorry? Who promised what?"

"Incoming." Jas repeated the word, and Hana gaped as he hung up on her.

She peered at the screen and her fingers drifted over the button to call him back before her mind had finished processing the message. The call connected again, and Jas sounded aggrieved. "No, Hanny!" he complained. "You shouldn't keep calling me! I'm giving you a very important message. Incoming, Hanny!"

"But I don't understand." Hana patted Sacha's wide flank as Jas consulted with someone at his end.

He released a sigh of exasperation. "Fine!" he grumbled. "I have to say '*tip-off*' as well, then. From Dad. '*Incoming*' and '*tip-off*.'" He hung up on her again.

Hana murmured the words to herself without comprehension. Sacha's head jerked upwards and her eyes flicked open as a heavy vehicle slewed through the gravel in the car park. The noise created a hissing sound which echoed off the walls of the courtyard.

"Incoming." Hana repeated the warning as the words tumbled into place like images on a slot machine. "Oh no!" She kicked the first aid kit towards the wall, the metal lid already falling to cover the bandages. "Stay there!" she shouted to Sacha as she ran towards the interconnecting gate and fumbled with the latch.

She slammed the gate behind her with enough force for the latch to click. Her bare feet drummed the concrete, grit digging into her soles. She took the steps onto the back porch in one giant leap and almost overshot the doorway. The keypad rejected her first attempt at entering the code.

Adrenaline flooded her body, overriding any sense of self as she pounded along the silent corridor. She emerged in the reception area in a rush and skidded around the desk. Karl rose to meet her as she aimed for Miriam Du Rose's old office and the radio control unit. She tried to sidestep him, realising too late that he intended to obstruct her progress. "No, you don't!" he snarled, snatching hold of her left wrist.

Pain from an old injury shot up Hana's arm and into her elbow. The trapped shard of glass which had evaded Mark's skill with a scalpel shifted and ground against her artery. Hana cried out and pushed against him instead of pulling. He hadn't expected that. She put all her weight into the action and drove him backwards into the office. He absorbed the force for both of them, but struggled to remain upright as the door creaked inwards at speed. Karl grunted as he clattered against a filing cabinet, his head tipping backwards at a horrid angle. But he didn't release Hana's wrist.

White hot pain and rage filled her vision, casting everything beneath a rosy glow. Karl popped upright and thrust her backwards, his irises alight with a dangerous fire. Hana used the weak point between his fingers and thumb to free her wrist with a forceful yank before dropping her weight onto her back foot.

She gathered all her energy and released the bunched fingers of her right hand. Karl's face didn't stand a chance against her protruding middle knuckle and, though the force of the impact sent a shudder up Hana's arm, it broke his nose. He gasped and bent forwards, clutching his face with both hands.

Hana whirled around and ran to the control unit, a shaking finger depressing the button. She leaned towards the microphone. "Base to One," she cried, her tone urgent and ragged. "Base to One, come in." She released the button and waited. It seemed an age before a voice crackled through the speaker.

"This is Two." David Allen's calm entered the room as a veiled hush. "Go ahead Base." He didn't say why Logan hadn't answered, but it didn't matter.

"Cops! Over!" she hissed. The air changed as a crowd surged through the front doors, their heavy footsteps pounding against the floorboards. More metallic slams echoed off the mountain as reinforcement vehicles arrived. Voices sounded in the cavernous reception area and Hana squeezed every tendon and muscle tight in her body as she waited for David to reply.

"Roger that Base. Affirmative. Out."

The air gushed from her lungs. They'd hide Tama.

She turned back to face the hotel manager, her chest locking with adrenaline and emotion. Her gaze fell on a fallen sheet of paper tucked inside a protective wallet. It leaned against the dustbin. Hilda's CV. Karl followed her gaze as he wiped his bleeding nose on his white sleeve. "You sent her?" He blinked and used his other hand to squeeze the bridge. "Bad luck, Mrs Du Rose." He squatted on the ground and dipped his head forward, dripping blood onto the carpet. His shiny shoes pointed in a ten to two formation like clock hands.

It seemed such an innocuous thing, to argue about Hilda's suitability for a receptionist's job when he'd clearly sent her away and called the police to report Tama's location. "Why?"

Hana ground through gritted teeth as the bell on the counter trilled for assistance from beneath an impatient finger.

Karl snorted and bloodied spray sprinkled his shoes. "Because you sent her. You're all crooked. I never supported the directors taking on this place. It's over for you now. Finished."

The bell rang again and Hana straightened her spine. "What did you tell Hilda?" she hissed, her voice low.

"I told her she was too fat." His lips parted as he stared up at her, his teeth stained with a pink hue.

Rage filled Hana's chest, a boiling, bubbling surge of pure venom backed by sympathy for Hilda's waning confidence. Plus guilt that she'd accidentally set her up to fail. Hana kicked him as the bell tinkled for a third time, and footsteps set off around the desk. The ball of her bare foot contacted Karl's exposed groin as he rose from his squat before her. She curved her toes backwards to ensure he got the full force of the hard bone as she drove it upwards. Horror filled his eyes, and he dropped like a stone to the worn rug.

"Can I help you?" Hana's entire body trembled as she met the detective at the office door. She slammed it behind her and blocked his access.

He stared at her, his lips parted and a sheaf of papers clutched in his left hand. "Warrants," he said, his gaze moving from her filthy bare feet to the state of her tousled curls. "Arrest and search. I'm meeting Karl Randolph. Is he here?"

"Fired." Hana's lips flattened into a sardonic smile. Bodie's cryptic message reached fulfillment. *Tip-off.* "Gross misconduct." She held out her right hand, the fingers stiff and dirt collected beneath her fingernails. "I'm Hana Du Rose. We own the hotel, but it's run by Charlton Events. And you are?" She dipped forward in polite expectation, though she recognised his face. He appeared taller in real life, with a slender grace destroyed by the TV screen.

He nodded and held out the sheaf of papers. "Detective Inspector Craig Marley. We believe Tama Hohaia is hiding on the premises. The top warrant covers the main building and all outbuildings, including the private dwelling of Logan Du Rose. The other authorises the arrest we expect to make."

Hana snatched the warrants, the corners bending beneath her fingers. "Okay," she said, her tone terse. "Please don't break down any doors. I can give you the keys."

89

Fly Mask

"Wait." Hana cast her gaze across the second of the printed sheets and frowned. The detective turned back to face her, his head tilted to one side. "Why does the arrest warrant list Tama Hohaia?" she demanded.

"Oh." The man flapped his hand between them. "He also uses the alias Tama Du Rose."

Hana shook her head and pushed the warrants against the man's chest. They crinkled against his jacket. "My son's actual name is Tama Du Rose. His father is Michael Du Rose. You can contact Michael in the Emergency department of Auckland General Hospital if you'd rather have authoritative verification. Tama has no alias." Her lips lifted away from her teeth as she spat the words.

The detective floundered. He peered at the sheet and his eyes flashed a darker brown as he realised the error. "He's Tama Hohaia on his birth certificate." His jaw showed through his cheek. "It makes no difference."

"Ah well." Hana released the sheets, and they fluttered to the floor between them. "It makes no difference because he isn't here."

"Your hotel manager thinks differently." Blond hair flipped across the detective's forehead as he tilted his face to smile at her. Victory tugged at the corners of his lips.

"Karl?" Hana raised her voice to ensure the hotel manager heard her. "Karl tipped you off?" She released a peal of laughter and shook her head. No sound emerged from the office and she sensed he'd thought better of crossing her again. "Oh dear," she said with a sigh. "Let me know which keys you want, and I'll make them available."

"You need to come with us, Mrs Du Rose." He stood his ground, and she shrugged. "My children are upstairs with their elderly grandparents. You'll need to wait for my husband. Give me a moment and I'll contact him." She didn't return to the office, but pulled her phone from her pocket. The detective's fingers twitched as though he wished to take it from her, but he stopped himself as she raised an eyebrow in question. Hana pulled up Logan's number and connected the call, praying he'd already left the muster and headed home. The cellphone tower offered reception in an arc level with their house on the ridge. She activated the speaker and held the device between her and the detective. Relief sent a tremor into her knees as Logan answered, his voice sounding strained.

"Yeah."

"Hi Logan." Hana infused her tone with feigned brightness. "The police are here. They want to search the property and expect one of us to be present. I've left Mac and Edin upstairs with Poppa Alfie for too long already. Are you nearby?"

"Half an hour away." His voice crackled, and she imagined him slowing Sonny to a reluctant trot. "Call Linc. He can stand in until I get down the mountain." He terminated the call, and Hana watched the detective wrinkle his nose. "Is it okay if I call the stable manager?"

He allowed it and Hana summoned Lincoln. By the terseness of his tone on the phone, she guessed Logan or David had already used the radio to provide details. "I'm two minutes away," Lincoln said, heavy breathing indicating he'd already set off walking towards the hotel. "Why is Sacha here?"

"Rawhiti said she just turned up and walked into her loose box." Impatience entered the detective's eyes, and a vein twitched in his forehead. The man blinked as Lincoln swore.

"What's wrong?" Hana tensed. "Are you okay?"

"Yeah!" he puffed. "Angry white problem heading your way." He ended the call, but not before Hana heard his footsteps scrunching fast across gravel. She had a moment to wonder why he'd headed towards the front of the hotel and not used the rear door. Then she heard the raised voices outside, interspersed with yells and the clang of dented metal.

90

Treeless Saddle

Sacha kicked in the side panels of a navy-blue transit van as she wreaked havoc in the hotel's turning circle. She dislodged the front bumpers of two marked patrol vehicles and turned her threatening rear end on anyone who ventured close enough to catch her. When an armed officer lifted his semi-automatic to his shoulder, Hana added her own hysteria to the melee. Lincoln's arrival achieved nothing, but when Logan trotted across the front lawn on Sonny, Sacha greeted him with a glee-filled whinny. Her tail lifted high, the blunted ends from Hana's work with the scissors making it resemble a woman's ponytail.

"Bad girl," Logan said, sliding from the saddle as Sonny slithered to a halt. He reached up and caught a handful of Sacha's remaining stumpy mane. "What happened to you?" He blinked in surprise at her wonky fringe and his gaze tracked straight to Hana. "Right." He answered his own question and didn't bother pressing the issue. Hana stood behind Sacha, her arms outstretched to stop the police officer from shooting her. The glint in his eye showed how much he wanted to depress the trigger and blow both the woman and the horse to kingdom come. "Sorry about that." Logan wrinkled his nose at the carnage and jerked his head towards a sign attached to a post. It stated in a clear font that neither the hotel owners nor the event management company were liable for damage to property while on the premises.

The detective's jaw ground against his cheek as he watched Logan catch up Sonny's reins and lead both horses towards the stable yard. Sacha's blue wall eye seemed to wink at Hana.

The gravel dug into the soles of her bare feet as Hana turned to survey the destruction. Lincoln tutted and shook his head. One blond eyebrow rose in question and she shrugged. "They want to search all the buildings and arrest Tama." Her voice sounded flat even to her.

"Righto," he replied, no concern in his tone. "Where do you want to start?" He lifted his chin and addressed the detective. The man consulted a printed map and jabbed at it with his finger. The excited buzz had abandoned the assembled group. Sacha had highlighted their human frailty in her whirling devilry. Reminded of Bodie's allegiance, Hana experienced a momentary flicker of guilt.

"You're welcome to grab a coffee in the hotel bar while you wait," she suggested, her tone sincere. No one moved, and the detective narrowed his eyes as though daring anyone to take up the offer. Hana released an inappropriate giggle. "I thought you might like it on the house but it's probably classed as bribery." She snorted, sensing herself pitching over the precipice into hysteria as the adrenaline faded from her bloodstream. Excusing herself, she left Lincoln to clear up her mess and pattered back inside the lobby.

She'd just reached the reception desk as Will's wheelchair hummed through the doorway to the museum. "What's going on?" he demanded. His finger paused over the controls of his chair and he surveyed Hana's rumpled, filthy state for a fraction of a second. Not tarrying for an answer, he spun his chair in a full circle and disappeared back into the museum. The door slammed behind him.

Karl sat in the single office chair and jerked as Hana entered the room. The castors rolled him backwards to clatter with the desk. "Where are the cops?" he demanded. "You've broken by dose." His speech sounded odd as he failed to form any sound requiring the use of functional nasal passages.

"Yeah, don't bother." Hana waved her hand at him. "Collect your things and leave. Otherwise, I'm calling the directors right now and making a formal complaint about your behaviour. You're rude, grumpy, entitled and misogynistic. Nothing gives you the right to call a job candidate fat. Just get out while you can still walk. At least that way, you'll get a reference."

"You assaulted be."

"I will in a minute!" Hana took a step towards him. "You realise the camera at the reception desk recorded you grabbing my wrist and dragging me backwards into here, don't you?"

The colour faded from his cheeks, leaving him washed out and pasty. "There are no cameras in dere!" He said the words, but Hana saw the doubt form as a haze in his eyes.

She twisted her lips and shrugged, daring him to contradict her. David Allen had fixed cameras everywhere a few years ago. She couldn't quite remember where but made a mental note to ask him. The events company hadn't wanted them all, and she suspected if one existed in the reception, it no longer filmed the conference guests who frequented the bespoke hotel location.

Karl didn't challenge her. Perhaps it was the pain in his nose, or the ache in his groin which made another argument unpalatable. "I wanted to keep you behind the reception desk to witness the cops arriving!" he spat, pushing his hand between his legs and leaning forward. "But not like this."

"Fantastic plan." Hana didn't hide her sarcasm. "Sorry, not sorry." She delved in a desk drawer and extracted a packet of baby wipes. "Clean yourself up and leave without a fuss," she ordered. "I'll wait." She leaned against the desk and folded her arms, not caring she resembled a banshee who'd been dragged backwards through a prickly hedge face first.

The police officers moved around the site on heavy footsteps. They shifted their vehicles into the staff car park to allow a wedding party from the third floor to leave. They checked everyone's identity but somehow missed Karl as he slipped from the hotel with a cardboard box filled with his personal items.

Hana used the ladies toilets to tidy her hair and wash the orange clay from her face and hands. She couldn't salvage her dress and phoned upstairs to ask Leslie to bring down something to cover it. Her heart sank at the sight of the mumu and she floated around behind the reception desk in two ginormous floral panels stitched together at the neck. She processed credit card payments and debated the usual minibar challenges with a smile. But her mind whirred with worry about Tama and Logan. But mainly Tama.

Reinforcements arrived during a lull between the departing day guests and an overnight group planning to discuss climate change. Hilda hovered on the threshold, her shoulders bowed and her chin tucked against her chest. Slumped in Karl's chair behind the desk, Hana rose to greet her. She tripped over the tasseled hem of the mumu and cursed. "Come in, come in," she urged, dipping to lift the sides and bunch the swathes of fabric at her hip. "Bloody thing!"

"I don't understand why you called me," Hilda began. "The other man said I wasn't suitable."

"Ignore him." Hana lifted the mumu over her head and Hilda's eyes widened at the stains on her dress. Hana dropped the garment onto the desk. "I fired him. Gross misconduct. He left an hour ago. I've sent a digital scan of your CV to the directors of Charlton Events. The CEO phoned just before I rang you. He wants to know when you can start."

"Here." Hilda gulped and stared around her. "Erm."

"I didn't realise you'd fully managed the Hilton Hotel in Auckland." Hana waggled her eyebrows. She hissed at the pain still tugging the fragile skin over the bridge of her nose. "This place should be a breeze."

"But what about Chester?" Hilda took a step backwards. "That sounds like a full-time role and my husband commutes to Auckland. We don't have any local family and Chester won't go to anyone else."

Hana eyed the office behind the reception desk as workable solutions whirled through her mind. She empathised with Hilda's dilemma but a warning tick in her chest prevented her being the answer to the woman's prayers. She sought a solution which didn't involve her doing all the free child minding. "That's your office," she said jerking her head towards the doorway. "Set it up with a nice sofa and perhaps a TV in case you need to bring Chester back here. You can employ a part timer and tag team with them while you do the school run or settle him. I'm sure you'll work it out if it's what you want. The events company interfere little with the running of the venue if they see a profit after they've paid the bills." She tilted her head to one side. "And it's definitely not the Hilton."

Hilda gave a slow nod. "I'd love it." She licked her lips and gazed down at her fingers. When she looked up at Hana again, determination filled her eyes with shiny sparks. "I'll do it!" she said, her mouth widening to a grin. "I'll make it work."

"Great!" Hana hadn't realised she'd held her breath until her lungs complained. "If you have time now I can show you the basics of the reception desk and give you a tour?"

Hilda nodded with enthusiasm. "Let me just text home and let them know." She tugged a pink covered phone from the handbag over her wrist. As her fingers coasted across the screen, she asked, "Why are there police officers everywhere? Was there a tornado or something because the vehicles look wrecked?"

Hana licked her lips and fingered the patterned edge of the mumu. She pressed the ball of her right foot over the toes of her left. "It's nothing," she lied, fixing her gaze on the chandelier which had witnessed six generation's worth of Du Rose antics.

"Most of them are leaving now. But anyway, you'll get used to it."

91

Spur Straps

Despite the use of dogs and a drone, the police officers didn't find Tama. Logan and Lincoln spent the day traipsing from one location to another. Hilda asked to sit at the reception desk to get a feel for the role, and so Hana showed the remaining officers around the hotel. They searched each room and inspected the housekeeping areas. But they prepared to leave as the muster crowd returned. The tired, bedraggled riders drove the last of the mobs into the valley for winter.

Hana stood barefoot on the front steps and drowned out the irritating voice of Detective Inspector Marley. She sensed the familiar rumble beneath her soles as an outrider appeared on the horizon. A wave of emotion built in her chest as Wiri materialised on the track above the paddock gate. He burst from the bush canopy, galloping alone. His horse threw a narrow trail of dust behind him on the reckless downhill. Tears pricked her eyes at the risk and the honour. A stampeding mob followed, a billowing cloud rising half a kilometre behind him and moving at speed. He had seconds to open the gate without dismounting and he managed it with a fluid ease, shoving it wide and backing his horse against the rear fence.

"Mama!" The scream chilled her blood and Hana jerked forward and raked the windows of the upper floors. "Mama! I here!" A tiny hand waved over the balcony rail of Alfie's apartment, and Hana held her breath. "Look, Mama!" The arm swung wide to point towards the mountain, and Hana skipped down the steps and shielded her eyes with a flattened hand. Leslie held Edin in a bear hug, the child's left arm gripped around her neck in a stranglehold. But her tiny face shone with excitement. "They coming!" She gave a whoop of elation as the first of the cream cows streamed through the opening. Phoenix appeared, using her horse to slow the mob while the men filtered them into single file. So fragile against the thundering cream bodies, the slender girl showed no fear. Her black curls streamed from beneath Hana's Jillaroo hat.

"Wow!" the detective exclaimed. "Are they children at the front?"

Hana nodded, unnamed emotions swirling inside her chest. "My children," she whispered.

Like spilt milk, the herd flushed through the gate and dispersed throughout the paddock. Tired and sweating, they milled around and bunched at the edges in their familial creamy groups. The last of the riders trotted through the gate and Wiri closed it behind them, bending to fasten the catch. He cantered across to Phoenix and their arms rose in a double high five.

"Mama! Cake!" Edin leaned away from Leslie, her fingers bunched over the top rail as she peered down at Hana. Her lips formed an upward curve and her chin flattened, the action taking extreme courage. Then her index finger rose and pointed straight at Detective Inspector Marley. "Not him!" she shouted. "Naughty man! Kick him!"

Hana winced. "No! We don't kick!" She wagged her finger at Edin.

"Yeah, we did kick." He pursed his lips and frowned. "But your folks were friendly. The cake tasted a bit odd. Was that your little lad sitting under the dining table?"

Hana nodded and forced herself to picture the scene. She'd left the detective in Leslie's less than capable hands. It seemed his search hadn't gone as planned. She wondered if he'd ventured as far as the roof garden but shoved away the question without verbalising it.

The officers left, and she stood on the steps for a while, watching as the riders corralled the herds into smaller denominations. Sunday's job would require checking each of the beasts through the crush to ensure they were uninjured and still had their identification tags. The stock hands would account for every one on the register and disperse them into the lower paddocks for winter. It was the only time of year they used JD's block of land up near the road. Jacob D'Arcy Du Rose. Hana sighed and whispered his name out loud, relieved to notice it caused less pain. "One day," she acknowledged with a sigh. "Maybe one day."

One day she'd visit his grave in the urupā and lay flowers for her children's great grandfather.

One day.

But not this day.

92

Western Saddle

Hilda proved a fast and enthusiastic study of the hotel's booking system. She stayed far longer than Hana expected and helped to check in the small group of climate change activists arriving for their overnight stay. Hana introduced her to the hotel's staff, and she fitted in with ease. When the reception closed for the night, she hugged Hana with genuine gratitude before leaving. Hana dragged her tired body upstairs to Alfred and Leslie's apartment.

"Ah, you bought back my mumu." Leslie grinned at her from an armchair in the lounge. She'd removed her teeth and the lack of structure gave her speech a curious lisp.

"Yeah. Thanks." Hana perched on the sofa next to Alfred and he rubbed her shoulder with a crabbed hand.

"You saw the last muster come home?" His grey eyes glittered in his wrinkled brown face. "Logan leaving early gave them mokos their heads, didn't it?" His speech bounced with victory. "He mollycoddles them. I never did that with my tamariki."

Hana pressed her lips together. She fought the urge to list Alfred's failings as a parent and a businessman. It wasn't an edifying speech, and she didn't wish to rekindle a fracture through mental exhaustion. Edin slept across Leslie's torso, her skinny legs dangling over the arm of the chair. A line of saliva left a trail across her pink left cheek and she snored. Mac lay beneath the dining table, his device clutched to his chest and the muted sound of a puppy yapped with forlorn urgency. Hana sighed. "You made cake?"

Leslie nodded. "Edie made cake. Gluten-free."

Alfred shuddered. "Tasted okay, but it looked like a giant beefburger." He cackled. "Leslie made that cop sit at the table until he finished. I thought he might choke."

Hana blew out relief through pursed lips. "Gluten-free? Thank you. That was thoughtful of you. We're seeing Dean on Friday at the hospital. Mark seems convinced that's the issue."

Edin farted, and Alfred wafted his hand across his nose. "That was a wet one," he remarked. "I hope they get her sorted and she stops that nonsense."

Hana nodded and paused as a crackle of static issued from behind the wall. "What's that?" She turned in her seat and pressed her palm against the patterned frieze behind her. "It sounded like the radio."

"Need to move it through here." Alfred jerked his head backwards but made no attempt to rise. Hana took the hint and pushed herself free of the sofa arm. Exhaustion added a numb quality to her thought processes. She opened the secret door leading to the roof garden and retrieved the handset from the first step.

"Why did you do that?" She dropped it onto the cushion next to Alfred and walked towards the French doors. Someone had removed the key from the lock, and Hana ran her index finger along the glass. It represented a milestone. Edin had ventured outside for a reason other than searching the car park floor for her dead uncle.

"Didn't want the boys to say where they hid Tama." Alfred's lips smacked behind her. "The volume toggle broke a while ago and the off button ages before that. The cops would hear it unless the charge died."

"Didn't the detective go onto the roof?" Hana turned with a frown at Alfred's guttural cackle. Edin stirred on Leslie's lap.

"Na. The wee one launched herself at him whenever he stepped near the wall. Leslie told him the kid didn't want him touching the birds on the wallpaper, so he didn't bother. Had a nosey around and left real fast after his tea and cake."

Hana narrowed her eyes. "So, is Tama on the roof, then?"

"Dunno where he is. Figured he rode to Dead Man's Gully at the northern end." His lower lip pushed upward to cover its mate. "Pay his respects to Kane, maybe."

"On horseback?" Hana shook her head. It's impassable.

"Na. They ditched the tack and turned his horse loose, but she didn't come back with them. She took a shortcut through the bush and arrived in the stable yard with that other one of Logan's hours ago."

"Sacha?" Hana's head jerked back and a bone in her neck clicked. "Sacha brought Tama's horse home?"

"Āe mārika. For sure. I heard Rawhiti on the radio just before we hid the handset." He released a high-pitched giggle. "That boy hates the white mare. She chased him around the stable yard. He had to take Tama's mount to the paddock and groom her there."

"She could still get him." Hana sighed. "I left the gate closed, and she jumped it to attack the police cars." She stared at a tui bird in the decorated canopy behind Alfred's tufty head. "But Sacha arrived ages before the police. How did Tama know to ditch his horse and hide before I did? I put the call out over the radio to David."

Alfred's eyebrows jigged on his forehead. "Did you think your son was the only snitch inside the police headquarters?" His lips formed a bow worthy of red lipstick. "Logan has sources even you don't know about."

"Right." Hana pushed her shoulders back to release the tension in her spine. "I might pop and see Sacha again," she mused.

"Just wait a minute." Leslie grunted as she forced herself upright in a rolling motion. She carried Edin with her and dumped her in Alfie's lap like a bag of bones. "I used that Googley thingamy you all play with. I think I found something out about them, Alderbanks."

Hana made a noncommittal sound in her throat. She very much doubted Leslie's prowess with a search engine. "Okay." She forced brightness into her tone. "I've tried most of the variations I can think of, but I'll look at what you found."

Leslie's hips shimmied in her dress as she wandered through to the bedroom. She reappeared with an iPad clutched in her fingers. The screen activated with a stutter and she used a stylus to tap something onto it. Hana stuck her hands behind her back to prevent her from taking over from the one person on the planet who used the stylus as intended. Leslie spun the screen to face her, and she frowned as she read the keywords. *'Serspitious deaths Alderbanks.'* She clamped her teeth over her tongue to stop her from pointing out the typos. Leslie persisted with the stylus, her breath rattling as it emerged through her nostrils. Concentration defined her wrinkles as deep furrows in her brow and beneath her eyes.

"Here it is." She smiled and jabbed the iPad into Hana's stomach. "Want some gluten-free beef burger?"

Hana gave a shallow nod and stared at the list of highlighted articles. The algorithm had corrected the spelling error and thrown up a column of suggestions. An electric knife whirred to life in the background as Leslie carved a wedge of crumbs from the concrete cake. She dumped a pile onto a plate with the hollow clang of rubble on crockery. The excess noise woke the children and Edin set up her familiar grizzle. Mac rose as though rebooted and fed his sad puppy its dinner.

"Police attended a suspicious death at the home of political candidate, Clive Alderbank, last year," she read under her breath. *"The three-year-old girl sustained injuries which concerned the medical examiner but were later attributed to a tragic fall down a stone staircase. The child was the daughter of the resident housekeeper. Mr Alderbank has thrown his hat in the ring for the candidacy of the Albany electorate."*

The article moved on to political manifestos and Clive's punt at becoming the next prime minister of New Zealand. Hana scrolled to the top of the page to the date and whistled through her teeth. "This is it," she breathed. "September 1969. I think Lana Alderbank killed that child. So, Antoinette moved Caroline north as a baby to protect her before risking bringing her here just after Logan's birth." She shook her head. "But what about the other daughter? It doesn't mention the younger Lana."

"It said the housekeeper's child died. The newspaper didn't seem interested in the Alderbank family." Leslie licked a crumb from her finger and cocked her head. Her lids closed, although her eyeballs moved beneath them. "Not bad," she said, turning and running her hand under the tap. "I'll ask that new fancy chef downstairs for a recipe."

"Ooh yeah. Get more of that chocolate pudding while you're at it." Alfred beamed in a smile which screwed up his entire face like a wrung out dishcloth.

Leslie gave a loud throat clearing and shot a warning glare over her shoulder to silence him. "Maybe the other girl wasn't born." She plunged her hands into the washing-up bowl and retrieved a shiny serving spoon.

"Na. She's older than me and definitely older than Caroline." Hana's brow furrowed as she stared at the patterned rug beneath her bare toes. Once Oriental and expensive, it had cushioned the feet of generations of Du Roses in various locations until the hessian backing showed through the wool. Perhaps Antoinette Du Rose had once stepped over it as she crossed a downstairs room into Reuben's arms. Hana sighed. "Why doesn't Lana remember Caroline then? She claimed she only found out about her recently after her mother suffered a stroke."

"Perhaps she wasn't there." Splish-splashing issued from Leslie's hands as she dumped cutlery onto the draining board. "The Alderbanks might have adopted both girls at different times."

Hana stared at the ribbons keeping Leslie's apron fixed around her wide girth. They fluttered against her skirt like bunting.

"Cake!" Edin grizzled. "Beef burger cake."

"Na, it's chocolate," Alfie soothed. He glanced up at Hana from beneath hooded lids. "What if someone else raised the older girl like you're taking care of this one?" He plopped a kiss on the top of Edin's dark head and she snarled at him like an angry lioness. She hid her grin against his chest when he roared back at her.

"Someone else raised her," Hana whispered. "Like who?" Thoughts of Edin's mother intruded along with her certainty that Caroline and Jennifer were sisters. A horrible possibility rose to the fore, one which explained everything. Hana dropped into a dining chair with a bump. "Oh, that makes sense," she whispered, musing over the problem. Pieces dropped into position with more clarity, losing their sharp jig-saw corners and melding together into an understandable picture. She rubbed her left eye with the backs of her fingers. "Do you still have Caroline's suitcase in the storage cupboard?"

"Caroline." Edin twisted her lips into a knot. She bolted upright on Alfred's knee. "Prison Mama?"

"Ooh," he hissed. "Not sure I know how to answer that one, moko."

"Yes." Hana nodded and smiled at Edin. "Caroline's your real mama."

"Noooo!" She squeezed her body into its crabbed, scrunched posture and gritted her teeth.

Alfred blinked at Hana and his shoulders raised to his ears in question. "Just leave it," she whispered. "It's a sort of progress."

Leslie wiped her hands on a tea towel and jerked her head towards the secret door. "It's through there," she said. Her gaze darted to Edin. "But we'll need to distract someone first."

The promise of cake formed a ready source of diversion. Alfred took both children to the bathroom to wash their hands. Hana and Leslie ducked into the passage behind the wall and dragged the heavy suitcase from a cupboard formed beneath the roof joists. "I hope the mice haven't got into it," Hana grunted as she dragged it onto the lounge rug. "We shouldn't open it here. It might trigger memories for Edin." She tilted it onto its end and Leslie helped to push it into the spare room at the end of the apartment. It took their combined effort to haul it onto the bed. Hana paused, her fingers fluttering over the zip. Then she put her hands behind her back. "You do it," she whispered. "I opened it to retrieve Horsey, but it feels weird going through her stuff."

Leslie shrugged. "She's lucky you fetched it from the campground after they arrested her. Otherwise, she'd have nothing to come back to when she gets released."

Hana cringed. "I should have checked for dirty clothes. Can you imagine facing freedom and thirteen-year-old unwashed knickers?"

Leslie grabbed the end of the zipper and hauled it around the circumference of the suitcase. The tight black fabric seemed to breathe out as the lid lifted. "What do you want from it?" Leslie demanded. She flipped back the lid and sifted through the mixture of a child's and woman's clothing. A tiny blue cardigan pitched onto the bedspread and Hana pursed her lips. Edin's fragile state made her nervous to reintroduce anything from her former life with Caroline. She fingered the soft wool between her fingers.

"I'll wash this and see if it fits her Horsey," she said, lifting it to her chest. "Perhaps if I reintroduce things by degrees, it might help her cope." A musty scent issued from the garment, and Hana closed her eyes. "We need to move this somewhere safer. I'll ask Logan to fetch it one night after I've put the children to bed. It's a shame to leave it in the roof space for another decade."

"So, what do you want?" Leslie pulled aside a pair of black trousers and a flowery blouse. Sounds filtered through from the kitchen as Alfred dropped a plate onto the table. It clattered against the wood, not breaking but surely damaged.

"Hairbrush," Hana whispered. "Can you see one in there?"

Leslie rifled through a washbag and produced a wide-toothed comb. Blonde hairs hung from it like streamers. Hana nodded. "Yes! That!" She glanced back at the doorway and tutted. "Do you have any clear plastic bags? I should treat it like evidence."

"Of what?" Leslie bobbed her hand, and the hairs danced.

"Her DNA." Hana reached out and took the comb, the smoothness of the plastic making her stomach clench. "Please, can you grab the bag? If I go in there, Edin will start playing up again, and I just need a moment."

Leslie nodded and her tights swished as her thighs brushed together. She crossed the room, and Hana listened to her scolding Alfred in the kitchen. "It's cracked!" she complained of the plate. "Look at it."

"You're cracked," he replied, his tone jovial. "Cracked in the head."

Hana heard Edin give a snort before inhaling crumbs. The humour turned to a cough, followed by grizzling. Leslie returned with the bag fluttering between her fingers. She peeled apart the opening and held it while Hana dropped the comb inside its rustling folds. They used the cardigan to disguise its presence and wrapped the bundle into a pillow case.

"I'm not sure what you're up to," Leslie commented as they emerged in the kitchen. "But I hope you know what you're doing."

93
Grazing Muzzle

"**Y**ou can't do a DNA test without both parties signing their agreement." Logan stamped on Hana's cunning plan from the outset. He tugged a clean tee shirt over his head and patted it down over his pectorals. "It's not legal."

Hana snorted. "When did you start caring about the law?"

He wrinkled his nose and buttoned his fly. "True. I might know someone who knows someone."

"Please call them?" Hana dipped her body and rubbed her stomach. The period had disappeared early, leaving an ache behind which painkillers hadn't shifted. "If I can compare Caroline with Jennifer, I won't need to get Dean to test Edin." She squeezed her knees together and groaned. "It removes a massive problem for me." Her eyes flared wide, and she raised her index finger. "And I could substitute Caroline's for Edin's. What do you think?"

Logan exhaled. "I doubt Dean wants involvement in any of this, babe. You're trying his loyalty to the extreme."

Hana whimpered and her shoulders sloped in defeat. Phoenix burst through the door, her curls flattened against her head. "I want straight hair," she stated, hurling herself onto the bed.

Logan pointed at her. "What did you do?"

"Cooking oil." She blinked and a single curl rose from her fringe. It waved like a flag amid its tortured companions as though beckoning for help.

Logan glanced at Hana for assistance before jumping into the fray by himself.

"Point number one. Ask before you raid the pantry.

Point number two. Please get off our bedspread.

Point number three. That won't work.

Point number four. Curls run in our family, so you're going to lose that battle."

Phoenix scowled and patted the top of her head. Her fingers shone with oil as she removed them. "What then?" she demanded. "How do I get beautiful?"

"You already are!" Hana huffed out a ragged breath. "Don't let the stereotypes flatten you into a clone!"

"A clone?" Phoenix popped to her feet as Logan tugged her hand until she stood upright. "Does a clone have straight hair?"

"No. I don't know." Defeat and exhaustion clouded Hana's vision. Disappointment laced the heady mix. She'd returned to the stables in search of Sacha but found only her empty stall. Logan swore he'd bolted the door, but she'd gone. Hana slapped her thighs with her palms and gazed down at her dress. "I need a shower," she said with a sigh.

"You just missed your slot." Logan hauled his daughter into the hallway with her hand. She continued musing on the hair type of clones. "Wash your hair!" His voice echoed off the ceiling, but the book shelves dulled his baritone. "And be quick. Mama's waiting for her turn." He walked back to the bedroom and studied Hana with a serious expression.

"I think I'll have a bath instead." She yanked her soiled dress over her head. She stood in the centre of the bedroom in her underwear. "Will there be enough hot water?"

"I'll raise the temperature on the thermostat." He stared at the ceiling. "You might have to wait awhile."

"Gosh." Hana sank onto the mattress. "Logan Du Rose is raising the thermostat. It must be Christmas."

He leaned against the door frame and raised his left eyebrow. "Are you accusing me of miserly behaviour?" He folded his arms across his chest. "I'm saving the planet."

Hana flopped back onto the mattress. She reached out at the last second and unclipped the voile, causing it to cascade across the gap and shield her from his view. "Come and get me when the water's hot," she demanded. "And a glass of red would be wonderful."

Hana slept through story time and Logan putting the children to bed. She only woke when a cool palm rested against her cheek. Her eyes slid open to discover Mac's nose was just a few centimetres from her own. She jerked backwards in shock and his eyes widened. "What's wrong?" she signed, her fingers moving in lazy formation of the words.

"Wiri snoring." His fingers rapped out the message and he spoke at the same time. One processor hung at a jaunty angle from the side of his head. A red curl coiled around it in an embrace.

Hana scrubbed her palms across her face. "Take this out then," she replied, tapping the processor with her nail. "Why are you in Wiri's room, anyway?"

"Tama," he whined. "Smells."

Hana groaned and gazed at the tiny lights shining from beneath the bed's ornate canopy. "Just get in here." She patted the bedspread, and he clambered up with dancing irises, having achieved his primary goal. He knee-walked across to Logan's side of the bed and burrowed beneath the sheets. Hana pointed to the side of his head and his slender fingers reappeared to disconnect the processor. He dropped it onto her pillow where it lay like a coil of grey wires.

Mac's mention of Tama drove her to search for him. She stuck her head around the door frame to find Mac's bed empty. Phoenix and Edin seemed to have swapped. She checked the other rooms in deference to the continual game of musical beds, but figured he hadn't risked returning home after the police raid.

"The children are all over the place." She yawned as she stepped into the lounge. Logan watched the news, his long legs stretched far enough to reach the rug. He tilted his head back to smile at her. Dark shadows hogged the space beneath his eyes.

"I saw." He yawned and stretched his arms above his head.

"Mac's in our bed." Hana dipped forward and clasped her arms around his shoulders. She leaned over the sofa to press her nose against his neck. "I don't know if I have the energy to run a bath."

"I'll do it." Logan waited for her to release him before standing. He reached for the remote and turned off the TV. The picture faded with a faint crackle until the screen became black and empty. "They're still hunting Tama."

"The bloody hotel manager made it too close for comfort." Hana picked at a loose thread on her bra. Beneath the muted lounge lights, its crisp whiteness faded to a dirty grey.

Logan slipped his arm around her and nudged her towards the hallway. He lowered his voice to avoid disturbing the children. "No. Tama thought he knew best. As usual." Irritation couched his speech as he edged Hana into the bathroom.

They reduced their conversation to whispers, which the tiled walls reverberated around the room. "Where is he now?" Hana asked.

Logan opened the tap and hot water tumbled into the deep bath. "Safe. We keep emergency gear in a few huts across the property. He has enough to survive. I don't know why he didn't go to one of them." He blinked and his jaw tightened. The dark bristles across his cheeks and chin seemed to rise in sympathy with his frustration. "David spent three days checking them all, and he was hiding in plain sight at the hotel."

"How did he stay there without food?" She perched on the edge of the tub and imagined Tama starving to death in Logan's old bedroom. He hadn't looked malnourished.

Logan humphed. "Wait till you see his bill for room service and movies." He upended a bottle of navy liquid into the bath and floral scented bubbles formed at the base of the cascading waterfall. "I'm not paying for it."

"I suppose it was clever to come home," Hana remarked. "Nobody expected that, and he would have stayed safe for longer if Raymond hadn't ratted him out to Lana's heavies."

Logan pursed his lips and released a non-committal grunt. He finished dispersing the bubbles with his hand and rose, drying his fingers on a nearby towel. "It's ready," he said. He pressed a kiss to the top of Hana's head and walked towards the door. "I'll bring the wine now."

He returned moments later with a glass of merlot and her phone. He laid both on a wooden stool next to the bath. Hana sank into the deep bubbles with a sigh. Dipping beneath the water level, she enjoyed the muted sounds of her own movements and stayed for as long as she dared. When she emerged and pushed water from her eyes, she heard her phone vibrating against the stem of the wine glass.

It took a moment for her to dry her fingers on the nearest towel and answer the call. Bodie launched without waiting for her to speak. "Hey, Mum. Sorry to bother you again. I just realised the medical examiner set Ari White's death around ten o'clock on the Sunday prior to Tama's disappearance."

"Right." Hana sank back into the foam with a sigh. Something bumped against the wall adjoining the bathroom, and Edin squeaked. She heard Phoenix sending her back to her own bed in another post bedtime switcheroo. She squeezed her eyes closed and opened them again. The overhead spotlights seemed bright against the darkness framed by the window. "I don't understand why you're telling me this. Wasn't Ari buried this morning?" She inspected a line of foam which eased along her wrist and onto her forearm. The hand which held the phone shone with droplets.

"He was." Bodie cleared his throat. "I guess I'm asking where Tama was that night? If he can secure an alibi, you won't need Lana Alderbank's statement. You can keep Edin and that means Caroline won't contact Izzie."

Hana's lips formed an 'o' of regret. She pushed herself upright, and the water surged to the plug end and back again. "Sorry," she hissed. "Caroline phoned me this morning. She won't tell Izzie anything. But you're right. Proving Tama's innocence will solve a lot of related issues."

"You trust her?"

"No." Hana swept her right hand through the bubbles. "I appreciated the call from Jas today."

"Good." The staccato rap of his reply suggested he wished to draw the conversation to a close. "Talk to Tama," he said. "Whenever you see him."

"Thank you. I will."

Hana placed the phone on the side of the bath and lay back in the warm water. But she couldn't settle. The question whirled around her mind. Where was Tama on the night of the murder? And why hadn't he offered the information without being asked?

94

Sport Boots

Hana emerged from the bathroom in a towel. She hunted for Logan and located him in the garage. He slouched in the camping chair with a tanned cowboy boot in his left hand and a cloth in his right. The slow buffing action created a shushing sound in the quiet room. The tang of saddle soap tickled Hana's nose. "Can you contact Tama?" she demanded.

"Why?" Logan lifted his left eyebrow to stress his question. His black lashes swished as he studied her. A pink line beneath his cheekbone betrayed his body's struggle to heal the cut.

"Bo just called me." Hana raised her phone in her left hand. "He wants to cut Lana's statement out of the equation. And he made me wonder why Tama didn't just offer an alibi for the time of Ari White's death."

Logan leaned back in the chair with a slow inhale. He stared at Hana through unseeing eyes. "That's an excellent question," he mused. "We never asked him."

Hana shrugged. "Because we all knew he didn't do it. I felt grateful to have him back in our care and it wasn't until the news release that it became an issue." She tilted her head and droplets transferred from her damp curls to her forearm and continued their downward journey. "We wanted to keep him safe from the Alderbanks' men and didn't realise Ari's death held any relevance." She raised her left palm. "So, where was he?"

Logan nodded. He placed his polished boot next to its dirty companion on the mat and rose from the sagging chair. Hana noticed the wince of pain cross his sharp features and bit her lip to stop her from asking questions he wouldn't answer. She gripped her towel tighter around her as Logan walked towards the base unit installed in a corner of the garage. He paused in thought for a moment before lifting the radio handset and changing the frequency to one Hana didn't recognise. She held her breath as he spoke. "One to Six. Come in. Radio check."

A litany of questions burst into Hana's mind and she squeezed her lips closed to prevent them from leaking out and irritating her husband. A line appeared in his brow and then faded as static crackled from the speaker.

"Six. Reading you loud and clear. Go ahead. Over."

Hana blew out her held breath and watched her husband as he debated something in his mind. His irises held a glassy quality. "Move to Bivouac Four at first light. Say again. Over."

The subsequent pause seemed endless. Hana sensed Tama formulating an argument and then dismissing it. If Logan asked him to move closer to home, he must have his reasons. After thirty seconds of internal wrangling, Tama complied, repeating Logan's request.

"Six. Moving to Bivouac Four at first light. Out."

Hana rose onto the balls of her feet and fidgeted with her towel as Logan reduced the volume on the base unit and replaced the handset. "Why did you move him?" she demanded.

"I can't ask him specific questions over the radio." Logan wrapped his arms around her and tugged her against his body. "We don't know who's listening."

"Fair." Hana nodded and her cheek shifted against his tee shirt. "Will you ride up to meet him? How long will it take? Can I come?"

Logan's chest rocked as he laughed. "Yes. An hour's round trip. No."

She tutted and tilted her head back on her neck. "That's not right!" she protested. "It's my question. I should be there."

"What about the children? Don't you have church tomorrow? You bunked off last week to meet Melissa."

Hana groaned. "I did." She squinted up at him. "And they're your children, too."

A laugh burst from Logan's chest. "Oh, I see where this is going. Are you planning to do a runner on me again, Mrs Du Rose?" He leaned back to survey her scowling expression. "Do I need to handcuff you to the bed?"

"In your dreams." Hana pressed her nose against his chest until the cut on her forehead pinched. "I don't remember where Bivouac Four is. We'd both need to go and I don't want to dump the children on Leslie again." Her brow furrowed. "Although she kidnapped the little ones this morning and made it clear, the invitation didn't include me."

"Tell you what." Logan lifted her chin with his forefinger. "How about this idea? I'll ask David to lead you up to the hut and I'll mind the children for the morning."

Hana twisted her lips as conflict set up an irritating tick in her chest. "What about church?"

"No promises there," he replied, cocking his head on one side. "But I'm sure I'll think of something."

"Sounds great." A smile spread across Hana's lips and her irises glittered. It faded just as fast. "What's the catch?"

Logan's smile matched hers, and he dipped his head to kiss her. She squeaked as he bent his knees and caught her in his arms, tossing her over his shoulder like a sack of potatoes. "Oh, there's always a catch," he growled, his voice a low rumble as he carried her along the hallway to the bedroom.

95

Fly Sheet

"I swear she has our place bugged!" Logan slammed the truck's rear door, and a warning vein ticked beneath his jaw. He glared at Hana as she climbed into the passenger seat. "Did you call her?"

"No!" Hana fastened her seatbelt and forced her mind to filter the last five minutes. Leslie had appeared without invitation, having borrowed David's work truck. She snatched Edin, Mac and Phoenix, cramming their booster seats onto the back seat. Wiri refused to leave.

"I'm taking them to church!" she'd insisted. Her brown finger jabbed in Logan's direction. "I know he won't." She'd waddled back to the truck and squished herself into the driver's seat. It had taken mere seconds for her to kidnap three willing co-conspirators. Phoenix waved to Hana from the front seat as Leslie bore her through the gaping entrance of the driveway.

Logan released a low growl in his throat and fired up the diesel engine. "I thought we'd visit Hamilton." Disappointment laced his tone.

Wiri's voice chirped from the back seat. "I'm still here, Uncle."

"Thanks." Logan glanced at the boy over his shoulder as he released the handbrake. "I bought tickets for the zoo this afternoon."

"Yey!" Wiri punched the air. "Where are we going this morning?"

Logan gave an angry huff. "I intended to take you all to church. Figured I could sit through one of Sam's sermons in the name of good parenting."

"Oh." Wiri sounded surprised and Hana pursed her lips and kept her gaze on the narrow lane. They passed the spot where Lana Alderbank had almost driven off the side of the mountain and she held her breath.

"I can do church," Logan grumbled to himself. "I'm not a total heathen."

Hana cleared her throat and rubbed a smudge of washing powder caked onto her jeans. "Will you still go to church?" she enquired, keeping her tone light.

Logan snorted. "Heck, no! Me and the boy can go to Hamilton early. I'll sort out the DNA task and then we'll visit the zoo. Maybe Jas and Hope might like to come instead."

"Yey." Wiri sounded less enthusiastic. He and Jas shared an uneasy relationship. In the spirit of truth and being the only child left, he related an interesting snippet of information. "Phoenix texted Nonie. She asked for help and said Papa wanted everyone to go to hell."

"What?" Hana spun around in her seat to face him. She peered through the narrow gap and almost bumped heads with Logan. "First, how did she text her and second, is that what she said?"

Wiri nodded. Conflict paled his healthy complexion as he realised he'd betrayed Phoenix on both counts. His shoulders slumped. "I'm not sure about the zoo," he whispered. "I'm scared of monkeys."

Hana lifted an eyebrow and won the staring competition as Wiri glanced away from her. He inspected the dark lines beneath his fingernails. "Okay. I feel bad now." His lower lip drew up to convey his misery. "She borrowed Ma's phone to text Nonie. And those were her exact words, but she spelt some of them weird. She wanted to send it to Pastor Sam, but I suggested Nonie might be a better idea."

Hana blew out a breath. "Thank goodness!" she hissed. She spun around to find Logan glaring sideways at her.

"Don't you use a password?" he demanded.

"I do!" She tugged her phone from the protective sleeve strapped to her biceps and swiped her index finger across the screen. "Look." She spun it to display the demand for a code.

Wiri sniggered. "It's 8418," he said. "HDH, but in numbers instead of letters. Hana Du Rose. 8, 4, and 18."

Hana slid lower in her seat. She cringed at the text her daughter had sent.

'Help! We're going to hell. Rescue us and take us to church.' She'd spelt two important words wrong, but Leslie had got the gist and responded as expected.

"I'll change the code," she whispered to Logan.

He shook his head and navigated the series of dangerous bends near the bottom of the mountain. His lips lifted upwards in a smirk.

Hana met David at the stables. Unlike Logan, he didn't invest in nurturing her fragile ego, and she tacked up Sonny without his assistance. He groomed Polly until the sun glinted off her coat, grinning to himself as Hana used the mounting block to clamber into the saddle. It took less than a second for him to spring onto Polly's bare back and catch up the rope threaded through her halter. He jerked his head towards Sonny's girth. "Are you sure that's tight enough?" he quipped. "His stomach isn't quite touching his spine yet."

"Haha." Hana gathered up her reins and glanced up at the azure sky. Not a single cloud marred the brilliant blue. "Logan asked Tama to move at first light. We need to go now or he might not wait for us."

"He'll wait." David patted the straps of the rucksack straddled across his shoulders. "I've got coffee in here. Logan said there's none left in Hut Four. Kid must be suffering from withdrawal by now." He urged Polly forward and her hooves clattered across the concrete.

❧❧❧❧ ❧❧❧❧

It took less time than Hana imagined, trekking up to the fourth hut on the extensive list. She acknowledged to herself, as she followed Polly's dappled rump through the undergrowth, she never would have found it alone.

David raised his fingers to his lips and released a loud whistle as they reached the craggy outcrop of a long ridge. Hana halted and leaned down to pat Sonny's sweating neck.

"I'm here." Tama appeared from behind a punga, pressing through a sea of ground ferns and wading towards them. Sonny inhaled in shock and lifted his front hooves off the floor. He shied backwards, and Hana clenched her stomach muscles and altered her balance. She swung him in an arc to take the heat from the movement and by the time he faced Tama again, he'd calmed enough to keep his feet on the ground. "Sorry." Tama approached, his face dirty and his shoulders rounded. He wore the same clothes he'd donned for the muster the day before. "Did you bring coffee?" he demanded, waving his arm behind him. "This hut's got none."

David dismounted and swung the rucksack from his shoulders. "Yeah," he replied, his tone businesslike. "You okay?" Polly nosed at the ferns near her hooves before lifting her head in disgust.

"Kinda." Tama offered a lame wave to Hana, but he didn't smile. A night alone in the bush had allowed his demons to return to taunt him. She dismounted and looped Sonny's reins over a nearby branch. The horse sniffed at the ground and then rubbed his cheek against Polly's rump. She released a snort filled with irritation but didn't raise her hind leg to discourage him.

"Want a hug?" Hana held out her arms to Tama, and he gave a shallow nod. His depression shrouded her head as she stroked his back with pats of consolation.

"Can I come back yet?" He murmured the sentence through down-turned lips as David unloaded the rucksack. A tin of beans rolled into the undergrowth as he released a catering sized container of instant coffee.

"No, sorry," Hana soothed. "But you can end this real fast if you answer my question."

"What?" Tama squinted at her and terminated the embrace. His fingers strayed to stroke Polly's flank in a lazy loop.

"Where were you on the Sunday before you went into hiding? Around ten o'clock that night."

The way his expression changed made Hana hold her breath. She knew in that instant he wouldn't tell her. A shutter slammed down over his misery and he bolted it from the inside and left her floundering. "Thanks for the gear," he said, forcing a fake smile onto his lips. "Let me know when it's safe to come back to the valley." He bent to help David transfer the groceries into his arms. They plodded off together and Hana saw a wooden door swing open from beneath a shadowy overhang.

She huffed in frustration and followed, picking her way through the ferns with care. An exposed kauri root almost cost her as she struggled to avoid stepping on it and listed sideways. A curse slipped free and then another as she bumped her shoulder against a punga's rough spines. "So much for Sunday," she hissed to herself. "What a potty mouth! You might well go to hell."

"What?" Tama emerged from beneath the outcrop, David close on his heels. Hana waved her arm towards the door as a curtain of ivy cascaded down to hide it.

"I want to see inside," she complained. "Two and eight are wooden cabins. How many more are hidden like this one?"

"About six of them." David's lips flattened as he hefted the empty rucksack back into place. He rolled his shoulders to ensure it didn't impede his movement. "Hurry though. I need to help the guys with the cattle we mustered yesterday." A radio handset crackled from a belt loop near his hip. Hana heard a male voice give a sit rep to the rostered controller. Toby replied from another portable handset.

Hana's inspection of the hut took less than a minute. It contained a set of bunk beds at its highest point, although the uppermost occupant wouldn't fit if they slept on their side. A cupboard contained the essentials and a stack of firewood leaned against a pot belly stove in the corner. Hana pressed her fingers against a chimney which disappeared through a vent in the roof. She turned to face Tama. "Please, tell me where you were?" she pleaded. "This could all go away right now."

Tama pursed his lips and set his expression to one of insolent dismissal. "You're not my keeper, Ma," he said, his tone flat.

"No. I'm just someone who cares about you." Hana spun on her heel and left him standing alone in the middle of the hut. She let the wooden door clang behind her and strode towards Sonny.

David didn't speak as they descended the mountain, perhaps repelled by the cloud of fury and disappointment following his companion. He took furtive glances over his shoulder and kept his opinions to himself. Hana's temper communicated through her rigid seat to Sonny, and he jogged and fussed until they reached the valley.

Hana untacked the gelding and treated him to the equivalent of a luxurious sponge bath as she considered her next move. She knew what to do but shied away from executing the dangerous maneuver. Tama wouldn't thank her, but neither would the recipient of her next phone call.

96

Buckle

Hana sifted through her phone contacts as Sonny gave a gargantuan buck and cantered across the paddock. He inserted himself into a group of grazing horses, enjoying a free day after their muster. Hana peered at the number on the screen and her finger hovered over the call button. A splinter transferred from the wooden fence and wedged itself beneath the tender skin of her wrist as she balanced her arm on the top rail.

"You need to just call it," she told herself out loud. "This is where it all started." Before she could provide another three reasons it was a terrible idea, she depressed her index finger and a plaintive ringing issued from the speaker. A hawk trawled the sky overhead, searching for lunch amid the scrubby grass. A mouse skittered beneath a hay bale, leaned at Hana's feet. She jerked aside and waited for the call to connect.

"Hi." The female voice held the gentle resonance of authority. Caution slowed the woman's speech and added an undertone.

Hana took a deep breath and launched into her story. "This is Hana Du Rose," she began. "I saved your number when you called about Tama not showing up for his shift." She paused to swallow and ploughed onward, determined to free the idiot boy from a noose created by his own hands. And his rampant libido. "I'm sure you've seen the news broadcasts and the public appeal by Detective Marley." She left off the rest of his title in a silent, futile rebellion. "I've discovered Ari White died around ten o'clock on the Sunday before you phoned me. Tama won't tell me where he was, so I need to confirm it for myself."

"Wait a minute." A door slammed and outdoor noises added themselves to the call. Tama's fire chief had stepped outside for a moment. Hana heard her swallow before resuming their conversation. "What's your plan?"

Hana blinked and frowned as Sonny followed Polly like a half ton shadow. They ambled to a locust tree at the edge of the paddock and sheltered beneath it. Sonny's muzzle drooped, but Polly yawned and shook her head, ever watchful. Hana cleared her throat. "My plan is to ask the woman Tama spent Sunday night with to make a statement to the police."

"Right." The clipped answer gave away nothing. Hana's lips parted as she prepared to demand a contact number for the office administrator Tama had mentioned many times. Privacy laws made it unlikely, but she'd already prepared an answer for that. She would offer her own number and ask the chief to encourage the girl to use it.

"I saw the news." The chief cleared her throat and Hana heard bird song and the muted strains of a coffee machine. "Is he okay?"

"Not really." Hana sighed. "He's terrified. A man is dead, Tama's in hiding, I got beaten up, and one of my children is under a constant threat of kidnap."

"What?" The word burst from the speaker.

"It's complicated." Hana exhaled. "It began with Tama asking questions about a fire which occurred here just over seven years ago. Now, it's become about a custody battle for our foster daughter." She flapped her hand to discourage a bot fly, which showed too much interest in her floral shirt. "I can't explain everything over the phone. But Tama's in more trouble than you can imagine. Otherwise, I wouldn't ask you to break all kinds of trust. You also need to investigate a man called Sid Alderbank. He knew Tama was looking into the fire."

"Sid? He works in the station."

"Yeah, well he's involved somehow."

"Right." The fire chief's voice became a whisper filled with regret. "And you're saying Tama won't reveal where he was, not even to stop the police charging him with murder?"

"Nope." Hana failed to hide her disgust. "Stupid boy." She inhaled and prepared to request the phone number she needed. But before she could formulate the sentence, the woman detonated her intentions.

"I'm sorry," the chief said. "I'll contact them now and fix it."

"Contact who?" Hana closed her eyes and shook her head. The chief had said *them*. She'd contact *them*. It sounded like more than one woman, and Hana gritted her teeth.

"Will you ask them to call me right back?" She kept her tone pleasant while berating a mental image of her randy son.

"I don't know if they'll do that." The woman sounded unsure. "But I'll call the police detective as soon as you ring off and I'll tell him Tama spent the night with me."

Hana stared at the screen, her lips parting in shock. Paulie's Sheila wandered across and lipped at the brim of Hana's hat before resting her muzzle against her shoulder. Hana's head emptied of suitable retorts and she pressed the disconnect icon with a shaking finger. Having killed the call, she prayed Tama's boss would do the right thing. She replayed her conversation with him at the school when he'd mentioned his broken arm. He'd already told her the identity of his love interest months ago and she'd fumbled an opportunity.

He spoke often of the office girls and other women he seemed to tow behind him in a misplaced sexual haze. But he'd only once mentioned his chief, and he'd been high on painkillers that day. He'd told her she was female, and that he loved her. And Hana had dismissed his garbled declaration as a passing phase.

She lurched for her hat as Sheila's teeth closed around it to drag it over the fence. "Have this instead," she said with a sigh, removing a slice of hay and dropping it into the paddock. The hat forgotten, Sheila buried her muzzle in the treat. She didn't see the regret in Hana's expression or how her irises glittered with unshed tears.

Tama had trusted her once.

And she'd failed the test.

97

Show Ring Number Holder

Hana kept her phone switched on all day, waiting for a call from the detective, which didn't come. She busied herself in the museum until Leslie returned from church with the children.

"Sam sends his regards." Leslie raised a bushy eyebrow and tilted her chin forward to stress the sarcasm in her statement.

"That's nice." Hana closed the lid of a glass cabinet after straightening a bonnet which once graced the regal head of Logan's great grandmother. She double checked the catch before turning the ornate brass key in the lock.

"He didn't." Phoenix frowned and splayed her tongue across the lollipop in her fingers. Red dye coated her lips and spread onto her chin. "Lying is naughty, Nonie. You'll go to hell."

"Okay." Hana placed her hand on her daughter's head and turned her to face the office. "We need a private word."

"Fine!" Leslie narrowed her eyes at the tattle tale. After anchoring herself on her pointy left shoe, she turned her body in an arc and set off towards the door. "Who wants gluten-free scones?" she demanded, chucking the comment behind her in a scattergun effect which hooked both Mac and Edin. They pattered after her without a second thought.

"What about me?" Phoenix popped the lollipop from between her lips and widened her eyes. She blinked as though denied oxygen. "I like scones."

"In a minute." Hana steered her towards the door and closed it behind her. "Sit." She indicated her chair.

Phoenix clambered onto the worn cushion and grinned as the seat swiveled to face the door. Hana raised a hand in warning, grimacing as she clamped her teeth over her lower lip. Phoenix dropped the sticky sweet onto the desk as she used both hands to force the chair back round to face her mother. Hana rose onto the balls of her feet to identify the sheet of paper bearing Logan's family crest, now blighted by a shiny red traffic light in its centre. She exhaled and leaned against the photocopier.

"Oh." Phoenix winced as she lifted the lolly stick and the sheet rose with it. She wasted valuable moments tearing it free and peering at the thin film of paper stuck to its reverse side. "Is this important?" She wafted the handwritten letter, which had been an outpouring of gratitude for a sizeable donation.

"Not anymore," Hana remarked. She sighed. "I need to speak to you about hell."

"Oh." Phoenix flattened her lips and jerked her head back. She dropped her hand, not noticing when the lollipop glued itself to her skirt. "Have you been there?"

"Not yet." Hana dragged her thoughts away from Tama's plight and collected suitable words into a coherent sentence. "Why are you so concerned about it? This seems to be a fresh fear."

Phoenix nodded. "Yeah. You can go to hell for cussing, complaining and getting into trouble." She counted the sins on her fingers. Hana prepared to speak, but the child hadn't finished. Her list moved into double figures, and she paused after twenty, having run out of fingers and toes. "Lots of things," she concluded. "Heaps and heaps of them. Not going to church is a big one." She tapped her forehead. "I'll use my noggin for such a massive sin."

"Right." Hana pursed her lips. "And who told you this? Not Pastor Sam."

"Going naked is another one." Phoenix glanced sideways at the desk and reached across to lift a pencil. "Can I start again and write them down for you?"

"I'm good." Hana fixed her gaze on a watermark staining the ceiling. The laundry sink on the first floor had overflowed two summers ago. She'd intended to get onto a ladder and patch it after the plumber fixed the leak, but hadn't yet found the time. Her mind whirred with replies for her daughter's latest topic and she wished she'd waited for Logan. He always knew the right things to say.

"Can I go now?" Phoenix tore the lollipop from her skirt and waved it in the air. "It's furry. Should I still eat it?"

Hana shook her head. "Probably not. Look, sweetheart," she began, her tone soft. "None of the things you listed are a single reason for anyone to go to hell."

Phoenix's eyes widened, and she rolled them in their sockets. "What if you did all of them at the same time? Mrs Collingwood is Scotlandish like Poppa Robert." Her features sharpened with intensity as she offered a reasonable impression of the old lady. "Nay lying!" she barked. "Nay thieving! Nay shagging thy neighbour's wife!"

"No! Thank you!" Hana crossed the narrow space in three steps and covered her daughter's mouth with her hand. "She did not say shagging!"

"Did!" Phoenix's eyes bugged over Hana's index finger, which muffled her protest. "Nay murder!"

"That's the ten commandments. But not quite like that."

"It's Scotlandish." Phoenix fluttered her eyelashes and pouted. She poked out her tongue and gave the lolly a tentative lick before wrinkling her nose. "I don't want Tama to go to hell. Did he kill a boy like it said on the radio?"

"No." Hana sighed and sank her bottom onto the desk. She wouldn't have done it if Will or Logan were present, and guilt forced her to rise again. She lifted Phoenix into her arms and took her place in the chair, snuggling the child against her chest. "Tama didn't kill anyone. The police will realise that soon and stop searching for him."

"So, he won't go to hell?"

Hana winced. "Not for that. If anyone can commit all ten sins at the same time, it's him. But look, the things you're saying are coming across as judgmental. We need to keep our eyes on ourselves and what we're doing. Worry less about other people and more about our own behaviour."

"But you don't go to church anymore." Phoenix sat upright and turned to face Hana. "You keep bunking off."

"No, I don't." Hana frowned, hearing Leslie's stock phrase emerge from her daughter's lips. "I go to church plenty. I've missed two weeks, and God knew exactly where I was and what I was doing. He's quite capable of telling me he's not happy about that. It's between him and me."

Phoenix frowned and peered at her red stained fingers. She took a moment to process Hana's revelation. "So, if I don't do lying and thieving and shagging and murdering, I'll be okay?"

"Please, stop saying shagging?" Hana hissed. "Mrs Collingwood didn't say shagging."

"She shouted it from her wheelchair at the front." Phoenix's chin wobbled. "Otherwise, I'm lying and I can't lie because I don't want to go to hell."

Hana groaned. "What does Wiri think about all this?" she asked, counting on the boy's common sense to piggy-back her out of the widening pit of confusion.

"He doesn't care." Twin dimples appeared in Phoenix's cheeks as she frowned. A half tooth behind her bottom lip heralded the first sign of adolescence. "He wants to go there just to see if Kane arrived. Then he'll come back and help me get to heaven."

Her children's complicated dynamic baffled her and left Hana speechless. They reasoned far beyond their reach and explored concepts she hadn't worried about at their age. She pressed a kiss to Phoenix's forehead. "Try to be your best self," she assured her, though the words sounded hollow. "It's all we can do. Love God and be kind to other people. That's all."

Phoenix poked a red tongue from between her lips and licked at the sticky mess hugging her left cheek. "That sounds easier," she concluded. "I can do that."

"Right, well, no more texting inflammatory messages to Nonie from my phone," Hana concluded. "It causes too much trouble."

"Okay." Phoenix beamed at her through lips the colour of blood. She straightened, shoulders already lightened of their load. "Please, may I go upstairs for scones now?"

Hana nodded. "Yeah. Let me lock up here."

"She said shagging."

"Yes, but *you* don't!" Hana flapped her hand at the child's bottom as Phoenix hopped from her knee. She accepted she'd never discover the origin of her daughter's fears of perpetual damnation. When she glanced at her palm, she discovered the lollipop welded to it.

❧ ❧

L ogan returned from Hamilton as the clock struck six. Phoenix showed her disdain for the milkshake stain around Wiri's lips and the fluffy skunk in his arms. "We bought you a meerkat," he declared, delving into a cloth bag swinging from his arm. Edin frowned at the miniature horse, which zinged through the air and hit her in the face.

"What's that?" Phoenix jabbed her index finger at the sloth, which Logan crawled under the dining table to present to his son.

"A sloff." Wiri balled up the cloth bag and shoved it into the bottom of the pantry. "They did nothing but hang from a tree like this." He pranced on the spot with both arms raised. His head sagged and his tongue rolled sideways from between pink lips.

"I didn't know you went to the zoo." Phoenix narrowed her eyes at Hana as though holding her responsible for the subterfuge.

"Ah well." Logan sank into a dining chair with a shrug. "You were supposed to come with us, but you set Attila the Hun on us."

"I did what?" Phoenix edged closer and Hana gave a frantic shake of her head from behind her daughter.

Logan wrinkled his nose. He drew his phone from his pocket and patted his knee. "Cuddle me and I'll show you photos of your meerkat. It's called Hans."

"Hans." Her features smoothed into a serene smile as she regarded her new toy. She clambered onto Logan's lap to inspect the contents of his photo gallery. Wiri appeared at her shoulder and they continued their own conversation. They scrolled through images of Bodie's children lined up next to a giraffe. Wiri held Hope's hand and used her as a buffer between him and Jas. Edin showed no interest. She crawled beneath the dining table with Mac and wrapped his sloth's long arms around her fuzzy horse. When the graze on her knee grew too sore to take her weight, she thudded onto her bottom and peered at the brown scab.

"The certain person at Bivouac Four might be off the hook." Hana pushed a mug of steaming coffee towards her husband. "It's both a great and terrible thing."

Logan lifted an eyebrow in anticipation as Hana spoke in code to him. Mac's deafness robbed them of the anonymity of sign language once the family learned it for his benefit. She told her story using complicated words she hoped none of them yet knew. Logan shook his head towards the end, not surprised by Tama's latest get-out-of-jail card. He sighed and rubbed his eyes with his left hand. "I delivered the DNA samples to my friend in Hamilton. He started the test this afternoon and promises to have results in three days at the earliest. I picked up a kit and dropped it in the postbox at the address you gave me. We'll have the facts soon, and then we'll take things from there."

Hana nodded. She stripped potato skins with a knife and dropped the creamy vegetables into a saucepan on the table. Water droplets splashed up with each new addition. "What should we do about Lana?" she demanded, her voice low. "Should I keep somebody away from school this week, just in case she stages another snatch?"

"No." He blinked and sighed. "She's safer there than here. The school has security and her teacher knows not to let her out of her sight." He glanced around the kitchen and his gaze wandered to the scenic panorama through the wide window. "You're too remote up here. And the hotel is filled with a constant stream of strangers. It only takes a second." He paused at the expression of horror which passed across Hana's face. She bit her lower lip and dropped the last potato into the water with a splash. "It'll be okay," he promised. "Lana Alderbank won't do anything until after the pediatric appointment next week. By then, we'll have answers of our own."

"Okay," Hana conceded, her voice faint. "I hope so, Logan. I hope so."

98

Girth Sleeve

Hana pored over an online news article about the two men who'd assaulted her at the hotel. She tutted with indignation at the extensive list of charges for which the judge remanded them in custody pending a trial. "It doesn't even mention what they did to me! Or how they intended to take Edin from school!" Her voice rose and Will stared at her over his spectacles. Her pique echoed around the workroom. "I still have the bruises."

"At least they're locked away now," he concluded. "I'd call that a result."

Hana grunted. "A result," she grumbled. "Not for me." Four painful days had passed since Logan delivered the DNA samples to his contact at the laboratory. Dean had called her about the kit delivered to him at the hospital, alongside a cryptic note relating to Edin. One day remained before Lana forced her to comply with the terms of their agreement. She'd assured Dean he wouldn't need to get involved, but with each passing day, she doubted herself.

Hana entered *Finlaggan* into the search function for the hundredth time and scrolled past items she'd already reviewed.

"Have you scanned the hotel plans yet?" Will laid down his magnifying glass and removed the cloth gloves from his left hand.

"In a minute," Hana promised. "I'm waiting for Bodie to let me know when the detective accepts the statement about Tama's whereabouts on the night Ari White died."

Will grunted. "And until then, you intend to surf the interweb and do no work? Those two things are not synonymous. You don't need your son to phone you in order to do your job."

Hana twisted her lips and forced herself to rise. "Fine," she grumbled. "I'll scan them now, but you'll need to switch places with me. I can't stand in front of the copier without tripping over your wheels."

"Rude." Will activated the switch on the arm of his chair and the motor whirred. He performed a precise turn which spun him into Hana's space. She dodged sideways at the last second and dragged her chair with her. "Pass those documents over here," he demanded, his tone curt. Hana pulled cotton gloves over her fingers before touching them.

"You're in pain." His gruffness betrayed his discomfort, and it kick-started Hana's compassion. "Can I get you something?"

Will tutted and used a twisted index finger to push his spectacles further up his nose. "A coffee from the restaurant might help these big tablets go down my throat, please?" He scratched around in a bag strapped to his wheelchair and extracted a translucent pot. The pills rattled inside as he set it on the desk.

"Okay." Hana stripped off her gloves and navigated the narrow space between the back of Will's chair and the workbench fixed to the rear wall. She checked for her bank card hidden between two layers of her phone case. "Milk and two sugars." She spoke as much to herself as to him, knowing his order after years of working with him. She closed the workroom door behind her and ventured into the reception area.

Detective Inspector Marley stood in front of Hilda, his hands wedged deep in his trouser pockets. His stance carried an air of insolence. Hana glanced around him and released a sigh of relief. This time, he'd come alone.

Hilda spun to face her, eyes aglow with enjoyment. "Hi Hana," she said with a smile. "This gentleman asked for you." She replaced the handset on the desk phone. Red polish glittered on her manicured nails. Competence and purpose oozed from her pores. In less than a week, she'd hired new staff, fired two who missed their shifts due to hangovers, and revolutionised the running of the hotel. A young man hurried from the corridor leading to the kitchen, skidding on the floorboards in shiny shoes. He strode towards Hilda, already gushing before he reached the desk.

"I can't find her." He panted in between words as though he'd run.

"She's here, Timmy." Hilda gave her newest employee a benevolent smile. "I forgot to ask you to check the museum." She reached sideways and dragged a fistful of tissues from a box near her keyboard and pushed them towards him across the counter. He pocketed two and used a wad to mop his forehead. A smart navy jacket hung from his sloping shoulders, a glossy name tag fixed to the breast pocket. "Take a few minutes to cool off before the wedding party arrives." She checked her watch with a flourish. "Ten minutes should do it, and then you can start depositing suitcases in bedrooms."

"Wedding party?" Hana took a step forward and frowned. "You're doing weddings?"

"This is an emergency one." Hilda's smile exuded confidence. Her uniform matched Timmy's. A pleated skirt complimented his neat trousers in colour. "The couple lost their venue on short notice. Mr Charlton phoned yesterday and asked if we had capacity to help a friend of his. The telemarketing conference organisers set up in the old library yesterday and didn't require any extra space. I didn't think it would hurt to impress the event company directors." She offered Hana a covert wink, which excluded Detective Inspector Marley. "I sent through the invoice and his friend accepted it and paid up front. The wedding planner and florist are decorating the ballroom as we speak."

Hana shrugged. "Fair enough." She blew out a breath. "I'm just grateful I don't have to deal with any of this stuff anymore." She turned her attention to the detective. "How can I help you?"

He cocked his head. "I think I'd like to start again," he said, his tone less presumptuous than on his last visit. "Do you have time for a chat?"

Hana nodded. She glanced back at the closed museum door and imagined Will struggling behind it to sift through decades of Du Rose artifacts without complaint. "You'll have to walk with me," she said, stepping towards him. "I'm on an errand."

Hana led the way alongside the sweeping staircase and headed to the restaurant at the back of the building. The rear doors stood open to the courtyard and groups sat around the scattered tables, drinking coffee beneath the wide umbrellas which protected them from the sun's harsh kiss.

"It's a pleasant setting." The detective waved his arm towards a vacant table, and Hana winced.

"I don't have time to sit," she said. "I'm already in trouble with my boss for slacking today. If I don't return, he'll send out a search party." The man's visit unsettled her. Tama's face had disappeared from the news broadcasts, but the detective's casual air irritated her. She wanted him to tell her he'd accepted Tama's alibi and then leave.

Marley followed her to the bar, blinking at the change of ambience. The event company restored the dark wood panels and added heavy embossed wallpaper above them to dampen the light streaming from the courtyard. Navy paint absorbed the glow from hanging chandeliers. It gave the room a secretive feel, as though diners stepped from the sunshine into an 1800s club for prosperous gentlemen. Hana ordered Will's coffee and one for herself and the detective. His eyebrows rose into his hair as she produced her bank card and paid.

"I assumed you got everything for free," he said, sinking into a nearby armchair.

Hana joined him, tucking her card behind her phone and laying it on the table. The whirr of the coffee machine added the backdrop to their conversation. "That's what most people think," she agreed. "But we leased the hotel to focus on the farm and the stables. We own the land and building, but nothing else."

He tutted and leaned forward, resting his forearms on the table between them. His wrists protruded from beneath his shirt sleeves, thin bones with knotty joints. "Can I call you Hana?" he began, his voice soft. She shrugged, tensing against a latent warning note behind the cordiality. "I'm Craig," he continued. "And I regret the circumstances of our first meeting."

Hana leaned back in her seat and observed him. Years of marriage to Logan had taught her when to remain silent. She didn't always succeed, but congratulated herself as she folded her arms across her chest and waited. The detective cleared his throat. "We received a phone call from a woman willing to vouch for Tama during the period we think Ari White met his death. I collected her statement this morning and can't see why she'd have any reason to lie."

Hana ground her teeth against her tongue to prevent her interrupting. When she released it, pain shot up both sides of her jaw and into her head. It had taken him four and a half days to visit Tama's station chief, the man's ineptitude causing a fireball of dismay to settle in her stomach. He'd called in to see her only because he happened to pass by on his journey south.

"When did she contact you?" She spat the question through clenched teeth.

Another throat clearing. "It's irrelevant." He flapped his hand in front of his face. "We've cancelled the warrant for your son. I thought you'd like to know."

"Thank you." Hana blinked as the barista set a cardboard tray in front of her. Three cups nestled in its molded compartments. She nodded to him and rose, dumping the police officer's coffee on the table in front of him. "So, you'll leave our boy alone now?"

"I still need to speak to him." He rose, snagging his cup in a fluid motion and lifting it to his lips. "We don't understand why Ari died wearing a cap belonging to Tama, or why we discovered his belongings in the boy's room."

"And you never thought to ask." Hana's lips twisted into a knot of disbelief. "This is about much more than a poor boy who died on the riverbank. My son is a detective in Hamilton. He's made numerous requests to speak with you over the last week, and you've rebuffed him. I suggest you listen to him." She lifted the cardboard tray and strode from the restaurant, hoping Craig Marley didn't follow her. With two hot drinks in her hand, she knew she couldn't trust herself not to act on impulsion. And drench him.

As she nodded to Hilda and pushed open the door to the museum, she lifted her drink and took a fortifying sip. Her phone trilled in her pocket and her hand shook. When she deposited her drink back in the tray and fished the phone from her pocket, Logan's number flashed on the screen. She stepped into the museum and let the door close behind her. The sip of coffee turned to acid on her taste buds.

99

Mounting Block

"Caroline and Jennifer are sisters, aren't they?" The door creaked closed behind her and she leaned against it. Will's gentle humming of a waiata carried across the quiet space.

"Definitely siblings." Logan breathed as though he talked while walking. She registered the click of his heels against concrete.

Hana laid the tray of coffee on a nearby cupboard. She lifted her right hand and flattened her fingers, trying to hold them steady but watching them vibrate as adrenaline coursed through her blood. "I'm relieved but also shocked," she admitted. Tentative steps took her towards the first of the archival cabinets. She peered beneath the glass at a letter written by Henri Du Rose to his wife, Phoenix. "What now?" She turned and leaned her spine against the wooden lid, jerking as it shifted in silent objection to her weight.

"Not sure." Logan cleared his throat. "The boy is fed up and wants to move again. What do you suggest?"

Hana warmed beneath the glow of her husband seeking her advice. She straightened her shoulders and imparted the detective's news to him. "Tama can come home. Marley wants to speak to him now about the clothing at Ari's place and the cap he wore. But they believe he didn't kill him because he was elsewhere."

Logan grunted. "Yeah, somewhere he shouldn't have been."

"Not our problem." Hana wafted her hand through the air, trying to catch minute dust motes as they danced in a light beam sneaking under the blinds. They moved away from her touch and she strode across the wooden floor to correct the source of corrosive light. The bottom rung of the blind tapped the windowsill as it lowered in obedience to Hana's tugging on its string. "That's between him and his chief. They can sort out their own issues." She twisted her lips in thought. "But it explains why she called me when he didn't show up for work. It makes sense now."

"Okay," Logan concluded. "I'll ride up to the hut and flush him out. Please, can you contact the detective and let him know?"

Hana turned back to the door before stopping herself. The soles of her sandals squeaked against the floorboards and Will ceased his humming. "No. I'll call Bo. Let him take the lead on this. I sent Marley away with a face like a slapped bum. Let's see how he likes playing second fiddle to a decent detective." She switched the phone onto speaker before calling up a text box and sending Bodie a message. Logan caught her groan as Bodie called her straight back, his icon strobing across the screen. "Bo's calling."

"All good." Hooves sounded in the background. "I'm trekking up there now. David lent me Polly for Tama to ride, so we should arrive back down here in about an hour." He rang off, leaving Hana to connect with her son.

"Tama's on his way home," Hana said. "Are you able to drive to our place to interview him? I don't trust that other clown."

Bodie snorted. "That other clown outranks me. Trumping him is akin to career suicide."

"Fine," she sighed. "He's hanging around here, anyway. Why don't you contact him and explain Tama won't speak to the police without you present?"

"I like that." Bodie's tone held a victorious lilt. "You're making me indispensable. But you realise he might refuse, as I have a conflict of interest."

"I don't see how." Hana lifted her cooling coffee and took a fortifying sip. "Tama is your stepfather's nephew. There's no blood relationship. Oh, that reminds me. Caroline and Jennifer are sisters. So, there's a whole other case for you too. Lana Alderbank stole Catherine Finlaggan from her pram in 1969."

Bodie blew a low whistle through his teeth. "Okay," he concluded. "I'm on it. See you in a couple of hours."

❦❦❦❦❦❦ ❦❦❦❦❦❦

Tama gave his statement to Bodie while Detective Inspector Craig Marley observed. Hana waited in the kitchen for them to emerge. She busied herself with more internet searching from Logan's laptop.

Leslie burst through the front door with a clatter as Hana sent another document to the printer in the home office. Leslie bustled across the room and slammed her index finger over the switch for the kettle. "I need a drink!" she exclaimed, hurling herself into the seat opposite Hana.

"Right." Hana's fingers tapped across the keyboard. "Lana Alderbank, isn't Lana Alderbank," she mused. "Her mother made her change her name to take over the running of Purple Primp. I found an article in an Auckland newspaper about it. Her name is actually Laura."

Leslie released an unladylike grunt. She patted the dining table with flattened fingers. "Listen to this!" she urged. "Raymond walked back into the hotel like he'd never left."

Hana shot upright, her shoulders aching from having hunched over the keyboard for too long. "Oh no!" she breathed. "Please tell me Logan hasn't seen him."

Leslie's eyes bugged like boiled eggs in her face. Excitement had given her brown complexion a ruddier hue. Sweat beaded on her forehead. "He saw him alright. Bounced the dude off the premises like a rubber ball." She cackled and squeezed her eyes closed. "He reminds me so much of his father. Nobody got the better of Reuben Du Rose." She released a sigh laced with lust for a man who'd never looked her way. Her paws lifted as though she caressed an imaginary bottom in her palms.

Hana made a gagging sound. "I don't want the images your dirty mind is creating," she complained. She leaned forward. "Is Logan injured?"

Leslie blew out a breath laden with equal measures of air and spit. Droplets spattered across the table. "Na, kōtiro. And he left the man's head on his shoulders, so that's something. But I'd pay good money to hear what he said to Raymond as he shoved him off the bottom step."

Hana exhaled and feared for Hilda's good opinion of her. She should have guessed it wouldn't last long. Leslie jerked her head towards the hallway and the closed double doors to the lounge. The rumble of voices reached her keen ears, and she grinned. "I'll brew tea for the boys in there," she said, making the table take her weight as she heaved herself to her feet. It groaned in complaint.

"No." Hana narrowed her eyes. "Leave them alone, please. I need this whole thing over. Bodie will ask if they want anything."

"Spoil sport," Leslie grumbled under her breath. She made herself a mug of coffee and dumped a second one next to Hana's elbow. "What are you doing?"

"Prevaricating." Hana shut down the browser and lowered the lid with care. "I need to inform Lana, or Laura, that we don't require her statement. Her blackmail has failed." She ran through a series of preparatory sentences in her head. Each one missed the mark.

"Do it now," Leslie suggested. She waggled her eyebrows in a curious, hairy dance. "I'll wait with you, just for support." She placed her coffee on the table and sank into a chair, resting her clasped hands across her stomach.

Hana tutted. "I can't do it with you staring at me!" She blinked as Leslie tilted her bottom upward and shuffled the chair so it faced the door. Her left hand swung back towards the table and her puffy fingers sought the mug handle like crabs side winding across a beach.

Hana lifted her phone and found Lana's number. She licked her lips before dialling and lifting the device to her ear.

"What do you want? Your appointment isn't until tomorrow." The tinkle of a cash register closing echoed in the background and Lana thanked someone. "Give me your email address and I'll write my statement and send it to you first thing in the morning."

Hana clenched her toes beneath the table. She rose and pushed her chair back, unable to sit still. Leslie turned her head to ensure she caught every word of the one-sided conversation, and Hana resisted using the speakerphone. It tied up her hands and gave her a sense of claustrophobia. She eyed the doorway, but Leslie had stretched her legs in front of it. "It's not about that," Hana said, her words sticking in her throat.

Lana gave a distinct huff and launched herself onto the offensive. "I knew you'd play games," she snarled. "No DNA, no statement. Your kid can rot in prison."

Hana cleared her throat. "He won't, because he has an alibi." She paused to let the wind leave Lana's sails and waited for her to stop her futile ranting. "We don't need your statement. I'm also sorry to tell you that Caroline is unlikely to be your sister. Her name is Catherine Finlaggan, and it's possible your mother stole her from her pram when she was six weeks old. It was all about the birth certificate your father entrusted to Antoinette Du

Rose for safe keeping. The gold didn't come from the General Grant. Only your father knows where he got it. It's evident he didn't realise Antoinette couldn't read, or that she wouldn't live long enough to do more than hide the box. I suspect the police will reopen the file regarding Catherine's kidnapping. They'll want to speak to your mother."

Leslie turned in her chair and gaped at Hana as silence greeted her revelation. She lifted her shoulders to her ears and spread her hands in a mute question. Then a click marked the end of the call. Hana peered at her phone. "She hung up on me." Her tone held a flat quality. She hadn't enjoyed the task and wished she'd persuaded Logan to do it. "I thought I'd feel like celebrating." Her lower lip curled down into a dissatisfied expression. With her left hand, she pressed her fingers over the healing cut on the back of her head. "But I just feel really sad."

Leslie shrugged and dropped her shoulders, her interest waning. She'd ended up with a ringside seat to nothing. "Is Logan gonna keep his room at the hotel?" she demanded. "I wanted to borrow it when my daughter from Australia visits in September."

"We've given it no thought," Hana admitted. "The ensuite bathroom is unusable."

Leslie wrinkled her nose. "I know your tane thinks we don't appreciate what he's done for us, but it's not true. He's a good boy."

Hana cocked her head. "Maybe you should tell him that once in a while."

Leslie blew out another wet breath, half raspberry. "Na, I don't think so. He's more like Reuben when he's stroppy. I like things as they are."

100

Endurance Crupper

Hana sat in the passenger seat of Bodie's car as they drove through the gates of the residential home. She fidgeted with the strap of her handbag as it provided a fortifying weight in her lap. Logan hadn't wanted her to make the visit, but Jennifer had insisted she act as the buffer between compassion and officialdom. Bodie had agreed.

"What happened at the appointment with Dean yesterday?" Bodie screwed his head around to peer through the rear windscreen as he reversed into a vacant spot. "I forgot to ask."

"Edin, let him take some blood." She pulled open the flap of her handbag and checked inside for her phone. "I still can't believe it. He's amazing with her."

"But he thinks she has Celiac disease?" Bodie secured the handbrake and pushed the gear lever into park.

Hana nodded, the movement shallow. "Yes. The local doctor missed it. We're officially the gluten-free Du Roses."

Bodie chuckled. He turned to face her, his expression serious. "Thanks for backing me on this, Mum. I got to stand front and centre on a current result and a cold case. Craig Marley has asked me to join his team in Hamilton on a permanent basis."

Hana tugged a red curl from her shoulder and inspected the ragged ends. "We should celebrate on Thursday evening. After Amy's hairdressing session with me and Mel."

"I have a better idea." Bodie dipped sideways and pressed a kiss to her cheek. "It's Easter next weekend and we're both on leave. Why don't we drive up with the children on Friday and make a weekend of it?"

"I'd love that so much." Hana cupped his chin in her hand and smiled. She could navigate the issue of church versus the Sikh temple another time. Her mind swooped to Phoenix's Easter plans. Her daughter had signed up to lead a chocolate egg hunt for the congregation's toddlers. Hana pushed her worries aside. She promised herself she'd make it work somehow. For her children.

Everything seemed to take too long at the reception desk. Hana signed a visitor's book and donned a name badge. She inspected the signatures above hers, wincing when she didn't notice the one she sought. Her knees trembled as she slipped her left hand through the crook of Bodie's arm.

An assistant led them along a corridor which reeked of floral cleaning fluid. It valiantly attempted to disguise the musty scent of old gravy. "In here," she said with a smile. "Gentleman wearing the bow-tie."

Hana stepped across the threshold of the open door into a combined lounge and dining room. She glanced back at Bodie after surveying the occupants dotted around the room in high backed chairs. Her eyes glittered with emotion. "She isn't here," she whispered. "We should wait."

Bodie straightened his smart uniform jacket and urged her forward. "Jennifer texted. She said she didn't want to hear it again," he whispered. "She'll come later but she asked if you could speak to him. Not me."

Hana's stomach twisted like a crocodile spinning its prey, though she hadn't eaten since the day before. "This wasn't what we agreed," she hissed, trying to turn back towards the corridor.

"But it's what we have to work with." Bodie took her arm and edged her towards the circle of empty chairs facing a television. Nerves assailed her, but she put one foot in front of the other until she reached a lone elderly man watching reruns of a black and white movie.

"Mr Finlaggan." He started, and she dipped her torso to accept the slender fingers he offered. Her hand closed around his and she experienced a moment of awkwardness when he didn't let go. Tiny bones as fragile as a kitten's gripped with unexpected strength. Headier food scents drifted across as lunchtime approached. A care assistant wiped the nearby dining tables with a pink cloth. She collected the crumbs into her hand and flicked the rest onto the patterned carpet.

"Sit, sit." Mr Finlaggan bobbed his head at the upright seat next to him and Hana obeyed. He kept hold of her hand and she rested her wrist on the arm of the chair between them. A nearby fan blew in a wide arc, spreading fetid air laced with the haze of mince and onions. "Have you met my wife?" He patted the empty chair on the other side of him. "Say hello, Deirdre." He glanced back at Hana with a conspiratorial smile. His blue irises sparkled from behind hooded lids. "I understand she's gone," he whispered. "But if I act mad, I might get the best drugs." He effected a wink, which made Hana smile.

She took a deep breath, and the joviality slipped from her expression. "I'm here about your daughter, Mr Finlaggan." She tugged her fingers from his grasp and reached into her handbag for the yellowed birth certificate. Dust motes sprang from the folds as she opened the fragile document with care. He cocked his head and frowned. Strands of white hair slipped from his bald pate and hung beside his left ear.

"Jenny? What's happened to Jenny?"

Hana gulped, her head shaking in a slow, uncertain motion. "Nothing." She raised her hand in placation and glanced at the care assistant. The woman bent to wipe the plastic covered seats at the table and didn't respond to Mr Finlaggan's obvious distress. "Jenny's fine. She's visiting later. I'm here about Catherine."

He blinked and stilled. The lights behind his blue eyes winked out, and Hana's panic increased as he sat motionless and staring. Then he exhaled, causing the whiskers of his white mustache to flutter. Hana sensed his world restarting again, guilt blossoming across her chest at the agony she'd caused. "Someone stole Catherine," he said, his tone dull. "We walked to the court house to register her birth and stopped on the way home to buy a cake. Deirdre left the pram parked outside the shop with me and Jenny. But she fainted, and the shopkeeper came to fetch me. I returned minutes later to check on the girls and Catherine had gone." He released a gargantuan sigh and shook his head as though to dispel the threatening cloud of memories which circled him. His stilted words revealed a story told many times over in the intervening years. "They took the baby and Deirdre's handbag. He leaned sideways and patted the delicate paper. "The birth certificates were inside it. That must be a copy." He closed his eyes and leaned his head back against the corduroy fabric of the seat. "We never saw our Cathy after that. She'd be fifty two now."

Hana's lower lip trembled. A memory raced to the fore of her brain, dragged from the annals of her and Logan's shared history. She'd sacrificed herself to save him and faced the prospect of never seeing her baby daughter again. She blew out a ragged breath, and the sheet bounced in her hand. "This is Catherine's original birth certificate," she whispered, stumbling over the words. "Our museum curator has verified it through his contact at the Department of Internal Affairs. We discovered it recently on our property in the north Waikato. We believe my husband's aunt kept possession of it, and we think we know who Catherine is."

"Is?" He blinked and pushed himself straighter in his seat. An involuntary twitch uncrossed his ankles, and he placed the soles of his leather slippers square on the carpet. "You know Catherine?"

Hana blew out a breath through pursed lips. She paused, regretting the hope which burgeoned in his rheumy eyes. "It's complicated," she began, "but yes. We believe she grew up on the property and Logan's family raised her as their own. When Antoinette died, Reuben continued to parent her until she left for university."

"University?" Mr Finlaggan puffed out his thin chest. His green bow-tie wobbled beneath his Adam's apple. Age spots dotted his forehead like snowflakes. "So, she did well then? A bright girl?" His chin trembled, creating a series of dents in his paper-thin skin.

Hana gave a reluctant nod. "She became a teacher, a good one, by all accounts." Her mind reacted against the next part of Caroline's sorry tale, and her heart rebelled. She backtracked, searching for a different route. "Mr Finlaggan, my husband's family name is Du Rose, but Catherine arrived with the name Caroline Marsh. Do you recognise either of those names?"

He gave a slow shake of his head. His stubbled cheeks acquired a sickly pallor. "I don't recall either of those." A tear slid from the corner of his right eye and tracked a meandering descent through the grey hairs. "Du Rose, you say? And they know who stole her?"

Hana shrugged and shook her head. "I'm sorry, Mr Finlaggan, but nothing is certain. It's all speculation. Anyone able to tell the truth is long gone. Antoinette went away for a time and returned alone in the late 1960s. Then Caroline arrived. Sorry," she corrected herself, "Catherine arrived. Antoinette kept this birth certificate along with a tablet of gold leaf." Hana held the paper on her palm like an offering and Mr Finlaggan leaned forward to peer at it. "It belongs to you." He flopped back in his seat, a sigh of exhaustion wetting his lower lip.

"So long ago," he said. "We'd given up hope."

"I understand." Hana laid the birth certificate on his lap. She reached out with tentative fingers and caressed the age spotted hand resting on the arm of the chair. Bodie's presence offered comfort, though he'd said nothing. She realised with regret that she hadn't introduced him or included him in the awful conversation. A glance at his taut expression showed he'd rather be anywhere else on the planet but stirring up agony for a harmless old man.

"I'm sorry to cause you such pain," she whispered. Logan's stellar advice reverberated as an echo in her mind, urging her not to disturb an old man in his dotage with shades of reflected grief. She hung her head and wished she'd listened to him. "I'll leave you alone," she said. "I'm very sorry. Jenny will arrive soon."

Her dress tightened around her thighs as she rose and turned to leave. The birth certificate fluttered to the carpet. Hana looked back to find Mr Finlaggan's gnarled fingers gripping a clump of the chair's worn fabric. His jaw hardened and his eyes sparkled with pain. "Is she dead?" he demanded, his gentle baritone backed by a whimper. "Is my girl dead?"

"No." Hana sank into the chair and the faux leather squeaked beneath her. She recognised the cruelty in leaving him with only half a story. "Caroline is still alive. And you have a granddaughter. Her name is Edin." She picked up the copy of the birth certificate and placed it back on his knees. Reaching into her handbag, she pulled out a photograph of Caroline, Kane, and a baby Edin. She'd printed it from Caroline's social media page after taking guardianship of her daughter, hoping to inspire the child with happier memories of her absent parents. The picture usually occupied a frame on Edin's nightstand and Hana lifted it to show Mr Finlaggan.

His gasp confirmed what she already guessed from a photograph Jennifer emailed to her. Caroline was the image of her birth mother, the missing piece between the elfin blonde woman and the man in the chair. "It's my Deirdre!" His voice lifted to a strangled wail and the care assistant dropped her cloth onto the table and turned to face them. He gripped the frame in both hands and drew the glass to his lips. His eyes closed as he pressed a kiss to Caroline's smiling face. His chest hitched and a low keening began deep in his chest. "My Deirdre," he sobbed. "My Catherine."

101

Day Rug

"So, her name changed three times." Hana shook her head and slumped against the bench in Miriam's rose garden. She released a sigh and her lips turned downwards as she considered Caroline's trauma. "No wonder she became so messed up along the way. The poor woman didn't know who she was."

Logan grunted and shielded his eyes from the sun. He lifted his cowboy hat from the bench beside him and settled it onto his head after running his hand through his hair. "I should ban you from my office," he remarked. "And the museum. My family history isn't safe around you."

"Sorry. I can't help it." Hana closed her eyes and released another deep sigh. "It's left me feeling quite sympathetic towards Caroline after understanding her history. She was born as Catherine Finlaggan, stolen by Lana Alderbank and renamed Caroline Alderbank. Then, Antoinette came across her while nannying in Auckland during a break from Reuben." She raised her eyebrow. "Perhaps after cheating with the unknown blond drover, or maybe because her husband loved Miriam. Either way, she rescued a child in danger and sent her to the family in the north as Caroline Marsh after the other little girl died." Hana shook her head. "What a tangled web."

Logan shrugged. "It's sad. Antoinette must have hidden the box in the shed at the back of the property, intending to give it to Caroline one day. But she died and Reuben never knew about it. He understood enough to send anyone away who used the surname Alderbank."

"Why change her name to Marsh, though?" Hana mused. "Why not Du Rose? It makes no sense. Antoinette and Reuben must have realised everyone assumed she'd played away and fell pregnant with Caroline. Your grandmother certainly did." She exhaled, and a frown bisected her brow. "The Alderbanks must have been terrifying enough to make her go through that for someone else's child. I wonder if she believed she'd taken Lana's daughter or if she realised she had a child which belonged to another family."

Logan blew out a low whistle and a myna bird answered him from a totara tree which sheltered the rose garden. "Based on Lana Alderbank's current behaviour, it doesn't take much imagination, does it? I got the impression she hated what her mother did to her, and yet she mirrors the same unhinged mentality. Family first. The same values as us, but backhanded." He used the heel of his boot to dig at a spiky puha lurking in the grass. Leslie would pull it up roots and all when she spotted it, turning it into a muscle rub during her next batch of rongoā. Logan flattened his lips and squinted sideways at Hana. "Who gets to tell Caroline all this?" He placed his hand over his heart. "Please say it's not me."

Hana shook her head and stared at a clump of fluffy leaved plantain which had invaded the lawn with its broad, protein filled leaves. "We don't need to do anything," she said, her tone soft. "I contacted her lawyer. He's driving Mr Finlaggan to the prison to meet her. Jennifer seems keen to accompany them. I hope it brings them all some peace."

Logan slipped his arm around Hana's shoulders and he tugged her against his ribs. His kiss against her temple warmed the skin, and she closed her eyes. "You're a good woman, Mrs Du Rose," he whispered. "Better than any of us deserve."

Hana checked her phone and slapped her left palm against her thigh. She rose from the bench and bent to kiss her husband. Her lips landed just shy of the healing cut. "Bo just arrived with the children. Are you okay to sit here for a while and I'll meet him in the car park?" Logan nodded and stretched out his long legs, relaxing on the bench. He shielded his eyes with his hand and watched the children playing a tag game on the grass. A bump against the underside of the bench made him dip forward to peer beneath it. Hana sighed and shook her head. "It's your youngest," she said. "I'll confiscate the game when I get back with the others."

"Okay." Logan leaned back with a sigh. "Tama texted earlier. He's arrived home. Said he's given Jordan notice to quit and his chief has suspended Sid Alderbank. He starts back at work tomorrow."

Hana punched the air with her fist. "I knew it! Sid Alderbank. No such thing as coincidence in this country. Two degrees of separation. I bet he suppressed the fire record because Lana asked him to."

Logan smirked and shook his head. He flapped his hand behind him. "You're such a conspiracy theorist. Go fetch your son."

"Mama!" Phoenix waylaid her by the jasmine arch leading through to the hotel. Her grey irises glittered with tears. "Jesus dies in a minute." She tilted her slender wrist to reveal the hands of her Mickey Mouse watch moving towards three o'clock. Mickey's inane grin conveyed a distinct lack of sympathy.

Hana turned to face her, bending at the waist and schooling her expression into one of serene control and competence. Behind her eyes, her mind ran in circles, wondering when her daughter might get the point of the Good Friday sacrifice.

"I know, sweetie," she soothed. "But he'll wake up again on Sunday. We talked about this, remember? I'm not buying plane tickets to Jerusalem."

Saliva burst from Phoenix's lips as they parted in a sob. "But we must help him. Quick!" Her voice rose in a wail and she pressed her palms against her mother's stomach. Her eyes narrowed as Wiri snorted at her. He stopped chasing Edin with Mac's sloth and collapsed onto his back with his elbows bent and his palms cupping his head. Phoenix's eyes narrowed, and she jabbed a finger towards him. "Mama! Wiri's laughing at Jesus! Tell him!" He grunted as Edin covered his face with Horsey's knitted body.

Hana glanced back at Logan as he dipped forward to persuade Mac from beneath the bench. The angle of his head told her he'd heard his daughter's outburst and opted out of providing a solution. They both knew she'd be all smiles in exactly forty-eight hours as she covered herself in chocolate egg.

Hana's heart clenched in her chest as her phone buzzed again in her pocket. "Bo and Amy are here with Jas and Hope," she said, forcing levity into her tone. She wished she possessed the words to disrupt her daughter's familiar Easter crisis, but only time and understanding could provide it. Even Sam had tried and failed. Hana held out her hand and smiled down at her daughter. "Come with me."

Phoenix shoved her hands behind her back and pouted. "Fine!" she snapped. "Bo's a police officer. He can help me save Jesus if you won't!" Her black curls bounced against her thin shoulders as she marched beneath the archway and stamped towards the car park. Logan's gaze met Hana's when she glanced back towards the bench. His irises danced with levity, and he clamped his teeth over his lower lip.

Hana lifted her index finger and jabbed it in his direction. "I'll get you later," she snarled.

Despite her tantrum, Phoenix was still a rule follower. She waited at the curb for Hana before crossing the car park to greet her half-brother and his family. Bo swung her into the air and she clamped her arms around his neck. Hana heard the low keening of her pleading Jesus' case to him.

"Hi Hanny." Jas pursed his lips for a kiss and let her wrap her arms around his neck. "I've grown since you last saw me," he declared. "Five centimetres."

"Wow." Hana kissed the top of his dark head before releasing him to embrace Hope. The elfin child resembled her Aunt Isobel with her glossy black hair and mahogany tinted complexion. Quiet and sedate, she mirrored Amy's poise as she beamed up at Hana and accepted her kiss.

"Where are the cousins?" Jas patted the camouflage combat pants encasing his hips and legs. A matching jacket from an army surplus store drowned his torso. "I need to do a roll call before we go to war."

Bodie rolled his eyes and shrugged at Hana. Jas couldn't comprehend the concept of aunts and uncles being younger than him. It was something else in a long line of things they'd given up trying to explain.

Phoenix frowned in Bodie's arms before wiggling her legs for release. She slid down his body and rounded on Jas. "War?" She cocked her head and folded her arms across her chest. "Do you do rescue missions?"

"All the time." Jas grinned at her, revealing missing incisors. His brown irises blazed with glee at her unusual interest in his army obsession. "Wanna be my sergeant major?"

Hana groaned. "Can we do it after the picnic?" Her voice held a strangled quality as she watched her daughter slip her hand through Jas' elbow. Phoenix rose onto tiptoes to whisper in his ear. Hope trailed behind them as the set a course for the rose garden.

"What's wrong?" Amy laid an arm across Hana's shoulders and kissed her cheek. "Trouble?"

Hana sighed and watched the coconspirators break into a run and jockey for dominance passing through the narrow arch.

"We need to persuade them to eat before breaking Jesus out of the Sanhedrin. I have a picnic ready in Miriam's rose garden. Leslie made cake. She and Alfie are joining us when he's had his nap."

"Huh?" Amy's head jerked back on her neck as she processed Hana's staccato sentences. She blinked, as though stunned. "Who's rescuing Jesus?"

"Oh." Bodie winced. He rubbed a hand across his mouth. "I forgot about Trauma Friday." His lips turned up in a grin. "Maybe Marcus could reason with her before next year? He's a vicar."

Hana gave an ineffectual wave of defeat. "So is Sam. But it's worth a try, I suppose." Her phone vibrated in her pocket and she slid it free. "Is this you again?" she asked, lifting the screen and shielding it from the sun with her hand.

"Nope." Bodie reached into the back of his car and hefted a box of snacks and fizzy drink into Amy's waiting arms. "I messaged you after we found a parking space. Must be someone else."

Hana groaned. "It's Lana Alderbank," she breathed. "Two texts saying she must meet with me."

Bodie's eyes widened as he slammed the boot lid and took the heavy box from his wife. "You can't speak to her!" he hissed. "She's part of an ongoing investigation. This is massive, Mum. Bigger than you realise."

Hana raised her phone in the air and shook it. "Then what do I tell her?"

"Tell who?" Logan's cowboy boots ground against the grit as he greeted the newcomers. He kissed Amy's cheek and nodded to Bodie. His eyebrow rose at the diabetes inducing contents of the box. "Want me to take that?"

"I'm good."

Hana tensed, waiting for the familiar awkwardness to descend over their joint gathering. She released her breath by degrees as the chirping of overhead birds banished its toxic influence on the gentle breeze.

"Cool. The children are excited." Logan turned and waited for Bodie to walk alongside him. They chatted about the weather as they traversed the car park and crossed the verge. Logan allowed Bodie and Amy to enter Miriam's rose garden ahead of him. The perfect gentleman. Then he ducked and stepped beneath the arch. Children's voices rose in an excited cheer.

"Cake!" Edin's shout sailed above the conifers and the kauri trees standing sentry over their hidden nook of wonder. "Want cake! And cheese! Cheese for Edie!"

"Prayers first!" Phoenix demanded, her tone petulant and forceful. "Then we're rescuing Jesus."

The tension left Hana's shoulders. Lana's text demands lost their potency beneath the headiness of family peace, and Hana dashed off a refusal before jamming her phone back into her pocket. She convinced herself that a page had turned and a pristine new leaf awaited a shiny future.

But it would have been a first for Hana Du Rose.

And she should have remembered that.

102

Kimblewick Bit

A my volunteered to put the giddy children to bed while Logan, Hana, and Bodie sought solace in the hotel bar. She waved them off at the front door before turning to her wrangling duties.

Hana sat in the back seat of Logan's truck, her brow furrowed as she watched the shrinking light over the porch. "I don't fancy her chances," she said, clicking her seatbelt into place. "Maybe I should have stayed to help."

"She's fine." Bodie smiled at her, tilting his head to stare between the seats. "A classroom filled with probationers can get quite silly." His eyes twinkled. "Or so she tells me. I'm sure she can wrestle six little kids into bed."

Hana ground her teeth and turned in her seat. "Have you met Edin?" she asked, her tone heavy.

She faced forward in time to catch Logan inspecting her through the rear-view mirror. His gaze implored her to cease treading the never-ending loop of worry and smooth his transition to friendship with Bodie. Hana dropped her chin in an acceptance of the challenge. This wouldn't have happened six months ago when the men couldn't stand to exist in the same room as each other.

The bar proved busier than Hana imagined. Resident guests mingled with locals to enjoy a glass of something with a basket of fries. She waved to the people she knew before picking the last vacant table outside in the courtyard. "I didn't know it got this much trade," she said, settling beneath the warmth of a patio heater.

Bodie nodded and sat down next to her. "They must go through a fair amount of gas," he remarked, twirling his fingers towards the heaters stationed next to each of the outdoor tables. Fairy lights turned the space into a wonderland alongside the flickering orange flames. Colourful blankets draped over the chairs for patrons who still felt the cold.

Hana lifted the patterned blanket from the back of her chair and wrapped it around her shoulders. "Fortunately, not our problem anymore," she remarked. A sigh escaped her lips. "This must be a real money-maker. I didn't know so many locals drove out here for a drink. I wish we'd thought of doing something like this."

Bo waggled his eyebrows. "And a time suck, getting it all set up every evening and finding someone willing to run it. Logan seems different without the hotel management hanging around his neck. It looks like an excellent decision from where I'm sitting."

"Yeah, you're right." Hana jerked as her phone vibrated itself across the table. She lifted it and stared at the text.

"Amy already admitting defeat?" Bodie grinned. "Perish the thought."

"No." The icy fingers of unease settled around Hana's heart and squeezed. She read the threatening text before turning her phone over onto its screen. She forced a smile onto her lips, pretending it was nothing for Bodie's benefit. But Lana's words burned like salt on a cut.

'You've ruined my life. I'm coming for you.'

She cleared her throat and leaned forward as Logan walked across the courtyard carrying a tray. He set a merlot in front of Hana and an orange juice next to Bodie. "Last of the big spenders," he joked, pulling out a chair on the other side of Hana. She eyed his soft drink and nodded. Her fingers shook as she lifted the merlot to her lips.

"At least I haven't let the side down," she quipped. "I'm out with a pair of lightweights."

Logan jerked his chin upward in response. "Early start tomorrow," he replied. Bodie's immersion into the Sikh faith prohibited intoxicants. Hana knew that even though her son didn't qualify his choice. Her phone buzzed again, and she forced herself not to look, wishing she'd left it at home. She slipped her hand beneath the table and laid it across Logan's thigh, grounding herself in his solidity.

Tama was safe, and Lana had lost her claim to Edin. Circumstance had stripped the Alderbanks of their power. Hana took a slug of her merlot, which proved too big in her haste. She choked and set the glass back on the table. A tickle rose into her throat and she dabbed her lips with the back of her hand. "I'll just nip to the bathroom," she said, her voice hoarse.

"You okay?" Logan frowned and cocked his head. Hana nodded, watching perception flare behind his grey irises. The flickering flame from the overhead heater turned them into the hue of polished granite.

"Fine," she replied. She laid the blanket over her chair and wove through the tables, back to the bar. A queue formed outside the ladies' toilet and she groaned and diverted to the hotel's dimly lit reception. She waved to the night receptionist and pushed her way into the bathrooms located behind the private corridor.

She used the toilet and flushed, taking the time to collect her thoughts. The main door gave a squeak of protest as someone else entered the room. The cubicle door next to Hana's clattered shut, and the lock clicked. She pushed back her shoulders and opened her door, walking forward to wash her hands beneath the warm water. The paper towel holder refused to disgorge more than a tuft of tissue and she busied herself pulling the rest free. The thing had jammed ever since the days of Miriam Du Rose's leadership. No one yet had replaced it, despite the luxurious makeover given to the bathrooms by the events company. Hana patted her hands dry with the tufts and reached into her pocket for her phone. She tutted, remembering placing it face down on the table. If Lana texted again in her absence, Logan would pick it up and turn it over. She tossed the fragments of paper towel into the rubbish bin beneath the sink unit. He knew her code and would unlock it. He'd see Lana's harassment before she'd had time to speak to him about it.

Hana turned and took one stride towards the door leading into the reception. She halted and apologised as the occupant of the cubicle adjoining hers pulled the door back and stepped into the walkway. The woman hadn't flushed the toilet, and it struck Hana as a momentary thought in the seconds after the knife slipped beneath her ribs and punctured her stomach.

It felt like a punch. The impact took her breath away in a smooth whoosh. She didn't realise she'd been stabbed until she glanced down at the blood cascading over the fingers which rose to investigate.

The woman didn't stay to survey the damage. She paused only to tug the purple headscarf over her hair and wrap it across her face like a niqab. The knife went into her pocket, the blade already retracted. The purple folds of her skirt absorbed the blood from her hands. Then she slipped into the reception area and glided through the front doors to the car park.

The receptionist smiled and bid her a good trip south, buying the story she'd told when she settled the bill for her hotel room minutes earlier. She glided down the front steps as though not touching the ground, unlocking the rented car she'd used since leaving hers at the panel beaters. A bite in the air heralded autumn, suiting her mood and her thirst for anonymity. A sliver of moon peeked from behind an angry cloud bank carrying rain. And she smiled for the first time in weeks.

Dear Reader,

I would love it if you could leave a review at your usual retailer.

I find the opinions of readers helpful and constructive. Reviews are the Holy Grail to an author as they cause our work to sink or swim. It is the bench mark for other readers and can determine whether our work will be successful and reach many or none. It doesn't have to be an essay or a literary criticism. A few words about what you liked would be most appreciated. The shortest review I ever received for my work was, 'Great,' accompanied by five stars and the longest was a whole video from a gorgeous woman in the USA. My favourite to date has to be the lady who said, '*I read until my eyes fell out.*' I keep looking at that one because it makes me laugh.
You can review on my website, ktbowes.com.
Go to the book's buy page where you can follow through to your own retailer and leave a review for me.

And hey, let me know when you've done it. I'd love to hear from you.

About the Author

K T Bowes is a bestselling teen and women's author.
Her novel, *A Trail of Lies*, was the winner of the genre award for Author's Cave in 2014.
Phoenix Du Rose was considered for the prestigious Ngaio Marsh awards for 2021 and *Her Quiet Legacy* in 2022.
K T Bowes is an Englishwoman in exile in New Zealand, swapping rugged cosmopolitan for mountain ranges and terrifying rivers. She loves Māori culture and has learned to weave flax using traditional methods. Her other passion is Rongoa Māori, which involves creating medicines from native plants. She is a student of Te Reo Māori.

You can find her hanging out on social media in the following places.
Check in and say hello. Maybe suggest she gets back to writing and stops watching cat videos.
FACEBOOK
https://www.facebook.com/NZauthorKTBowes/
TWITTER
https://twitter.com/ktboweswrites

INSTAGRAM
https://www.instagram.com/k_t_bowes

Also by this Author

The Hana Du Rose Mysteries Series:
Logan Du Rose
About Hana
Hana Du Rose
Du Rose Legacy
The New Du Rose Matriarch
One Heartbeat
The Du Rose Prophecy
Du Rose Sons
Du Rose Family Ties
Du Rose Vendetta

The Hana Du Rose Mysteries (Generation Z)
Phoenix Du Rose
Wiremu Du Rose

The Calculated Risk Series:
The Actuary
The Actuary's Wife
The Actuary in Trouble

The Heart of The Actuary

Troubled series for teens:
Free from the Tracks
Sophia's Dilemma
A Trail of Lies
Gone Phishing

Escaping the Back Country NZ Series:
Pirongia's Secret
Deleilah

Standalone novels:
Artifact
Demons on Her Shoulder
All Saints
Her Quiet Legacy

Humorous Cozy Mystery Series from New Zealand
Dead Straight
Bad Hair Day
Side Parting